Th Covenant

Tormod Cockburn

A "Mysterious Scotland" novel.

Set among The Cairngorms

Mys.Scot

First published by Mys.Scot Media in 2023

Copyright © Tormod Cockburn, 2023

The moral right of the author has been asserted

Print ISBN: 978-1-915612-09-0

E-Book ISBN: 978-1-915612-08-3

Cover photo credit: Gavin McCormack, Getty images, licensed by Canva

This is a work of fiction. Names, characters, places, and incidents are the products of the author's imagination or are used fictitiously. Any resemblance to actual events, locales, or persons, living or dead, is entirely coincidental.

For updates and free books, we invite you to join our Readers Syndicate. Either click the logo above in a digital copy or see details at the back of this book.

Mys.Scot

Dedication

For Kirstie

Until the next time we walk. Somewhere among the mountains.

Also by Tormod Cockburn

The Bone Trap
The Ness Deception
The Stone Cypher
This Jagged Way
The Ice Covenant

Chapter 1

<u>Airth Church – six months ago</u>

Tapping the accelerator a few times, Raphael steers his machine down a country lane and coasts towards a group of middle-aged men lingering along the verge. Caught briefly in his headlights, they turn, nod a 'thank you' for his considerate driving, and then look back to their task. They are dressed in camouflage jackets, watching the river with night vision lenses mounted on tripods. Slipping past them, he guides the machine into a field and under the shadow of an ageing sycamore. With a last throaty roar, he hits the ignition button and turns off the engine.

Kicking out the bike stand, he lets the machine settle and takes off his helmet. He cradles it in his lap, and with his legs still astride the machine, he ponders what the next few minutes will bring. Just another night. Just another mission. Though if he's honest, and he's always honest, he's not looking forward to this assignment. He's grown attached to his charge; this odd red-haired human with all his strange ways. Of all the people he's guarded, this man has become one of Raphael's favourites. This side of the great reunion, he's going to miss Gill McArdle.

'Nice bike', says a human voice behind him.

'Thanks', says Raphael, without turning around.

'I'm a bit of a bike buff. Isn't that a Triumph Bonneville T120?'

'You're close. This one's a T140.'

The man doesn't respond straight away. 'Can't be. The 120s are the latest. Where'd you get it?'

'I have contacts in the trade', says Raphael. 'How's the bird watching?' He gets off the bike now and turns around. The man facing him is dressed from head to foot in army-surplus gear. He's of average height and a little overweight.

'Pretty crap. We're about to pack up for the day.'

'You looking for the Lesser Yellowlegs?'

'Yes.' The man blinks twice at Raphael's sword, slung over the back of his leathers. 'Are you a birder? Cause you don't look like a birder.'

'I take a passing interest', says Raphael. 'If it's the Yellowlegs you're after, swing your optics twelve point five degrees west and focus on the landward side of the carse. Give it a couple more minutes. I'm sure she'll be along.'

The man stands silently, perhaps assessing the merits of this unusually specific advice.

'Give it a try', Raphael says. 'If it's thin pickings this evening, what have you got to lose?'

'Do you fancy joining us?' asks the man.

Raphael thinks. 'Thank you. Perhaps. I have a little …. business to take care of first.'

'Okay then.' The man looks at his watch and seems quite relieved to take this as an opportunity to scuttle off. 'Thanks, pal. And if the Yellowlegs doesn't show, you okay if I bring my mates over and show them your bike?'

Raphael nods, before watching him go. Then with a heavy heart, he turns and looks uphill towards the ruins of Airth church. In this gloomy dusk, it is just another abandoned building. It was formerly a place of community and worship, but today, a terrible blackness is descending, and this isn't simply the absence of daylight. An ambassador of the dark realm is coming, and it's Raphael's job to make sure he plays by the rules.

He stands watching the last rays of daylight seep away. In the distance, he can hear excitement among the bird watchers as one of their number catches their prey in the lens of a night vision camera. And for a moment, Raphael's happiness for their success contrasts with the great sadness he feels inside. Like the rest of his kin, emotions do not come easily to him. The great span of his existence, combined with the panoply of human emotion he has witnessed; shock, joy, anger, and above all – fear, make him emotionally immune, except in the most poignant of moments. He's accepted today's assignment knowing that to refuse would place him among the dark ones. That is unimaginable, and in truth, Raphael knows there's a higher purpose to all this living and dying. He's been guarding one human after another for millennia. They all die eventually. Many passing after lives of no consequence, while others grasp their existence as a very precious thing. To protect his own heart, Raphael has held very few of them dearly, but this present human in his care had seemed so promising.

Raphael shakes his head. He doesn't need to check his watch to know the time, but he does anyway, out of comfort from a very human habit. And at the appointed hour, Raphael begins to climb the hill. Simultaneously, he feels his body tense as the darkness spews its ambassador out into the human realm.

It is night.

It is time.

Stepping over a fence and in amongst the ruins, he selects a place where he can monitor the proceedings but not influence their outcome by his presence. Leaning back against the wall of the old church he stops and looks at the sky. The sun went down an hour ago and he can identify the major constellations. He's picking out a few of his favourites when he hears the clink of metal fencing. A glance in that direction confirms that Gill McArdle, the *Sword-Bearer*, has slipped behind a protective barrier and into the grounds of the ruined church. In a few seconds, he'll pass within a metre of Raphael's position, though McArdle won't see him. So, in the meantime, he folds his arms, the leather of his biker-jacket emitting a gentle "huff" as his right arm closes over his left.

He stands silently, listening as the *Sword-Bearer* crunches past, walking upon leaves on the other side of the wall. Raphael allows himself an ironic smile. McArdle thinks he's being discreet – if only he could realise how much noise he's making, picking his way around the hole in the ground where the Airth Slab lay for one thousand years. McArdle shuffles and pokes for a few minutes. Then with a sigh, he makes his way through the remaining trees to the fence line to get a clear view over the Firth of Forth. Raphael watches discreetly. McArdle is scanning the horizon in the dimmest of twilight. If he drops his gaze a few degrees, he might even notice Raphael's bike, parked at the bottom of the field.

While the *Sword-Bearer* has stepped away, Raphael can hear the ragged breathing of another creature nearby. Whoever the dark realm has sent is crouching high in the crumbling remains of the clock tower. It's a good position and he'll have the upper hand when McArdle returns. Raphael releases a frustrated groan. It doesn't matter that he's giving away his own location, because the creature already knows where he is. Those are the terms of this contest. For once, Raphael isn't allowed to intervene, regardless of his misgivings. Perhaps if the *Sword-bearer* had more time to prepare? If he'd been granted a few years of training, and some sense of what was at stake. But he's inexperienced in matters of faith, and even fresher to the blade. Even if luck existed, and the *Sword-Bearer* had it in abundance, he still wouldn't stand a chance.

The creature gives a sharp intake of breath. The *Sword-Bearer* is coming back; hands in his pockets as if he hasn't a care in the world. And in a moment, that'll be true, because McArdle won't be in the world. The man stops again and stares at the hole. What in heaven's name does he expect to see that wasn't there five minutes ago? Raphael resists the urge to run around the other side of the wall and bellow at him. But even a warning is out of the question. The rules of this contest are clear. His protégé must face this darkness alone.

But suddenly, something unexpected is happening.
The *Sword-Bearer* is abruptly alert to the creature! Without any clues, other than the unsaintly stink coming off the thing, McArdle senses it is near. The creature knows it too, and acts. A lump of masonry from the tower! The *Sword-Bearer* seems doomed, and yet the man's instinct tosses him out of harm's way.

'Bravo!' Raphael whispers. 'My boy goes down fighting.'

The creature meanwhile has already descended to the ground and has his lance ready to finish the kill. McArdle slithers backwards, but the seconds are ticking and in these last moments, Raphael can't bear to watch. He turns his head away and waits for the end.

The clang of blade against blade jerks his attention back to the fight. McArdle's sword! With nanoseconds to spare, he lifted it against his attacker. The creature wasn't expecting that. Lights from the hotel car park skitter across the battlefield and the creature hides his face. The *Sword-Bearer* is injured, but not so badly he can't flee. He's up like a hare and away, dragging his sword behind him. Raphael laughs with surprise. This battlefield manoeuvre isn't pretty, but at least it gets the job done. The crash of the metal fencing tells him McArdle has fled. Against the odds, he's survived.

Tentatively, Raphael pushes up from his hiding position and walks over to the fallen masonry. He can detect the outline of the creature now, his profile just visible as he lingers in the shadows, hiding from the light of the cars.

'How did he know?' the creature rasps.

Raphael shrugs. 'He's a *Sword-bearer*. His gifts emerge quickly.'

Feet drag through dry leaves as the creature walks out of the shadow. He wears a long black robe, fashioned from soft leather and imprinted with fiendish symbols. Raphael can't see his face, though the creature wears a sash of high office.

'You warned him! You've cheated on our terms', spits the creature.

'I didn't warn him, as you well know.' Slowly, Raphael turns to fully face the voice. 'Reveal yourself.'

With a hiss, he tosses back the hood of his robe.

Raphael fights to suppress a gasp. 'Ah! Sariel, my old friend. I wondered if it might be you.'

'You cheated! I'll take this to the court. Let's see what HE has to say.'

Raphael's laugh is suppressed to no more than a chuckle. 'Lies, lies, always lies. Your father makes so many of them. Face it, Sariel. You lost today.'

The creature steps towards him, so its face is bathed in cold blue light, and Raphael sees Sariel's face for the first time in centuries. Scarred and grey, the once noble angel is but a wraith, a shadow of his former self.

'I get two more chances', Sariel bleats. 'Or will you cheat me of those too?'

Sadly, Raphael nods. 'Three chances to destroy the *Sword-Bearer's* flesh and blood. And if he does survive, your master cedes to him the right to declare *The Torn Isle*. Those were the terms, though truth be told, I'd never have struck such a bargain.'

'And yet HE did. Perhaps HE'S more of a dupe than you realise?'

Slowly, Raphael starts to walk away. 'You'll not be quickly parted from your foolishness, Sariel. I think this conversation is over.'

'Two more chances, Raphael', Sariel cackles. 'To make the *Sword-Bearer* no more than a blood stain on history.'

'Then I'm sure I'll see you again soon, old friend', Raphael calls over his shoulder. He stops for a moment and smiles. 'Try to get out more. Do you good to spend a little time in the light.'

Raphael strides towards the fence line with a spring in his step, while behind him Sariel mutters curses and lies. The field is now washed in rising moonlight and Sariel chooses not to follow. Reaching his motorbike, Raphael collects his helmet. In the distance, he can hear the excited chatter of the birdwatchers. Clearly, they're delighting in their shared experience. Celebrating nature, despite the havoc humanity has inflicted upon Eden's garden. He pauses once more to look down at the river as he comprehends the solemnity of this moment. What might be possible if McArdle survives? The enemy has made a strategic blunder. A territory is now in play. 'One down, two to go', he whispers. 'A battle for *The Torn Isle* has begun!'

Picking up the pace, he walks to join his new acquaintance and an encounter with a rare little bird.

Chapter 2

Ratho Village – 3 weeks ago

Detective Constable Alexander Lillico waited for the lights to turn to green before carefully mounting the humpback bridge over the Union Canal and into Ratho Village. He remembered The Bridge Inn was almost immediately on the right, so he pulled over and slid quietly into an empty bay. It was 9 pm and the heavy rain beating down on the roof of his car accentuated the darkness. Chief Superintendent Macfarlane was late. Or maybe Lillico was early. Either way, the temperature was falling, and winter wasn't far away.

At 9.15 pm, Macfarlane's 4x4 pulled to a halt opposite him. The lights flashed once and Lillico sighed, pulling on a rain jacket. Privilege of rank. The Chief-Super gets to stay in his own dry car.

'Good evening, Alex', said the familiar voice. 'Sorry to drag you out on such a dreich night.'

'No problem, sir.'

'Have you been home since you came off shift?'

'Not yet, sir. Been catching up on some paperwork.'

'You could have taken that with you.'

'No need, sir.'

'No one at home for you?'

'No.'

'Pity, at your age and stage of life.'

'Enjoy my own company, sir.' He left a slight pause. 'And when the alternative is living with my mother ...'

'I remember being your age', said MacFarlane, cutting in. 'Long days on the job, then home to sleeping kids and a wife who hadn't talked to a soul all day. Back then, I wondered if I'd ever get through it, but I did.'

'Maybe it's for the best, sir.'

'Someone will be along. Just haven't met the right girl, eh?'

'Indeed, sir.' Lillico looked at the man, eager to crystalise the reason for this conversation. It certainly wasn't a social call, and he'd no curiosity for the Chief-Super's domestic arrangements. Past or present.

'How's the Mackinnon trial going?'

Lillico swung his gaze to stare at the falling rain. 'I'm sure you've read the reports, sir.'

'I mean from your perspective?'

Lillico tried not to sound defensive. 'Detective Inspector Mackinnon is flailing about. Seeing who else she can bring down with her by trying to spread the blame.'

'You think she's guilty?'

'I know she is, sir. I was present when Kevin Cranston was beaten to within an inch of his life. So, I know what happened. It's simply a question of whether or not the jury believes me.'

'You must be worried about your own career?'

'From what perspective, sir? As a Detective Constable on the big organised crime case that hit the rocks, or as the junior who shopped his own DI?'

Macfarlane smiled. 'Oh, they do say that about you. "Mind out for Alex Lillico", they say. "He cuts to the chase so fast he'll spin you off the road".'

Lillico almost flinched. Instead, he turned and stared at his superior, carefully blocking emotion from creeping across his face. 'They can say what they like, sir.'

'I'm sensing a little pain, Constable. Anything you care to talk about?'

Lillico ignored the comment. His professional standing was weak and the Chief-Super wasn't trying to be his friend. 'Away from Bathgate like this, sir? I assume there was something you wanted to ask me?'

'Yes. Back to the chase. In short, I might have an opportunity for you to rehabilitate yourself.'

Lillico didn't think he needed rehabilitating, though the system he served could do with a refurb, and he doubted that was on the Chief-Super's agenda.

'I see you're on temporary secondment to the new *Special Investigations* unit', Macfarlane continued. 'How's that going?'

'It took DI Mackinnon two years to decide she hated my guts, sir. In the current direction of travel, I suspect DCI Wiley might achieve that in a fraction of the time.'

'You find him a hard man to work with?'

Lillico looked out at the rain. 'No more than many others, sir. DCI Wiley seems to hate everybody and everything. Especially if it means he has to work for a living.'

Macfarlane snorted a laugh. 'Oh, on that we're agreed.'

'Perhaps we're both wondering if he's the right man for the job, sir.'

Macfarlane tossed his shoulders about as if shaking off an insect without having to employ his hands. 'Some of the wider management team think he's a Detective who gets results. Others have reservations about his work ethic. Slightly murkier questions around his associations. In short, I'm yet to be convinced he's competent. And if he is competent, I'm not sure he's straight.'

'Why was he appointed?' Lillico was tired of this dance, so he left a long pause before adding the obligatory, 'Sir.'

'Lack of other candidates …' Macfarlane looked away. 'Perhaps a sense that if he did fail in this job, he might be easier to dismiss.'

'And you're telling me this, because?'

'I've been granted authority to run a deeper background check. To be completed before our "Acting" DCI gets his name written on a door.' Macfarlane paused to wag his right forefinger in the air. 'And after Wiley has had a couple of months in the job, I'd like to hear your opinion, Lillico. After all, you're renowned for your honesty.'

'Thank you, sir.'

'If that sounded like a compliment, Alex, trust me it wasn't. After torpedoing Mackinnon's organised crime case, the only viable career move for you going forward is with *Professional Standards*. And you do realise that any new hires in that department have to pay the membership fee?'

Lillico sunk back in the soft leather passenger seat and battled to keep tension out of his voice. 'You want me to go undercover?'

MacFarlane snorted. 'You've neither the training nor the instinct. I want you to carry on doing your regular policing job while compiling a dossier on Wiley's methods and integrity.'

Drawing a deep breath, Lillico released it slowly. The ordeal of giving evidence on the Mackinnon trial had shown him how worried he was about his job; the sense that his own morality was somehow at odds with the police force that employed him. And now, like manna from heaven, here was a way out. 'Count me in, sir.'

'Really? I thought you'd need a little convincing.'

'You don't think I'd lie to you, sir?'

Macfarlane laughed at that. 'No. I believe you. Just thought this might be a harder sell.'

'I'll go where I'm needed, sir. Do whatever is lawfully asked of me.'

'You *might* need to lie to DCI Wiley. In case he's suspicious of you.'

Lillico shook his head once. 'Won't be needed, sir. I'll be discreet.'

The Chief-Super leaned over and rather awkwardly, they shook hands. 'Right. First thing in the morning, I want you to carry on at *Special Investigations* without mentioning this chat. DCI Wiley is about to get landed with a big murder case. His performance will determine if he has a future in Police Scotland, or not.'

'Very good, sir', said Lillico, preparing to leave.

'One last thing.' Macfarlane dug an envelope out of his jacket pocket. 'For your information, you passed your Sergeant's exam last month.'

'I did, sir?'

'And despite a few mutterings from senior officers dismayed at your performance in the Mackinnon trial, I am authorised to give you this.'

Macfarlane held out the envelope. 'Congratulations', he said flatly.

After three heartbeats, Lillico reached for the envelope but found Macfarlane didn't release.

'The promotion is deferred until the first of November. For the time being you'll remain a Detective Constable.'

Lillico bit back his frustration. 'Why?'

'It's your camouflage. I believe DCI Wiley would be intimidated by a DS. Posing as a DC, you're more likely to see the inner workings of the man.'

Lillico said nothing.

'Is there a problem, Alex? Perhaps you see a potential conflict between this assignment and the whiter-than-white persona you've created for yourself?'

'I'll work it out, sir.'

Macfarlane released the envelope. 'Go home, Alex. I'll be in touch in due course.'

Glasgow – one week ago

Oscar sat in an unmarked white van looking out at rain falling on the Kelvin Way. Or at least it seemed to be raining. In truth, the sound of the ice drumming down on the van's roof hinted at soft hail. A Glasgow autumn. Cold and damp in malicious harmony.

Shivering, Oscar resisted the temptation to switch on the engine and drive some heat into the freezing vehicle. Doing so would attract attention. Instead, with no heat, no music, and no movie downloaded to a phone, the minutes passed slowly.

And the first hour.

And the second, while Oscar fended off the chill.

Finally, around 2 am, there came the sound of another vehicle reversing up to the van's rear doors. Oscar remained still, noiselessly blowing warm breath onto icy hands, primed to flee if the meeting went bad.

Listening. Decoding every sound.

From this new arrival, the sound of doors opening and closing discreetly. In the van's wing mirrors, figures dressed in black, their features shrouded, passed through the line of sight, followed a few moments later by a blast of cooler air as they opened the back doors in Oscar's van. The voices were too muffled for Oscar to hear anything, which was the objective during these irregular proceedings.

No faces – that was the deal.

Not now.

Not ever.

Sitting nervously, Oscar twice felt the van tilt a little as two people stepped into the body of the vehicle, grunting as they struggled with their load. Then a 'bump' as they deposited the cargo on the floor, followed by mutterings and profanities Oscar couldn't quite hear. Then the rear door closed again and a few moments later, their vehicle started up and slid off into the night.

Oscar studied the rear lights of the departing vehicle until they disappeared in the billowing folds of driven hail. Stepping out of the van and around to check the rear doors were secure, Oscar half-opened one door to check on the load. A single body, wrapped in black roofing felt, which in itself was a good thing. Easier to work with and a lot quieter than black plastic. Another reminder this Drumchapel crew were such professionals. Closing the door, Oscar flexed cold fingers, climbed back into the driver's seat, and carefully drove away.

Chapter 3

Stonehaven Harbour – present day

It was a cold, dark Friday evening in late September and Gill McArdle stood alone.

Rain was driving in from the sea as he took a deep breath and stepped outside the protective barrier and onto the concrete apron of the south pier. Gripping the railing with his left hand, he leaned over the water and observed with satisfaction that the ebb tide was well established. A glance around the amphitheatre of stone houses confirmed there was no one watching him. And while lights illuminated many windows, drawn tight around this horseshoe bay, the curtains were all closed. And why not? No one would be bothered on a wet and windy night to mind some guy standing too close to the water.

As he thought about his father, he recalled Gordon loved nights like this. There could never be enough weather for the old man. Little more than a year ago, he would have stood where Gill was standing now, with his hands dug deep in his pockets, looking at the sky, smelling the air. Then he would have shuffled home and muttered about developing areas of low pressure, the weakness of the gulf stream and the approaching equinox. Gill smiled weakly. Yeah, it was Gordon's kind of night.

Gill sighed and unscrewed the canister. He waited until the wind swirled again at his back and slowly upended the container. Half the earthly remains of Gordon McArdle dropped in a heavy stream, straight into the water. The other half formed a billow of dust that blew away in the wind.

'Goodbye, Dad', he said quietly, watching the last ashes gust out over the water. He stood and wondered how he should be feeling at this moment. Sadness the old boy was gone? Relief that his suffering was over? Glad they'd had time to mend their relationship? Yes, all of that, but more. Something he couldn't quite articulate. The frustration of unfinished conversations. The departure of this last living link to his birth family. The Earth spinning on its axis, as time ticked away.

He brushed the rain off his face with his free hand. And, he realised, there might be a tear. Quite possibly the blown remains of his father. Anyway, it was finished now. He turned on his heels and walked the twenty paces to where Salina and Fiona waited for him in the shelter of the harbour wall.

'All done', he said.

'You doing alright?' Salina asked, draping her arms over his shoulders.

Gill stared back into Salina's dark eyes. Sparkling with intelligence; warm with compassion, Gill was certain he wanted to stare into her eyes for the rest of his life. And it was long past time he did something about that.

'Aye', was all he said.

'Sure?'

He caught her hips and squeezed her. 'On so many levels, I've never been better. I mean, I'm gonna miss him. But I got him back, Sal. Before the end. So much to be grateful for.'

Salina pulled him into a hard embrace and he was thankful she didn't press him. Being grateful didn't stop his heart aching.

'Marine Hotel, or, The Ship?' said Fi, rubbing her hands against the autumn chill.

Gill slipped his spare hand into hers. 'In memory of Dad, let's do both.'

Two days later, approaching his Dundee office, Gill stopped suddenly, caught by an unexpected tremor of grief. He took a second, leaning against one of the trees planted to soften the austere rear wall of the Caird Hall. Was this the way life had always been? You bury the last of your family and then carry on as if nothing had happened? Probably, yes. Because anything else could leave you imprisoned by circumstances you couldn't change. Maybe he should have accepted Cassy's advice and taken a few days off? But it was too late now. Perhaps later in the month, after the next magazine hit the shops. Taking a deep breath, he beat back the emotion, then pressed into the start of a new day.

And so, it was with a little false bravado he thumped his laptop down on his desk and shook rainwater off his coat. 'Morning, Cassy. Hell of a weekend.'

'That's four wet ones in a row. I'm getting webbed feet.'

'You had a gig this weekend. How did it go?'

'*Calum's Road* were AWESOME as usual, but the driving! Dornoch of all places. I'd no idea being famous would be this tiring.'

Gill folded his arms and stared at her. 'Let's not give up on the day job just yet. You're not quite famous.'

'Just because you haven't seen us yet doesn't mean we're not in demand. We've another six weddings to do this side of Christmas.'

'Well, in that case, I'll need to talk to you about a date …'

Cassy swept up her mug and headed for the coffee machine. 'The diary is filling up fast, Gill.' She smiled over her shoulder. 'Better be quick.'

'I was hoping you could fit me in. Like a mates-rates thing?'

'Email me', said Cassy, walking away. 'I'll run it past the booking committee.'

'If you're grabbing coffee, can I have one, please?'

'You don't have time', she called back. 'Tony wants to see you right away.'

Gill took a deep breath. As the editor, *Mysterious Scotland* was his magazine. But Tony Farquharson was the publisher and had nursed the title through its turbulent birth and beyond. Gill might be its adoptive father, but Tony still demanded visiting rights. He'd spent Gill's first year with the paper cajoling the editorial team to get more organised, then spent the second year wringing his hands every time Gill's research took them into controversial territory.

Gill chased away his weekend blues and donned a professional smile before knocking on his boss's door. 'Hey, Tony. You wanted to see me?'

'Gill. Come in. How was your weekend?'

Gill shrugged. 'Family time on Saturday. Then I dropped Salina for a flight to Florida first thing this morning.'

'Nice! Holiday?'

He shook his head. 'Deep sea submersible in the Gulf of Mexico. They're doing a series of dives over five weeks. Marine biology of the wider Mississippi Delta, or something like that.'

'Ah, well, if she's away that long, you'll need plenty of work to distract you. Did you hear about Killiecrankie?'

'You talking about the roadworks collapsing?'

Tony was tapping an image on his desktop that Gill couldn't see. 'Looks like the retaining embankment they were building was too steep. Became so saturated it just dissolved back into the hillside.'

'That makes a change from the *Rest and be thankful*.' He paused, realising Tony wasn't just making conversation about the latest road to be demolished by a landslip. 'But what's that got to do with us?'

'What it might represent', said Tony. 'Is an opportunity.'

Gill pulled a chair over to Tony's desk and sat down uninvited. 'I'm listening.'

'I'd a call from … from a … golfing pal last night', said Tony, stumbling. 'He's got a contact in the Scottish government with oversight for the Transport Department. Anyway, he got a shout early Sunday morning about the damage at Killiecrankie. Long story short, there'll need to be emergency repairs, including a broadening of the road.'

'That won't be popular', Gill muttered. 'Adding that extra carriageway to the A9 buried a big chunk of the Killiecrankie battlefield site.'

'Exactly. And that's despite trying to keep the footprint of the new road as small as possible', Tony continued. 'Which is probably why they built the bank too steep.'

'The law states that any road extension is subject to environmental impact and archaeological review', said Gill. 'So it'll be a pain in the ass to get done in a hurry.'

Tony smiled happily. 'Which is the reason my golfing buddy called me. Because of the road's importance, my friend hopes he can accelerate some of the legal due diligence. There's going to be a generous budget and so, long story, short, he's asking if we're interested.'

Gill sniffed. 'Sounds like you're being offered a bit of grace and favour, Tony.'

'Maybe. But they've phoned every agency north of Manchester and they're struggling to find a team to do it.'

Gill thought for a second. 'Battlefield sites are always fascinating, but it's a bit outside our usual way of working. We normally dig with a goal in mind. This would just be a fishing expedition.'

'Agreed. Which is why I'd never fund that kind of dig. But in this case, the DoT would be paying for the whole thing.'

'Ah, I see. And how big is the site?'

'The embankment extension will be twelve hundred metres long and twenty metres deep.'

'Bloody hell, Tony. That's huge.'

'But maybe only four hundred metres cover the battlefield.'

'Still, that's …' Gill rushed through some mental maths. 'Eight thousand square metres. Call it two acres in old money.'

'Meaning, we'd need to crew up.'

'Big job, in a hurry. We'd need about a hundred folk.'

'My friend was thinking about your various university contacts?'

'Undergrads at best, Tony. Huge logistics. No idea how we'd supervise that many.'

'We have the skills though. And we could outsource some of the tasks. The budget would be a blank cheque.'

'Aye, but what do we get out of it? I could run myself and our best people into the ground for a fortnight and not have more than a musket ball to show for it.'

'That's fair.'

'I'm not saying no. I mean, you're the boss. But where's the mystery?'

Tony shrugged. 'Just that another piece of Scotland's heritage landscape is about to disappear forever under tarmac.'

'Oh, I see. And here's *Mys.Scot*, doing its bit to preserve what we can?'

'Exactly. I think "Citizen science", is the phrase you'd want to deploy. Lots of happy Scottish men and women, digging their hearts out to preserve our shared heritage.'

'You should be in politics, Tony.'

Tony ignored Gill's sarcasm. 'Let's see where my friend nets out. In the meantime, can I ask you to think how we could resource it?'

'Okay. We're ten days from closing issue 28, and as usual, we're in good shape. I can probably find a morning this week.'

'This one's urgent, Gill. And I need to get back to my contact. Can I say when you'll visit Killiecrankie?'

Gill puffed out his cheeks. Maybe hard work was the most constructive response to all his sadness. 'Okay then. Let's say Wednesday morning.'

Chapter 4

Two days later, Gill was sitting in a traffic jam, inching forward and tapping the steering wheel in frustration. He was going to be an hour late. On a typical trip north up the A9, he would sweep through this stretch of road with barely a glance to the left or right. He'd usually ignore the rolling, wooded countryside, topped with inaccessible crags, and instead, he'd plough on with his journey to somewhere inevitably more beautiful. Pitlochry, a few miles to the south of the site, was considered the gateway to the Highlands, and the landscape around Killiecrankie was the first place the mountains started to tower above the highway. He'd climbed nearby Ben Vrackie with his brother as a teenager and remembered looking down on the A9. From the vantage point of a Munro, you could see this route was the only road penetrating the high ground as it wound its way north to Aviemore, and Inverness beyond that. When you stopped to look at it, the landscape was really quite beautiful – a pastel mix of everything lovely Scotland had to offer.

The section of road running by Killiecrankie was threaded through a narrow pass and had been a single-carriageway for most of its existence. Only in recent years had the transport authority begun the challenging work to add a second carriageway onto the tenuous embankment that carried the existing road. And it was this road extension that had now collapsed. As he joined the contraflow, he watched for the 'works exit', and finally dropped out of the traffic. Donning a hard hat, boots and high viz waistcoat, Gill walked away from his car.

Scott Shannon was a slightly built man in a heavy blue parka squeezed under an orange jacket. As Gill approached, Scott lifted his hardhat to sweep away strands of wispy fair hair, before reaching to grasp Gill's hand. The noise of slow-moving traffic made it difficult to talk, so Scott steered them into a portacabin sitting on the damaged side of the road.

'Sorry I'm late. Should have thought about the lane restrictions.'

'No worry. It's bad at the moment, but it'll settle down once folk learn to adapt.'

'Are we far from the landslip?'

Scott jerked a thumb over his shoulder. 'Another three hundred metres that way. I've got engineers examining the site, so it's a good time to go and take a look.'

'What happened?'

Scott shrugged. 'Optimistic design assumptions on the initial build, plus all this rain we've had. The drainage under the new road didn't cope. Especially when the carriageway started to act like a reservoir wall.'

Gill glanced out at the hillside, sweeping down from the road and tumbling towards the River Garry. 'It's brutally steep.'

'Aye. The site's a mixture of old and new trees. Without them, the landslip might have run all the way to the bottom and hit the railway line.'

'I'd forgotten about that. It's right on the river I recall.'

'Pretty much. And it's complicated, running a river, a railway and a dual carriageway through the same wee gap.'

'Right then. How can I help?'

'Before we crack on with the reinstatement, Tony says you guys will be able to help me tick the archaeology and conservation box?'

Gill allowed his head to bob from side to side. 'We're certainly looking at it. I've put a shout-out for volunteers. Our office manager is advertising the dig on our website, and has contacted everyone on our mailing list. But we'll need to see how it goes. My goal for today is to understand the practicalities.'

Scott beckoned him over to a series of site drawings pinned in a row on the wall. 'This section in red is where we had the slip. Everything downhill for a hundred metres is just mud and rubble at the moment. I'll need a safety all-clear before we even start to move it. If you decide to help us, this section in green will be available to your guys from next week. It's the footprint of the widened road area where the surviving embankment looks sound.'

'Can you show me where the roadworks sit in relation to the battlefield site?'

Drawing his finger across the map, Scott focused Gill's attention. 'The part of the A9 we're concerned with is a mile north of where the old dual carriageway stopped. So, the whole section between Krankie village and the bridge where the A9 passes over the B8079 needs to be strengthened, which is about one and a half kilometres.' He tapped a point close to the river, marking a stone memorial. 'This is the Claverhouse stone and roughly marks the centre of the battlefield. The landslip is two hundred metres north of that point.' He stopped to smile. 'If you want to brush up on your history, it's where Clan Ranald on the Jacobite side bore down on the Ramseys in the government army.'

'And is the land all open?'

'It is now. The spill tore through an area of newly planted trees. The old road configuration had trees covering most of the hillside, but they were cleared for the widening scheme last year. That pushed the boundary line between new and established trees about one hundred metres below the new road. Fortunately, the more established forestry prevented the slip from reaching the B8079, or the railway line.'

'Hell of a site', said Gill. 'To do what's required, in the time available; I'll need a big crew.'

Scott nodded. 'We've an established service base a mile south of the village. There's parking there, toilets, and a canteen. Your people can park there and use the shuttlebus we operate during daylight hours.'

'And I need to understand the Health and Safety environment. I want to brief folk before I bring them in here.'

'Which is mostly what my job is all about.' Scott smiled. 'Let's go get some mud on our boots. I'll walk you through the whole thing.'

The hour-long drive back to Dundee saw Gill in the office for early afternoon.

'Yuck', said Cassy as he walked into their section. 'Didn't you have time for a shower after you finished?'

'What can I say? There's a one hundred per cent correlation between being an archaeologist and getting mud on one's trousers', said Gill, flicking through some post on his desk.

'How did it go?'

'Scott is a level-headed kind of guy. I can work with him.'

'Ed Johnson was looking for you. As usual, he sounds stressed.'

Gill's shoulders sagged. He wasn't on great terms with his old university professor in St Andrews. And to his sadness and regret, Gill knew this was due to the lack of professional courtesy he'd shown his old mentor. 'I thought he wasn't speaking to me?'

'That's what I said! And when I'd reminded him, he confirmed he wouldn't trust you as far as he could throw you. But he still needs a chat at your earliest convenience.'

Gill grunted acknowledgement but didn't say anything.

'You'd think being a university professor would add a bit of swagger to his life', Cassy continued. 'I mean there you are, at the top of your career. You're seriously successful, you're highly respected and you have a bank account full of cash. Really, what is there to worry about?'

Gill looked up. 'There are so many misconceptions in that statement I don't even know where to begin.'

Cassy ignored him and carried on talking. 'But the volunteer sign-up page on our website is going like a fairground. We've got north of seventy offers and rising.'

He glanced at her over his post. 'Not sure why you're so chipper about it. This is gonna be a shedload of work. You do know that?'

Cassy just smiled while her fingers flew over her keyboard. 'Doesn't bother me. I'm amazing.' She paused and looked up. 'In fact, I'm so dazzled by my own brilliance, I almost forgot you have a visitor.'

'Who?'

'An old pal. I've stuck him in the conference room.'

'Cassy …'

'And I'll need the room back by 3 pm. Cat mag editorial meeting.'

Gill dropped his paperwork back on his desk and peered across the office pens to get sight of his visitor.

'Oh, bloody hell, Cassy. Couldn't you have told him I'd left the country or something?'

Cassy carried on typing. 'I'm your office manager. If you want me to do personal security, you'll have to pay me extra.'

'Inspector', said Gill, stepping into the conference room and managing a forced smile. 'What a pleasant surprise.'

George Wiley turned from his hushed conversation with the younger man seated at the table beside him. 'Ah, McArdle. You're probably not aware I've had a bit of a bump-up since we last spoke. It's Detective *Chief* Inspector these days.' He stood to shake Gill's hand but almost recoiled when he saw Gill's clothes. 'I've gotta say, normally you look like shit, and today is no exception.'

Gill glanced at his trousers, then at the two men in turn. 'Honest Perthshire topsoil, Chief Inspector. Nothing else.'

Wiley pointed at the younger man. 'This is Alec Lillico. He's my Detective Constable.'

'We've met', said Gill, nodding in Lillico's direction. 'Back in March, DC Lillico charged me with trespass at Airth church. And he took a statement from me after I was attacked on the Isle of May.'

'Thanks to your professor friend, the trespass charge didn't go to court', said Lillico.

'And the people who tried to throw me off the island still haven't been caught', Gill responded.

'Not yet', said Lillico. He was a head taller than Wiley, lean to the point of being skinny and not yet out of his twenties.

'Sure', said Gill, waving a hand as if dismissing his own complaint. 'So, DC Lillico. I do hope you're enjoying rubbing shoulders with Scotland's finest.'

Lillico glanced from Gill to Wiley but said nothing.

'Isn't this sweet', said Wiley. 'We're all playing along nicely. Like a regular bunch of pals.'

'What can I do for you?' Gill asked wearily.

'There you go, Alec. It's like I said. And just like you. A man who gets straight down to business.'

'Just busy, George. Just busy.'

'With my recent promotion came a new role', Wiley began in a pompous voice. 'I've been lifted out of regional policing and now I'm seconded to a new unit called, *Special Investigations*. My role is to bring expertise to cold cases. Plus any active investigations that require a high degree of lateral thinking.'

Gill blinked twice and wondered if George Wiley and "lateral thinking" had ever as much as passed in the street.

'As I've been presented with a difficult case, I've been authorised to leverage civilian resources to bring fresh insight.'

'Ah!' said Gill. 'I was under the impression this was a social call. And now I suspect I'm about to be … *leveraged*.'

'No need to get sniffy, McArdle. You haven't even heard what it is yet.' Wiley wagged a finger at him. 'Because, knowing your history, I think you'll like it.'

Gill dropped his open palms on the table. 'And I doubt I'm going to stop you telling me about it.'

Wiley flicked his chin at his junior. 'Show him, Alec.'

From the floor beside him, Lillico lifted a black evidence case onto the table. Then he reached inside and pulled out a clear plastic bag, containing what looked like half a kilo of fine white gravel. Wiley took it from him and slid it across the table to Gill.

Gill caught the bag and took it in his hands to examine the contents. He immediately dropped it and pushed it away to arm's length. 'Sorry, but that's disgusting.'

Wiley pulled a self-satisfied smile. 'Isn't it just.'

'Wiley, please tell me why you're polluting my conference room with a bag of human teeth?'

'Because, Mr McArdle, I've got a little mystery on my hands.'

'Aside from professional curiosity, what's this to do with me?'

'Because, when the shit hits the fan, your problems generally end up in my in-tray. Seeing as how Alec and I are so short-staffed, I thought it was about time I got one back.'

Chapter 5

Gill bought himself a couple of minutes by leaving the room to organise hot drinks for them all. George Wiley had never been an easy man to work with, so it rankled with Gill that he should turn up in Dundee looking for favours. Laying the coffees on a tray, he forced himself to cool down. At very least, he had to hear them out, so he shook some professionalism into his face and returned to the conference room, where he nodded to the officers to begin.

'Three weeks ago', said Wiley. 'A member of the public was on the Cairngorm plateau. Nice sunny autumn day. Cold but no snow cover. On one of the trails, while he was descending a mountain called Ben Macdui, our eagle-eyed retired dentist spotted something on the path. Recognizing it as a human tooth, he almost ignored it until he saw another, and then another. He called the police and after an extensive search of the paths, the team gathered what you see in front of you.'

Gill gave a curt nod. 'Like I said, it's disgusting but I'm struggling to see a crime here.'

'All the teeth were healthy when they were extracted from their hosts. Some show signs of dental work but most do not. "Crying shame to see good teeth like that go to waste", said our dentist.'

'These wee holes', said Gill, pointing at one of the teeth in the bag. 'Was someone trying to make a necklace?'

Wiley shook his head. 'Police lab taking DNA samples. And that's where it gets interesting. We've only had one hit so far, for a chap called David Fleming.'

Gill pushed the bag of teeth all the way back to Wiley. 'Have you asked Mr Fleming if he's missing any teeth?'

Wiley took the bag and clutched it in his meaty right hand. 'We can't. He's been missing for over twenty years. Under the seven-year rule, he was declared dead ages ago.'

Gill thought for a second. 'That puts a different spin on it.'

'Yes, it does. I'm waiting for more results, but the only thing we know for certain is that we have teeth from twenty-five different individuals.'

'And apart from Mr Fleming, you've no idea who the other people were?'

'Nationally, only about ten per cent of the Scottish population is in the DNA database. That means we'll never identify the majority of these people. In fact, Alec here thinks we've been lucky to find one.'

'You're presuming these people have come to some kind of unfortunate end?'

'There might be some reason why their perfectly healthy teeth would end up on a hillside, but if there is, I'm struggling to see it.'

'And your reason for bringing this question to me?' asked Gill.

'Alec and I have had this on our desks for a fortnight now, along with other enquiries. We're getting nowhere, so I said to him yesterday, "Alec-boy, we need some fresh eyes on this little mystery." And that's when I thought of you.'

'Not sure what expertise I can bring.'

'The origins of the Great Glen disaster. ScoCion's foul play on Orkney. I could go on, but you're like a creepy-crawly, McArdle. You find your way into all the cracks.' Wiley peered at Gill with porcine eyes. 'And now, after all the support I've given you, I'd like you to find me a crack in this case.'

'Thanks, Detective. I'm truly flattered.'

'See it as a wee challenge to hold in your back pocket while you're wandering around getting shit on your trousers. Maybe you could take a walk up to Macdui yourself and see if you get any inspiration?'

'Really quite busy, George. I've got a massive new dig starting next week at Killiecrankie.'

'That's nice. What're you hunting for?'

'It's a battlefield site. Just off the A9.'

'Well, that's just down the road from the Cairngorms. A nice walk up Ben Macdui would be a relaxing stroll for you.'

Gill wasn't sure what to say to get this man to leave his office. He settled on a platitude. 'Sure. I'll see what I can do.'

Wiley took a slug of tepid coffee and stood to leave. 'Great. And in return, do let me know if there's anything I can do to help you at Killiecrankie.' He shrugged. 'Perhaps Alec here could direct the traffic or something?'

The rest of Gill's afternoon was devoured preparing for the Krankie dig. The task he was avoiding was to return Ed Johnson's call. And when he got around to it, the conversation proved less than satisfactory.

'To be honest, Gill, I'm asking you to postpone this one', said the Professor. 'The new term has only just begun, so our undergrads should be attending lectures.'

'Normally I'd agree with you. But this dig's urgent.' Briefly Gill explained the road reinstatement.

'It's the wrong time of year' Ed grumbled. 'You're going to be standing knee-deep in dirty water that's two notches above freezing.'

'It's archaeology, Ed. It's always mountain tops or boggy bottoms; we rarely get to be comfortable.'

'Well, in the circumstances, I'll be emailing our students to recommend they pass on this one.'

'I'm sorry to hear that.'

'But as ever in this institution, your reputation precedes you. While the management team regard you as discredited, the student base thinks you're some kind of archaeological rock star. Somebody spotted *Mys.Scot's* shout out for volunteers and after that, I gather it was wildfire.'

'My apologies. We weren't targeting your students behind your back.'

'So, in the circumstances, the only thing I can do is to turn a blind eye to any students who are missing for the two-week duration of your dig. But to be clear – the university is neither encouraging nor taking responsibility for anyone who chooses to go.'

'No problem. We have our own insurance and there's a decent care package for volunteers on this one.'

'That may be, but it's October, Gill. It's cold and wet in the Scottish Highlands and just about the worst time to start a dig.'

Gill did his best to mollify Ed, but he came off the call with an unpleasant realisation. The eighty-plus volunteers already signed up on the *Mys.Scot* website weren't in addition to a workforce from St Andrews – they were the bulk of his crew. And that wasn't the end of his problems.

Tony was in touch to say that external funding had been agreed for *Mys.Scot* to undertake the Krankie archaeology. And as soon as the dig got a green light, he'd called Fiona. 'Sorry, Gill. I'm in Hampshire from the third week of October. There's a big archaeological team working the ground in advance of a new highspeed line.'

'But you're here for the first week. Could you get me started?'

'Sure, if I don't mind going to Winchester absolutely knackered, with a dose of trench foot and a head cold.'

'You mean, fresh from a *Mys.Scot* dig. Inspired and with the wind in your sails?'

'I'll think about it, Gill. But it's best if you keep looking for someone else as your site supervisor.'

'I was sorry to hear about your father', said Rosemary Solomon as they walked along Dundee waterfront during his lunchbreak the following day. He was still bogged down in the details of the Krankie dig and was grateful he'd booked this meeting with her.

'It was his time', said Gill. 'And he was incredibly peaceful at the end. He was breathing steadily until suddenly, he wasn't.' They were strolling away from the town and the V&A museum where he'd bought coffees a few minutes before. Gill had met Solomon through an acquaintance going by the name of Barcode Charlie. Along with a Jewish museum curator of Iranian descent, Adina Mofaz, the three of them each carried a peculiar supernatural gift. The nature and purpose of these gifts were still unclear, and Solomon, with her own sense of calling, had become a mentor to all three. But they were a rag-tag outfit and so far, there had never been a moment when all four of them had been together.

'I enjoyed meeting Salina', said Solomon, pulling him out of his reverie. 'Though, I had the sense she was checking me out.'

Gill dug his free hand in his pocket. 'That's because she was. I value her opinion.'

'Thank you. That's honest. Do you think she was serious about her offer?'

Gill reviewed the conversation in his mind. Solomon had been a secondary school teacher and these days she was employed by a local charity recently set up by Gill. Working with others, their project brought volunteers into the local college to read with disadvantaged young people. 'I know she'd love to help', he said. 'Managing her diary so she can be with you regularly … that will be the challenge.'

'I understand. Perhaps she could help us when we're launching our service to secondary schools. She's very charismatic. Young people will come leaping to any activity she endorses.'

Gill smiled. 'She's a powerhouse.'

'And what did she make of me?' asked Solomon.

'She made a connection with you. Sal and I have spoken about her volunteering for our project, but she wanted to meet you first. She wouldn't have signed up if you didn't inspire her.'

'Sorry', said Solomon. 'Let me rephrase. What did she think of this obscure little group you're part of?'

Gill paused before responding. 'Like me, she's fascinated to see what's next.'

Solomon reached across and picked a small piece of debris off his waistcoat. 'You could say the same thing for me and Charlie.'

'Do you ever wonder why the whole thing isn't clearer?'

She examined the scrap and discarded it. 'That's the problem with the Creator of the universe. He's got all the time in the world.'

Gill grunted his ascent. 'I understand now why you were so vigilant the day you and I first met.'

'I'm glad. I didn't mean to offend. But one half of me didn't want the crystal armour to be real. And the other half had no idea how to proceed in the event it was.'

'And now we know it is real, how do we proceed, Solie?'

'We gather. People with gifts of armour, like you, Charlie, and Adina.'

'Have you had a chance to spend any more time with Adina?'

'Twice since you and I last talked. Have you?'

'I don't have happy memories of our previous encounters.'

'That's not answering my question.'

'No, Solie. Apart from greeting her at the *Desperate Dan* statue, I haven't seen Adina since the night she swung a gun in my face, and then, I ended up selling her a rock for two and a half million quid.' He took a sip of coffee, surprised by how angry he sounded. 'How is she?'

'She's very uncomfortable with all of this. She felt compelled to accept Raphael's gift but finds the uncertainty maddening.'

'And what do you make of her?' asked Gill when Solomon didn't offer up any more detail.

'She's terrifying', snapped Solomon. 'Just like you.'

'Terrifying?'

'In what she doesn't know. And for the incredible things she might be capable of if she lasts the course.'

'What kinds of things?'

Solomon glanced at him and away. 'Adina isn't like the rest of us. She doesn't suffer doubts or uncertainties. Her gift grants her rock-solid belief and astonishing mental clarity. And because she's so logical, she finds it distressing not to know its ultimate purpose. As the armour group moves forward, looking for our collective calling, I believe it will be Adina who sees it first.'

Gill considered this and found himself agreeing. 'Has Charlie seen her since the incident at the *Desperate Dan* statue?'

'Yes.'

'How did that go?'

'I spent most of my time translating.' Solomon tossed a frustrated shake of her head at the sky. 'Charlie and Adina are from opposite sides of the tracks, if you know what I mean. Adina missed three out of every four words Charlie uttered. And her vocabulary is so high, I needed to parse her comments back to Charlie in bite-size pieces. I mean, they got on okay, but the only thing they have in common is their involvement in this thing.'

Gill smiled. With his shaven head, building-site physicality and prominent neck tattoo, Charlie was a daunting character. But he brimmed with decency. And after all was said and done, it was Charlie's faith and determination that brought them all together.

'What did you and Adina talk about?'

Solomon's gaze flicked upwards while she remembered. 'Adina talked about her encounters with Raphael and told me how she got to know The Nazarene. Has she told you her story?'

Gill shook his head.

'Ask her. It will blow your mind.'

'I will. Anything else?'

'We spoke about how Scotland has changed through the ages. As a Jewish Arab, she's got an unusual fascination with this country.'

'In what sense?'

'There are similarities between Iran and Scotland. Iran was once the cradle of the three big world faiths. And Scotland was once a place of vibrant faith. But now that same belief has decayed into a despised religion.'

Gill grunted his assent. Even with his changing mindset, he'd never once felt the urge to visit a church. 'Does she ever doubt?'

'Her gift is the helmet, Gill. That means she's very certain about what she believes. And very determined to discover what's ahead of us.'

Gill thought back to his own experiences accepting the challenge on a blustery Orcadian moor under the ancient gaze of the Brodgar Stone Circle. 'Sticking with us will cost her', he said. 'But she wouldn't have joined if she wasn't in for the long haul.'

'And you?'

'Can't hide from it. Past running away.' He ran his left hand through his hair. 'Guess I'm in.'

'I believe you', she said. 'And have you achieved any insights into what's going on?'

'Like you, I can see a pattern for this in *The Book*. The armour, I mean. There are six pieces. So far, we have the sword, shield and helmet.'

'Meaning we still need people representing the belt, breastplate and shoes.'

Gill concurred. 'I believe they'll turn up. Once they do, things might become clearer.'

Solomon's face stiffened as she stared out over the river. 'You do realise this thing we're involved in will be opposed?'

'In what sense?'

'Yin, yang, Gill. One supernatural force equips you with an unnatural power. You have to anticipate another supernatural force will resist you.'

Gill shrugged. 'Maybe we'll stay under the radar. At least until we're organised.'

Solomon turned more serious. 'The demon that attacked you at Airth back in March; have you ever sensed it again?'

Gill shook his head. 'I'm hoping it was a one-time thing.'

'Don't be so sure. Despite the rather misleading way good and evil are portrayed in our culture, demons don't get to wander the earth at will. There are permissions to be sought.'

'Forms to be filled', Gill added.

'Don't mock. I'd advise you to research this. The day might come when you'll need to be sure of your rights.'

'Okay', said Gill. 'The authority of demonic powers to walk on the earth. I'll add that to my list.'

'Good. I want you to walk me through your conclusions the next time we talk.'

'Ever the teacher', said Gill.

'Trying to craft success from the poorest clay.'

'Oh, Solie', said Gill, nudging her in her ribs. 'You seem stressed.'

Solomon busied herself hunting for something in her pockets. 'I'm fairy godmother to a rabble of half-formed superheroes, and a well-meaning auntie to every struggling reader in Scotland's fourth city. Why should I be stressed?'

Gill laughed. Solomon was growing on him.

Chapter 6

'Right, guys', said Gill, calling their informal meeting to order. 'There's a good chance I'm going to be in the field all of next week, so as far as possible I want to complete issue 28 this week. In a moment, Cassy will bring her usual laser focus to help us achieve that, but first, I've got some team news.' Gill glanced around the faces to make sure he had everyone's attention. 'You'll be aware no one has successfully claimed the cat mag's sweepstake for a couple of months now. But today, I'm pleased to announce a victory. Larry has cleared the pot with his prediction back in April that *Mys.Scot* would go six months without a death associated with one of our stories.'

'Aye, lads and lassies. I called it', said Larry tossing a hand through his long grey hair with more than his usual swagger. 'Last year wuz carnage. I sussed we were due a dry spell.'

'Excellent job, Larry. The first round at our next team drink is on you.' Gill waited until the murmurs of appreciation died down before making his next announcement. 'And in other news, having agreed to the permanent expansion of the *Mys.Scot* crew with Tony, I'm pleased to announce Mhairi has accepted an offer to switch from temp to full time.'

'Go girl', cried Cassy as they all gave an embarrassed Mhairi a gentle clap.

'No gettin' away noo, lass', Larry called.

'Aw, thanks Larry', Mhairi crooned. 'It was either this or take a job in childcare, really.'

'Well, that's a ringing endorsement', Craig gasped with mock offence.

'Thinking about it …', Mhairi continued. 'Working with you guys feels a bit like working in childcare.'

Gill flashed a look at Craig. 'We creative types need a steady hand to keep us on track. You know; mother us from time to time.'

'In that case, is there any chance of a coffee and a pack of bickies?' Craig shot back.

'Honestly!' cried Mhairi. 'You guys!'

Gill waited for the kids to quit flinging sand at each other. 'Cassy, as mother-in-chief, can you give us the running order for this week?'

Cassy seemed relieved to leap in and reported where everyone was at with their various tasks, plus any urgent next steps. Issue 28 was almost in the bag, and much of the thinking on issue 29 was already underway. There was plenty of work to do, but these days, there was always a clear plan. They held a quick-fire discussion, followed by a round of refinements and job swaps. The team had a convention. The week following an issue going to print was spent fleshing out the immediate next edition. This freed the following two weeks for development work on future issues. The fourth week in the cycle was a mad dash to the finishing line to get the next magazine prepped and uploaded to the printer. Under pressure from the Killiecrankie dig, the forthcoming week was the one the team needed to compress.

'What's the sudden excitement at Krankie?' Craig asked.

When Gill didn't reply straight away, Cassy stepped in. '*Mys.Scot* is leading a citizen science project. We're leveraging our readership to do a compressed study of a battlefield site before it's lost forever.'

'Aye. PR bullshit', muttered Craig. 'But what are we actually looking for?'

'Entirely speculative', said Gill. 'The whole area was thoroughly excavated a few years ago, so I'm not expecting any gigantic breakthroughs.'

Craig waved his right hand in front of him. 'And that's worth you being out of the office for what, a fortnight?'

'We'll get something out of it', said Gill. 'I'm sure we will.'

'And then there's yon *Toothfairy*', said Larry.

'Let's agree not to call it that', Gill said quickly. 'You'll have spotted Detective *Chief* Inspector Wiley in here yesterday. He brought in a case he'd like our help with.'

Larry leaned forward in his chair. 'Soons a bit mair interestin' than yon Krankie dig. Wha's the angle?'

Briefly, and confidentially, Gill told him.

'So, nothing we're ever likely to get permission to publish?' said Craig.

'I guess.'

'Unless there's a link to the other little story you're brewing', said Mhairi with a hint of mischief.

'Please, Mhairi', said Cassy. 'A single sighting does not a mystery make.'

'What's this?' asked Craig.

'Nice wee enigma', said Larry, digging Craig in the ribs with his elbow. 'You an the boss man cud tak a wee walk in the glens taegether. See wit you can find.'

Craig just looked puzzled and held a hand out to Gill for enlightenment.

'I'll explain', said Gill. 'It comes from the fact we had a report of the *Old Grey Man* in our logs over the weekend.'

'Old Grey Man?'

'Monster that stalks the Moontains an' glens', said Larry. 'Aw the while lookin' fair an Englishman to drag to his lair.'

'That's not even close to the legend, actually', sniffed Mhairi. 'I think, based on the data, you'll find he prefers to eat Scots.'

'Aw weel. When we write it, we might need tae juice it up a bittae.'

'*The Grey Man*', said Gill. 'Is one of the oldest Scottish myths. A tall, grey humanoid figure famous for chasing walkers off mountain tops. In our sighting report, he was seen near the peak of Ben Macdui, which as I'm sure you're all aware, is Britain's second highest mountain.'

'*The Grey Man* is most likely explained away by rare optical illusions', said Cassy.

Larry tapped the table to show his offence. 'Nae, lass.'

'I googled it', Cassy protested. 'And despite our illustrious editor's propensity to believe in supernatural mumbo-jumbo, this particular myth is just horse shit.'

'No smoke without fire', Gill whispered, rearranging the papers in front of him.

'Larry's right. You could go look for it', said Mhairi, smiling.

'Aye. On your own time', muttered Cassy.

'Wait, wait, wait', said Craig. 'You're saying someone actually saw this thing?'

'Aye, like I said. On Ben Macdui last weekend. A hillwalker left a long breathless message on our answer machine detailing how he was chased off the mountain by an ominous presence.'

'And you believe him?'

'I think we have to agree he saw something', said Gill. 'Whether it was a natural phenomenon or a spectre, we'd have to go and see for ourselves. Fancy it?'

Craig thought about this and seemed a bit taken with the idea. 'I suppose we could take a wee dander. It's been ages since I did a Munro.'

'Okay, let's do it. Is Friday week okay for you? We'll need to stay overnight so we can be on the hill at first light on Saturday.'

'Aye. I'm up for it. Need to check the snow before we go, but it's early yet. I'd be happy to give it a shot.'

'Hang on', said Cassy. 'Risk assessment! Chance of being consumed by a mythical monster is a tiny fraction of one per cent, and the chance of dying in an avalanche is what – about five per cent?'

'It's October. The avalanche risk won't be that high', said Craig.

'Craig, you're working with other risk factors here', said Cassy, jerking her biro at Gill.

'We'll be careful', Gill droned.

'If you're both knocking off bright and early next Friday', observed Cassy. 'What exactly will you be looking for on company time?'

Larry smirked. 'The lair of the *Auld Grey Man*, Cass. A cave scattered wi the banes o' lang deid hikers. Yon'll be Gill's next big breakthrough.'

'You coming too?' asked Craig.

'No way, pal.'

'Come on, Larry', Gill urged.

'I cannae climb the stairs wi oot coughin.' No way 'am goin' up a hill.

The meeting petered out and Cassy shooed everyone back to their desks. As Gill gathered his stuff to go, Cassy shut the conference room door, trapping him inside.

'Oh, no', he said.

'What?' said Cassy.

'You're about to resign, aren't you?'

Cassy's baggy shirt billowed as she flung her arms out in a dramatic flourish. 'Yeah, *Calum's Road* are playing Wembley next weekend. Then we're off to New York to launch the American leg of our worldwide tour. I think my journey with *Mys.Scot* is coming to an end.'

'Please, Cassy. Don't mess with me.'

'The thing is, Gill. I'm bored. You and Craig get to go play in the woods. Why am I always stuck at my desk?'

Gill looked at her, eyes blinking. 'You're the office manager. I think the clue's in the name.'

'Take next week', she continued. 'I'm half organising the logistics for Krankie, and you're doing the rest, which is all the on-site administration. But you hate that kind of work, so you'll be crap at it. And then you'll probably piss off because there's more interesting things to do. Which means, I'll be stuck here, back in Dundee, firefighting whatever chaos you create.'

'You'll be sending issue 28 to the printer.'

'We're already ahead of the game on that.'

'And issue 29 will need your guiding hand.'

'Done, all done', Cassy droned. 'BOR-ING.'

'Okay, Cass. What do you suggest?'

'Take me with you. Stick me is the same cheap hotel as you, separate bedrooms, and let me do my thing, but do it on site. I've got my phone. With a portacabin and half-decent Wi-Fi signal, there's not much I do here I can't do out there. Meanwhile, I'm freeing you up to do your archaeology stuff.'

'Do you have any idea how wet it could be next week? Have you seen the forecast?'

'I was raised on an island, you know. I do own outdoor clothes.'

'But Cass …'

'It sounds like you don't have Fiona. And there are bound to be situations I can handle better by being in the field. Besides, Mhairi is staff now. She can cover the phones.'

Gill wasn't sure if he was more concerned about Cassy's welfare in the field or what might happen in the office during her absence. 'If you're certain?'

'I'm sure, Gill. I'm fed up hearing all the stories second-hand. I want to be where the action is for a change.'

'Don't know what you said to her', Mhairi whispered, nodding at Cassy's back. 'She's all smiles since this afternoon's meeting.'

'Aye', said Gill. 'We'll see if it lasts. Listen, when you get in tomorrow, can you help me with this *Toothfairy* thing?'

'I thought we weren't calling it that?'

'Yeah, but on reflection, it's useful shorthand.'

Mhairi thought about this for a second, then smirked. 'Sure. What do you need?'

'There are a thousand ways to die on a mountain', said Gill. 'And The Cairngorm Plateau is the biggest lump of high ground in Scotland. Can you research the deaths on the mountain over the last few years? I want to know who died. And I need a list of people who disappeared who might have died, and if you can find it, a list of unidentified bodies.'

Mhairi shook her long brown hair off her shoulders and peered at Gill. 'Is this data to help you find the *Toothfairy* or the *Old Grey Man*?'

'Either', said Gill. 'Possibly both.'

'I see. Nice we can do our bit to help the police.'

'Yeah, well. It's *The Grey Man* that really gets my juices flowing.'

'Good job Larry made his prediction when he did. Not a single death reported in *Mys.Scot* for ages.'

'Aye', said Gill. 'I've got a nasty feeling it could be a heavy month.'

'Your request is going to take some time. But I'll try to get you something by late next week.'

Gill spent Friday morning working with Larry, Craig and Mhairi making the final changes to issue 28, plus setting up the website and social media feeds working to build interest in next month's stories. Friday afternoon was the regular publisher's meeting, so that left Friday lunchtime for Gill and Cassy to pull the logistics together for Killiecrankie. Cassy's skills and rejuvenated enthusiasm ate up the tasks so that when he returned from the meeting, most arrangements were in place. Anticipating a few days out of the office Gill was starting to look forward to it. He was just about to wrap up his week when his mobile rang.

'Afternoon, Fiona.'

'How's it going?'

'Mad dash to the finish, but we're all set for Killiecrankie next week.' He chewed on his lip for a moment. 'How are you feeling about helping us for the first week?'

'Something annoying just happened.'

Gill's heart sank. Fiona was a friend, a relative, and the best site supervisor he'd ever worked with. 'What's going on?'

'I was speaking to the site director at Winchester and dropped your name into the conversation. He got a bit excited by our association and insisted I take the full two weeks with you before joining his dig.'

Gill clenched his right fist and shook it happily. 'Oh, that's nice of him.' He left a lengthy pause and put on his calmest voice. 'Though, I'll have to look at the roster again. Make sure I can still fit you in.'

Fiona laughed. 'Piss off, Gill. You've got me for two weeks max. I'll see you Monday.'

'Fi', Gill called. 'Thank you. And also, thank you for last weekend. I know Dad would have wanted you there.'

'We're family, Gill. It's what we do.'

Chapter 7

Almost 7 am and Oscar looked out the window towards the golf course where the first glints of sunlight announced another new day. Tonight's package was almost processed, and the remaining procedures of draining and labelling were all that lay between a long night's work and bed. The foul smell that had filled the room in the past hours was almost gone and only the lingering industrial pickle-like aroma of the formaldehyde lingered in the air. These concluding tasks ticked past with practised efficiency until finally, the stainless-steel mortuary door clicked closed. Sighing with tiredness, Oscar went through to the office and checked the work diary for the upcoming days. Today was Saturday, which shouldn't have been a surprise, though in fact, it was. Wondering for a second when this working life could finally stop, Oscar stopped and checked the date. It was 5th October. Only three more weeks until this work was done. Three weeks until this covenant was fulfilled.

Shoving hands in pockets to search for car keys, Oscar's fingertips rippled against objects, cold and smooth.

'Getting sloppy!' muttered Oscar irritably.

Gripping the objects and then letting them rest in gloved hands, these weren't the kind of things you'd want to see escaping in the laundry.

Squatting and reaching for the lowest drawer in the filing cabinet, Oscar rummaged at the back until fingers found an old metal coffee tin. Oscar shook it gently and felt its weight. With a flourish, the six perfect human teeth slid from the gloved palm and joined the many others already in the tin.

'Almost time for a ramble', Oscar said quietly.

Chapter 8

Leaving Dundee bright and early, Gill and Cassy were up at Krankie for 7.30 on Monday morning, with Fiona arriving shortly after. It was raining, just as it had rained most of the weekend. Scott Shannon met them and took them to their new HQ, basically, a portacabin in the field next to the carriageway. The fact the hut had been placed on a section of the designated dig site seemed an irrelevant detail Gill decided not to debate.

'Miserable morning', said Scott after the introductions.

'How's the site looking?' asked Gill.

'No sign of any more slippage if that's what you mean. But the ground's saturated so we'll be alert to any movement. I do have something to show you in a minute. What's your plan?'

'We've volunteers and equipment arriving between 9 and 10 am. We'll brief our people in batches and set them working in four teams. Fi, do you want to cover some of the detail?'

Fiona nodded. 'This dig is due diligence, so we won't actually excavate anything unless the ground looks promising. It's all been surveyed before so we're not expecting to set the world alight. We'll do an initial sweep with metal detectors and ground-penetrating radar. Gill, that's assuming we have enough people from the Uni with appropriate skills?'

'Aye, more or less.'

'Then we'll log everything we can spot from ground level and make some executive decisions about where we sink our spades.'

'Great, well you'll have the site pretty much to yourselves for the full two weeks. That's apart from the engineers who'll be wandering around trying to figure out how we fix this mess.'

Gill looked at his watch. 'Cassy. Can I suggest you get back on the shuttlebus and start to muster the early arrivals in the canteen? I want to do the Health and Safety briefings before they set foot on the site, and we might as well do it somewhere out of the rain.'

'Aye, aye, boss.'

'Fi, you're with me. Scott has something to show us.'

'Bloody hell', said Fiona under her breath. 'This is gonna be complicated right from the starting gun.'

They stood above the main landslip, looking downhill towards the river, surveying the thirty-metre-wide slick of mud and stone. Prominent in the dark earth were the paler streaks of human bones.

'We didn't see them at first', said Scott. 'But all this rain seems to have flushed them to the surface.'

'Any idea where they came from?' Fiona asked.

'I've looked at the past archaeological surveys', said Scott. 'They mark a couple of burial pits. I'm guessing the landslip ripped them apart.'

'Aye', said Gill. 'On battlefield sites, we normally identify these bone pits, then leave them be. They're designated war graves.'

Scott nodded at the hillside. 'Well, now they're exposed we can't leave the bones here. What do you reckon?'

'You know as well as I do, Scott. This will need to go to the Procurator Fiscal.'

'Aye, but it's not like it's a murder scene', Scott protested.

'Nevertheless, the law is clear', said Fiona.

'I know some people I can reach out to', said Gill. 'Let me say hello to our volunteers and then I'll make a few calls.'

Scott nodded anxiously. 'And after we've had the police slow us down for a few more days, what then?'

Gill looked at Fiona. 'Gather, record and remove. If the bones were older, they might go to a museum, but this lot? We'll probably need to plan their reburial at some stage, but that can be done later. Fi, what do you reckon?'

Fiona, however, was staring at the sprawling rubble, dotted with human bones. 'There's something weird about this. Can't put my finger on it.'

'What's bothering you?'

'Dunno. When I figure it out, I'll let you know.'

'I think I know what you mean', said Scott, turning away from the landslip. 'This place feels like the haunted house of road construction.'

Gill laughed. 'That's surprising coming from the mouth of an engineer.'

Scott shook his head. 'Maybe it's the presence of human remains, but once you've been hanging around here a few days, wait and see if you agree with me.'

'Duly noted', said Gill. 'But in the meantime, can we agree not to discuss ghost stories in front of our newbies?'

An hour later, Gill stood in the contractor's canteen briefing the first batch of volunteers, while Cassy manned the door, checking in new arrivals. She was sensibly dressed for the outdoors but with a few theatrical touches like a blood-red scarf with matching fingerless mittens.

'Welcome, folks', he shouted over the rumble of voices. 'Grab a seat please, and I'll run through some Health and Safety before Fiona briefs us on what we'll actually be doing today.'

After fifteen minutes of housekeeping announcements, Fiona called out lists of names to place people in teams. 'We're about fifty-fifty in terms of novices versus people with archaeological experience, so you will all be buddied up. Do please take instructions from your mentors and don't be afraid to ask if you're not clear.' She looked across at Gill. 'Anything to add?'

Gill had been chewing on a form of words and took the floor again as all faces turned to him. 'Everybody, I do have one important announcement.' He waited until the last voices died down. 'You'll all be aware this is a battlefield site', he said, looking around to make sure he had their attention. 'On a summer's morning back in 1689, a small Jacobite army ambushed a larger government force as it wound its way along the River Garry. As battles go, it was short and bloody.

Between two and three thousand men on both sides died that day. As was the custom, they buried their dead where they fell. Survivors dug grave pits to allow speedy interment of the bodies.' He stopped to clear his throat. 'What I want to alert you to is the likelihood you will encounter human remains during these excavations. In fact, I've seen one spot already this morning where human bones have been exposed near the surface. For that reason, we'll issue you all with protective gloves and masks. Please don't touch human remains without alerting your team leaders.'

Gill hesitated, thrown back to a memory of how he'd lain trapped beside the long-dead bones of a man who'd once been his friend. That experience on Orkney still had the power to keep him awake at night. Noticing his pause, a ripple of nervous whispers broke out around the room.

Coming back to himself, Gill moved to address their worries. 'Look, folks. It is one thing for professionals to be doing this job, but as volunteers, I don't want you to underestimate how upsetting it can be to hold in your hands a human pelvis, skull, or whatever. I'd like you to think about that on your way down to the site. And if at any moment you have qualms, let us know so we can deploy you in the area least likely to have human remains.'

He glanced around the silent faces. 'Okay, looks like we have a minibus full, so Fi, if you want to take the first group down, Cassy and I will brief the next cohort.'

It was late morning before Gill saw the last group escorted onto the site and into the hands of the various team leaders. With a gasp of relief, he found Fiona had recruited several experienced students, including three of his original waterhorse team. Having accepted hugs from Hailey, James and Emma as they arrived on site, he put them to work as Fiona's lieutenants. With that done, he was free to make a phone call.

Gill didn't particularly dislike DC Lillico. They'd had a run-in; that was true. But the man was a little too straight – a little too much by the book for Gill to be at ease around him. So, his options were either, to call Wiley and most likely find himself palmed off to another department, or he could just call the police helpline and be passed from one desk to another without anyone grasping the urgency of his situation. Or, he could bite the bullet and talk to the one competent individual in his phonebook who'd most likely get the job done. Swallowing his pride, he manned up and made the sensible choice.

'DC Lillico. Gill McArdle here … Yeah, good thanks. Hey, you know the way I'm doing DCI Wiley a favour on the *Toothfairy* thing … Sorry, but I can't think of an easier short-code. I don't mean to be disrespectful. Anyway, I'm at the Krankie battlefield site and I've human bones to report to the Procurator. Would you mind being our liaison? … Hard to tell how many. Let's say forty individuals for now and we'll pin down the number once we move forward.'

He listened for the response. 'Great. Thank you. I'll see you later.'

The morning's rain was relentless. By early afternoon, Fiona reported discontent in the ranks, and they decided to call a halt for the day. The police would be arriving soon, and Gill judged it best if they had the entire site to themselves. Cassy moved amongst the wet, weary workforce to thank them for their time, while Gill and Fiona sheltered in the portacabin and reviewed what had been achieved.

'We've got a grid established over the entire site, and apart from the landslip area, it's all pegged up. We made a start with the metal detectors, but there's no point dragging the ground radar about in this rain', Fiona began.

'We've got a weather window tomorrow morning', said Gill. 'We can make a start then.'

Fiona nodded. 'I'll work from the outer perimeter. Let the guys get familiar with their kit before we approach the heart of the battlefield.'

'How are our troops holding up?'

'Just the first day. We're bound to lose a few as the week wears on. Great to have most of the Harris crew. The energy they're bringing is unreal.'

'I didn't think they'd be available.'

'Emma and James are doing master's degrees and Hailey now works in a Perthshire brewery. But when she heard about this dig being almost on her doorstep, she begged her manager for some time off.'

They were interrupted by Scott sticking his head around the door. 'The boys in blue just turned up.'

'We've done an initial sweep', said DC Lillico two hours later. He was standing with Gill and Scott, in the shade of a police van, taking what looked like a very welcome sip of coffee. 'As you say, there are bones throughout the soil spill. My guys reckon they're consistent with the battlefield context.'

'After this length of time, it's unusual for any bones to survive, said Gill. 'So, the crypts must have been dry enough to slow the decay process.'

'And you're certain these are war casualties?'

'There's no consecrated ground in the area of the landslip. No record of family burial sites, plague pits or any other reason to see so many remains in the one place.'

'Fine', said Lillico. 'I'll double check with church records, but I'm happy to proceed on the assumption these are field-buried casualties.'

'Are you telling us we can crack on?' said Scott.

Lillico shook his head. 'Not as easy as that. We'll need a pathology report on all the bones you recover. We'll send someone to work alongside you. They'll check there are no contemporary remains before we release them for reburial.'

'Hang on', said Scott. 'The logistics of this could get quite complicated. We have minimal storage capacity here.'

Lillico lifted a hand. 'There are agencies who can handle this kind of thing. People who could transport and store everything you find.'

Scott coughed. 'Aye, at who's expense?'

Lillico ignored the question. 'We've a list of morticians, approved by Police Scotland. I'll sort something.'

'Once that's in hand, we can press on?' Gill asked.

'Yes. One of our pathologists will be present while you're recovering the bones. If you have any questions, chat with them.'

'And if they're not about? Can we call you?'

'I'm hoping I won't have any day-to-day responsibilities up here, so best if you contact the pathology people', said Lillico. 'When do you think you will proceed with recovery?'

Gill looked at Fiona. 'As soon as we get a break in the rain.'

Chapter 9

Alex Lillico said he had a list of police-approved morticians, but when questioned by Gill, he admitted DCI Wiley had already selected a preferred firm. For his part, Gill was delighted. Lossuary was a renowned business with exactly the skills they needed. Better still, Gill had used their services several times in the past. Their senior director, Pete Gibson, had the benefit, not only of being the cheeriest mortician Gill had ever known, but also the most flexible. Of average height and slight build, with thin, wildly flyaway hair, the spritely sixty-something looked well past the normal retirement age. Dressed in black Gortex over a simple black suit, he held an earnest smile as he grasped Gill's hand and shook it vigorously when they first met in Fiona's makeshift HQ the following morning.

'Great to see you again', said Pete.

'Thanks for coming so quickly.'

'No problem', said Pete. 'I've worked this trade in one form or another for fifty-five years and the one thing I know for sure about the dead is that the living like them tidied away as quickly as possible. Talk me through your situation.'

Briefly, Gill did so.

'You'll want to bring up the bones to a covered area on the roadside. From there we can box them, label them and remove them to our premises at Falkirk.'

'The police will want to view them at some point.'

Pete beamed an even bigger smile. 'We've done a few of these jobs before. We'll pack the boxes here, before drying the bones at our facility. Then they'll be sealed again until the pathologist has done their thing.'

'Are you sure you have space? Early indications are we have the remains of several dozen different individuals.'

Pete reached out and grasped Gill's arm. 'You've seen Lossuary. Unless you find more than a thousand, we'll be fine.'

'If we find that many, the Transport Authority might decide to build the road over the top of us', muttered Gill.

'I'll get you a dedicated team. I'll be doing the paperwork, taking photos of the box contents, and overseeing storage and catalogues back at Falkirk. And you'll have Hamish and Gary doing the collections. They can help with some of the heavy lifting.'

'Thanks. At the moment we're only scheduled to do a two-week dig. I've no idea how the bones will impact that timeline.'

Pete chuckled. 'I've been here before. Two government agencies working with completely different priorities.'

Gill nodded. 'The road service wants to start the reinstatement as soon as possible, while the police take their time ensuring no crime has been committed.'

'Which reminds me. You said there's a police pathologist around somewhere?'

Gill pointed through a dirty window. 'The lady in white overalls. I think her name's, Beth.'

Pete beamed with happiness. 'Think I've worked with her before. I'll just go and say hello.'

Tuesday afternoon wore on and the rain returned, again. Fiona released the volunteers a little ahead of schedule and beckoned Gill to walk the site with her. The grid pattern was now augmented with flags of different colours and in a few places, actual excavation had started.

'We're getting back on track despite the slow start', she said. 'As long as the volunteers keep showing up, we'll burn through this lot over the next couple of days.'

'Great. Then we can move one of the teams to the fringe of the landslip. Scott's engineer is certain there's no immediate risk of further collapse.'

'How's Cassy enjoying her first on-site?' Fiona asked with a mischievous smile.

'Finding lots of good reasons to hang out in the canteen. She's made volunteer relations her highest priority.'

'Not enjoying all the rain and mud?'

'Since her walking boots started to leak, I haven't seen her smile once.'

'Where have you guys been staying?'

'A guest house at Blair Atholl. I love it, though Cassy is bored to bits.'

'For goodness sake, Gill. Send her back to Dundee!'

He shook his head. 'I'd never hear the end of it. She stays. Stays and stays and stays, until the moment comes when she's had enough.

Wednesday morning brought no change to the weather. Fiona led a team onto the top end of the spill site and started to nibble away at the tonnes of earth that had washed out of the road embankment. Within three hours, they had gathered enough bones to fill two trestle tables, located on the roadside surrounded by a dirty-white marquee. Gill found Cassy, standing at a distance from the remains. She was sheltering under an umbrella, watching Pete Gibson's crew, recording and boxing the bones.

'You alright?' Gill asked.

Cassy gave a flick of her chin and shook herself out of whatever daydream she inhabited. 'Just trying to imagine these bits as people.'

Gill nodded. 'It's tricky when they're disarticulated. Easier if you have a complete skeleton.'

Cassy shuddered. 'That would be even worse.'

They watched Hamish close the last of four boxes and load them into the back of a white van. 'Come on', said Gill.

'Where are we going?'

'I want to show you the other end of Mr Gibson's operation.'

'Is that really necessary?'

He studied her uncertain face. 'It's part of the archaeologist's job, Cass. We lift these objects out of the earth and we're responsible for what happens to them.'

'Not sure I need to see that bit.'

'And it's an hour each way in a warm, dry car.'

Cassy's face brightened immediately. 'I'm in.'

They followed Pete's van to an industrial estate at the edge of Falkirk and watched it reverse against a roller door. Pete directed them to the reception area where they signed in and had their photos taken by a smart piece of security kit. The building was entirely anonymous from the outside and it was only in reception that the company revealed its brand name. '*Lossuary. Specialists in recovery, preservation and storage of human remains.*'

'A long time ago, we used to be a regular family firm of Funeral Directors', Pete explained to Cassy as he led them through the building. 'Then the business got quite competitive around here with the big nationals muscling in. For a long while, it looked like we might have to close.'

Moving from a dingy corridor into a harshly lit room full of brushed steel surfaces and cabinets, Gill could see the room was scrupulously clean. He caught no whiff of decay, though a strong smell of disinfectant stung his nostrils.

'Then in the summer of '88, there was a massive fire on an oil rig', Pete continued. 'It was a terrible business. Hundreds of deaths, meaning hospital morgues were full and the victim's bodies were stored at multiple locations across Scotland. It was before the days of DNA analysis so identifying the dead was a logistical nightmare. My father, who was close to retiring, won an emergency contract to act as a clearing house. We had the funereal skills and most helpfully, the space to do the job quickly, and with dignity for the dead.'

He pointed to a glass-fronted wall partitioning off a large bay of chiller drawers. 'We built up something of a reputation. And now, in the terrible moments after a large tragedy, this is often where the victims are recovered.'

'Sounds gross', said Cassy, under her breath.

'Technically, yes', said Pete. 'It is a dirty job by any stretch of the imagination. But as the saying goes, somebody needs to do it.'

'This is your entire business model?' asked Gill.

'Yes. Multiple death situations. Logistical support for police pathology units. Unidentified remains. And a wee side-line in aurochs', added Pete, after a pause.

'What?' snapped Cassy.

'The creature we recovered from the banks of Loch Ness', Gill explained. 'It came here to be cleaned. We're donating it to *The Ness Explorer* Exhibition once they've finished their rebuild.'

'Ah!'

'Had any disinterments like our battlefield site?' asked Gill.

Pete shrugged. 'From time to time. Situations where human remains have to be lifted from consecrated ground. A new motorway cutting through a graveyard; that kind of thing.'

'Do you ever get nightmares?' asked Cassy.

Pete laughed. 'By the time I was twelve, I was doing human embalming for my Saturday job. I'm past having nightmares.'

Gill shivered. It had been less than two weeks since he'd said goodbye to his father's earthly remains, and so far he'd experienced none of Pete's ambivalence around dead bodies.

The older man led the way to a warehouse area and used a remote control to start the roller doors lifting upwards. A minute later, Hamish drove the van inside and Gary lowered the door.

'We don't shift anything from the vans until the doors are closed. We don't want to risk upsetting a passer-by.'

'What happens next?' Gill asked.

'Our boxes are heat resistant', Pete said. 'We take the lid off and place the container in a low-temperature kiln. We want to dry the bones so there's no chance of disintegration while they're in our store.' He led them from the warehouse back into the space full of large, brushed steel appliances. Gill thought it looked more like an industrial kitchen than a morgue.

'We can do any necessary treatments here', said Pete. 'And then it's off to the ossuary.'

He moved to open a double set of doors but stopped so abruptly, Gill almost ran into him. 'I would just say. Some people find this next section upsetting. It's partly the smell. We'll happily clean our equipment until the cows come home, but you can't do much about the stink of old bones.' He glanced at Cassy. 'I'm happy to just describe it to you, if you'd prefer?'

Gill looked at Cassy and could see she was giving serious thought to sitting this one out. 'Yes, or no?' he asked.

Cassy swallowed. 'Would Salina be jealous if you held my hand?'

Gill laughed. 'You're not serious?'

She frowned at him. 'It's okay for you. You dance with death three times a week and twice on Fridays. The closest I ever get to death is the corpse of the yucca tree that sits by the coffee machine.'

He took her hand reluctantly and together, they followed Pete into a large, dark room.

'What did you make of that?' Gill asked as they drove away.

Cassy looked at him before answering. 'Like an Amazon warehouse full of old bones.'

'It feels strange', he said. 'Being around so many dead people.'

'I found the kitchen freakier. What do you think they do in there?'

Gill imagined what some of Lossuary's customers might look like. 'Honestly, Cass. You don't want to think about it.'

Cassy obviously thought about it for a second. 'Ah! Yeah. Yuck!'

'Anyway, in the context of the work we're doing, it's helpful you've seen it, but you never need to go back there.'

'Tell you one thing', said Cassy after a few moments' silence. 'If I ever wanted to commit a murder, it would be a brilliant place to hide the body.'

Chapter 10

The week carried on and to everyone's relief, Thursday brought dry weather and the chance to really make progress with the dig. Fiona and Gill consented to the use of earth-moving equipment and now two small diggers gently exposed new areas of the landslip to the archaeologists' eyes.

'Totally against normal protocols', Fiona grumbled.

'In theory, we're wrapping it up a week from now so it's the only way to cover the ground', said Gill. 'Besides, the sooner we're done, the sooner you can skip off to sunny Winchester.'

Fiona stood up and painfully straightened her back. 'You make it sound like I'm a lightweight.'

Gill glanced at her agricultural hips and the muscled forearms that would make a wrestler proud. 'Never accuse you of that, Fi.'

He was saved by his phone ringing. 'Hey, Craig.'

'Hey, boss. Are we still walking on Saturday?

'I'm game if you are.'

'All that rain we had fell as snow on high ground, so it will be hard going in places. But it's too early in the season for avalanches, so I'm good as long as we're properly equipped. If we make an early start, we can approach Macdui from the north and be back in a pub before it's properly dark.'

'Let's go for it. Do you want to book accommodation in Aviemore?'

'I was thinking we could take my campervan. It's not luxury and you'll still need a four-season sleeping bag, but it means we can camp near Loch Morlich and be on the hill for first light.'

'I like the sound of that. Can you pick me up in Krankie on your way through?'

'Sure. I'll be there by 5 pm tomorrow. But before you go, Mhairi wants a word.'

'Tell her I'll call her back in twenty minutes. I need to find somewhere I can take some notes.'

Rather than go to Fiona's portacabin and risk multiple interruptions, Gill decided to slip away to the canteen, boarding the shuttlebus up on the carriageway and weaving through traffic until he was deposited at the contractor's base. It was heading towards 'home' time, so there weren't many customers looking for refreshments at this time of day.

'Hey, Mhairi. How was your week?'

'Good so far. Quiet without Cassy here. Is she doing okay?'

'Having a ball', Gill lied.

'And you?'

'Soaked to the skin most days and not even close to doing any proper archaeology, but we'll get some context material we can write up.'

'Good. Thanks for returning my call.'

'No problem. A quick question first on issue 28. Did you get it away okay?'

'We reviewed the proofs this morning and delivered it ahead of schedule. Means I've had time to start looking at historical records for deaths in the Cairngorms.'

'Excellent. Did you find many?'

Mhairi sighed. 'Where do I start? Those mountains are real killers.'

'Just talk me through what you're seeing as a topline.'

'Let's start with aircraft. There've been numerous crashes over the years.'

'Numerous as in dozens?'

'More like many hundreds. Almost six hundred aircrew died in multiple crashes on the Cairngorms in 1943 alone.'

'That's crazy! Though I guess there must have been a lot of novice pilots around due to the war. Delivering new aircraft to forward bases and all that.'

'And that continues after the war. There's a famous crash site involving an Oxford transport plane that came down in 1956. That's just one of many.'

'Any chance you could send me a list?'

'It doesn't exist, Gill. I daresay I could compile it with time, but you'd think there would be a memorial, or a book of condolence or something.'

'What about walkers and climbers?'

'Again, it's a long, heart-breaking catalogue, but at least there are accurate numbers. I've compiled a list of casualties and where they died.'

'I remember there were some harrowing tales. Parties of school kids and the like?'

'Aye. Particularly the 1971 disaster.'

'What about unidentified bodies?'

'A small number over the last fifty years', said Mhairi. 'Again, I'll include that in my email.'

'Any mention of bodies with missing teeth?'

'Absolutely none.'

'Last question. Do you have a list of named individuals who were thought to have been lost on Cairngorm but whose bodies were never found?'

'That one is a bit more subjective. And like the aircraft, there isn't a single exhaustive and reliable source. But I compiled a list of half a dozen names.'

'Thanks, Mhairi. This is brilliant. Let's keep going and regroup later. See if we can see any patterns in your data.'

'No problem.'

'Can I ask a last favour?'

'Shoot.'

'The Publisher's meeting tomorrow afternoon. Can you take along our working plan for issue 29 and stand in for me?'

'Don't you want Larry or Craig to do it?'

Gill just managed to restrain an expletive. 'I'd normally ask Cassy as they'd both refuse. Which reminds me; be confident.'

Mhairi seemed puzzled. 'Of course. Don't you think I'm normally self-assured?'

'Absolutely. It's just that Tony likes his editors to be punchy and concise.'

'I can do that.'

Gill thanked her and hung up. Poor Mhairi, he thought. If she made a single stutter, the editorial team on the cat mag would hunt her like an injured bird.

Gill started his Friday with a pre-booked call from Salina. She was onboard an oceanic exploration vessel six hundred kilometres south of New Orleans. Despite the isolation, the data link was sufficient to allow them a video call. In the week she'd been gone, this was the first time he'd seen her face to face.

'Good morning, mystery man', she murmured sleepily.

'Good evening, my love. How's it going?'

'First dive today. Mainly to test the machines. We get going in earnest tomorrow.'

'And how's the weather?'

'Hot and sticky. You?'

'The exact opposite. Scotland's winter has arrived grumpier than usual.'

'Pity. Sometimes October can be lovely.'

'We've got a break in the rain this coming weekend. Craig and I are going to climb a hill together.

'Nice. Send me some photos.'

'Sure.'

'Before I forget. Is there any chance you could do me a favour?'

'Anything, Sal.'

'It's mum's birthday the weekend after next. I meant to organise some flowers before I left and completely forgot.'

'I can do that.'

'You sure?' There was warmth in her voice, plus a tiny bit of scepticism. Salina knew he had a habit of forgetting things.

His fingers danced over his phone screen. 'I've made myself a reminder. I'll either deliver in person or order something decent. What does she like?'

'Hmm. Lilies, white roses and sea holly would be great. If you can find them.'

'You got it.' He left a pause. 'I won't let you down, Sal.'

She giggled mischievously. 'You'd better not.'

'How are things on the boat?'

'Good. The facilities are compact but decent. And the crew is almost half and half, male and female, so no one's at risk of getting their bum patted.'

'Glad to hear it', said Gill, remembering some of Salina's earlier travails. 'And the DSV?'

'Solid little ship. We're gonna get on fine.'

'It's hard to imagine you working at such depths.'

'Aye, we'll be down as low as three and a half thousand metres. Almost as deep as the Titanic.'

'Oh, Sal …'

'No need to fret. The tech's amazing.'

'I'm sure it is.'

'Don't become a worrier, Gill. Besides. You're not exactly in a risk-free occupation.'

'I'm a reformed character', Gill blustered. 'These days, I'm allergic to mild peril.'

'Oh, aye. Glad to hear it. And are you gonna take care on the hills?'

'Absolutely. Craig has loads of experience so he's in charge of Health and Safety. But hey, it's the Cairngorms, not the Alps. If you're sensible, what can go wrong?'

They chatted back and forth for a few minutes and all too soon their allotted time was up.

'I'll wait until I've got my dive schedule for this coming week, then I'll book another call. You can tell me all about your walk.'

'Be safe', he said, signing off. He listened for a click at the other end of the line before releasing a juddering breath. Salina Ahmed was his closest friend and his greatest weakness. He loved her so much, he couldn't imagine carrying on with his life if she wasn't around.

After his call with Salina, he left his accommodation and shook off his fear for her by pushing into a short but earnestly uphill run to the Falls of Bruar. Standing downwind of the waterfall, the mist rising off the river blended with the morning drizzle coming off the mountains to form a refreshing natural shower. He would have lingered if it hadn't been for the midges. Abundant despite the autumn nights, and seemingly impervious to the weather.

After a shower, he gritted his teeth for a call with Tony. Although Mhairi was standing in for him, Gill's boss didn't like it when his editors missed the weekly team meeting.

'I'm not hearing anything that's going to give us much of a story', said Tony, once Gill had summarised the dig to date.

Gill suppressed his frustration. 'Boss, you're the one that wanted us to take this dig. And maybe the articles won't quite be Waterhorse-level exciting, but we've got a citizen science project that will see *Mys.Scot* do its bit to preserve an important battlefield site.'

'Nothing at all on the *old-Gill-McArdle-sensor* of yours?'

'Just that if we stay here much longer, we're all gonna get trench foot.'

'Alright. Keep me appraised.'

'Will do. And Tony?'

'Yes?'

'Make sure the guys are gentle on Mhairi. I'd hate for her first publisher's meeting to be a grilling.'

'Mhairi!' snorted Tony. 'She's got more wit about her than anybody else in the room. I'm more worried about what she'll do to the guys on the hobby mags.'

'But the cat mag …'

'Trust me, Gill. And honestly, I'm not sure why you don't already know this, but Mhairi will be fine.'

When Gill arrived back at the dig a couple of hours later, Fiona and Cassy were deep in conversation. Fiona was gesticulating at the site ferociously. Even from a distance, her body language broadcast unhappiness. Cassy was nodding and scribbling on a clipboard.

'What's up?' he asked, zipping up his coat against the cool air.

'Because of the weather window, some of the keenies want to work through the weekend', said Cassy. 'We think that's probably a good idea.'

'Are you sure? We've lost two dozen already. The attrition rate will get worse once they get tired.'

'I dunno', said Fiona. 'I think we're getting down to a core. And frankly, anything that lets me get back to digging with a trowel rather than an industrial earthmover feels worth the effort.'

'Your call', said Gill. 'But I won't be able to be here.'

Fiona pulled a face. 'Salina cut your shore leave? And you're not even married yet.'

'Salina is diving off Mexico for the next few weeks. Deep sea submersible. I'm trying not to think about it.'

'Gill has organised some boy-time', said Cassy, nudging Fiona with her elbow. 'They're gonna climb some mountains and then drink lots of beer.'

'Craig is picking me up this afternoon. And strictly speaking, it's work', Gill protested. 'And there's nothing wrong with a couple of real ales after a full day's exercise in the exhilarating splendour of Scotland's highlands.'

'You sound like a bloody brochure', muttered Fiona, glancing at her watch. 'Shall we dispense with the flowery language and go grab some lunch?'

Chapter 11

They took packed lunches and walked downhill, away from the noises and smells of the road. The autumn was well advanced and most of the deciduous trees had shed their leaves, carpeting the valley floor with reds, browns and orange leaves. The lack of foliage made it easier for them to wind their way to the river, drawn as they were by the roar of the mountain spate, fuelled by the recent rain. They picked their way along a narrow trail almost overcome with blaeberry bushes and emerged into thin sunlight. Then they hunted along the river until they found a large flat rock and spread out their lunch.

'That's better', sighed Fiona, sucking in a deep breath and turning her face up towards the cloud-veiled sun.

Cassy meanwhile had crawled to the rock edge and was peering down into the river. Fast-moving water, the colour of whisky rushed past them, with short waterfalls linking a series of dark pools of uncertain depth. 'Did a soldier really leap this river?' she asked, a little incredulously.

Gill glanced at Fiona, who held up the cheese sandwich she was eating and beckoned Gill to carry on. 'That's the legend', he said. 'Donald MacBean. A government soldier fleeing the Jacobites.'

Cassy sniffed and didn't look convinced. 'It must be, what, eighteen or twenty feet? Hell of a jump.'

'If your life's in danger, you can do almost anything.'

'You would know', Cassy grunted, pulling back from the edge. 'Was Donald part of the English army?'

Gill shook his head. 'Krankie was a battle in a Scottish civil war. England and Scotland were still separate nations back then, though they shared a monarch. This fight was mainly Scots against Scots.'

'What was it about then?'

'Religion, on the face of it. England and Lowland Scotland had picked a Protestant monarch. But the highlanders were mainly Catholic. They wanted to restore the Catholic King James. Hence the word, Jacobites.'

'But the good guys won, right?'

'Good guys? That depended on what side you were on. But yeah, the Jacobites carried the day. But their general was killed on the battlefield and the whole rebellion ran out of steam a few weeks later. Meaning lots of people had died for nothing.'

'Typical bloody religion', muttered Cassy, before glancing back at Gill. 'Sorry. I know you have your own convictions.'

Gill shrugged. 'When it comes to all the wars fought in the name of religion, I totally agree with you.'

Cassy unzipped her lunch bag and poured herself a coffee. 'What's the point of it then?'

'Most human cultures have a concept of God. The notion runs pretty deep in our psyche.'

'Aye, but to have a bloody battle because of what? Different religious practises? Seems such a waste.'

'There are other considerations', said Fiona with her mouth full. 'Religious wars were often fought as proxy battles between one power base and another. In the case of the Jacobites, you could argue they were fighting to preserve a way of life. The clans and their chiefs; their dress and their language. Religious differences were just the rallying cry.'

'And if your clan chief told you to pick up your broadsword and go fight, you did it because that was your duty', said Gill. 'Also, your chief was your landlord, so you could argue it was a case of, go fight, or watch your family starve.'

Cassy ripped the lid off a pack of fresh pasta while she thought about this. 'Maybe that made sense back then. But it's the twenty-first century, Gill. We're all free of these expectations. What on earth makes you want to be religious?'

'If you look at our culture, I'm not sure we are free', said Gill. 'And I'm not religious. I simply have beliefs that are grounded in my experiences.'

'Yeah? What experiences?'

Since his first clumsy coffee shop conversation with Cassy, six months before, Gill had refined his thoughts. He took a deep breath and lit the touchpaper. 'Magic', he said.

'You what?' spluttered Cassy.

'The word isn't perfect, but "magic" seems the closest expression for it. Put it this way', said Gill, patting the rock with his free hand. 'Let's say I had an encounter with the supernatural. Something I cannot explain by the laws of physics or any other natural law. You'd understand me if I said I was curious about that?'

Cassy nodded once.

'You know me. I'm a scientist first. I want to understand cause and effect. So, if I can only rationalise my supernatural encounter by reference to something I'll call "magic", then it seems sensible to investigate.'

'But seriously, Gill. Rabbits out of hats? How would this magic thing even work?'

'It'll be like any other natural phenomenon. It will follow rules.'

'Is that a smoked salmon sandwich?' Fiona interrupted. 'I'm eating a three-day-old piece from the canteen while you and Cass are on the posh stuff?'

'We're staying up by Bruar', Gill explained. 'The shop is pricey, but the food is first rate. We've been trying to catch the last orders in their restaurant.'

Cassy reached out and grabbed his wrist. 'Yes! The venison rump last night was … AMAZING.'

Fiona took another disdainful look at her sandwich and tossed it in the river. Then she eyed Gill's lunch bag. 'Give us a look then.'

While Gill passed it over, Cassy pulled them back on track. 'Rules of magic. Sorry, Gill. I'm not following.'

'Physics, chemistry, biology. All the forces of nature follow rules. Like how the water got to be in that river. And how that river shaped this valley. And how this valley impacts the rest of the environment. Because it is governed by the same Creator, this magic will follow rules. And its practise will have consequences.'

Cassy's eyes flashed at Fiona, who laughed. 'Don't stop him, Cass. This is hilarious.'

Gill felt his face flush. 'It does sound a bit mad. It's certainly subjective.'

'And you think you've figured out these so-called rules?' said Cassy.

'I'm still trying to nail them', said Gill. 'But basically, I see two rules. The first in this. There is a supreme being, let's call him The Creator.'

'Him?' said Cassy.

Gill flicked a hand at her. 'Let's not get stuck on pronouns. And this Creator has a son who once visited our world, plus a representative who still lives here on Earth. You have to heart-of-hearts believe in all three of them for this to work. That in effect is the cost of operating in this magic. You have to acknowledge the Creator and his representatives. With me so far?'

Cassy nodded. 'But what can this so-called magic actually do?'

'That's the second rule. It can do anything.'

'Anything?'

Gill nodded. 'Turn water into real ale. Bring the dead back to life. Stop the sun in its tracks for a few hours. Anything.'

'You're quite, quite mad', said Fiona, now happily munching on a red wine and haggis-flavoured sausage roll she'd found in Gill's bag.

'What's the catch?' said Cassy. 'There has to be a catch. Otherwise, everybody would be doing this stuff.'

'Yes', said Gill. 'The catch is this. The magic is unpredictable. Sometimes it works. Sometimes it doesn't.'

'Sounds a bit pointless then', said Fiona, licking grease from a mud-stained finger.

But Gill could see Cassy wasn't satisfied yet. 'The magic only works if you're trying to do something, or change something, that aligns with the Creator's desires and intentions.'

'You're saying I couldn't use this magic to win the lottery?'

'Unless it was in the Creator's plan to entrust you with absurd amounts of wealth, then, no.'

'Sounds like this Creator keeps all the good stuff for himself.'

'Not at all. I think his posture towards humanity is one of generosity. But at the end of the day, it's kinda logical the magic works to serve his intentions. Otherwise, he'd just be a great big vending machine in the sky.'

'Give me an example?' Fiona demanded.

'Well, take this job I do', said Gill. 'The Creator already knew my academic career was toast, so at just the right moment, this job came up. And I think you'll agree', he said with a smirk. 'I'm perfect for it.'

'And it serves your Creator's desires, how?'

Gill glanced back up at the dig site where the mud-stained hillside was just visible over the tops of the trees. 'At some level, I believe I'm fulfilling a calling. I'm designed to do this job and somehow, it sits within the Creator's purposes.'

'Still not getting it', sighed Cassy. 'If he's a supreme being and all that, how would we even know what he wants?'

'We have a book, and we have his representatives. And to an extent we can have human mentors, but that's a really good question.' Gill leaned across and gave her a fist bump. 'Right there, my diminutive friend, you just hit the nail on the head.'

Cassy turned and looked at Fiona for inspiration. But Fiona just shrugged. 'Only a week 'til the full moon. Hopefully, the dig will be done by then, before Gill gets down on his knees and howls at it.'

Gill grinned sheepishly at them but said nothing.

'Aw', said Fiona, leaning over to give him a clumsy hug. 'We do still love you. But magic? You're bonkers, Gill McArdle.'

The tailbacks through the Krankie roadworks meant it was almost 6 pm before Craig's campervan, coughed and staggered into the contractor's rest area.

'Tell me this traffic eases', he moaned as Gill appeared. 'This old girl hates staggering along in first gear.'

'Aye. In about two hundred metres thataway', said Gill, indicating north.

Craig nodded. 'Okay, then. Jump in and show me the wide-open road.'

'She's a grand old van', said Gill, glancing around at the boxy interior full of faded plastic.

'Aye. And she's more miles on her than a London taxi.'

'What's the plan?' asked Gill, hoping that at least a small amount of Friday night alcohol would be on offer.

'Fish supper in Aviemore, then up the road to Loch Morlich. We can camp there both nights.'

'No chance of a pub stop?'

Craig cracked a wicked grin and thumbed his hand over his shoulder. 'That, my friend, is all taken care of.'

Chapter 12

The weather forecast for Saturday had been fine and dry, but as Craig and Gill left the campervan and walked out from the Aviemore ski centre at first light, they found the mountains shrouded by a thin mist.

'Not what they promised us', said Gill, already regretting the previous night's session had ended with a youthful Islay malt whose raw peat smoke had been tamed with too much caramel.

'Aye. Any thicker and we'll have to call this off', said Craig. 'Have you ever been on the Cairngorm plateau?'

'Only in fine weather. You could see half the mountain tops in Scotland from up there. What about you?'

'A few times.' Craig shuddered. 'Walking the Cairngorm plateau in the mist is dead eerie. Unless you keep your head and a firm grip on your compass you can easily lose all sense of direction.'

Gill tapped his phone. 'I've got Google Maps.'

Craig shook his head in despair. 'Your battery won't last long in the cold damp air.'

'I guess.'

'The thing about the Cairngorms, Gill, is you need to keep a clear head. Don't be distracted by one member of the party wanting to go in the opposite direction. I've seen a group make navigation decisions based on the force of personality rather than map reading skills.' Craig stopped and shivered.

'And if this mist turns to a sullen black rain, you're wet to the skin in no time, and your kit gets heavier with the extra moisture. You get so desperate to get off the hill, you make unforced errors. That's when people get hurt.'

'Well, we're here now. Shall we take a look?'

'Aye. But let's go carefully. I promised Julie I'd keep us safe.'

'Agreed', said Gill. 'It's your call. If at any point you don't like the look of it, we'll bail out.'

Leaving the campervan, they walked past the ski centre and joined a wide service track that wound back and forth between the struts supporting the funicular railway. Built in the early 2000s, and the highest railway in Britain, the service had been closed on and off for a decade. Ultimately it seemed, the infrastructure would become an ugly decaying scar on the mountainside.

An hour of steady walking took them to the Ptarmigan restaurant and half an hour beyond that took them to the top of Cairngorm Mountain.

'Cracking view', said Craig sarcastically as they crunched over frozen snow and into the shelter of a small brick weather station. Although it wasn't windy, the mountain peak seemed to agitate the mist, making it fast-moving, as if the ground and visible air were two separate conveyor belts moving in opposite directions. Gill found the whole effect rather unsettling.

After they'd lowered their rucksacks, Gill pulled out his flask and poured them both a coffee. 'Aye. Could be better. What do you reckon?'

Craig opened his OS map and indicated their present location. 'Let's be careful to keep well to the south as we descend onto the plateau. There are two north-facing corries in the shade of Cairngorm Mountain that could catch us out.'

'You're sure you're happy to continue?'

'Normally I'd plan to exit by skirting past Cairn Lochan and walk the path back to the ski centre, but if this mist lingers that route won't be safe. Today, I'd suggest we pick up the pace and walk beyond Ben Macdui and then exit off the south face of the mountain using this path here.'

'That'll take us into the Lairig Ghru', observed Gill. 'That'll mean a long walk home.'

'It's either that or return by the route we came and end up descending Cairngorm in the dark.'

Gill glanced at his watch. On a leisurely Saturday morning, he wouldn't normally be out of his bed by now, so there'd probably be enough daylight for Craig's plan. 'Understood. Let's walk for two hours and then review.'

They finished their drinks and set off into the mist, descending Cairngorm Mountain towards the plateau. Had he been on his own, the poor visibility would have been enough to make Gill turn back. Although he took comfort from Craig's cany disposition, Gill admitted to himself he was starting to feel anxious. For a few moments, he allowed himself to be distracted while Craig struck out across the icy heather. While he wasn't paying attention, a thick patch of mist moved through, and he briefly lost sight of his walking partner.

'Wait up', Gill called, picking up his pace for a few seconds until the outline of Craig's body started to materialise again. Just at that moment, a squawking, fretful chuckle exploded from near his feet and Gill dived to one side to avoid the source of the noise. He rolled over to find Craig laughing at him.

'Mind the wildlife, boss', Craig chided.

'What the hell was that?'

'Black grouse. Watch out, 'cause they're gregarious. There'll be more.'

'Sorry. I was miles away.'

Craig heaved him to his feet. 'Just birds, Gill.'

He dusted himself down and they started walking again. Soon they were following a thin path across the vast wilderness of the high plateau. The longer they walked, the more Gill understood Craig's caution. The mist deprived them of landmarks and the lumpy ground all looked the same. Without Craig's firm grip on his compass, they wouldn't have known where they were. And all around them, just a few miles in each direction, the plateau ended in sharp drops and cliffs. While it was one thing to safely access this slab of high ground, it would be quite another to get off it again safely.

In the event they didn't see any more grouse, however, a little while later, four dark shapes, about the size of donkeys came wandering towards them.

Craig gripped Gill's wrist. 'Watch out. It's the local mafia.'

'What?'

'Reindeer. They'll probably frisk us for carrots and mince pies.'

Gill had heard about the Cairngorm reindeer but never encountered them before. Unlike their native cousins, this invasive species had no fear of humans.

'They eat lichens', said Craig. 'So, the local forest managers aren't bothered by them.' He dug in his pack for a large plastic lunchbox. 'They're also quite partial to raspberry sandwiches, but don't ask me how I know that.'

The appearance of the reindeer combined with a slight thinning of the mist seemed to lighten their moods. Gill told Craig about how he'd fallen out of academia and into the *Mys.Scot* job. In return, Craig spoke about his adoption as a teenager by an east coast crofting family and his love of old motorbikes. He asked Gill about his father's death and how that affected him, and finally Gill gave voice to his fears for Salina and her regular visits to the ocean floor.

The time passed as they talked and so it was late morning when they arrived at the coordinates Lillico had given them. Ragged strands of police tape fluttered from four metal bars that indicated the centre of the search area where multiple human teeth had been discovered a few weeks earlier. Although they stopped and looked around, there was nothing to see as the whole area carried at least thirty centimetres of compacted snow. Behind them lay the bulk of the Cairngorm plateau. To the south lay the long incline that would take them up to the snowy top of Ben Macdui. And to the west and below them, occasionally just visible through swirling mist, lay a long straight valley called the Lairig Ghru.

'Corrour Bothy is down there if we get stuck', said Craig.

'I thought all the bothies were demolished?'

'Not that one. It's the natural halfway point for anyone walking Braemar to Aviemore.'

They both stood silently for two long minutes beside the police tape. The wind was even lighter here and only the eddies of mist drifting past their faces told them the air was moving at all.

'It's bloody remote up here', said Gill.

'Do you think that's why the *Toothfairy* chose this spot?'

Gill shrugged. 'Maybe. We're about as far from human habitation as it is possible to get on our congested little island. But I just don't get it.'

'What?'

'Why dispose of the teeth here? If it was simply a case of getting rid of them, he could have chucked them in a wheelie bin, or in a river or umpteen other places. Why come all the way out here?'

'Some kind of ritual', ventured Craig. 'Or maybe this place is important to him?'

'A sacrifice.'

'Pardon?'

'Maybe he is offering a sacrifice of some kind.'

'Like a religious thing?

'Maybe.'

Craig rubbed his gloved hands together and waited for Gill to finish.

For his part, Gill wasn't sure what he was looking for. He just wanted to take in the scene and see if anything spoke to him. But after a few minutes lingering in this desolate spot, he heard nothing.

Craig heaved his daysack back on his shoulders. 'Lunch on the top?'

Gill studied the dark brooding presence of Britain's second-highest mountain. 'How far?'

'An hour. No avalanche threats on this side as long as we stick to the saddle.'

He glanced at his watch. 'Let's crack on.'

They put their heads down, walking steadily, and aware they were approaching the day's midpoint. Any lingering at this stage would mean finishing the walk in the dark. And the hiking wasn't getting any easier. Compressed snow started to give way to the kind of boulder field typical across many of Scotland's higher peaks. The weathered pillows of rock were covered in a sheen of ice, so they stopped to pull on shoe spikes to give them grip. As they gained height, they were aware of lighter skies ahead and before the long, the mist thinned. When finally, they emerged onto the mountain top, they were standing in bright sunlight under a clear blue sky.

'Oh, my, goodness', said Gill, his eyes adjusting to the dazzling light as he studied the horizon, gradually twisting through three hundred and sixty degrees. The whole landscape below them was an infinite carpet of fluffy white clouds. Around them, and punching through this layer, stood the peaks of several mighty mountains. Nearest were the westerly Munros along the opposite side of the Lairig Ghru, while in the distance he could make out several more.

'Cairn Toul', said Craig, pointing at a nearby peak. 'And that one is Braeriach, I believe.'

'I've never seen temperature inversion before', said Gill.

'Because of the early snow', said Craig. 'The cool air sinks to the valley's floor leaving a warmer layer above. It's really quite beautiful.'

The two sat and ate their sandwiches in silence; revelling in the landscape, sitting upon an icy desert island surrounded by an ocean of frosty white air.

'Don't get too cosy', said Craig. 'Got a long walk home.'

Gill nodded and packed away his lunchbox, reluctant to tear himself away from the incredible scenery.

Craig texted his wife to update her on their progress, their planned exit route and an estimated time when he would next make contact. The details they gave her could be lifesavers in the event they got into difficulty. Then they started to descend.

Almost immediately, Gill felt a dark chill in his spirit. 'Ooh', he said. 'Did you feel that?'

Craig turned and looked at him. 'What?'

'Just … something', said Gill.

Craig turned away and started walking again. 'Probably your salami sandwich. I don't know what you were thinking of. That wee bugger will be coming back on you for days.'

Gill shook his head. He was letting the mountain spook him again. Probably his underlying anxiety about the physical dangers lying between here and the car. He hadn't noticed Craig had stopped until he ran into the back of him.

'Look', said Craig, pointing downhill to where the mountain cast its shadow onto the fog bank below.

'I'm not seeing whatever it is you're looking at', said Gill.

Craig stood up straight and waved his arms over his head. Detecting movement in the shadow, Gill saw Craig's outline waving back at them.

'It's him! *The Grey Man*', said Craig. 'So cool. Never seen this before.' He stepped away from Gill and up onto a rock, causing his shadow-self to split into two; one figure for Craig and one for Gill. They both waved and laughed.

'So weird', said Craig. I don't get how the optics work. At this distance, our shadows should be so diffused they'd be invisible.'

'Something to do with the mist', said Gill, trying to recall an article he'd read. 'Somehow the layers of mist form a lens that allows a sharp image to coalesce, even in bright sunlight.'

'No spectre after all', said Craig. 'No ghosts or ghouls. Just the simple application of physics.'

They laughed some more and waved at each other, not yet tiring of their boyish game. Until once again, Gill felt a chill in his spirit. Craig was still having fun, but for Gill, a rising sense of danger punctured his consciousness. Thinking about it, he hadn't felt like this since that dark night in Airth churchyard.

A snowball whistled past Gill's ear and hurtled down the hillside. Instantly, he felt the weight of his blade on his left shoulder. A quick glance at Craig suggested he couldn't see it.

Another large snowball came flying. Then a third, catching Craig powerfully on his shoulder and sending him slithering off the rock.

'What the heck', he shouted as he fell into an untidy heap on the ice.

Gill turned and looked uphill for their attacker. Snowballs might be fun in the playground, but this guy wasn't playing safe. He pulled his left hand to his forehead and shielded his eyes against the sun. Scanning left and right, he couldn't make anyone out.

'Look', said Craig, pointing at their shadows.

Gill followed his direction. Their two shadows were still distinct, though huddled. Off to the left of their silhouettes, on higher ground, a third, far taller man was getting to his feet. The figure stooped to pick something up. Then he stood and threw.

'Bloody hell', yelled Craig as a block of ice the size of a football flew over their heads. 'Hey, pal. Watch it', he yelled as the figure crouched again.

Gill ran a few metres back up the mountain, looking for their assailant, but still could see nobody. He heard the sound of air being displaced, just as a granite rock as big as the last snowball landed beside Gill, exploding against another rock and spitting out fragments in every direction. Gill felt his ear sting and reached up a hand. His fingers came back bloody.

'Gill! We need to bail', yelled Craig.

They were up and running, their shadows reflected on the mist tumbling over each other in their rush to get down the hillside. The third figure was moving too and stooping to gather something. Moments later, a rock the size of a basketball came whistling through the air and landed in front of them. Craig spun sideways to avoid the rocky shrapnel and fell hard on his right side.

'Who the hell is that guy?' Craig wheezed as Gill rushed to his aid.

'Dunno. I didn't see another soul when we were up top.'

'Not seen another walker since before the reindeer', said Craig, rubbing a bruise on his chest.

Another larger rock exploded behind them, covering them both in sharp fragments of granite.

'Can you run?' said Gill.

'Aye.'

'Let's get out of here.'

Linking arms, they accelerated to a shuffling scurry, while rocks and ice rained down around them.

Chapter 13

'What was that all about?' asked Craig as they reached the Corrour bothy an hour later. The low stone building, an old two-roomed croft, sat at the mouth of the glen and offered two routes off the hills. Strictly speaking, they didn't need to stop, but Craig wanted to recover before turning towards home. The bothy had no power or water, but it had a roof and a door, so better than nothing. Craig was jumpy, darting from window to window, scanning the approaches in case something had followed them. The dash down the mountain had exhausted him. Until he'd had a chance to eat and drink, Gill didn't think Craig had much left in the tank if they needed to flee again.

After Gill had prepared mugs of tea, he asked Craig to show him his injury.

'You're bruised', he said. 'But the skin isn't broken. Your jacket took the brunt of it.'

'Aye', said Craig, thrusting his hand through the fist size hole in his Gortex. 'That's two hundred quid down the drain.'

'We're fortunate that's the worst of it.'

'Seriously, Gill. What was that thing?'

'What makes you say it's a thing?'

'Boulders that size?' said Craig, turning back to look out the windows. 'Are there any myths about *The Grey Man* being a Scottish yeti? Cause if there aren't, I'm seriously gonna start some.'

'Maybe just some kid messing around.'

'Aye, and ma granny is the Loch Ness Monster.'

'Once we've caught our breath, we need to decide; north to Aviemore or south to Braemar?'

Craig shook his head. 'This path doesn't come out anywhere near Braemar. It finishes in a National Trust carpark in the middle of nowhere.'

'North, then?'

Craig nodded. 'Do you think we'll see that thing again?'

Gill studied his own senses before responding. The oppressive darkness he'd experienced as they left the peak was gone now. 'I don't.'

'If it comes for us in this valley, we don't stand a chance.'

'Come on. Drink up. Let's get to your van and thereafter, post haste, to Rothimurchus, where we collapse into the Woodshed Bar until closing time.'

Craig glanced at his watch. 'I hope they're open late because this walk is gonna take us hours.'

Raphael watches from the top of a stone buttress while the *Sword-Bearer* and his friend escape off the mountain. The mile-long slope down to the valley floor forms a gentle concave, forming a stone and heather amphitheatre capable of seating one million souls. Perhaps, that's why Sariel chose this place for his ambush. In his mind's eye, he would have cast himself as a gladiator, slaughtering the indigenous slaves for the amusement of his master. Except this time, the slaves escaped.

Behind him, Sariel hisses and spits in anger. It's still in the demon's power to pursue McArdle and his friend, but it seems like he's having second thoughts.

'Two chances down', Raphael calls out. 'Just one to go.'

'You warned him again!'

'We both know that's a lie.' Raphael allows himself a smile and admits he's hoping his boy might yet survive this. 'And I'm coming to realise, you've got terrible aim.'

'It's this human body', Sariel bleats, pointing at his sinewed arms. 'So limiting. So pathetic.'

'The terms agreed oblige us both to surrender our higher forms.' Raphael stops to stroke his black leather jacket. 'I find it insightful.'

'Ah! Now you see how fragile they are. So unworthy of HIS attention.'

Raphael considers his response. 'We both know they're not fragile when they're wearing the armour.'

Instantaneously, Sariel arrives at the foot of Raphael's lookout. 'McArdle only has the sword. And yet, you're so certain he'll survive! Oh, that's naughty, naughty, Raphael. You know how HE feels about pride.'

'And the Creator knows the *Sword-Bearer* better than I do. If I've made any error here, Sariel, it is only to underestimate him.'

'Enjoy it while it lasts', says Sariel with a cunning smile.

Raphael shakes his head in despair at his old friend's malevolence. 'What's the plan for your last attack?' He allows himself a playful shrug. 'Are you going to throw rocks at him? Again?'

Sariel is already walking away. He turns to look over his shoulder and sneers. 'All you seem to see are my failures. You haven't the wit to comprehend how I'm herding him to his death.'

'Oh, so your poor stone-throwing is part of a cunning plan?'

'Watch and learn, Raphael. I've got something very special prepared.'

Lillico didn't normally work Saturdays. Not if he could help it. He coached a kid's football club first thing in the morning, then headed over to the coast for a walk, or took himself to the cinema if it was wet. He'd shop for groceries in the afternoon, then pop and see his mother for a few hours. After that, on some weekends, he'd catch up with old university pals, or classmates from the police training college. Too often, however, he'd spend the rest of the weekend alone. Sometimes, especially on a Sunday, he would close his eyes and try to hear the still, small voice that had seemed so silent these past few years. He missed the voice. Its calming influence had steered him through his difficult teens. And now, with his career teetering on the brink, he wasn't sure he was still on the right path. Frankly, he'd give anything to hear the voice again. In the meantime, he'd carry on, in the hope his life was somehow travelling in the right direction.

This week, McArdle's battlefield crew and their short notice decision to work through the weekend had thrown a curve ball into the Lillico's normal plans. Beth Peyton, the pathologist who covered the weekday shifts, wasn't available this Saturday or Sunday, and no one else in her department was putting their hand up for it. That meant the responsibility was his. That said, he didn't have the skills to don a white suit and go picking over the excavations. He could however show up at the end of each working day and cast his eyes over anything they'd found. He could look at the log and open a couple of the boxes. If there was anything out of the ordinary, he could trust his copper's nose to sniff it out. In all likelihood, it would be mundane, and he could head back home and salvage what remained of his evening.

It was stretching into the second half of the afternoon when he drove his unmarked police car into the temporary layby created for the works crew. He moved carefully and only briefly showed blue lights while he nosed out of traffic. Parking up where he wouldn't block any works vehicles, he walked over to the staging area set up by the Lossuary team. One of the magazine girls was there, standing in shapeless walking trousers and a matching jacket. She was totting up numbers on a clipboard, clutching a cheap biro in a dirty red mitten.

'Afternoon', he said. 'Looks like you've had it dry today.'

'It's official', said the girl, her intelligent, dark eyes barely visible over a bright red scarf. 'Scotland has finally run out of rain.'

'Surely not? I can investigate if you like?'

'No need. I know where most of it is. My boots, my jeans, my skin.'

Lillico wanted to ask a question, but the girl wasn't finished yet.

She pulled down her scarf a little to reveal naturally red lips and high cheekbones. 'And I've worked out why the Jacobites picked this spot for their skirmish. I mean battlefields are meant to be muddy, horrible places. And this hillside is a shitstorm of mud.' She paused. 'Sorry. Can I help you?'

He flashed his warrant card. 'DC Lillico. Checking on today's finds.'

'Sure. Yeah, sorry. I remember you now.' She scratched the back of her head with her biro. 'I'll find you the list of what we've got so far. Fiona is still finishing off so she could tell you if we saw anything out of the ordinary.'

'Fiona. Site supervisor, right?'

'Yes. She's in the field. Can't miss her.' The girl flicked her eyebrows. 'She's the muddy one.'

Lillico thanked her, then took the implied advice and returned to the car for disposable white overalls and boots. Then, following the signage, made his way down to the dig. Since he'd last been here, the landslip area had been cleared of its weightier rubble and now, various flags and markers decorated the scar. Left and right of the collapse, much smaller excavations peppered a mile-long strip adjacent to the road.

He found Fiona with her hands on her hips, staring down at the trees shrouding the passage of the River Garry through this narrow glen. She was muddy from head to foot and seemed preoccupied.

'DC Lillico', he said, assuming she wouldn't recognise him.

'Hiya', she said, only half turning to face him.

'Difficult working conditions I hear.'

Fiona flicked her chin at the forest. 'Aye. First the rain, then the mud. Mind you, it's the constant noise and smell of the traffic I hate. Give me a nice, lonely field in the middle of nowhere any day of the week.'

'Tough gig. At least it won't be a long one.'

'Can say that again', said Fiona, continuing to stare at the forest.

Lillico cleared his throat. 'Find anything interesting today? Anything I should take a look at?'

Fiona slowly shook her head. 'Same ol' crap to be honest.'

'Right', said Lillico, uncertain how far he should push this.

'But now you're here, there is one thing you could help me with.'

'What's that?'

She pointed at the woods with a single forefinger. 'There's some bugger down there who's been watching us the last two days. I'd happily warn him off but apart from tiny glimpses, I haven't got a fix on him.'

'Probably one of the local kids mucking around. They'll be curious.'

Fiona shook her head. 'No kid. This is a big guy. And I can't be sure, but from the little I've seen, I'd say he's naked.'

'Oh', said Lillico. 'In this weather?'

'I can't be sure. One of the others saw the same thing.' She wiped her mouth with a dirty sleeve. 'Some kinda freakin' weirdo.'

Lillico sighed. 'I'll take a look.'

'Please', said Fiona. 'Normally I'd run my own security, but a big naked guy in the woods? I'm not being paid that kind of money.'

Lillico considered ploughing into the woods as he was. But he'd made certain promises to his mother, so instead, he returned to his car, removed the white overalls and fitted his duty belt. Checking it was complete with the usual essentials, he decided to supplement his gear with a robust torch.

'Just some weirdo in the nude', he told himself. 'Easy to scare off. Arrest if necessary.' He nodded. He was being quite logical. Why then did he suddenly feel so nervous?

When he returned to the field, Fiona had abandoned her forest watch and was loading tools and equipment into a scruffy portacabin. He walked past where they'd been talking and stepped into the woods. Once he was well below the treeline, he stood still for two long minutes, listening for any unusual sounds. Incidental birdsong rippled through the trees, and as a constant backdrop, the river tumbled over rocks and pools. He had to decide on a direction, so he started to walk upstream as noiselessly as possible. For one hundred metres, he saw or heard nothing out of the ordinary. Then two hundred metres, then three hundred. He was about to abandon the hunt when he heard a blackbird being disturbed some forty to fifty metres away. The bird's alarm call heightened his own anxiety and he told himself not to be so stupid – he had the law on his side. And if that wasn't enough, he had a weapon and the element of surprise. Reducing his speed, he clenched the torch in his right fist and moved slowly forward.

A few minutes later, he had his first sight of the man. Just a glimpse – a flash of skin between the distant bare branches of a hawthorn. And what skin! The man must have been doing this all day; his skin grey and wet.

Lillico gathered his phone to call for backup. But the density of trees plus the depth of the valley masked the phone signal. His quarry might have seen him now, raising the stakes in their game of cat and mouse, so he moved on, his trajectory taking him up hill, but well within the tree line. And another grey flash, flitting between two tree trunks. He considered calling out, then trying a sprint to run the man down. But his target held the high ground and would have the upper hand in any race. Instead, Lillico decided to outflank him, dropping to the river and making faster progress along the riverside path. He stepped past the trunk of a huge beech tree and paused to take his bearings.

'We shouldn't be doing this', said a voice behind him.

Lillico spun around to find an immense olive-skinned man staring at him. He was leaning against the tree, with his hands tucked behind his buttocks for comfort. He was dressed in black biker's leathers with a matching black belt, decorated with a motif of a roaring lion. Oh. And a sword slung at an angle across his back. Lillico had the strange sensation he'd seen this man before. Someone he'd arrested? A known criminal? But it had been a long time ago in a fog of circumstances Lillico had forgotten.

'Afternoon, sir', said Lillico. 'And who might you be?'

The man gave the most fleeting of shrugs. 'That's not important right now. The question that ultimately will need an answer is, who are you?'

Lillico pulled out his warrant card and held it close to the man's face. 'DC Alexander Lillico. I'm going to need you to come with me.' He stared at the man, exerting more confidence than he felt. If this man resisted him, Lillico would in all likelihood be overpowered.

The olive-skinned man looked surprised and pointed up the slope into the darkest patch of trees. 'I hope you're not confusing me with that creature. That thing passed this way a few minutes ago.'

'That wasn't you?'

The man tilted his head and smiled. On reflection, Lillico knew he'd asked a stupid question. The man's clothes, his colour. 'Okay. Where'd he go?'

'Back to wherever in hell he came from', said the man.

'I'm still going to need you to accompany me.'

'I've committed no crime', said the man evenly.

Lillico nodded at the sword. 'How about, carrying an offensive weapon in a public space?'

The man's face puckered into a gentle smile. 'This place doesn't seem especially public, DC Lillico.'

'I don't need to justify the rules.'

'Would it help if I told you, most people can't see my sword? In fact, most will never see it.'

'We'll go to the nearest station', Lillico countered, not knowing exactly where that was. 'Cover a few routine questions.'

'I like your belt', said the man, pointing to Lillico's duty belt.

'My belt?' said Lillico, sensing he was being distracted.

He threw his right hand behind his back and freed the handcuffs from their pouch, but just at that moment, his belt buckle gave way and the whole contraption fell to the forest floor. He dived to recover it and when he looked up, the leather-clad man had disappeared.

'Show yourself', Lillico called, moving around the tree to the most obvious hiding place. But the man wasn't behind this tree, or the next. Frustrated, Lillico decided to forget about Biker-guy and continued walking in the direction where he'd last seen the naked man. He wasn't tiptoeing through the forest anymore. He was direct and purposeful; more than a little frustrated and ready for anything. But when he emerged from the far end of the dig site twenty minutes later, wet and a little muddy, the fight had gone out of his limbs. Remembering he wanted to get back home, he strode across the field towards the portacabin by the shortest route possible. Fiona was locking up as he arrived.

'See anything?'

'Just a glimpse. But he got away from me. I'll try again tomorrow.'

Fiona peered at him with a weary, puzzled look on her face. 'You okay?'

'If you can show me your log of human remains', he said, ignoring her concern. 'I'll give it a once over and then we can both get on with our evenings.'

Chapter 14

Gill woke up stiff and cold on Sunday morning. He stared up at the ceiling, suspended just an arm's reach from his face, and wondered where he was. A groan from another bunk sounded a lot like Craig and Gill remembered he was in a campervan.

'Cold in here', said Craig. 'Stay where you are for a minute, and I'll get the gas on.'

Gill obeyed without speaking. He moved his limbs a little and took stock of his situation. In the event, it had taken them so long to walk back to the van the previous evening, they'd only managed an hour in the pub before closing. Two real ales. No, three. Then a whisky chaser back at the van. Younger men would have burnt the midnight oil, but Gill and Craig were beyond tired, and the alcohol eradicated any remaining desire they had to talk. It wasn't his head that hurt; it was every muscle in his body. Yesterday's walk had topped out at twenty-one miles and felt more like thirty because of the snow. The long walk home via the endless Lairig Ghru had been completed in darkness and aching silence.

'I like your van', said Gill as the first draft of warmer air kissed his face.

'Kids love it. Julie loves it. Personally, I'd prefer the flexibility of a tent.'

'Make sure you put your fuel costs on expenses. And your jacket.'

'Thanks', said Craig, putting a small kettle on the stove.

'Decent pint last night', said Gill. 'I was ready for it.'

Craig didn't reply.

'Are you alright? How's the bruise?'

'Gill. Two questions', said Craig, ignoring Gill's enquiries.

'Sure.'

'Firstly, what was that thing yesterday?'

Gill hunched into a sitting position in his sleeping bag and ran a hand through his hair, trying to bring order to the chaos. 'I don't know.'

'Can we agree it was dangerous?'

'Yes', said Gill. 'And there'll be a rational explanation, probably.'

'Take your word for that', said Craig, pausing to drop teabags in cups. 'Second question. Why are you treating this like it's the most natural thing in the world?'

Gill turned over in his bunk and looked down at Craig. If he could have made it sound rational, he'd have explained the occasional appearances of a man Gill understood to be his guardian angel. And that would have been the obvious thing to do if Raphael had suddenly materialised yesterday. But he hadn't seen Raphael in over a year and seeing the distressed expression on Craig's face, he decided chatting about angels wasn't going to help. In the end, he said something simpler but equally true. 'A little over two years ago I went into a bog and dug up a waterhorse skull. From that day forward, everything changed for me. The impossible became possible. The natural touched by the supernatural.'

Craig shook his head and turned to watch steam wisping out of the kettle. 'I hope that works for you, Gill because it sounds like a stretch for me. I'll give you this - whatever that thing was, it didn't seem natural.'

'Agreed. And let me throw out a wild idea of my own. I'm wondering if that thing we saw might be linked to the *Toothfairy*?'

Craig rubbed his stubbled face with the back of his hand. 'Yeah. I see where you're going. My bet is that thing eats hill walkers, and then just spits out the pips.'

Four hours later, after a big fry-up and a short, aching walk around the wooded paradise of Loch an Eilein, Craig's van pulled up at the contractor's carpark at Krankie. Gill transferred his gear to the boot of his own car and hobbled back to give Craig an awkward, blokey embrace.

'I enjoyed it', said Craig. 'Aside from the whole rock-throwing-monster-thing, it was a great laugh.'

'I enjoyed it too', said Gill. 'Great to hear some of your stories.'

Craig raised a hand in farewell. 'If you ever fancy renovating an old motorbike, you know who to call.'

Gill watched until Craig was safely on the carriageway, then hobbled down to the dig to see what was happening. He could see from a distance there was no one on the south end of the site and when he finally reached it, the portacabin was empty. Hearing distant voices, he limped along to the landslip area and found a small team, clustered around one confined area.

'Look at the state of you', said Cassy, coming in the other direction. She was smiling again. Four consecutive days of dry weather had done her a lot of good.

'Yeah, I'm fine thanks. You should see the other guy.'

'Did Craig have to keep stopping to let you catch up?'

'Are you suggesting I'm not fit?'

Cassy shrugged. 'I'd say you're run-for-a-bus, fit. Not ... Craig, fit.'

'Thanks.' He nodded at the cluster of workers. 'What's going on?'

'It's a skeletal mother lode. Fiona thinks we've reached the exposed bone pit.'

'I'll go and take a look.'

He made his way along a makeshift path, nodding at one or two volunteers he recognised. Fiona, true to form was on her hands and knees with a trowel. She noticed him and unsmiling, got to her feet. 'Guys, take a fifteen-minute break. I need to go over a couple of things with the boss.'

Nervously, Gill waited for the volunteers to clear away. 'What's up?'

Fiona dusted her hands on her overalls. 'We've hit the source of all the human remains, obviously. But that's not the main thing.' She glanced around to make sure they weren't being overheard. 'I've worked out what's bothering me about the bones.'

'Which is?'

'They're all stained as we'd expect, and many are broken, pre or postmortem. But there's no significant deterioration. On any of them. We assumed the bone pit would be dry, but it's not. It's as waterlogged as the rest of the site.'

'But surely, bone fragments … surviving scraps of rotted bone?'

'Nothing, Gill. It's like they've been in the ground for months instead of centuries. I don't know what, but there's something weird going on here.'

A few hours later, Gill was just about to leave the site and head off to his accommodation when DC Lillico arrived to make his housekeeping call.

'What's up?' said Lillico, seeing Gill limp towards him.

'I've had a tiring weekend', said Gill. 'On top of an already tiring week.'

'Business or pleasure?'

'I took a walk on Macdui with a friend yesterday, and we visited the spot where the *Toothfairy* sprinkled his calling cards.'

'Oh, yes?'

'Consequently, I have some thoughts for you.'

'Anything urgent?'

Gill thought about their encounter on the mountain. 'It'll keep for tomorrow. We should have your boss around.'

'Fine. Bathgate or Dundee?'

'Actually, could we do it here? I need to be on-site for a few days and there's something I want to show you.'

'Is this about our nude stalker?'

Gill pulled a face. 'What?'

Lillico shook his head. 'We can talk about that tomorrow as well.'

Gill nodded and flicked a thumb over his shoulder in the general direction of the dig. 'Can you tell me one thing - what has your pathologist made of the Krankie remains so far?'

'She isn't working this weekend, so we haven't spoken.'

'Get an update from her. Fiona is surprised by the lack of decay on the bones. I'd like to know what your expert thinks.'

Chapter 15

Looking around the portacabin on Monday morning, Chief Inspector Wiley looked uninspired by the accommodation. In the absence of a table, and because the plastic chairs were covered in mud, most of them had elected to stand. Wiley and Lillico held notebooks, while Fiona slouched in a chair with her arms folded, making it clear she'd rather be somewhere else. Outside, celebrating the start of a new week, heavy rain lashed the roof of the hut.

'When I asked you for a favour, McArdle, I was thinking you would use that big-assed university brain of yours to throw some fresh thinking at our little dental problem. I didn't think you'd tie Alec up for half the week, digging the foundations for a road extension.'

Gill smiled at the red-faced officer. 'Sorry. I needed to call somebody in Police Scotland, and you did offer to help.'

'We'll come to that in a minute', said Wiley. 'First, I hear you visited the mountain?'

'Yes. I wanted to see the context.'

'And?'

'Well, it is intriguing. Why walk so far to dispose of something you could literally chuck in a litter bin?'

'Most likely, he removed the victims' teeth to make it less likely they'd ever be identified', said Wiley. 'Beyond that, I'd say the killer is trying to make a point.'

'I take it the teeth were just dumped on the path? They weren't arranged in any ritualistic configuration?'

'Scattered along the path, like bird seed', said Lillico. 'No obvious pattern. The only difference is the amount of weathering on the teeth.'

'Suggesting they've been scattered on more than one occasion?'

'Yes. And scratches on the enamel suggest some of them had been there for years.'

Gill nodded. 'Then it has to be the location that's important to whoever placed them there.'

'Something about that particular spot?' Lillico clarified. 'Like a death?'

'Or a marriage proposal, or a declaration of divorce.' Gill continued. 'Something so significant he ritually comes back to this spot over and over again.'

'Maybe it's where he was standing when he heard his business was bust, or that he'd won the lottery', Wiley grumbled. 'Basically, any human emotion under the sun. I must say, all this useless speculation is getting my Monday morning off to a flying start.'

'I don't agree, sir. It helps us think about motive', said Lillico.

'What about the teeth?' said Wiley, ignoring him. 'I mean, why leave teeth?'

Lillico held out his hands. 'Maybe symbolic of something?'

'Or a metaphor', said Gill. 'A reference to something that's as frustrating as … pulling teeth?'

Wiley scowled at him. 'Ha, bloody, ha.'

'Or something sacrificial', Lillico continued. 'Where it's easier to bring in teeth as a substitute for an entire body.'

'You two are very entertaining', said Wiley. 'Maybe I made a mistake putting you together. Do either of you have anything solid to go on?'

'Yes', said Gill.

Wiley waved at him to continue.

'Last Saturday, when I was on the hill with Craig ... we were attacked.'

'Attacked, how?' said Wiley.

'We were beginning our descent. Someone came from behind us and started hurling snowballs.'

'Hold the bus', snarled Wiley. 'Snowballs, Lillico! Get on the phone and issue an APB.'

'And then the snowballs became rocks', Gill continued. 'Small ones at first, then boulders.'

Wiley looked at Gill with an expression that questioned his sanity. 'Who'd be throwing boulders at you?'

'I dunno. They were on higher ground and had the sun behind them.'

'You're sure this wasn't just a rockfall?' asked Lillico.

Gill shook his head. 'There was a temperature inversion that day. We could see our own shadows cast onto the fog bank. We saw a third figure.'

'How big were these rocks?'

'Initially, they were just a few kilos. The last couple must have been twenty, thirty, even forty kilos.'

Wiley cleared his throat. 'Kind of unlikely, don't you think?'

Gill shrugged. 'That's what we saw.'

Wiley's face puckered into a sneer. 'First time we met, you thought you were being hunted by a killer unicorn. That didn't turn out to be true.'

Gill left a long pause while he measured his response. 'You're right. I am, in every sense, an unreliable witness. And yet. Here you are, looking for my help.'

Wiley pointed his biro at Lillico. 'Alec here will take your statement, if you like. But I'm not linking this to our original investigation. We've enough to do as it is.' He nodded at Fiona. 'Miss. Can you tell us what's so interesting about these bones?'

'They've been in the ground for three hundred and fifty years', Fiona drawled, her head hanging low to emphasise her boredom. They should have faded away by now, unless they were buried in a dry crypt, which they're not. Or if there was high acidity in the soil to prevent bacterial corruption. And that's not the case here either.'

'Which suggests?'

Fiona sighed. 'You need to look very carefully at what we've found because there's a chance these remains are contemporary.'

Wiley's eyes opened wide. 'Alec. Did you know about this?'

'We only started speculating about it late yesterday afternoon. I could see the information was important, which is why we've come down here this morning. But I didn't see it as sufficiently urgent to disturb your Sunday evening, sir.'

'And the pathologist?'

Lillico shook his head. 'She hasn't mentioned anything.'

'But she's on-site today?'

'So I believe.'

'Well, let's go and speak to her then.'

Wiley and Lillico made to leave but Fiona held out a hand. 'Aren't we going to talk about the other thing?'

'What other thing?' Wiley barked.

Lillico looked at Fiona. 'We had a stalker here on Saturday. Maybe Friday as well.'

'A what?'

'A guy in the buff, watching us from the woods', said Fiona.

Wiley raised a quizzical eyebrow at Lillico.

'I went down to take a look, sir. I had him in my sights for a few minutes but couldn't catch him.'

'Any crime committed? Assault? Indecent exposure?' Wiley huffed.

'Borderline', said Lillico, looking at Fiona for confirmation.

'It weirded me out', said Fiona.

Wiley opened the door and looked up at the dark grey sky. 'I doubt he'll bother you this week.' He glanced around the room. 'Alec will keep an eye out for you. Assuming he's not busy doing someone else's job.' He tapped Lillico's elbow. 'Meanwhile, can we find the pathologist so we can finish up here and get back to civilization?'

They started to troop out of the portacabin and towards the landslip, but Gill hung back and caught Lillico's attention. 'Wiley was dismissive when we talked about the teeth. But Macdui is so remote, the *Toothfairy* has to have some connection to the place.'

Lillico drew his hands to his hips and looked towards the tree line. 'I agree. Once I've got him out of the rain, I'll talk to Wiley about it on the way back to Bathgate.'

'I've had our researcher review all the deaths on the Cairngorm over the last sixty years. I can ask her to share her data with you, if you like?'

Lillico nodded. 'Yeah. Please do that. If I find anything interesting, I'll let you know.'

'And as one favour deserves another, can you tell me why you're so certain this is definitely a murder investigation?'

Lillico glanced at his boss, making sure he was well out of earshot. 'Don't know why he's reluctant to share this with you, but we've established two more identities connected to the teeth.'

'And they are?'

'That's not relevant to your involvement in the case.' Lillico paused, then continued. 'But suffice to say, all three of the victims identified are on the missing person's register.'

'Ah, so one day they're walking around and the next, the only trace of them is their teeth on a hillside?'

Lillico nodded. 'And that's all I can say.'

'Are these people linked in any way?'

'Really, Gill. I've said too much already.'

'Okay. But the more you trust me, the more I can help you.'

Lillico gave a weary nod. 'I'll keep working on my boss. See if I can get you more information.'

There was no sign of the pathologist on the dig site, so they moved up to the despatch area and found a small but energetic lady, supervising boxes being loaded onto a Lossuary transporter. Somewhere in her late fifties, she wore all-in-one white protective overalls, topped off with eyewear pushed back over her close-cropped grey hair. She greeted Gill and Lillico by name, then peered at George Wiley.

Lillico took the lead. 'Beth, this is DCI Wiley. He's recently transferred from the Highland Division to lead the new *Special Investigations* unit.'

'Chief Inspector', said Beth, lifting a gloved hand in greeting.

'I'll get straight to it if you don't mind', said Wiley, pulling his coat collar tighter against his neck. 'As this roadworks situation has been dropped on our existing case load, I'm rather hoping we can tidy it away quickly.'

'Due diligence is the law when it comes to the discovery of human remains, Chief Inspector.'

'Nevertheless, we're not solving a crime here. I'd like your observations so far, so my DC and I can get back to some proper police work.'

'It'll all be in my report', said Beth.

'Granted', said Wiley. 'But I'm standing in front of you, and I'd like an overview.'

Beth paused what she was doing and fully turned to face Wiley. 'We've got a historical burial site that's been disturbed by a landslip. We are recovering remains to a commercial facility where they will be studied, before reburial at some later date.'

Wiley glanced at the nearest box and quickly back to her face. 'Nothing unusual to report?'

'The bones are in remarkable condition, given the age of the grave.'

'Remarkable, how?'

Beth looked at Lillico and back to Wiley as if weighing this as a trick question. 'Bones of this vintage are extremely rare. They've normally disintegrated by now.'

'You're saying the bones might be contemporary?'

'I don't think that's a reasonable conclusion given the context of the finds.'

'But they could be?'

'It's possible. That'll be clearer once I have them in the lab.'

'But you didn't see fit to mention this to my Detective Constable?'

Beth's body language closed like a clam shell. 'Chief Inspector. I'm a humble civilian contractor. On average, I work four days a week for Police Scotland, and two more for local university labs. At the moment, I'm juggling four cases for you people. I've got a murder, a rape and a beating that resulted in life-changing injuries. As much as I appreciate your desire to tidy this away quickly, this job …' she jabbed a finger towards the dig site. 'According to my supervisor … is a box-ticking exercise, and as such, he's assigned it the lowest priority in my workload.'

'I'm just …'

Beth cut Wiley off. 'If you have a problem with my work rate, please take it up with my manager. In the meantime, you can expect my final report five working days after we complete the bone recovery stage.'

'Fine', bristled Wiley. 'I look forward to it.'

Wiley strode towards his car without another word. Sheepishly, and with a little flick of his eyebrows to Beth, Lillico followed him. Wiley ripped off his protective suit and tossed it onto the back seat, before slamming the door. Waiting just long enough for Lillico to get into the passenger seat, Wiley drove off.

'Arrogant shite', Beth muttered, lifting a box and sliding it into the van.

Gill waved politely at Wiley's departing car. Like Beth, he knew Wiley wasn't good at first impressions. But she'd leapt down the man's throat at his first provocation and was needlessly making an enemy. Whether that was down to tiredness or short temper he couldn't tell. Nor was it on his list of priorities to find out. Knowing he needed to spend the afternoon in Dundee he headed for his car. There were things to sort back in the office and it would be a welcome opportunity to grab some fresh clothes, and a night in his own bed.

'Checking in', said Gill as he strolled into the *Mys.Scot* pen. 'How are you all doing?'

'Stiff as a board', said Craig. 'And still a bit rattled by our weekend encounter.'

'Told anyone about it?'

'Only Julie. And I'm not sure she believes me. She reckons we were low on oxygen, or high on alcohol, and just imagined it.'

Gill straightened his back and tried to keep his voice from sounding condescending. 'It was the Cairngorm, not the Himalayas.'

'Aye. That's what I said.' He paused before continuing. 'But we'd been battling through rough conditions. Speaking for myself, I was pretty tired already. Maybe it was just kids throwing snowballs and we panicked. Lost our perspective?'

Gill thought for a second while he measured his response. 'You've got a pretty big bruise for someone having snowballs thrown at his back.'

'What ever happened, we're still here to tell the tale, Gill. But I'll not be back to Macdui in a hurry.'

'How are things on the next issue?' said Gill, switching tack. They chatted for a few minutes about one article that Craig was working on, and Gill promised to send his feedback by the end of the day. He'd just started working on it when Mhairi finished a long telephone call.

'Thanks for sending your Cairngorm data to DC Lillico', he said. 'I'm wondering if you'd have time to do some follow-up?'

'Sure. What do you need?'

'I'd like to focus on Ben Macdui and get a bit more depth on incidents involving injury or loss of life. Let's ignore aircraft accidents – keep to people walking on the hill.'

Mhairi thought for a second. 'I can pull those from the old journals of *The Cairngorm Society*. I don't think they're digitized but I saw them as PDFs last week. Anything else?'

Gill took a second to frame his next question. 'I'd like to dig a bit deeper into any mythology attached to that particular mountain.'

'Fairies, ghosts, water spirits, that kind of thing?' she said as if Gill's request was the most normal in the world.

'Anything at all. Especially anything that relates to the *Old Grey Man*.'

'Sure. I'll have to juggle alongside magazine prep, so I hope you're not in a hurry.'

'As and when you can', said Gill. Like Craig, he didn't plan to climb Scotland's second mountain any time soon.

Chapter 16

That evening, Oscar's van drove into the Edinburgh-bound motorway services at Harthill, and holding to the service road running through the grounds, slid past the main carpark and into the far reaches of the site. Ignoring the exit ramp, the van found its way to a piece of isolated tarmac, in a blind spot well removed from any of the security cameras, and carefully parked up. It took a minute for Oscar's eyes to adjust to the dark and render it safe enough to exit the cab. It was almost midnight and the only other vehicle using this overflow area was an old Mondeo tucked in a far corner. Oscar wandered towards it, hands in pockets, and checked the car. Then, satisfied the vehicle was cold and likely to be there for a long time, walked briskly back to the van. Time for a few last-minute checks - driver's door locked; backdoors slightly ajar. With things all set, the stroll back towards the petrol station, bathed in a pool of orange light, took two minutes.

Crossing the covered footbridge and down into the services situated on the westbound carriageway, Oscar glanced at a clock. With ten minutes to kill before the predicted appointment, there was time to amble into the café and buy a coffee and a roll. Then it was back up to the footbridge to stand over the eastbound carriageway, watching the late evening traffic speed by; enjoying the strange sense of motion created by cars, rushing like a river below.

The white van was visible from here and when headlamps appeared, entering the overflow area, Oscar gripped the handrail and watched intently.

But there's no danger here.

Standing at this distance.

No risk of seeing faces.

A transaction, that's all.

Taking another bite of roll; chewing slowly as the vehicle turned in the carpark and reversed to the doors of the van. For a time, the headlamps were extinguished. A few minutes later, when they lit again, the vehicle slowly turned down the exit ramp and merged back into the traffic.

Oscar stood and finished the coffee without any sense of hurry. Keeping a wary eye on the van for a few minutes in case the gang should return. Finally, with the roll and coffee cup discarded, Oscar strode back to the vehicle so this Monday night's work could properly begin.

Chapter 17

He didn't admit it, but like Craig, Gill was struggling to come to terms with what had happened on Macdui. And so, he did what he always did when confronted with a mystery and refused to accept what he'd seen at face value. He needed data. And perhaps a different perspective that might explain their experience. Normally, he'd have delegated this kind of technical question to Craig, but the incident had unsettled Craig even more than Gill, so that didn't seem fair. And science wasn't Mhairi's comfort zone, so he'd have to do this one himself.

Finding a little free time on Tuesday afternoon, he started to enter search terms in Google that reflected his experience. Soon he found a thread built around a concept called *The Third Man*. Taking a deep breath, he called up a list of articles reporting this concept and dived in. He'd been reading for half an hour when he had a breakthrough. One of the papers had been co-written by a name Gill recognised. Straightaway, he dialled the author's number.

'I'm trying to reach the eminent brain scientist by the name of Arnold Broadbent', said Gill when the call connected.

The pause at the other end was just a beat. 'I ken when someone's trying to butter me up, matey-boy.'

'Do you? How much buttering would I need to do to get your help with something?'

'Quite a bit, Gill. You could start by sending this fellow scribbler a news story, from time to time. The traffic on this helpline seems to be all one way since our little get-together on Orkney.'

'Well, I might have something for you soon. I'll spare you the details just now, but *Mys.Scot* is working on a scientific story that I could eventually share with you.'

'Glad to hear it. And in the meantime, in light of this offer of fair exchange, how can I help you?'

'I gather you ran some experiments on human cognizance before you switched to journalism.'

'For my PhD. Particularly on what happens in the human brain under stressful conditions.'

'I was in a stressful situation two days ago.' Taking a deep breath, Gill recounted his encounter with the *Old Grey Man* on Macdui.

'You're sure this thing was throwing rocks at you?'

'That's what we experienced. Craig got clipped by one.'

Gill listened to Arnold's breathing for a few moments before deciding to push him. 'Any ideas?'

'You know there are lots of reasons why you might have imagined this', said Arnold. 'You said it had been misty until you reached the peak?'

'Yes. If it hadn't been for Craig's navigation skills, I'd have been lost within minutes.'

'Humans are social animals. Isolation and low blood sugar caused by strenuous exercise make you more susceptible to imagination. Add in the poor visibility and a sense of not knowing where you are increases the effect. From Ernest Shackleton through to the present day, there are numerous reports of climbers and polar explorers experiencing a presence accompanying them during a stressful journey.'

'Okay.'

'It's sometimes called the *Angel Myth*', Arnold continued. 'You know, in the sense that people in trouble believe they are being watched over and put the experience down to angels, or whatever. When really, it's just your brain creating a sensed presence which places the social ape back in community.'

'You're saying you don't believe in angels, Arnie?'

'I work for a science mag, Gill. Of course I don't believe in angels. What's happening in these situations is a neurological response to periods of extreme stress. To religious folk, this manifests in their imagination as an angel or some culture-specific god. Secular folk on the other hand might express it as an entity or force. "May the force be with you", and all that stuff. In either scenario, this phantom companion is experienced as a help; overcoming the psychological pressures of the experience.'

'And this sensed presence, does what? Encourage? Help carry the load?'

Arnold grunted. 'They're make-believe, Gill. They couldn't even wipe a snowflake off your nose. Didn't you have an imaginary friend when you were a kid? A friendly little playmate to keep you company in the schoolyard when all the real kids didn't want to talk to a wee ginger-bap like you?'

'No', said Gill, deciding to keep his personal experiences with angels out of this conversation. 'And while last Saturday's walk was challenging, it didn't qualify as mountaineering or a polar trek. I don't think we were under that kind of stress.'

'You were on Macdui, right? Britain's second-highest mountain. On higher peaks, lack of oxygen exacerbates the effect, and scientifically minded climbers who reject a spiritual dimension interpret this as a deterioration of brain function.'

'Macdui is thirteen-hundred metres. Everest is almost nine thousand. I doubt oxygen was a factor on Saturday.'

But Arnold wasn't listening. 'Hypoxia. That's shortage of oxygen to mortals like you and me. It makes us more vulnerable to this kind of experience and can even lead to out-of-body experiences. Basically, a failure of the brain to process sensory information.'

'What about the fact that Craig and I felt anything but protected? We experienced it attacking us.'

'Well, that's another line of thought. You have to remember humans are wired for predator detection. Strolling in the countryside at night, or walking alone down an empty street, we're generally afraid of the dark. And if we're under stress, this leads to hypervigilance that might detect a threat even though none exists.'

Their conversation was interrupted by someone talking to Arnold. 'Sorry, matey. Gonna have to go. Was that helpful at all?'

'Thanks, Arnie. Useful perspective.'

'I'll send you links to some websites. Meantime, I'll wait to hear about this scoop you have for me.'

Gill signed off the call and laid the phone down gently. Arnold's perspective was grounded and reasonable, and some tiny part of him was asking an important question. All of Gill's encounters with Raphael had happened in moments of extreme stress. Could his embattled brain have imagined his angelic friend? Could it have conjured up this helper to aid his fight or flight? But Salina had seen Raphael. Charlie and Adina too. If Raphael was make-believe, then he kept a wide circle of friends. But to logic this out, if Gill believed Raphael was real, just as his experience with Craig on Macdui was real, then he was trying to reconcile two sets of unnatural encounters – one good, and one bad. And he remembered how, once they'd begun their descent, the mood on the mountain had become so menacing. That reminded him, he'd detected this same black atmosphere once before.

Then he groaned to himself as he acknowledged the likely identity of their mountain assailant. Solomon had warned him about this. The demon from Airth churchyard was back.

Towards the end of his working day, Gill requested to meet Solomon. For a change of scenery, he suggested they meet on the esplanade at Broughty Ferry. This was the old fishing village on the eastern fringe of Dundee City, that had been his home for over a year.

'How are you?' she asked as they began the mile-long stroll along the new seawall.

Gill smiled. Getting to know Solomon was like hiring a therapist. 'I'm good. Heading into a manic spell at work.'

'You looking after yourself?'

He nodded. 'Doing my best. You?'

She nodded her assent and for a few minutes, they talked about their charity and some urgent items of business. When that was tidied away, they walked in companionable silence along the shore.

After a time, Solomon spoke first. 'Broughty Ferry. It's significant to you?'

'I have a flat above an ice cream parlour. I like it here, so Salina and I have offered on a house.'

'Here on the shore?'

'Aye. Near the old lifeboat shed. Salina would go insane if she couldn't be near the sea.'

'Pricey though?'

'Not St Andrews numbers. But we wanted a bigger place with a bit of garden. We've decided to sell my dad's old place, so I think we can swing it.'

'Good. I hope you'll be happy.'

Gill nodded but said nothing. Selling Gordon's Stonehaven house was the right thing to do. But he'd still miss it.

'I was thinking about you on Saturday.' She glanced up at him. 'Do you mind me asking what you were doing?'

He gave an involuntary flinch of his chin as he absorbed her question. Her frequent and uncanny insights meant there was no such thing as a casual conversation with Solomon. 'I was hill walking with a friend.'

'And?'

'And, we were attacked. By someone capable of throwing rocks the size of a basketball.'

'Oh, Gill', said Solomon, turning in alarm.

'And before you ask, it does look similar to my encounter at Airth.'

Subconsciously, Solomon pulled her left hand to her lips while she thought. 'A second attempt to harm you. I hope you're taking this seriously.'

'I am', he said. 'I take it bloody seriously whenever anyone tries to kill me.'

'Come on, Gill', said Solomon impatiently. 'Use your knowledge of *The Book*. For example, do people see angels every day?'

Gill thought about this. 'No. Only when they bring messages or interventions.'

'Meaning?'

'Meaning, the Creator sent them.'

'And what about demons? Do they trot through history killing people at will?'

'Clearly not. Humanity would've been toast by now.'

'But there are examples. Name me one.'

Gill gritted his teeth. He'd had a history teacher at high school who sounded just like Solomon. 'Book of Job', he said after a moment. 'The devil goes into the Creator's throne room to demand three attempts to destroy his servant, Job.'

'And for reasons known only to Himself, the Creator allows it. Within the confines of the negotiated parameters, the devil or his demon could then attack at will.'

Gill was struggling to buy this line of reasoning. 'But you're talking about one of the big names in *The Book*. Why would the same circumstances apply to me?'

Solomon stopped and for a few moments reached up to grip his shoulders. 'The logic of this applies to everyone who believes. Think about it another way. Why shouldn't it be you?'

Gill took a deep breath, and she relaxed her grip. 'I guess.'

'The demon came three times for Job. If I've heard you correctly, Gill, he's already hit you twice.'

Gill swallowed. He really didn't want to think about this at all.

'You need to talk to Adina and Charlie', Solomon continued. 'You are under attack, and they need to be aware.'

Gill nodded. 'I'll speak to them both today.'

'Do. And Gill?'

'Yes.'

'The armour group. Someday soon, we all need to be in a room together. At the moment we're too fragmented. Too easy to pick off.'

'I'd agree. But good luck convincing Adina.'

Chapter 18

Back at Krankie on Tuesday morning, Gill braced himself for another long session in the cold and mud. Conscious of the fact the site would be winding up in a few days, Gill pulled Cassy and Fiona into the portacabin for a meeting straight after lunch. Fiona had sourced a couple of spare tables from the canteen and any archaeological finds from the last few days were spread across them.

Using gloved hands, Cassy picked up a powdery white ball. 'This is a musket bullet?' she asked, bright-eyed.

'Aye', said Gill. 'As you can see, they're all lead and all slightly different sizes.'

'Why would that be?'

'They made their own munitions back then. Some folk made bullets that perfectly fitted their muskets, and others were limited to whatever mould they had available.'

'And some of these would have killed people?'

Gill shrugged. 'Maybe. But they had very limited range compared to modern guns, and I doubt these wee balls flew straight and true.'

'Bloody deadly at close range', muttered Fiona. 'The Jacobites would have taken a hammering as they ran down the slope towards the government guns.'

'But they had muskets too?' said Cassy.

'Yes, but the highlanders were happier with swords and axes. They would have run at the government line; taken a single shot at the enemy, then dropped their guns and charged into the lines.'

'Highland charges could anticipate fifty per cent losses', agreed Gill. 'But once the Highlanders were in close with their blades, they were deadly.'

'Got a couple of these', said Fiona, pointing out a pair of rusted steel spikes.

'What do you reckon they are?'

'Krankie was one of the first places the government troops used bayonets. Not very flexible against a Highlander with a sword but better than wasting time reloading a musket you might never get to fire.'

'And this looks like the firing mechanism from a musket.'

'Aye, though it will take a patient soul a month to coax what's left of it out of all this rust.'

'It's so exciting', said Cassy. 'I can't believe I'm touching stuff lost on a battlefield hundreds of years ago.'

'Sure', said Fiona, flatly. 'No offence, but it's all quite routine.'

Gill reached over and gave Fiona's shoulder a friendly nudge. 'You look a bit low. Are you missing us already?'

'Just pissed with all this rain', said Fiona. 'And I hate doing archaeology in a hurry. No offence, Gill, but why are all your digs such a frenzy?'

Gill shrugged. 'Mainly because we're opportunistic, under-funded suckers for unreasonable deadlines.'

Fiona pointed at the tables. 'I'd guess this is just a fraction of the stuff we'd find if we were doing the dig professionally.'

'I agree. But we're doing what we can in the time available. We've still got the police crawling all over the most interesting part of the site. Meanwhile, the Department of Transport people are tapping their watches and asking why we're not finished yet. Eight weeks from now, this whole area will be buried under concrete and tarmac.'

'Well before they fire up the bulldozers, can I alert you to another wee problem?'

'Sure.'

Fiona moved across to the site plan and pointed to a rectangular box drawn in the upper part of the spill site. 'This is the bone pit.' She glanced around at Gill to make sure he was paying attention. 'As of this morning, it's all been cleared. We're just scanning for any interesting bits and pieces before Scott comes begging to fill it all back in again.'

'Yes, great job. So, what's the problem?'

'We're still finding bones in here', said Fiona, stabbing at the map.

Gill leaned in closer. 'But that's uphill of the pit.'

'Maybe everything got churned up by the landslip?' said Cassy.

Fiona shook her head. 'Thank you, ladies and gentlemen, but the next most obvious source of bones is …?'

Gill's shoulders sagged. 'There's another bone pit.'

Fiona nodded. 'Yep. And having had a wee sniff around, I'd guess it's about here.'

Gill looked at where she was pointing. 'Right in the belly of the collapsed road.'

'That's what I'd conclude.'

'Ah shite', muttered Gill, anticipating another week in this miserable muddy hole.

'Yep', said Fiona, matter-of-factly. 'All sorts of logistical implications.'

'No one's gonna like this news', said Gill, after a sigh. 'Let's go speak to Beth and Scott.'

'Can't we just leave them?' said Scott, his eyes darting from one face to another.

Beth shook her head. 'The law is quite clear. If we have human remains disturbed by construction, we need to gather and inspect.'

'But it'll just be more of the same!'

'Nevertheless, my supervisor is playing this job by the book. I can ask him, but I doubt he'll be open to any suggestion we leave the bones where they fell, just because we're in a hurry.'

'In a hurry!' said Scott, thrusting his right hand up towards the surviving carriageway. 'Half of Scotland passes by here every day. The average speed in the roadworks is under ten miles an hour. The economic impact of this … well, it's huge.'

Beth shrugged. 'Your boss can talk to my boss. At the end of the day, we're all working for the same team.'

Scott appealed to Gill. 'In the meantime, can your lot crack on? We really need to finish this.'

Fiona's hands came to her hips. 'No way I'm sending unpaid volunteers into the heart of that landslip before the ground is stabilised.'

'My people told you already. It's safe.'

'The back of that gully is almost vertical', snorted Fiona. 'And it's weeping with moisture, so the ground is clearly still saturated.'

'I have to agree', said Gill. 'If we're to dig any further, we need protection.'

Scott ran his hands through his hair. 'But that'll take, say thirty pieces of tempered steel, inserted by a piling machine. Could take me the rest of the week to source that. Longer to get it in place.'

'Best crack on then', said Fiona, offering Scott a thin smile.

'In the meantime', said Gill. 'We'll wrap up the rest of the site. We'll get these long north-south strips finished and ready to hand back to the contractor.'

Scott still didn't look happy. 'I'm going to kick this upstairs. We can let the boys and girls with the big pay packets sort this out.'

The meeting broke up, and Gill walked Fiona back to her portacabin. 'No pressure', he said. 'But how long do I have you?'

'Close of play on Monday', she replied. 'Unless …'

'Unless, what?'

'If we do find something worthwhile, I'd probably be able to swing another week out of Winchester.' She peered up at him. 'What's that old McArdle-sixth-sense saying?'

Gill sighed. His sixth sense was still absorbed trying to figure out what the hell happened to Craig and him on Saturday. Around here …' He paused to glance down the length and breadth of the dig. 'All I sense is bureaucracy, bones and ice-cold mud.'

Wednesday brought yet more rain and shrank the ranks of *Mys.Scot's* volunteer army to a hardy few. Scott announced that the steel and crane to pin the extension to the dig site would be in position by Friday morning, meaning the embankment would be stabilised forty-eight hours later. That implied Gill had just Monday to work the newly discovered bone pit with Fiona before she was released to pastures new. In the meantime, she would focus on the dig areas outside of the main landslip and seemed content to work out the week at a more methodical pace. That meant there was little he could add to Fiona's team other than an additional pair of hands. Consequently, he started to feel the tug of the office. Mhairi, meanwhile, at Gill's suggestion, had alerted Cassy that her desk was buried under incoming mail and message notes. Hearing that, Cassy announced, "reluctantly", that she felt the rest of her week would be better spent back in Dundee. So, at the end of their working day, like the government survivors from the battlefield three hundred and fifty years before, they tucked their tails between their legs and retreated to the lowlands.

Chapter 19

Gill spent all of Thursday reviewing articles for the next issue and drafting a few pieces of his own. The rest of the team manoeuvred around Cassy trying to work out if she'd enjoyed her time in the field, or hated it. To Cassy's evident irritation, Mhairi nagged her to switch off the fan heater she constantly had simmering at her feet. For her part, Cassy developed a stinking head cold and fretted she would be unable to play at the next *Calum's Road* gig in two weeks' time. Mhairi rather frostily suggested that whether in the office or in the band, Cassy wasn't indispensable, and eventually Gill had to intervene to prevent a bust-up. He waited for a moment when Mhairi was away from her desk, then sprang to Cassy's side.

'Tomorrow', he told Cassy as red-eyed tears threatened to stain her normally unflappable exterior. 'Take a sick day. You are tired. You are cold, and you're probably a bit in shock from all the stuff you witnessed these past ten days.'

'I'm fine', she sniffed into a hankie.

'Ninety-nine days out of a hundred you are more than fine. In fact, you excel. But I want you to take a day off. Maybe two. Get yourself well.'

'Mhairi is being a cow', said Cassy, sullenly.

'Maybe. Or maybe you're utterly wrung out and not up for your usual banter.'

Cassy blew her nose. 'Yeah, but on balance, I think you should fire her.'

Gill fought to suppress a smile. He knew when Cassy joking, even if the joke held barbs. 'We've only just hired her. On your recommendation.'

Cassy sneezed. 'Send her to Krankie then. With a pick and shovel. And a couple of body bags.'

Gill nodded. 'I might just do that. But only if you take some time off.'

'I do feel pretty shit. Is it okay if I knock off early?'

'Sure. I'll take Mhairi into the conference room and give her a firm talking-to about her snippy attitude. In the meantime, you go home and take a long, hot bath.'

'Okay, and now you're patronising me.'

'I know. It's a bloke thing. Like a factory setting.'

'But you'll definitely yell at her?'

'I promise.'

'Okay', she said. 'I'll see you on Monday. Will you be going to Krankie?'

'Maybe in the afternoon. There's a case review planned for Lossuary first thing Monday morning. I'll catch you by phone or in person after that meeting.'

Cassy nodded and gathered her stuff to go.

Gill moved away from Cassy and flicked his chin as Mhairi returned to her desk. 'A word, please.'

Mhairi gathered some files off her desk and wordlessly followed Gill to the conference room, where he closed the door and sat down opposite her.

'Am I in some kind of trouble?' she asked.

Gill nodded energetically. 'Absolutely not. But while Cassy is still watching us, can you look suitably chastised?'

'Okay …'

'And for the next few minutes, I'm going to tap the table in front of you in an authoritative manner, while you tell me what you've found out about life and death around Ben Macdui.'

'I've not quite finished that.'

'No problem', said Gill, tapping the table ferociously and scowling at her. 'I know you're doing great work. And I'm so glad you've joined the team. Can you tell me what you found out so far?'

'Right. Well, the biggest incident was years ago, back in November 1971. Known as the 'Cairngorm Plateau disaster', five children and an assistant leader died of exposure having got lost in deteriorating weather.'

'Yeah. I've heard of that one. They were heading for a bothy or something?'

'Their plan had been to climb Macdui and then drop down into the valley and overnight in a hut called the Corrour Bothy.'

Gill nodded. 'Craig and I were there briefly last weekend.'

'But the conditions became so bad they decided to follow their agreed emergency plan and seek refuge in another spot called the "Curran Shelter." By then a blizzard had started that would last three days. They couldn't find the refuge, so they were stranded in the open for two nights.'

'Yeah. This one is tragic.'

'And controversial', Mhairi continued, trying to look downcast and remorseful while Cassy prowled around the *Mys.Scot* pen, occasionally glancing at the room. 'The official enquiry decided that places like the Curran Shelter encouraged reckless climbing and should be removed. By the summer of 1974, they'd all been demolished.'

'But that didn't solve the problem?'

'People continued to die. I'll mail you the list I've pulled together.'

'That's a sobering place to start. Anything else?'

'Smaller incidents by comparison. Parties of two or three and plenty of individual deaths. Folk falling or getting lost in the snow. As I said, I've a lot to do. I'll drop it into an email.'

'Thank you. I don't mean to rush you.'

'That's alright. Has Cassy gone?'

'Aye. Just.'

'Thanks. I'll text her later and apologise.'

'Give it a day', said Gill. 'People in here joke about *Mys.Scot* being "Body Bag Monthly", but there's some truth in it. Even if they're just bones, these are real human lives we're touching, and I know from personal experience that it can be genuinely distressing. When Cassy's had time to reflect, I think she'll realise how much of a shock she's had.'

'Not a great advert for going on a dig, really', said Mhairi, standing up.

'It's rarely a halfway house', said Gill. 'You're either bored to death or handling death's consequences.'

Later that Thursday afternoon, DC Lillico spotted Beth in the roadside marquee just as the last Lossuary truck of the day was loading up. He waved to catch her attention as he walked towards her.

'Heard the good news?' she said cheerily.

Lillico groaned. 'I'm beginning to hate this place. Can't believe we'll be at it another week at least.'

'Leave it to me', she said. 'No need for us both to be freezing our pips off in this godforsaken valley.'

'Thanks, but I've got a couple of other things going on here.'

'How nice for you. Anything I should know about?'

Lillico grabbed the waistband of his white overalls and hitched it up a few centimetres. 'Have you seen anybody spying on the site?'

'Spying?'

'You know. Creeping in the bushes; scaring the dig crew?'

'Not that I've seen or heard.'

'Nobody mentioned anything?'

'Scott thinks the place is haunted. But hey, that's engineers for you.'

'And the Lossuary guys are doing a good job?'

'At this end, certainly. I'm only here for the second half of the afternoons so Fiona covers the rest. And so far, I've only attended their Falkirk unit a couple of times.'

'I've heard it's pretty slick', said Lillico. 'For an industrial-sized funeral home.'

'It is, which is useful as I'll be spending a lot of time over there.'

'Trying to make sense of all the bones we gathered?'

'Aye. Human jigsaws for the empathetically challenged.' Beth flashed a rather obvious glance at her watch. 'Listen, do you mind if I crack on? I've got a class this evening.'

'Sure. I'll catch Fiona and probably see you tomorrow.'

'Maybe. Based on my workload, I'll be in Falkirk more than Krankie over the next few days.'

'Working the weekend?'

'I'm a contractor, Alex. They pay me by the day. And with all the bones we've hauled outta here, there's plenty to do.'

Distracted by his phone ringing, he gave Beth a business-like smile and stepped away a few feet.

'Lillico. It's Chief Superintendent Macfarlane. Can you talk?'

Lillico glanced around. 'I can, sir.'

'I'll get straight to it. I'd hoped by now to get an update from you.'

'Our big murder case is still ongoing, sir. We're splitting our time between that and another potential crime scene.'

'The human bones at Killiecrankie?'

'Yes.'

'A complete distraction. You shouldn't be wasting time on it.'

'The Procurator Fiscal put it on our desk, sir. It is a cold case and all that.'

'I can make a call. Get it shifted.'

'Actually, sir. Can you leave it with us? A substantial portion of the remains appear contemporary.'

'You're saying these could be recent killings?'

'DCI Wiley and I are considering the possibility someone has been using the old battlefield site as a dumping ground. On an industrial scale.'

Macfarlane chewed on this new information. 'Are you linking this to the killer DCI Wiley rather distastefully calls, the *Toothfairy*?'

'We've no evidence that's the case. We've got pathology working to verify the exact age of the bones.'

Macfarlane grunted. 'And what is DCI Wiley doing to capitalise on this new lead?'

'Following up on victims as we gather identities from the teeth DNA.'

'Really? Well, we'll see where you net out. I'll expect a full and frank report, Lillico. If you simply cover for him, and Wiley is bent or lazy, or both, then he'll ruin your career too.'

'Acknowledged, sir.'

Macfarlane hung up without another word. Lillico stared down at his phone and fretted for a second about what would happen to him if Wiley was ultimately found wanting. And it wasn't wasted on him that both he and Wiley were tainted goods in the eyes of their colleagues. If they didn't get results soon, they might both end up directing traffic.

He looked back to where he'd left Beth loading up her boxes. She was busy and seemed done talking to him, so he decided to touch base with Fiona. In case she asked, and because it was the right thing to do, be decided to exercise due diligence towards Fiona's stalker. He began by scanning the treeline for the grey-skinned man. Seeing nothing that caught his attention, his gaze drifted over the treetops, across the river and onto the rocky hills beyond. This was the first time the view hadn't been obscured by rain. And it was pretty! A natural and unspoilt part of Scotland. Too steep to be farmed. Too rocky to carry agricultural forest. A verdant paradise, if it wasn't for the mud-brown wound of the spill site, spreading its ugly scar across the land.

Bypassing Fiona's portacabin, he walked to the other end of the site and dropped downhill into the woods. For the next twenty minutes, working from tree to tree, he retraced his steps from the day he'd encountered the forest stalker. Walking this time in the opposite direction, he saw no sign of the stalker, nor the leather-clad guy with the fancy belt.

He found Fiona logging the few finds of the day and laying them in plastic boxes. She had her back to him and on reflection, Lillico decided she would be more than a match for any lurker in the woods.

'Just swinging by', he said, stepping into her line of sight. 'Any more problems with your snooper?'

Fiona looked up at him. 'Not that I've seen today. I feel his eyes are on us but can't say from where.'

'Take my number. If you spot him again, call me. I can get a couple of uniforms out here ASAP.'

'Thanks', said Fiona, before picking up a trowel and tapping the table with it. 'Pretty sure I'll be alright.'

Lillico decided to say nothing.

'I'm only around a few more days. After that, this is Gill's gig.'

Lillico looked back across the wrecked landscape. 'I'm sure he can't wait.'

Chapter 20

Oscar slid the white van into a parking space on Broad Street and waited. It was early yet, but from here, there was a clear line of sight up the flight of stone steps leading into Stirling's Tolbooth Theatre. The door itself was accessed through an archway below a square clock tower, brooding beneath the darkening sky. There was still time to eat before showtime, so Oscar rummaged for the pack of supermarket sandwiches acquired on the drive up to Stirling. Now the only thing to do was wait.

Sitting where it was, Oscar's white van was only a street away from Roddy Canmore's house. Not that a social call was on the cards. His was another face Oscar didn't want to see. Not that they had any direct association, but over the years, snatches of conversation had been overheard in parked vans, loitering in laybys in the middle of the night. No, Oscar didn't know Roddy Canmore. Rather, it was the lingering suspicion that, indirectly, the man was a client. Tiny scraps of evidence. Coincidences a good Detective couldn't ignore. But that wasn't Oscar's business. And if, on these trips to Stirling, Oscar did bump into Canmore … well, sure, they'd no grounds to even know each other.

Ten minutes later, three lassies made their way up the street. Just young things in black leggings that left little to the imagination. Kids from the local Uni; Oscar watched them chattering for a moment at the base of the stairs while one of them sent a text. Their loud voices, brimming with confidence reached inside the van and headlined how nervous these girls actually felt. Oscar had seen their type a thousand times before. If you faced down their bluster; spoke over their nonsense. Asserted yourself. You could lead people like that. Be the one cool head that everyone turned to when the pressure was on. And when they finally mustered the courage to climb the stairs, Oscar lingered in the van and imagined their shrill introductions.

Two more figures. Male. Older. They strode to the steps and walked inside, so engrossed in conversation that they didn't as much as glance at the white van. Oscar sighed and then shook the stiffness from limbs that knew too much work and not enough rest. Knowing it was time to make a move, Oscar put on the mental mindset needed for moments like this. Ready to step into that building; adopting the voice, the movement, the character, of someone in authority.

Reaching into the van's glove compartment, Oscar pulled out a cloth bag. Extracting the Glock G19, the weight of the weapon was always a surprise. A confident flick slid open the magazine. Satisfied, Oscar slipped it into its usual hiding place and cautiously climbed out of the van.

Mounting the steep stone steps.

The climb is slow and deliberate.

Hands deep in pockets.

Reaching the top, the door swung open to reveal a tired hallway. Following the sound of voices into a brightly lit room, young people stood in groups. The young women from the street were in animated conversation with a group of boys. The older men were pouring over sheaves of notes, tapping the papers as they discussed a plan of action. Oscar stood at a distance from them until someone detected this new arrival.

'Oscar', said one of the men who'd arrived just before him. 'Good to see you. We're just making introductions.'

'Grand', said Oscar.

The man glanced left and right. 'Did you bring it?'

In response, Oscar gave a single slow nod.

'Let's see it then.'

Oscar listened to the young voices bubbling around the room. 'I need you to witness my armoury check. Confirm the absence of the firing pin and ammunition. So, it's best we go some place private where we won't scare the kids.'

'Of course. And thank you. We couldn't have pulled this off without you.'

Chapter 21

The following morning, Lillico had been at his desk for two hours before he saw his boss walk past.

'Alec. Anything new?'

Lillico lifted an email he'd printed off. 'I'm still working through the names Gill McArdle's crew sent through.'

Wiley gesticulated at Lillico's email with a fat forefinger. 'You outsourcing your desk work?'

'It's a list of anyone who died on Macdui these last sixty years. And I recall sir, it was you who asked them for help. If they turn up anything useful, I'll obviously corroborate it.'

'Is it giving us any leads?'

'I've cross-referenced their list with the four *Toothfairy* vics we've identified, so far. Unfortunately, none of the names overlap.'

'Were you expecting them to?'

'Just a line of enquiry, sir. I've started tracking down the nearest relatives of the four identified victims to see if the Macdui names mean anything to them. And of course, the names of the other mountain casualties. See if we can detect any relationships.'

'No disclosures to McArdle's team, please, of these Missing Persons being deceased. I don't want to alert the *Toothfairy* that we're on his trail.'

'Got it.'

Wiley nodded and started to move off. 'Sir', called Lillico. 'Did you hear the Krankie dig is running for another week, at least?'

'I heard. The damn thing is never-ending. Have we received a pathology report yet?'

'Nothing official. Just the anecdotal conversations about the contemporary appearance of the bones.'

'Right. I'm gonna put some pressure on Beth. See if we can get an interim report.'

'Are you going to alert her to the possibility the *Toothfairy* might have used the battlefield as a dump site?'

'Nope', said Wiley. 'I just wanna hear the facts.'

Taking the opportunity to spend the weekend away from the muddy works at Killiecrankie, Gill spent Saturday doing some chores and finding flowers for Salina's mum. Towards mid-afternoon, he texted Salina's dad, Waquar, to check when he would be home from his weekend golf. As Gill suspected, his suggestion to 'pop round' was warmly augmented by an offer to stay overnight. Relieved Waquar would be at home, Gill accepted. He liked Salina's mum, though she was a woman burdened with vocal opinions. And he was slightly shy of Salina's three sisters; each of them slightly younger, smaller renditions of Salina, like a collection of nested dolls. But Waquar had become a friend. And whenever the opportunity allowed, he and Gill met in Glasgow's Café Gandolfi, to drink tea, talk business and argue about politics.

Two hours later, Gill parked in a leafy avenue in Shawlands, on Glasgow's southside. Naurah answered the door and after a warm embrace, Gill handed her the flowers.

'From Salina. And me. Happy Birthday!'

'Ah, thank you, Gill. My favourites! How did you know?'

'Salina's suggestion.'

'Sea holly', said Naurah, stoking the leaf of one of the prickly pale blue flowers. 'They're what Salina likes best.'

'Funny you should say that', said Gill, stepping into the house with its warm embrace of cooking smells. 'I was going to ask you about Salina's preferences.'

Naurah hefted her eyebrows. 'You've been seeing my daughter for over a year, and you don't know what flowers she likes?'

'I have a general idea', said Gill defensively. 'I was thinking about flowers for a special occasion.'

'Oh', said Naurah. 'What are you suggesting, Gill McArdle?'

'Let's wait until Waquar gets in. Then I'd like to run an idea past you both.'

After an extended wait for DCI Wiley at their Bathgate office on Monday morning, Lillico drummed his fingers on his steering wheel. They were going to be late for their appointment. As a consequence, he wasn't exactly chatty on the drive up to Falkirk. Not that he put his foot down, though he ran close to the speed limit all the way up the M9.

'You can blue-light it, if you're stressed', said Wiley.

'Not exactly protocol, sir.'

'Aye, but it's a privilege of our occupation.'

Lillico gave a single shake of his head and focused on the road.

'And I think that's your problem right there, Alec-boy.'

'How do you mean, sir.'

'By the rules. By the book. Trying to succeed in a job that's impossible unless you learn where to cut some corners.'

Lillico measured his response. 'Isn't that our job? Make society a better place by helping everyone follow the rules?'

Wiley spat out a laugh. 'No one follows the rules, Alec. You'll do better once you learn which rules are the most bendy. It's a question of not getting caught.'

'And if you are caught?'

Wiley shrugged. 'You do what everyone else does and cover your arse.'

Lillico said nothing.

Wiley stared at him. 'Do you have a problem with that? No, don't answer that question. I saw your record before you joined me. "Scrupulous to a fault", said your previous DI.' Wiley shifted his bulk in the passenger seat and turned to look out the window. 'Which was just before you shopped her to Professional Standards.'

Lillico sighed. 'I had a good working relationship with DI Mackinnon. For most of the time we worked together.'

'Collapsing her case like that. You were lucky not to get nailed in a disciplinary.'

'All I did was tell the truth', said Lillico, evenly.

'You put the bollocks on a colleague's witness statement. "Yippee!" shouted the defence lawyers as they rushed to savage the Procurator's case, just because Alec Lillico had to kneel before his conscience.'

'My colleague lied. I wasn't about to join her.'

'And what? The accused weren't guilty? Wasn't that your job - to put the bastards away?'

'I was sorry to see them get off. But if we, the police, abuse the truth, then we're all on a slippery slope.'

'The slope's been slippery a long time', Wiley huffed. 'You're too naïve or idealistic to realise it.'

'I know where I am with the truth.'

'What does that mean?'

'If I tell a lie, even a little one; before long I'd have to tell another one to justify what I've said. Or how I acted. Or even how I thought. So, I'd be building layers of lies upon lies and before long, I'd be so far from the truth, I'd not even see it on the horizon. By then, I'd have no idea where I was. No idea how to get back.'

'Sounds great', said Wiley. 'Meanwhile, back in the real world, we have crimes to solve. I tell you what, Alec. If you ever do to me what you did in the witness box to your previous DI, I'll make your record stink so bad, the only thing left for you to do will be to flush your career away. Got that?'

Lillico nodded. 'By the way, sir. You'll find in time I don't respond to *Alec*. It's Alex, sir. Or Alexander, or DC Lillico if you prefer.'

Wiley leaned his elbow on the passenger door and looked away. 'Suit yourself.'

Driving in silence for the rest of the journey, Lillico left the motorway and drove along the A9 until he saw signs for the logistics park. He wound his way past a variety of industrial buildings until he came to one indicated by the Satnav and noted it was unmarked. He parked up and switched off the car. Wiley unclipped his seatbelt and walked off without waiting for him. Lillico got out and rubbed the back of his neck. Anticipating the forthcoming meeting, he couldn't help feeling sorry for the pathologist.

Beth was dressed in white overalls as usual. With her stood Pete Gibson, Gill McArdle and Fiona Hamilton from the dig site. All of them lounged against the various upright freezers while two Lossuary staff worked in the background, ferrying boxes from the ossuary onto the stainless-steel tables in the morgue.

Lillico caught snatches of a macabre story Pete was relaying to Gill, while the latter listened intently.

'Afternoon, gents', Beth said sarcastically, spotting their arrival. Sheepishly, Lillico reciprocated.

'McArdle. Why are you here? This isn't a spectator sport', said Wiley.

'Representing the road contractor. And I'm taking over from Fiona as site supervisor on Monday.'

Fiona leaned against a work surface, with her arms folded. 'Any reason we're doing this meeting now? I thought the Fiscal didn't need a report until all the remains had been catalogued?'

'Sorry', said Wiley. 'Is there somewhere else you need to be?'

Fiona lifted up her palms. 'Yes! Winchester. A few days from now.'

'Nothing yet from the new bone pit?' asked Lillico.

Fiona shook her head. 'The piling machine was behind schedule when it arrived on Saturday. Consequently, they're still working. And I'm glad to be offsite, to be honest. The noise up there is horrendous.'

'Can we crack on?' said Wiley.

Beth pushed off the work surface. 'Apologies. Even after the drying process, they do rather smell. Thanks, Hamish and Gary', she said, indicating to the two that she would take it from here. She waited until they left the room before she began. 'Right, folks. We're reviewing a selection of human bones collected from the Killiecrankie battlefield site between 12th and 25th October.'

'Why just a selection?' asked Wiley.

'We've run out of work surface', Beth said flatly. 'What you can see in front of you are a dozen of the ninety boxes collected so far. The others are in the ossuary and can be inspected today if required. And, Pete, we have, what? A further eight that arrived yesterday and are still in the kiln?'

Pete nodded.

Beth began passing out slim binders of printed sheets. 'This is my report, sorry, my interim report. It lists all the finds, their general locations and my observations.'

'Thanks, Beth', said Lillico. 'Would you mind summarising for us, then DCI Wiley and I would like to take a look ourselves.'

'Sure. First off, the majority of the remains were disarticulated, meaning the bones from the burial pit had been scattered by the force of the landslip. That incident also damaged the majority of the bones. As we reached the heart of the burial chamber, we found twelve articulated skeletons. Examination of these proved they were all male, young to middle-aged and in reasonable health at their time of death.'

'And therefore, consistent with battlefield casualties', added Fiona.

'Indeed. Using the Lincoln Index, I've estimated that we have the remains of at least seventy individuals.

'And the age of the bones?' asked Wiley.

'As we've previously discussed', Beth began. 'These bones show an unusual lack of weathering. That is to say, the normal processes of deterioration where the bones soften, and flake doesn't seem to be happening here.'

'Why would that be?' asked Gill.

Beth glanced at the floor. 'There must be some form of natural preservative in the soil, although for the life of me, I can't figure out what it might be.'

'Pete. Have you ever seen anything like this?' asked Lillico.

Pete shook his head and smiled a broad smile. 'And I've been in this game a long time. Even in oak boxes, old bones are usually no more than smoke and shadows.'

'So, the bones are contemporary?' said Wiley.

Beth shook her head. 'There's no sign of modern medicine. No hip replacement, knee joints, no pins or plates. And most telling of all; no sign of modern dentistry. Any superficial dating we've applied suggests the bones are seventeenth century.'

Wiley glanced at Lillico. 'Repaired teeth could have been removed, right?'

Beth suppressed a smile. 'I think you're forgetting how poor dentistry was back in the late seventeenth century. Extraction was the typical response to any advanced tooth or gum decay. No, I'm pretty certain the bones are as old as we thought they'd be. I just can't explain the preservation. At least, not yet.'

'Was the location of the bone pit well known?' asked Wiley, turning to Fiona.

'It wasn't on OS maps, if that's what you mean. But its approximate location was indicated by previous archaeological surveys.'

Wiley grunted an acknowledgement. 'Could contemporary corpses have been added?'

Fiona flashed a look at Gill. 'Given how close the pit was to the new road, I think that's unlikely. Normally I'd have been able to prove or disprove your theory by using ground penetrating radar to tell us if the ground had been recently disturbed. But since the embankment collapsed …' she said, trailing off.

'Have you used carbon dating on the bones?' asked Gill.

Beth nodded. 'I've sent off samples. Should have a first estimate on Monday. But really, even if the bones are seventeenth century, the numbers might be off.'

'Why?' Wiley demanded.

'Carbon dating is most useful on older remains. Think thousands rather than hundreds of years', said Beth.

'And it's useless for anything younger than mid-twentieth century', Gill added. 'Carbon pollution and atomic bomb tests skew the data from about 1950 onwards.'

'I'm getting left with questions, rather than answers', growled Wiley.

'Can we handle some of the skulls?' Lillico asked.

Beth swept her right hand towards the steel benches. 'Wear gloves, please, but be my guest.'

The meeting fragmented with Wiley and Beth staying in the morgue while Lillico walked into the ossuary. Pete followed him and pointed out the part of the bones store dedicated to the battlefield remains. Lillico's glance at Pete wordlessly asked for a little space, which Pete acknowledged by returning to the main room.

Lillico had never held a human skull in his hands. Opening the first box, he paused for a moment and steadied himself. Then carefully, respectfully, he lifted the first skull and inspected its teeth. Brown with age, with only two worn molars clinging to each side of the upper jaw, it seemed a fragile thing. He gently replaced the skull in the box and used both hands to select another. A full set of teeth on the upper jaw, but the lower jaw was missing. He replaced the skull.

He carried on in this vein for fifteen minutes until he came across Gill McArdle doing much the same thing, but coming in the opposite direction.

'What are we looking for?' Gill asked.

Lillico took a moment to finish examining a jawbone. 'Anything that might suggest the *Toothfairy* passed this way.'

'I'm struggling to match the shiny white teeth you brought to my office with these old things.'

'Yeah. This idea looked good on paper. Not so sure now.' Lillico sighed in frustration. 'Come on let's go back through.'

Back in the main room, Wiley clenched a skull in his palm, held as far away from his body as he could manage without dropping it.

'Alas, poor Yorick...' muttered Fiona in the background.

Wiley sniggered. 'The problem here is, we don't know him well. Whoever he was.'

Pete swept in and recovered the skull from Wiley's clasp. 'Gentlemen, ladies. Let's show due respect.'

'Beth', bellowed Wiley across the room. 'You reckon Krankie yielded seventy skulls?'

'Yes.'

'How long would it take to get a DNA analysis from all of them?'

Beth's shoulders slumped. 'You've got to be kidding me.'

Chapter 22

Following the meeting, and after a roadside coffee, Gill dropped Fiona back at the dig site. Torn by a sense of duty towards her and repelled by the ear-splitting bangs emitted by the piling machine, he was saved by a text from Mhairi requesting a catch-up. A quick text exchange with her also confirmed that Cassy was back at her desk, so he experienced a defensive urge to test the temperature in Dundee. He apologised to Fiona for shooting off and promised to return by late afternoon to relieve her and take over the site supervisor role.

Back in the office around lunchtime, the first thing he saw was Cassy and Mhairi returning from the coffee machine with smiles on their faces.

'You're looking better', he said, addressing Cassy.

She grinned. 'Better slept and all dried out. Thanks for chasing me home last week.'

'You could have taken longer.'

She shook her head and glanced at Mhairi. 'Had a few things to sort out.'

Mhairi clasped Cassy's shoulder. 'Gill, we're going for a team drink on Thursday. Want to come?'

He thought for a second. 'Yeah, that appeals. Give us a chance to spend some of Larry's winnings.'

'Not one of Gill's old man pubs', groaned Cassy. 'Somewhere with a bit of life.'

'Oh, please. It has to be real ale. Or a half-decent Guinness if nothing else.'

Cassy wiggled the fingers of her left hand in the air as she walked away. 'I'll think about it.'

Gill sighed and looked at Mhairi. 'You wanted to see me?'

'Yeah', she said, slightly seductively as she drummed her fingers on his chest. 'Let's go to the conference room again, and then you can give me another imaginary bollocking.'

'What have you got?' said Gill, opening a fresh document on his tablet.

'I'll email you the details', said Mhairi, switching back into her professional mode. 'But I've been having some fun with this Macdui *Old Grey Man* thing.'

'There's data on it?'

'Yes. Under a variety of guises. I think the 'Macdui Yeti' was my personal favourite. Or 'Am Fear Liath Mor', which is the older Gaelic name for the same phenomenon.'

'It goes back aways?'

'Oh, yes. Older than the Loch Ness Monster, may she rest in peace.'

'By the look on your face, I'm guessing you've got more contemporary accounts?'

Mhairi smiled. 'We start to see solid information, from 1925, when an eminent mountaineer called Professor J N Collie, described being chased off the peak of Macdui by a 'Big Grey Man.' He reported hearing heavy footsteps crunching in the gravel behind him and turned to find a tall figure approaching him out of the mist. When he ran away, it chased him, hurling stones.'

'Was this guy legit?'

'He was a serious individual. And he delivered his report to a respected mountaineering committee.'

'Alcohol … madness?' Gill queried.

'Clean sheet as far as I can see. But it was a hundred years ago so I can't exactly trawl his social media to get the measure of the man.'

'Okay, so it's potential evidence for a creature that may either haunt or inhabit the mountain.'

'Next up is a guy called Peter Densham. Back in May 1945, he was a reputable mountain rescue team leader and part of another credible mountaineering group. He reported a sudden drop in temperature and the impression of someone standing near him. He also mentions the crunch of gravel as someone approached and a feeling of apprehension.'

'Yeah, but it was probably misty. Surely your guy was being weirded out by the conditions?'

Mhairi shook her head. 'He'd experienced the Cairngorms' worst conditions and had a record of putting his life on the line to save others. The only reason we have a record of this strange encounter is because the witness was so credible.'

'Any more?'

'Next one is from the '50s. A well-known Cairngorm climber called Alex Tewnion described being charged by a creature that was so real and so menacing he discharged three shots from his revolver.'

Gill choked. 'Why would he be carrying a gun?'

'Maybe he was a pal of Densham. Hearing that tale, I'd have carried a gun on Macdui.' She glanced at her notes. 'Have you heard of the *Third Man* phenomena?'

Gill nodded. 'I read a little about that. It's about climbers experiencing a benevolent force who comes alongside them in moments of crisis. *Third man*, because he's been known to accompany groups of two climbers in distress. My take is it's experienced by folk who've pushed themselves too far. People reaching into their deeper psyche for the resources to survive.'

'Okay, well the *Old Grey Man* seems to be a Scottish version. He's similar but altogether more sinister. It's more like the angry spirit of the mountain, attacking walkers and striking down aircraft.'

'Jeepers, Mhairi. You've got more of this stuff?'

'So far, I've got to 1956.' She glanced at her watch. 'Couple more hours until home time. I'll have added a few more incidents by then.'

'Thanks, this is fascinating. Listen, I've got to get back to Krankie for a couple of days. Can you mail me this list?'

Fiona stood at the door of her portacabin and pulled a long breath of damp air into her lungs. This was her last shift and for once, it wasn't raining, though the air was thick enough to spread on toast. She'd tried to resist looking at the weather forecast for Winchester for the coming days. Resisted, and repeatedly failed. The app on her phone confidently predicted low to mid-teens, all the way through to Christmas. After this mud bath, she deserved a change. She'd even begun to fret that as her new job progressed through to the end of June, it might even get too warm. She smiled. A different problem for a different day. For now, this was her last stint on the Krankie dig. They were in good shape, so at 5 pm this evening, she'd shake Gill's hand and walk away from the mud, the rain, the constant odours of diesel exhausts and the irritable grind of traffic winding its way through the roadworks. Time to go work somewhere else.

She pulled on her filthy rain jacket and trudged across the improvised gravel path that took her to the second bone pit. Emma was already there so with her help, they pulled back the blue tarp. This pit was much smaller than the first and a lot deeper. Mercifully, no bones were showing above where she stood, so it was reasonable to assume that this was where the archaeology could stop, and the contractors come back in. First, she had one last mystery to solve. They'd stopped digging on Sunday evening after multiple human backbones had been found. Probing at one, Fiona had deduced the corpse had been buried in a crouching position. Sensing they had done enough for one day, they had stopped. Now, she was here to finish the job.

Working with Emma and two others, they peeled back the earth around the remains.

'Weird', said Emma. 'We've got six different skeletons, all presenting in the same posture.'

'Almost as if they're crouching', Fiona added.

'Or kneeling?'

Fiona sighed. 'Poor buggers. They probably dug this hole themselves and were told to curl up in it. Then had their lives ended at the point of a lance.'

Emma gave a little shudder. 'That's horrible.'

'Let's not assume', said Fiona, standing up and waving to attract Hamish's attention. 'Let's dig them up and see what we find.'

Hamish slithered down beside them.

Fiona passed him a plastic case. 'Over the next few hours, can you take a few photos? Something we can show Beth tomorrow to give her context?'

Hamish grunted an acknowledgement and wandered back to his boxes.

Through the rest of the morning, Fiona and her small remaining team picked away at earth and bone, collecting the individuals into separate containers and carefully stripping away the earth. By breaktime, the six had been recovered.'

'There's more beneath them', Fiona sighed. Their helpers had already excused themselves and now Fiona and Emma worked alone.

Emma wiped her nose. 'I'm seeing the same here. Looks like they're in identical crouches.'

Fiona's back was aching as she stood up. 'Let's take a break.'

'Sure. I have coffee. Wanna share?'

'Please. Are you a smoker Ems?'

'No, never. You?'

'Never. But if I'm ever on another dig like this, I might need to start.'

Emma started pouring drinks. 'It's so grim. Those poor men.'

'Yeah. It's the way they're packed in. I try not to, but I can't help imagining their final moments – crouching there in terror while the men alongside were run through with pikes.'

'Oh, Fi, don't. You'll break my heart.'

Fiona grunted and flicked her head at the sky. 'At least it's stopped bloody raining.'

The two women sipped their drinks in silence for the next two minutes, each lost in personal thoughts.

'Right', said Fiona. 'Let's get our professional heads back on. I really want to reach the bottom of this hole before I hand over to McArdle later.' She squeezed Emma's arm and the two reluctantly stepped back to the trench to recover the next layer of bodies.

Hamish came and went with boxes, which blessed Fiona because it wasn't part of his job. When down at the dig, he took a few shots from relevant angles and showed them to Fiona. She nodded, requesting a few close-ups and several from above, which Hamish took by going up to the carpark and creeping to the edge of the steel piling.

By 4 pm, the second row of bodies had been recovered. Emma looked tired and Fiona caught her glancing at her phone.

'Ems. Go, if you need to go. You've been brilliant today.'

Emma smiled. 'I think we're about there, don't you?'

Fiona stepped carefully around the pit. 'Oh, sorry. There's one more.'

'Let me just send a text, then I'll jump back in. You take the head. I'll take the feet. We'll have him boxed away in no time.'

With the end in sight, the pair chatted happily for half an hour. They reminisced about the Callanish dig two years before, and what this jewel in their respective professional crowns had done to their CVs. Emma spoke about other fieldwork she had done and her aspirations to work in academia. Fiona increasingly said nothing. A chill had come upon her, and she wondered for a while if she was coming down with flu. It was only when Emma stood up and said, 'He was a big old bugger', that Fiona came back to her senses.

'Ems. Step out of the pit would you.'

'But we're almost done.'

'I'm hitting pause on this one.'

'I've got a femur here that wouldn't look out of place on a horse …'

'Emma!'

'Sorry. Yes?'

'Out of the pit. Right now.'

Emma obeyed, scurrying up the boards and onto the apron of the excavation. 'What is it?'

'Give me a hand with the tarp', said Fiona, following her. Together they grabbed the corners of the heavy blue plastic.

'What the hell?' said Emma, catching a glimpse of the last skull in the pit.

'Tell everyone you see, that's us finished for today. Thank Hamish for me, but ask him for my camera back.'

'Fiona. Tell me what's going on?'

Fiona held her hands up. 'Honestly. I don't know. Come back tomorrow. I'll have more for you then. Or maybe, Gill. I'm not sure.'

'If you're certain?'

'Ems, you've been brilliant. We just might need to take our time on this next bit.'

Emma nodded, looking slightly chastened, and went off to find Hamish.

Fiona grappled for her mobile. In a moment she'd phone Gill McArdle. She nodded to herself and took a deep breath. Yeah. In a moment. Right now, her hands were shaking too much to do anything.

When Gill took Fiona's call, he was heading north on the A9, passing Bankfoot. He listened to what she had to say and after hanging up, he immediately called Lillico.

'Constable. Where are you?'

'Just passing Pitlochry. I'll be on-site in a few minutes if you need to get away.'

'No, I'm heading there myself. I'm about twenty minutes behind you. Listen, before you arrive, there's been a development.'

'What's up?'

'I haven't seen for myself. Do you know if Beth is available?'

'She's at Lossuary for a couple of days.'

'Can we pull her back in if it's an emergency?'

Lillico was quiet for a few moments. 'I'll prime her. We can call somebody out if it's important. Gill, is this something to do with the *Toothfairy*?'

It was Gill's turn to be quiet. 'I don't think so. Something different altogether.'

Chapter 23

Four hours later, Gill worked silently in the bone pit opposite Fiona. Lillico had called Beth and in turn, she had summoned a lighting rig and a support team. Now, under a blaze of artificial light, Gill picked away the earth from whatever this thing was. The sight of the emerging bones impacted everyone who saw them, and during the early evening, Gill noticed Beth slipping away to retch quietly in the background. Rationally, these were just bones. Rationally, this was just another body falling to the skilled hands of a pathology team who'd recovered their fair share of bodies over the years. But there was something irrational about this moment. Working near the skeleton, Gill felt repelled and imperilled, as if the bones might be giving off deadly radiation that right now was shortening his life. In fact, Beth, at first sight of the creature had gone to her car and returned with a basic field issue Geiger counter, just to confirm that working in the pit was not a danger to life. Even with that reassurance, he felt a personal blackness just being near it. And from time to time, he would get up, take a minute, and walk away.

'Your boss coming down?' he asked Lillico, during one brief respite from the pit.

Lillico shook his head. 'He's had a couple of drinks, apparently. He'll see us in the morning.'

Gill looked at the dark, starless sky. 'In the circumstances, I don't blame him.'

'Any ideas?' said Lillico, gesturing at the bones.

'I'm better with routine stuff like waterhorses and loch monsters', Gill shot back. 'This one's beyond me.'

'Okay, well when you get to a point, I think we should wrap up and rest. Tomorrow is going to be a long one.'

Gill nodded. 'Tonight, I'm gonna sleep with the light on.'

The following morning, George Wiley stared down into the bone pit. It was 8 am and he stood with his left hand pressed against his forehead. 'What on God's earth is that?'

'We don't know', said Gill. 'Come closer and have a look if you want.'

'No thanks. You describe it from there.'

Gill nodded and crouched near the figure. 'We have the skeletal remains of a humanoid figure, of two point eight metres in height, or a little over nine feet. The narrow configuration of the pelvis suggests the creature was male, but that's just an assumption at this stage. The length and width of the principal leg and arm bones suggest the deceased was extremely muscular.'

'What about the skull, McArdle?'

'The skull is the strangest part of all. About double the size of a typical human, the face appears abnormally flat. The eye sockets are approximately double what we'd expect and whereas a human's eyes sit at the midpoint of the skull, the eye sockets in this creature centre in the lower third.'

'What are those two little holes?'

'I'd guess they're airways.'

'Am I the only one who thinks it looks like an alien?' asked Wiley.

'On this occasion', said Gill, scratching the side of his head with a muddy thumb. 'I'm inclined to agree with you.'

'Should we be wearing hazmat suits?' asked Lillico.

Fiona spat out an angry laugh. She'd been around the thing for more than twelve hours and now she was tired and sullen.

'Probably a bit late for that', said Beth. 'I'll do a full tox report once I have it on a slab.'

Wiley gesticulated at the grave. 'Any other remains in the vicinity?

'Fiona recovered twelve bodies before reaching this one. They were all presented in a ritual fashion. As far as I can see, there's nothing further', said Gill.

'Let's get it lifted', said Beth. 'I'll get it transferred to Bathgate.'

Wiley shook his head. 'There's no need for a whole new group of people setting eyes on this thing. Take it to Falkirk. Has anyone seen Mr Gibson?'

'He's on his way', said Beth.

'Good. Let's keep this tight. Who's got photos of it?'

'Just me', said Fiona.

'Right. Can you pull the memory card out of your camera and give it to Beth. For now, she's to be the custodian of this thing.'

'Hang on', said Gill, suddenly realising this dramatic discovery could be swept under a bureaucratic carpet. 'This isn't *Area 51*. We've potentially found something of huge significance. You can't just hide it away.'

Wiley pointed at Beth. 'I've got a police pathologist telling me we've got an unusual corpse. That means it's evidence, in what's already an ambiguous situation.'

Gill's exasperation was rising. 'He's been dead for the best part of four centuries. You're not exactly investigating his murder.'

'Don't worry, McArdle. You and this … this … alien will get your moment in the sun together', said Wiley, flicking his forefinger at the bones. 'But in the meantime, until we know exactly what it is, I don't want anybody blabbing about it in a pub.'

Gill wondered if anything in heaven or hell could shift the smile from Pete Gibson's face. He'd expected the old man to recoil. Instead, he leaned in close, deeply curious about the new find. He chuckled! He actually chuckled, as he tapped Gill's arm and said, 'You don't see one of those every day.'

'Pete, please tell me you don't ever see one of those, any day of any week, ever!'

Pete looked down at the thing and shook his head. 'I once had a body swapped for a life-size rubber model of E.T. But that was just a joke.'

'I guess it's a laugh-a-minute in your trade.'

Pete beamed. 'You'd be surprised. Now. Let me go and find a container for this big fellow. Then we can get him back to Falkirk and you can have a detailed look at him under some bright lights.'

'He's a rare one', said Fiona, watching Pete's disappearing back.

Gill just grunted before nudging Fiona's elbow. 'How're you doing?'

Fiona lifted her gaze from her feet to his eyes. 'Been doing this job for years. This is the first time I've ever found something that troubled me.'

'It's a weird one.'

'I'm gonna be able to picture that ugly skull for the rest of my days.'

'Do you want to leave? You're already a day late for Winchester.'

Fiona used her grubby gloved hand to wipe her nose. 'I had a brief conversation with my new gaffer.'

'Oh, yes? What did you tell him?'

'I didn't use the words "alien skeleton", but I did mention we have a waterhorse-level find up here. Obviously, I couldn't be more specific, and I think his patience is wearing thin, but I've got a few more days.'

'Thanks. But don't let me do you out of a job.'

'I don't particularly want to be around that thing, so yeah. I won't linger.'

'How much did Emma see?'

'Plenty. And she saw how I reacted. I've made her promise not to say anything.'

'Is she still on-site?'

'She is. I've let everyone else go. Sorry you didn't get to give the survivors a big send-off.'

'I'll do a big "thank you" in the magazine.' Gill watched Pete and Hamish appear with a stretcher. 'Are you joining us in Falkirk?'

Fiona shook her head. 'Emma and I will finish in the pit. See if we can see anything else worth reporting.' She paused for a few moments. 'Do you think this will extend the dig?'

He couldn't quite suppress a dark smile. 'Depends if we end up excavating the A9 looking for a flying saucer.'

'Och, please, Gill. You can't be serious?'

'Honestly, Fi. If this guy is the real deal, this story is going to be global news.'

'Good luck with that', she said, walking away.

Chapter 24

'I'm almost certain it's human', said Beth, her voice muffled by the face mask and visor she now wore.

The *Jacobite Alien*, as Pete Gibson had now christened him, was laid out on the steel table before them in the Lossuary mortuary. His skeleton was disarticulated, but to Lillico's eyes, surprisingly complete.

'You're certain?' said Wiley.

'I won't be absolutely sure until I get the DNA results. I'm talking to a specialist later this afternoon, but your alien is most likely some poor foot soldier with a hormonal disorder.'

'At nine feet tall?' spat Wiley.

'Sure. The tallest man ever measured was Robert Wadlow. He was just a whisker shorter than our chap.'

'What about the other features?' asked Gill. 'Like the weird skull.'

'Most likely deformities caused by hormone problems.' She drew a breath. 'But there's one feature you haven't seen yet.' She leaned over the skeleton and used the point of her biro to indicate a line of connected bones lying behind the pelvis. 'This is his coccyx.'

'His cock-wots-its?' demanded Wiley.

'His tail bone', said Beth curtly.

Gill stepped in closer. 'But that must be over two feet long.'

Beth nodded. 'Yes. And quite possibly its cartilage extension was twice as long again.'

'Hell of a mutation', Gill breathed.

'Sorry, someone please explain', Wiley demanded.

Beth pointed at the offending bone. 'Our strange trooper had a tail, Chief Inspector.'

'And you still think it's human?'

'We all have tails. It's just that in a normal human specimen, the tail is regressed to the point where it's occluded by buttock muscle.'

Wiley flinched as he tried to comprehend what Beth was telling him.

'Your tail, Chief Inspector, is buried in your fat arse', she said.

Wiley reddened and looked like he was about to explode. Lillico meanwhile had spotted a new message on his phone. 'Sir. Can we step outside for a second? Something just came up.'

Still transfixed by Beth's smug gaze, Wiley didn't move. 'I don't want you bringing anyone else in on this', he breathed. 'No experts, no colleagues and no pals. Not without my explicit say so.'

'How on earth am I meant to make progress?' Beth protested. 'And don't say Google, because I've tried, and frankly, the material so far isn't helpful.'

'Not going to repeat myself', said Wiley, reciprocating her glare.

Ultimately, it was Beth who broke the standoff, turning her back to him and leaning over the bones.

'Is it just me or are people ruder since Covid?' asked Wiley as Lillico steered him outside.

'She's been working long shifts, sir. Best to let that one pass.'

Wiley didn't say anything for a moment, though Lillico doubted he'd forgive Beth's insolence in a hurry. Which was ironic, considering how he routinely treated people.

'What's so urgent?' Wiley asked.

'We've had DNA hits off two more *Toothfairy* victims.'

'Excellent. Are we seeing a cluster yet?'

Lillico shook his head. 'There's still no pattern. The latest identifications are a spinster in her sixties, from Alloa, and a retired bank manager from Galashiels.'

'Any link, no matter how tenuous, to the other victims we've identified?'

'None as far as I can see. There's still a chance we'll identify some of the remaining nineteen.'

Wiley lit a cigarette and pulled hard on it. 'Twenty-five people, Alec. That's almost as many as Fred West and Denis Nilsen put together.'

'Agreed, sir. And personally, I'm dreading the day the newspapers get hold of it.'

'Do you think I was wrong to involve McArdle?'

'No, sir. Because, until we find a cluster linking at least some of the *Toothfairy* victims together, we're going to need all the help we can get.'

As Gill walked back on site later that afternoon, Fiona turned to meet him.

'What's the news at Falkirk?' she asked.

'Beth thinks he's human, but I'm not so sure.'

'What's her reasoning?'

'That he was just some poor bugger with a congenital disorder.'

Fiona nodded, looking relieved. 'He would have terrified the government soldiers. All that ugly height bearing down on them.'

'Why is Pete so certain he was a Jacobite?'

'That's my fault. The remains were found at the top of the hill where the early Jacobite casualties would have fallen. And when Wiley asked me if we'd found anything else in the pit, I mentioned a couple of jacket buttons. A quick check online matched them to some Jacobite items found here during a survey in 2016.'

'Good work. Anything else to report?'

Fiona shook her head. 'Fragments, but nothing worth mentioning. And the base of the pit is definitely the bottom. As far as I can tell, the ground beneath is undisturbed.'

'That's a relief.'

Fiona nodded but said nothing.

'Are you doing okay? That was a disturbing find.'

'Yeah. I'm grand. Hey, we dig up bones for a living. You gotta hope for something interesting from time to time.'

'How's Emma?'

'She's a bit freaked out. I've asked her to be discreet, but we can't compel her to stay silent. One way or another, it's only a matter of time before someone leaks this.'

'Of course. Maybe I'll have a word. Beth should be finished with her first raft of tests by this time tomorrow and we'll hopefully have it nailed by the day after. If we can keep it out of the news until then, that would help.'

Fiona kicked aimlessly at a clod of earth. 'Can you ask her to run a chemical analysis of the bones?'

'Sure. What are you thinking?'

'Emma and I were kicking around for any explanation of why the bones in both pits carried so little weathering. I can't see any reason for it, so it sets me thinking about the big guy. Maybe there was something in his constitution that acted as a preservative across both pits.'

Gill thought about this for a second. 'I can't think of any naturally occurring chemical in the human body that would have the effect you're talking about. And not at that kind of scale.'

'Fair enough. Worth asking the question. I've taken a batch of soil samples and they'll be on the last van going to Falkirk.'

'Good thinking.'

'Does this mean we can wrap up the site?'

'That's up to DCI Wiley and co. But I think we should finish tomorrow. We can leave it to DC Lillico to fight it out with

Scott about when the bulldozers come in. Shall we have another crack at deciding your last day?'

Fiona immediately nodded. 'Tomorrow, if that's okay. That way I can travel south on Thursday.'

Gill reached over and gave her a muddy embrace. 'Definitely. Get away this time and no distractions.'

Gill took Wednesday morning in the office. He still had a couple of weeks until his next print deadline, so he spent most of the morning topping up the online feeds and contributing to several debates on the *Mys.Scot* website. He also dropped in some teaser material on the Krankie dig, though he was careful not to hint at their star find. But Cassy had noticed he had news. She could spot it in his body language, of course. So, he told her, which was only fair. But then Cassy mentioned it to Mhairi, who let it slip to Craig. By lunchtime it was clear he'd have to get a lid on the situation, so straight after lunch, he pulled the full team into the conference room and reviewed progress on the dig so far. He scoped out potential articles and took suggestions from the team about how they could link these recent finds with other stories. Eventually, he threw the meeting open to the team and waited for Cassy to ask about the *Jacobite Alien*. And when she did, he told them everything he knew.

'How many bodies in the end?' said Craig.

'Between eighty and ninety. Plus one big ugly alien', Gill replied.

Craig glanced across at Larry and in unison, they both shook their heads.

'And I thought we were on a roll', muttered Craig. 'Ruddy cat mag.'

Gill could see Mhairi's brain was spinning.

'You're all acting like this is normal', she said. 'For a man to be that large and with such severe deformities … it's incredible he was fit enough to fight in a battle.'

'Yon big fella wuz runnin' doon hill', Larry observed.

'Yes, but these kinds of disorders. He would have struggled to walk, never mind run.'

'Maybe he was their mascot?' said Craig. 'A big guy to strike fear into the opposition?'

'Or a champion, like Goliath in the Bible', said Mhairi.

Gill leaned in towards the centre of the group. 'Folks, if we have discovered alien remains, or some kind of alien/human hybrid, we need to be one hundred per cent certain before we report it. That means we have to use the time before Wiley lifts his reporting embargo and do some thinking on this. Craig, when you get a minute, can you research the specific human diseases that could cause this kind of deformity?'

Craig nodded.

'Cassy, can you use your highland connections and see if there are any clan histories that speak of large fighters? Even deformed ones.'

'Got it.'

'And Mhairi. You're our high priestess of myths and legends. Can you take a look at the broader field of human history and see what you can see.'

'There be giants!' Mhairi whispered, making Cassy giggle.

'Wot about me, boss?' said Larry.

'Your mission, should you choose to accept it, is to get us through this week without anyone outside this team getting wind of the *Jacobite Alien*.'

'Meooww!' whispered Larry.

Chapter 25

On that same Wednesday, Lillico was having a frustrating morning. Shortly after his boss arrived, he was summoned to Wiley's office.

'I see pathology have sent over another batch of DNA results', said Wiley, dispensing with any greetings. 'Anything useful?'

'We've now identified nine of the *Toothfairy* victims which is way more than we expected. And the Krankie bones have yielded thirty-two usable profiles. Unfortunately. When I compare the two groups, I find zero overlap.'

Wiley flicked his chin. 'Still early days.'

Lillico shook his head. 'Actually, we've plucked the low-hanging fruit from both groups. The remaining unidentified *Toothfairy* victims probably aren't on the DNA database. And as for the Falkirk bodies, we've got samples from the best-preserved bones and we're not likely to get reliable profiles from many more.'

'Any of the Krankie profiles already listed on the national database?'

'None so far, which reinforces the original hypothesis they are battlefield remains rather than anything fresh.'

'We're certain there aren't contemporary bones?'

'Yes. Beth is reviewing the bone and soil samples. There must be some other kind of preservative effect going on.'

'What about that list of Cairngorm casualties you got from McArdle's team?'

'They pulled together forty years of deaths and disappearances on the mountains. They could only give us names and ages, but there's no overlap between folk missing on the mountains and any of our nine identified *Toothfairy* kills.'

'I'm beginning to wonder if the Cairngorm connection is spurious', said Wiley, picking up a sheaf of files. 'Nearly all our named vics came from the central belt. They didn't go missing in the mountains. They're from different areas, different professions, and no particular social class. We need to start digging into the backgrounds of these people. Spot the link. Figure out who might want them dead.'

'I've got a list of next of kin. If we're going to do a lot of legwork, I'll prep a couple of route plans so we can use our time efficiently. Which makes me think. What do you want to do up at Krankie?'

'Let's push Beth to get a final report to the Fiscal this week. If I get one more call from Transport Scotland begging us to release the site, I'll damn well go up there with a shovel and fill in that hole myself.'

'If we're going on the road this week, sir, is there any chance I could send the names of our nine vics to Gill's team? They might see something we can't.'

Wiley shook his head. 'As of yesterday morning, all they want to babble about is aliens. I'm regretting I ever involved them.'

Towards the end of Wednesday afternoon, Gill found Fiona in her portacabin, taking down the site plans and sliding them into a plastic folder. 'You're going to miss this place.'

'I am not', said Fiona, without looking up. 'Pish weather, pish mud and another dash to the finish line to meet *Mys.Scot's* intolerable deadlines.'

'It's the new archaeology', said Gill. 'Same amount of excitement, delivered in the time it takes you to watch a TikTok video.'

'With a fraction of the planning, and barely enough crew to get the job done.'

'I think you'd agree these were exceptional circumstances. Where we're standing will soon be under twelve metres of rock and tarmac.'

'Och, I know. Push comes to shove? I just hate hurrying away.'

'I'll let you know what's happening.'

'I don't think much will be happening now. We're all closed up. Mr Gibson is away home to Falkirk to count his fortune, and even Beth is sitting in an office somewhere dashing out her report.'

'Actually, she's in Falkirk too. Wiley's orders, but yeah, point taken.'

Fiona stepped towards him and gave him a hard embrace. 'You'll let me know when they figure out what that thing was?'

'I will.'

She released him and gathered up her bags. With Gill shouldering her laptop, they exited the cabin and locked the door.

'As if this site wasn't weird enough, there's also our resident flasher', said Fiona.

'You mentioned him. Does he actually flash?'

'No, but he must be creeping around in the buff to look like that. And the team saw him three times. It's a wonder we haven't found him lying dead with exposure.'

'Well, he can have the place to himself now. If the police return with picks and shovels, he can try strutting his stuff with them. Either way, I think our role here is done.'

Fiona raised her face to bathe in the cold, softly falling rain. 'This time next week, if the forecast is right, I'll be working in shorts and a t-shirt.'

Gill glanced at the rain-laden sky. 'Brilliant. Send me a postcard.'

Thursday morning saw the team reconvene with everyone wanting to discuss story ideas to exploit the *Jacobite Alien*. The task for today, however, was to feedback on the myths and legends that might help explain the discovery. It soon became clear they'd all struggled with their respective research tasks. Cassy pleaded pressure of work so Gill let her go first.

'Right then. Shall I start with references to giants in clan records?'

After a nod from Gill, Cassy reeled off half a dozen short paragraphs she'd constructed from her research. The work was hurried and Gill detected nothing that piqued his interest.

'Summing up', said Cassy. 'I found a few references to big or mighty warriors but nothing like the chap you found at Krankie.'

'Okay', said Gill. 'Anything in the myths?'

'If you want to get a bit legendary, we could talk about Benandonner.'

'Never hear of him', said Craig.

'Scandi fitba player', said Larry. 'Played fer Rangers back in the nineties.'

'Benandonner was a Scottish giant', said Cassy, tossing Larry a smirk. 'Who wanted to challenge his Irish equivalent, the slightly more famous Finn McCool, to a fight. With his very cool name, it was supposed old Finn was up for a wee bit of a barney because he built the Giant's Causeway, so they could meet and do battle. As Finn made his way across to Scotland, he saw Benandonner in the distance. Thinking he looked much bigger, taller and stronger than Finn, the Irish laddie scooped up a clod of earth and threw it at Scotland, forming the Isle of Man.'

Craig sniffed. 'So basically, it's a baseless legend.'

'Absolutely', said Cassy. 'Pure, unadulterated myth. Can I go now? I'm still really behind.'

Gill thanked her and nodded at Craig. 'You're up.'

'Right. Biological reasons for gigantism in humans.' Craig began. He passed around a few colour prints of abnormally tall men, mostly in period dress. 'Here are a few examples. I have to say, the mechanism for this isn't well understood. It can't be predicted and doesn't seem to have any reliable course of treatment.'

'The drug companies won't touch it', said Mhairi. 'There will never be enough cases to justify the billions they'd spend researching the condition.'

Craig nodded. 'It's caused by an excess of growth hormone and sufferers seem to develop it around puberty. They develop a benign tumour in their anterior pituitary gland, leading to overproduction of the growth hormone.'

'Would it explain the weird skull and tailbone?' asked Gill.

'Not directly. I guess he could have been unfortunate enough to suffer two rare types of abnormalities, but I think it's unlikely. Sufferers of gigantism tend to have weak hearts. To throw another congenital complexity on top would have left our guy gasping for breath, even on a good day.'

'Could he have carried Neanderthal genes?' asked Mhairi.

'Odds are against that', Craig replied. 'I can't find any record of Neanderthals reaching Scotland. They were a Eurasian species and are thought to have been extinct forty thousand years ago.'

'Homo sapiens only made it to Scotland about thirteen thousand years ago', said Mhairi. 'Which isn't surprising considering the weather. That and the crappy rail network.'

Gill smiled and tapped the table gently. 'But don't all humans carry some Neanderthal DNA?'

'Western Europeans do', said Craig. 'But it's well mixed in. I don't think it gives us any leads on the *Jacobite Alien*.'

Gill nodded and glanced at Mhairi. 'Over to you. Let's see if you can save the day.'

Mhairi scratched the back of her head. 'I'm only going to offer you myths and legends, really. Nothing as solid as Craig was talking about.'

'Yeah, but for completeness. And don't forget the work you did for me on Orkney. That gave us the best possible theory for what was going on.'

Mhairi glanced at her notes. 'I can email you full details if you like. I found the Greeks, Romans, Norse and Hindus all have their own myths about giants. Let's say we ignore the unrealistic ones that claim giants over one hundred feet high. If we do that, there does seem to be a high degree of similarity in the remaining legends.'

'How do you mean?'

'They all talk about warriors, or venerated mighty men. Rather than being the clinically damaged humans Craig was talking about, they appear endowed with supreme abilities.'

'You're saying they had supernatural powers?'

'No. Just that they were supremely strong, or long-lived. In the Apkallu tradition, which is associated with Sumeria, they were regarded as incredibly wise. I found a few websites proposing these giants were the first aliens to live on Earth.'

'How so?'

'They looked strange. Some were compared to birds. Some to reptiles and others to fish.'

'Sounds unhelpful', said Craig.

Mhairi winced. 'It was a long time ago, and it's all so tenuous.'

'Do these myths have a common root?' Gill asked.

'There's no smoking gun, but I do have a smouldering wisp of a theory rising over one potential idea. Have you heard of the Nephilim?'

Gill nodded. 'I've read about them. First few chapters from the book of Genesis.'

'Like in the Bible?' said Craig.

Gill nodded. 'Feel free to leap in, Mhairi, but I think the story goes that the fallen angels; the ones who sided with Lucifer, went down to Earth and took brides from among the human population. They sired a tribe of super-sized humans who became known as the …'

'Anakites', added Mhairi. 'A thorn in the side of the Jews as they journeyed towards their promised land.'

'And thought to have been destroyed during the wars that established the first Israeli kingdom', said Gill.

Craig cleared his throat. 'Boss, I can see by the look in your eyes that you're enjoying yourself. But what has any of this got to do with that box of bones sitting in Falkirk?'

Gill sat quite still and tried to analyse the feeling that had just come over him. Excitement? Fear? The simple pleasure of the chase? He wasn't sure. He did know one thing. There was a story here. Whether it was one he'd ever have the guts to print …

'Boss?'

'Yeah. Sorry. Mhairi, anything else?'

'The Nephilim disappeared from history at the time of the Biblical flood and their descendants soon after. So I've nothing else to add.'

'Okay, guys. Thanks for your input. Let me gather my thoughts and then we'll regroup.'

Gill touched base with Cassy back at her desk after the conference room cluster broke up. 'You okay?'

She looked up and smiled. 'Yeah. Just a bit behind after a few days out of the office. Sorry I had to bail. Good meeting?'

'Helpful, but inconclusive.'

He glanced over her shoulder and cast his eye down the lists of numbers on her PC. 'How's the subscription base holding up?'

'Better. We seemed to have recovered the ground we lost after our Orkney controversies.'

'Yeah, that was the Marmite issue. Doesn't seem to have hurt us in the long run.'

Cassy pointed at her screen. 'And look at the overseas subscriptions. It amazes me anybody wants to get a magazine posted halfway around the planet when they can pay half the price to see it all online.'

'Power of the brand, Cassy. Besides, we're switching to print-on-demand in the US next year. That'll save a few air miles.'

She huffed. 'You sound like Tony.'

'Yeah. I should really start dressing the part. Red braces. Shiny suit. The very embodiment of the contemporary, forward-looking editor.'

'Let me know the day you decide to dress like that. Just so I can get my resignation in early.'

'But seriously, Cass. You had a challenging few days out in the field. How are you doing now?'

She threw him a smile. 'I wanted to see a dig. Now I have. And I'm back here in the warm and dry, running the show the way I like it.'

He backed away in mock offence. 'You think you're the one running the show?'

'Gosh, yeah. A few days with the office running without me? It was almost a train wreck.' She sat up a little straighter and stared at her screen. 'I'm really awfully busy, Gill. You're dismissed.'

Gill threw her a sloppy salute and returned, smiling, to his desk. Top of his emails was a note from Beth, headed 'DNA results are in for J-A.' His pulse ticked up as he hovered over the unopened email. In this moment, he felt the same curiosity he'd experienced the day they'd lifted the Orcadian slab. On that occasion, his instincts had been buzzing. Today, his inner voice was strangely subdued. Despite his excitement to see these results, his inner voice anticipated only darkness.

With a deep breath, he opened the attached screenshot and scanned the contents. To his surprise, Beth had included two charts rather than one. From his limited knowledge of human phenotypes, he realised the first chart carried the polymorphic markers predicting the human appearance and ancestry of the *Jacobite Alien*. The peaks in the data indicated his hair, eye and skin colour, alongside the considerable details documenting his individuality. The second chart had a completely different set of numbers, employing phenotypes he didn't recognise. Unfortunately, her email contained no interpretation of the data. He tried calling Beth but went straight to voicemail. Instead of leaving a message, he emailed back to set up a meeting with her for the following morning. Shrugging off his disappointment, he was packing up his stuff to join Larry and the others at a bar when a text popped onto his phone. Realising it was from Solomon, he read it and sighed.

Instead of words her message consisted of two question marks.

Chapter 26

He texted her back with a request to meet ASAP. And she responded with an offer of 6 pm under the V&A.

A short while later, while arriving at the meet point on the river side of the museum, Gill saw Charlie, standing a little way off, his eyes alert for danger. Gill nodded at him, and Charlie nodded back, before returning his gaze again to the perimeter. He couldn't see Charlie's shield, but like Gill, Charlie was learning to control the manifestation of his weapon; ready to deploy it at a moment's notice. With Charlie keeping watch, Solomon and Gill could talk freely.

'Well?' she snapped as he approached her through the dusky, rain-stained arch.

'Well yourself', he replied. 'You texted me, so you go first.'

Solomon considered this for a second. 'I sensed you're having another little brush with darkness.'

'Darkness? I was reading a DNA chart when you texted.'

'Ah', she said calmly. 'And I'm sure that was all perfectly routine.'

He stepped up close to see her face clearly in the poor light. 'When you say, "you sensed?" I tell you what, Solie. I'd really love to know how this sensing thing actually works?'

'You've seen me do it before. And the girl you met on Harris.'

'Ailsa.'

'Yes. Ailsa. She could do it too.'

Gill bobbed his shoulders.

'And you do it yourself. Though you're always in too much of a hurry to realise when it's happening.'

He laughed. She'd never insulted him before. Under the unwritten constitution of Scottish culture, that meant they were becoming friends. 'How do I already do it; this sensory-thing?'

'You described it at our first meeting. You said you sometimes stand before an archaeological dig, and you know right there and then if you're going to find something significant.'

'That's just instinct.'

'Oh, is that what we're calling it now? Well, let's just say that I had an *instinct* to be in touch with you this afternoon. And now I see your face, I'm glad I did.' She peered at him for a long second. 'If you've finished your little tirade, can we talk about darkness now?'

Gill gave a shallow nod and stared over her shoulder at the River Tay, more than a mile wide, flowing silver in the dusky light. 'What do you know about the Nephilim?'

'Only what I've read. I've not given the topic much thought, to be honest.'

'They were seen as half-angel/half-human abominations. The early Jews exterminated them.'

'That's what *The Book* says', said Solomon. 'It's hard to know which parts of that particular story were literal and which are metaphors.'

'What would you say if I told you we have the remains of a Nephilim stored in a box in Falkirk?'

'I beg your pardon?'

Briefly, and in confidence, Gill told her about the find in Krankie, plus the preliminary DNA results. 'And there's more. We've had sightings of a large grey man; naked, and watching the dig site where the bones were recovered.'

'I see.'

'And … and, as I mentioned to you last time we talked, I was walking on Macdui with a friend two weeks ago, and something attacked us. Something big enough to toss boulders like they were snowballs.'

'You think all these circumstances are linked?'

'Well, I've got my instincts and you've got your little sensey-thingey. They've both got wee red lights flashing, so yeah, I think they're linked. And somehow, they both tie back to my demon encounter at Airth.'

Solomon gathered her arm in his and without asking, steered them into a slow walk along the riverside pathway. 'These bones. How long has the creature been dead?'

'Twenty-seventh July 1689.'

'That's very precise!'

'Killiecrankie. The day of the battle.'

'But the apparitions you saw in the forest around the dig site - they appeared to be living flesh?'

'I didn't get to see it, but that's what I've heard.'

'Gosh. Very rare for something like this to happen.'

'Like what?'

Solomon sighed. 'Look, Gill. This is the less comfortable aspect of whatever it is we're involved in. To understand what I'm saying, you have to remember that the fathers of the Nephilim were considered to be demons.'

'Define demon for me, Solie. Just so we're on the same page.'

'They are angels formed by the Creator, but who then rejected His majesty and tried to set up a kingdom under Lucifer, the highest ranked fallen angel.'

Gill nodded. 'That's why I'm seeing fleshy apparitions. They're a demon/human hybrid?'

Solomon shook her head. 'I doubt it. They haven't existed for thousands of years.'

'But we keep seeing one. Most likely, it's what attacked me on Ben Macdui.'

'No, I'm certain what you're experiencing is a demon, briefly manifesting as a human. Like Raphael manifests whenever he wants to talk to you.'

'How do you explain the bones then?'

'I can't.'

'Using your logic, there would have to have been a human and demon coupling back in the mid-seventeenth century.'

'Agreed. Which would be totally against the rules, of course. Mixing with humans that is. But you can't expect a demon to behave with a social conscience.'

'Indeed. That would kinda defeat their purpose. We've got one living in the office photocopier. He's a wee bugger.'

Solomon rolled her eyes and continued. 'Good and evil, locked in a continuing battle, seem to have arrived at certain rules of conflict. One of those is that they do not appear as humans in physical form, unless a particular person, or piece of territory, or historical moment, is closely disputed.'

'I've heard that described as a "thin place", said Gill.

'That's a good Highland word for it. We know demons are outnumbered and outgunned, so they don't parade themselves in human society for fear of accelerating their end.'

'Maybe they manage to mess up humanity without having to put in personal appearances?'

Solomon exhaled a long slow breath. 'Indeed. We're all so selfish and gullible.'

'You think?'

'Just look in the mirror, Gill. And yet, HE thinks you're special.'

Gill balanced her gentle rebuke with the nagging scepticism lurking in his own mind. His chat with Arnold Broadbent was weighing on him. Not for the first time since he accepted a supernatural dimension to his life, he wondered if it was rational. Arnold had spoken so convincingly about *The Third Man* syndrome, it had given Gill cause to question if his own experiences were genuine. Had he, in fact, conjured Raphael in moments of stress? Was this voice he occasionally heard in his head just his own brain's efforts to help him endure? And was *The Book* just a carefully constructed fiction imagining a non-existent god's interaction with humanity? When he stopped to reconsider the "evidence" that had rocked his worldview, it all seemed so subjective.

'Am I "special", Solie? Or do I believe that because it's a desirable sentiment? A warm, fuzzy feeling to take to bed every night?'

She released his arm and spun to face him. 'Very good question, Gill. But answer it this once and then don't ever ask it again.'

He held out his hands to her. 'How do I answer my own question?'

She formed a wrinkled fist with her right hand and struck him lightly on the chest. 'By letting this conversation go full circle. By being honest with yourself about what this fledgeling instinct is actually telling you.'

Gill thought for a second. 'I only get my instinct when I'm on a dig site.'

Solomon threw her hands out from her sides. 'Then pretend you're on a dig site, Gill. Gather data in the same way you would in the field.'

'How do I do that? It's so hypothetical.'

'By practising! Every opportunity you get, every situation you're in; ask your instinct a question. Let her answer. Walk through your day and see how these situations play out. Then look at your data. On balance, is the spoken intuition in your head better than your brain at decoding your day-to-day interactions, or not?'

'Her?'

'Don't change the subject. And let's experiment right now. Go on. Ask her if you're special.'

Gill stood glaring down at his friend and nodded. He waited for a few moments while his discomfort subsided, then silently, internally, and rather awkwardly, he asked his "instinct" the question.

'Well?' Solomon demanded, some two minutes later.

'I got nothing.'

'Try again.'

Gill sighed and waited. 'Again. Nothing.'

'One more time.'

Gill glared at her and while he was constructing a riposte to tell her what she could do with her daft experiment, his head swam. He reached for the wall to steady himself and found that Solomon had grasped his free hand. This time, she stayed silent. Just looked at him and waited.

Gill hung his head. 'It was like opening an oven door; that blast of heat you get that almost takes you off your feet. A huge awareness that I'm loved.' He swallowed. 'I guess that means I'm special.'

'There you go. Now, which side are you on?'

Gill flinched. 'What were the choices again?'

Solomon lifted her free hand and pressed it against her forehead. 'For goodness sake, Gill. Ask the voice!'

He took a second. In fact, he took several. And then he asked this presence, augmenting his intuition, where he should stand.

He sighed. 'I can either stand with evil, or stand with good. Or can hang around in the middle pretending the choice doesn't exist, and basically become cannon fodder.' He shrugged. 'I'm with the good guys.'

'Right. That's progress. But it's also an admission.'

Gill blinked at her, willing her to go on. 'Good and evil are locked in a war', she said. 'Armies shooting at each other.'

'I heard the voice say that on the day I first believed.' He winced. 'Does that literally mean, shooting?'

Solomon shrugged. 'I guess they were shooting at one another in Killiecrankie, but generally, I'd say it's meant figuratively. And that's why you need your wits about you if you sense any demonic activity. Thin places, Gill. THIN PLACES!'

'Thanks. I'll work on that.'

She took his arm again and for ten minutes they walked again in unsettled silence. Then they turned and walked back, discussing the few words in *The Book* that described the Nephilim. Eventually, they returned to the spot where they had begun.

'I'm very careful with pronouns these days', said Gill.

'Well, you have to be', Solomon replied.

'I couldn't help but notice you referred to your inner voice as feminine.'

'I did, didn't I.'

They stopped and Gill folded his arms. 'As it's kind of a God-give-me-guidance voice, I thought it would be male.'

'I'm sure it is for some people.'

'But for you. It's female?'

'Yes. And she has a name.'

'And are you gonna tell me?'

Solomon hitched her bag further up onto her shoulder and made ready to go. 'Ask her. When she's ready, I'm sure she'll introduce herself.'

'Solie!'

But she was already walking away. He watched her go, then drifted over to the sloping concrete walls of the museum, allowing his head to rest against the cold stone. His thirty-minute conversation with Solomon had answered a couple of his questions, but posed twice as many more. About par for the course.

But he had heard a name. Raphael had mentioned a name before and hinted at her supremacy. Gill wracked his brain, but the name wouldn't come. Catching the lesson in Solomon's words, he stopped and asked the voice. Rather lamely, he stood and stared at the river for several long minutes, trying to hear his inner voice. But he was starting to tire of Solomon's exercise.

He gave up and glanced at his watch. Cassy and the rest of the team would already be ensconced in a town centre bar. It was time to join them. As he turned away, he caught a murmur of the voice. And the name she gave sparked a memory in Gill, of a day long ago near the stones of Callanish.

'Aura', she breathed.

Chapter 27

Beth was bustling around the Lossuary "kitchen" when Gill arrived the following morning. Bizarrely she was singing to herself, a tune Gill recognised from his school days; "America", from *West Side Story*.

He tapped on the door, and she turned around and smiled. 'Ah, here he is.'

'About your dodgy DNA.'

'Which is clearly not as exciting as I thought it would be. In my naivety, I assumed you'd hightail it over here yesterday afternoon.'

'Considered it', said Gill, glancing warily at the remains of the *Jacobite Alien*, laid out on a steel table. 'But my team were having a social thing. I didn't want to miss it.'

'No problem. Listen, before we get to that, I think I've figured out why the contents of the Krankie bone pits are so well preserved.'

Gill gave a low whistle. 'That was fast work. Please, tell all.'

'It's just chemistry', Beth shot back. 'I found residue of gunpowder in most of Fiona's soil samples. Looks like a load of it was dumped in the second pit. As the powder oxidized, it leached something into the groundwater that preserved the bones. It will take an expert to figure out exactly what happened, but my guess would be the reaction over decades would have leaked hydrogen peroxide into the higher pit, and from there, down into the lower burial pit.'

'Gunpowder! Why would they even do that?'

Beth presented a flamboyant shrug. 'Maybe they buried the *Jacobite Alien*, then in retrospect, somebody decided to blow him up. In the event, the powder must have got wet. It didn't go bang. Instead, it left the nitrates and sulphates to do their weird thing in the soil.'

Gill stood blinking at her. 'You're sure? I mean, the effect you're describing covered a wide area downhill from the bone pit. Why was its impact so uniform?'

Beth waved a hand to hush him. 'I've done my bit. Let's leave it to the forensic chemists at Bathgate to sort out the details.'

'Okay.' Gill tried and failed to keep the disappointment out of his voice. 'At least we can tell George Wiley that Krankie doesn't hold any *Toothfairy* victims.' He shook off the letdown and got his head back in the game. 'Let's assume that's one mystery solved. How about our deceased friend's DNA? One of the charts you sent looked strange.'

'Yes. I'll show you.' She moved across to her laptop and pointed at the charts on her screen. 'Do you know how to read DNA charts?'

'I'm not an expert, but yes, I've used them.'

'The peaks on the first chart are exactly what I'd expect to see. They tell me our man was white-skinned, red-haired and probably prematurely balding. There are a bunch of smaller peaks that are consistent with his clan connections.' She looked up at him. 'So far so good. But if you look at the second chart, we find his DNA had markers for something completely different.'

'I noticed those. What do you think they are?'

'Very complex DNA. Probably only a tiny part of his full genome, so someone will have to do more work on that.' She paused. 'The thing is, Gill. I know enough to say this section isn't human DNA.'

Gill nodded slowly as if this announcement was the most natural thing in the world. 'What is it then?'

Beth dropped her hands on the table. 'At the moment, I don't know.'

'Somebody, somewhere must have seen this before?'

'Wiley still has this locked down. I don't know what he's afraid of, but he won't even let me talk about this challenge with my colleagues.'

'Meaning you can't throw it out to a bunch of universities?'

'I should be able to, but Wiley's orders are strict. And he has the seniority on this.'

'That's annoying.' Gill shot a glance at the bones. 'Can you speculate?'

'The obvious suggestion would be hybridization of some kind. Begs the question, though. Hybrid of what?'

'Sounds like he might be part alien after all?'

'Come on, Gill. Work with me on this! He's human but part something else. I'm not sure what.'

'Okay, what about another near-human species? Chimpanzees for example.'

'That's where I was going.' Beth pointed at her chart again and dropped several more rows of peaks onto the chart.

'Even if it were biologically possible, which it isn't, none of the great apes carry DNA in this range.'

'Something extinct, then. A hominid of some kind. An ape that was a halfway house between our species?'

Beth brightened. 'Yes! Of course. Way back in time. Maybe even a hominid that hasn't been discovered yet?'

'Now you're thinking!'

She slumped forward again. 'But until Wiley lifts his embargo, I can't test this hypothesis.'

'I'll speak to him. There are ways we can do this quietly without making a fuss.'

'Yes. We could reach out to the top genetics labs by the end of the day if I had his say so.'

'In the meantime, I've a good desk researcher in my team. Without divulging the source, she can look for any creatures matching the DNA you've identified.'

'Okay, but you're bending the rules there. You should check with Wiley first.'

Gill snorted. 'I know what he'd say. On one hand, he's desperate for me to help, and on the other, he's happy to tie my hands behind my back.'

'As long as we've agreed, if there's any blowback from …' Abruptly, Beth stopped speaking. Her lips open in mid-speech. Her right hand held up with fingers splayed; motionless.

'Beth?' Startled, Gill studied her frozen face. 'Beth!' But she did not flinch. He waved his hands in front of her face. He touched her outstretched fingers and found her to be a statue of her normal self.

Panic started to rise in his chest. And then he heard a sound. A rasping, hissing, clicking voice halfway between a growl and a purr. He spun around to face the stainless-steel table to find a naked, grey-skinned creature, sitting cross-legged on the work surface beside the bones. Gill recoiled. Even in this repose, the creature was more than a head taller than Gill. Its head swivelled to look at him and for a moment the jet-black eyeballs met his gaze.

'… our favourite Detective, then that's on you', Beth continued.

Gill kept staring at the steel table, but the creature had disappeared.

'You okay?' asked Beth, squinting at him.

He turned to face her. 'Did you see that?'

'See what?'

'Just for a second, there was a creature perched on the table.'

'What? Like a rat of something?'

'No. A big grey thing. Like a man, but bigger. Like the *Jacobite Alien*, but with flesh on.'

Beth studied his face for a moment then slowly shook her head.

'Maybe I'm losing it. But for a few seconds, you were frozen in mid-speech and this thing was just sitting there.'

She let several long seconds pass. 'Are you winding me up?'

'No! Honestly. It was right there.'

Beth turned back to her computer. 'Don't hang around the dead, Gill. It's clearly not good for you.'

'Beth, I'm not messing around!'

'Look, I'm really quite busy', she said, turning back to her work. 'I've already sent you the DNA results but keep them to yourself for now. If you could persuade Wiley to let me throw this out to a wider professional circle, I'd appreciate it.'

Gill murmured his agreement and couldn't stop himself from looking around for the creature before he literally backed out of the room. When he reached his car, he was shaking uncontrollably. 'What the hell was that', he whispered.

Chapter 28

Gill returned to the dig site by lunchtime. He parked his car and glanced at the contractor's canteen. But on reflection, decided he wasn't hungry. Whatever had happened at Lossuary had shocked him. The cold hand of logic told him he had imagined the experience. And the part of him that tended towards anxiety fretted he might have a brain tumour and be on the cusp of losing his sanity. Through all that, a part of him was hounded by insatiable curiosity; he needed to understand what had happened in Pete Gibson's lab. To reconcile these competing logics, he couldn't help but remember Solomon's advice – that the Airth demon might come for him again. Shuddering, he reflected on this different encounter. This time, he'd actually seen the thing. And in a manner, Gill couldn't quite fathom, the creature reeked of evil.

All of this was circumspect. If and until he saw the creature again, he needed to carry on with his life. Resorting to base instincts as he walked onto the dig site, he found himself alert to danger, like a deer sniffing the wind. He was still musing about all of this when his phone rang. It was his boss, Tony Farquharson.

Gill forced himself to sound cheerful. 'Hey, Tony.'

'Gill. I've got Mhairi with me and we're just prepping for the publishers meeting.'

'Yeah, sorry I can't make it. Fiona did her best for us, but she had to head south to her contract in Winchester. So, I'm holding the reins for the last few days up here.'

'That's fine. She did a great job last week.' Tony paused. 'Thing is, Gill. Mhairi's hinting that you might be onto a very significant story but tells me she's been sworn to secrecy.'

'Yeah', said Gill, knowing he should have anticipated this moment. 'We found something strange at the dig on Monday. Something in the Krankie bone pit. The pathologist kicked it up to the boys in blue and they've put a news embargo on it for the moment.'

'Okay', said Tony. 'Can you tell me anything?'

'It's significant', said Gill.

'More significant, or less significant than, say, finding a waterhorse skeleton?'

Gill stroked his chin with his free hand and measured how to respond. 'Potentially more.'

Tony paused. 'And how do you see this progressing?'

'They've done a DNA test that they've just shared with me. The results aren't clear. We'll need to do more work to figure out if we've dug up a freak of nature or, whether, just possibly, it's something very special.'

'Special enough to warrant reworking the upcoming issue?'

'Almost certainly. Or the issue after that, if it takes a while for the news embargo to be lifted.'

'By which time the majors might be on it', said Tony.

'Maybe. But we're the guys on site. We have all the inside data.' Gill paused to consider for a second how this story could play out if indeed, the Jacobite carried alien DNA. 'Tony, the other folk that might try to capitalise on this are the highway agency and their contractors. If this does become a big story, I've no idea who owns the media rights.'

'Leave that with me', said Tony. 'I'll chat to our legal guys. And as the site is close to wrapping up, I might put a call into my golfing buddy and find out what he's heard.'

'Who's that?' Gill heard Mhairi ask.

'The guy who put us onto this dig', Tony replied.

'Issue 29 will definitely need some additional material', said Gill, butting back in. 'At a very minimum, we need to capitalise on the citizen science aspect of our dig. And of course, use the opportunity to do a full historical spread on the battle itself and its back story.'

'If I see Larry twiddling his thumbs, I'll get him to start working on that', he heard Mhairi say.

'Okay', said Tony, wrapping up the call. 'Needless to say, as soon as you can, please fill me in on this enigmatic discovery.'

Towards the end of the afternoon, Gill spotted Lillico emerging from the woods below the dig site. They'd touched base earlier to confirm the dig was now concluded, and the road contractor would be back at work the following Monday.

'You bird watching or something?' Gill called out.

Lillico shook his head. 'Having a last look around. Fiona's team were bothered by someone lurking in the trees.'

'The allegedly naked woodsman?'

'Yeah', said Lillico. 'I spotted him once, though he got away from me.' He shuddered. 'Not a pleasant looking bloke.'

Gill's curiosity kicked in. 'In what way?'

'Tall, rangy looking man.'

'Anything else?'

'Grey skin, the colour of a corpse. Why do you ask?'

Gill grimaced. 'Just sounds weirdly familiar.'

Lillico jerked a thumb over his shoulder. 'The guy in the woods. You've seen him?'

'Not here', said Gill, wishing he could cut the conversation there and walk away. 'I saw something this morning while I was down at Lossuary. Beth was updating me on the *Jacobite Alien.*'

Lillico just stared, waiting for Gill to go on.

'Nah, it was nothing', said Gill. 'Probably just my imagination exploiting my tiredness.'

'Really?' Lillico made a little show of looking around. 'You got anything more urgent to talk about?'

Gill shoved his hands in his pockets and stared at his feet. Then, slowly, he described the creature that had manifested beside him at Lossuary that morning. To his surprise, the Detective Constable kept a straight face.

'What do you think it was?' Lillico asked.

'Honestly, Detective. I'm grasping at straws to explain it.'

'Go on. Try me.'

Gill shrugged. 'If the creature we've boxed up and taken to Falkirk does have an alien origin, maybe it could manifest? I mean, its bones might contain some weird alien tech.'

'Are you seriously considering that as an explanation?'

The suggestion didn't offend Gill. And he knew it wasn't the most outrageous thing he'd ever said. 'It's better than the alternative', was his defensive shrug.

'Which is?'

'That it was supernatural', said Gill before he could stop himself.

Again, to Gill's surprise, Lillico didn't smirk or feign disinterest. Instead, he climbed up the last bit of the bank until the two men stood side by side.

'What?' said Gill. 'Are you going to arrest me for believing in heaven and hell?'

This time, Lillico did smile. 'I just might. Those are unpopular notions in twenty-first century Scotland.'

'The longer I live, the less popular I become. And believe me when I say, I started on a low base.'

'That'll be your ginger hair', said Lillico, dryly.

'Anyway', said Gill, ignoring Lillico's teasing. 'Freaky grey guy wandering in Krankie woodland, and another haunting Lossuary. Quite a coincidence.'

Lillico glanced around. 'I don't believe in coincidence.'

'Me neither', said Gill, noticing a text coming in from Salina. 'Sorry. I'm gonna need to take a call.'

'No problem. Let me know if you figure out our grey phantom.' Lillico offered Gill his outstretched hand. 'It's been good working with you. After today our paths might not cross again.'

Gill reciprocated. 'Take care, Constable.'

As he watched Lillico walk to his car, Gill had a sudden urge to call him back. He couldn't explain it, but he had a sense of unfinished business with this man. But he didn't call as he didn't know what to say. His muddled thoughts were interrupted by his phone ringing. It was Salina.

'Just had five minutes and I'd thought I'd grab you. Did mum like her flowers?'

'Loved them.'

'You found a reliable courier?'

'Delivered them in person. For which I was rewarded with a beautiful meal and an evening playing board games with your sisters.'

'That must have been fun.'

'Basically, I got my ass kicked.'

'Aw, darlin'. They fancy you, that's all.'

'Well, they may not be daredevils like you, but they sure push for victory at all costs.'

Salina laughed. 'Sounds like my girls! How's it going on the dig?'

'Fine', he lied. 'How's life on the ocean floor?'

'We've stepped up the pace of the dives. The skipper is keeping an eye on a deep area of low pressure out in the

Atlantic. If it brews up into a hurricane, we might need to run for cover.'

'Are you in danger?'

'It's not officially a hurricane yet. And its trajectory is east of Florida, so we should be fine. Besides, this is a strong old boat. She can paddle through anything.'

Gill murmured an encouraging platitude that was intended to make him sound reassured.

'What about you? You've been quiet', she continued.

'Ah', he said. 'This dig has turned a bit weird.'

'In what way?'

'We found an unusual skeleton. Hard to describe what it is. And the cops have done a real number on this dig site. We've had a pathologist and other staff here every day.'

'Because of the human bones?'

'Aye. There were concerns for a while the bones were contemporary.'

'Grief. How're you coping?'

Gill battled with his conscience for a few moments while he considered whether he should tell her about his strange experience in the Lossuary bone store. 'It's all a bit unsettling. But today was the last day of the dig so things should calm down now. And it's just been so dreich. Bring me a little sunshine and tell me something about your work.'

He listened for a few minutes as Salina talked happily about some of the wildlife she'd encountered on her dives. 'And there are these dragon fish that would be worthy of your magazine. They're like something out of a sci-fi flick.'

'Ah, but can we tie them to Scotland?'

'No chance. They're just fascinating.' They were interrupted by a timer going off on her phone. 'Right. I need to go shortly. We're back in the water in thirty minutes. Got anything nice planned for the weekend?'

Gill cleared his throat, nervously. 'I might go back to Shawlands and hang out with your beautiful sisters.'

Salina giggled. 'They're gorgeous, aren't they?'

'Too pretty for their own good. Mini-Salinas. Without the battle scars.'

'Just don't let them beat you. Choose something long and tactical, like *Risk,* or *Ticket to Ride.* That's the way to break them down.'

'Ah, the inside track. I'll do that.'

They signed off and Gill tried to take encouragement from how positive she sounded. But now, in addition to diving at unimaginable depths, Salina might have a hurricane barrelling towards her. Gathering his worries into words spoken in his mind, he repurposed them as prayers for her safety.

He was still thinking about her when he arrived in Shawlands the following morning. The whole family was present and a raft of notepads and plans lay spread about the kitchen table.

'I got the information we discussed', said Gill tapping his phone. 'Did you have any luck with the measurements?'

'She made me wear a fat suit', protested Nadia, Salina's next oldest sister.

'I did not', howled Naurah. 'Your sister has muscles on her muscles, so I simply added a little padding.'

'Girls, girls', muttered Waquar, arriving beside them and laying a coffee press on the table. 'We've got two hours before we leave for Fife. And there's so much to do.'

Chapter 29

Early the next morning, Oscar sat in the Aviemore centre car park looking at the mountain and fretted the light covering of snow could force a rethink of today's plans. The engine was still running to fend off the abhorrently cold air. But it was a Sunday, and for October's closing gasps, the conditions weren't too bad. Checking the forecast again, Oscar faced the reality there wouldn't be many more chances like this before winter arrived. Keenly aware of that promise, made so many years ago, this orphan child of the mountain remained determined to fulfil a sacred duty. Because soon this work would be done. The debt finally paid. There were a few final scenes to be worked out in what would be the final act. Meanwhile, today, in the crisp white light of a brand-new morning, Oscar would take a sacrifice to the mountain. And remember.

The trek took five hours. Having done it so many times before, the walk was long but efficient. South through the Lairig Ghru, followed by an angled assent towards Macdui onto the Cairngorm plateau. The flatter ground gave Oscar time to catch a breath before quickening the pace. Before long, a slim patch of water known as Lochan Buidhe was visible on the landscape, so tracking northeast, Oscar strode on alone.

The exact coordinates of this pilgrimage were in the base of a little hollow. Today it was pooled with slushy snow and

Oscar observed again how things had changed in the thirty-three-year duration of this covenant. For the first half of those years, this area had been snow-locked from late October to April or May. Those conditions made this perilous journey even more poignant. But global warming had stretched its cloying breath even here and nowadays, wet boots and prematurely thawing snow cornices presented bigger hazards than lung-crushingly low temperatures. And today, with mapping software, satellite telephone, and location apps, the threat isn't the same. These tools hadn't been available half a century before when the four of them had crouched together. 'Hang on, Oscar', dad had murmured. 'It won't be long now', over and over, and occasionally, mother. 'If you listen carefully, you'll be first to hear the helicopter.'

But hours had passed. And the helicopter hadn't come. And as the heat had ebbed from their bodies, Oscar had fallen into a confused dream that in later years was recognizable as the onset of hypothermia. After their murmuring stopped, a new whisper began. A rasping, hissing, clicking voice demanding someone be accountable for this crisis. That it was somebody else's fault. And all the while urging Oscar to take revenge.

'Join me, Oscar. Together, we'll make them pay. Will you join me? Yes. YES!'

Oscar's next conscious thought had been of strong voices. Male voices. Close. Urgent. Sensing daylight through eyelids frozen closed and arms pinned by mother as she held her child in a final act of eternal love. Crying out, in a voice cold and hoarse as the men outside this macabre cocoon shouted out in excitement. Finally, on the cusp of rescue, Oscar's eyes wrenched open to see mother's gaping mouth; lips dark blue against pale blue skin. Horrific and yet intimate. Oscar's last thought before consciousness ebbed away was that mother had perfect teeth.

Was it a silly thing, Oscar wondered?

To bring this offering, year after year?

To redeem mother's teeth by bringing the teeth of strangers?

It wasn't just teeth Oscar had promised these long-dead kin; it was revenge. After a gap of many years, Oscar had returned as an adult to the mountains, lingering for days in the face of hunger and difficult weather. For a time, death had seemed like an option, but the hissing voice returned from time to time whenever Oscar felt weak. Payback! Revenge! Speaking of killings and curses! And so, over time, it became Oscar's life's purpose to spread pain around the families responsible for this havoc. The teeth? They were just garnish.

The voice. The hissing voice. Oscar considered it and shuddered. Even though it brought strength, there was one certain thing. When this quest was over, Oscar hoped never to hear that voice again.

Oscar sat in the hollow and pulled out the last photo of them all together. These days a weakened memory needed this old image to accurately recall their faces. Studying the photo, expressing devotion by the shedding of tears, Oscar's ritual climaxed as it always did with a curse, uttered against the roll call of the guilty. And on their children until the thousandth generation. The sons and daughters of the people who murdered Oscar's family. It had been a long list all those years ago and now only one household remained unscarred. And by this time next week, as recompense for what they did, they too would meet the punishment they deserved.

Oscar opened the tin recovered from the office filing cabinet and gathered the first handful.

Aiming for Macdui's peak.

Scattering an offering of enamel with each slow stride.

Chapter 30

Monday morning came, and the *Special Investigations* team were still trying to see a pattern amongst the name *Toothfairy* victims. Through a mixture of Wiley's short working hours and the sheer complexity of tracking down relatives of the victims, they had decided to go their separate ways on the previous Thursday and Friday. Working alone was completely against protocol, of course, and was further "proof", Wiley believed, that the senior ranks should bulk out their humble unit. And being honest with himself, Lillico suspected his boss would take the opportunity on Friday to knock off early. But in the event, Wiley reported back on a total of eleven interviews he claimed to have done in person over two days. Alongside his obligation to make a final appearance at Krankie, Lillico had managed just nine. Now they were into a new week and Wiley was impatient for progress.

'What have we got?' barked Wiley as Lillico prepared to walk him through several charts he'd created off the back of their interviews.

'I ran the data through a statistical package this morning. And we're still seeing a random sample across the entire Scottish population', said Lillico. 'I see no discernible pattern by age, gender, social class or occupation. They watched different media, borrowed cash from regular sources, and any financial investments they had when they died were quite pedestrian. Several have had minor brushes with the law which is what put them on the DNA register. But the only thing they all have in common is that none of them are minors.'

'Okay', said Wiley. 'What does that tell us?'

'The absence of a pattern suggests they're not the victims of a serial killer. Unless it's some psychotic individual, killing at random.'

'Those guys tend to get caught. They're too driven and prone to leave a trail of clues, whereas our killer has been operating undetected for at least thirty years.' Wiley tapped the board with the faces of the nine known *Toothfairy* victims. 'These victims are unconnected because the people who wanted them dead are independent of each other. The reason we're not seeing a motive is because no two motives are the same.'

'You're starting to think they were contract kills?' said Lillico.

'That's where I'm leaning.'

'What about the Drumchapel crew? If they're involved this could give us our first solid lead.'

'Admire your enthusiasm, Alec, but the time frame doesn't fit', said Wiley. 'Not unless The Galloway brothers have been killers since kindergarten.'

Lillico tucked his hands into his armpits. He should have spotted that himself.

'Let's run through the logic one more time', said Wiley, waving a fat hand at the faces on the board. 'If our vics were high profile criminals, or personalities, or whatever; their disappearance would have caused a stir. Someone would have detected a connection and started to build a case for us. However, our vics are so unremarkable, no one notices they're missing, apart from their immediate family. Because their disappearances follow no pattern, they all end up in different case files. They go on the Missing Persons register and no one ever connects the dots until finally, their teeth end up together, scattered on a mountaintop.' He tapped the board. 'And it's this randomness that makes me think they must all be assassinations.'

Lillico nodded his assent.

Wiley pointed at Lillico's laptop. 'I want you to use our nine *Toothfairy* victims to create a profile of other potential victims. You know what I'm saying. Mr & Mrs Joe Ordinary. No young people. No wealthy folk. Then I want you to trawl the Missing Person files and create a list of people matching that profile.'

'Sir, the parameters are so broad, there will be hundreds of …'

'Let me finish, Alec. A proportion of your profiles will have DNA records attached that weren't on the National Database due to privacy requests. Let's lift all of those.'

'But if those records are private …'

'Effectively, we're reopening those cases. Phone the relatives and get permission if you have to. If there's no DNA on record, then beg a hairbrush or toothbrush; anything we can lift a sample from. Anything we can do to widen the list of identified victims. Enough names to find some logic in all this mess.'

Lillico blew out his cheeks. 'It'll take me a couple of days, but I'll get right on it.'

He got up to return to his desk, but Wiley lifted a hand. 'My least favourite pathologist has been spamming me about getting a press release out on the *Jacobite Alien*.'

Lillico paused, caught off guard by being asked for his opinion. 'Are you going to let her?'

As Wiley looked at Lillico, the constable saw Wiley's head give a barely perceptible shake. 'Not yet. If the suits upstairs make us face the media, it'll be a distraction. Let's park that for McArdle to handle somewhere down the road.'

Lillico nodded. No doubt there'd be a university somewhere that could explain the Jacobite's distorted physique. 'At least we can be confident there's no link between the battlefield bones and the *Toothfairy* victims.'

'No. But there might be a link between the *Toothfairy* victims and Lossuary.'

Lillico thought about this. 'How, sir?'

'Think about it, Alec. We've a significant number of victims, disappearing without a trace, over decades, leaving just a few teeth scattered on a hillside.' Wiley paused to make sure Lillico was keeping up. 'Where else would be better to dispose of bodies than a bone store?'

Lillico chewed on this unpleasant proposal. 'They could dispose of fleshy parts using their cleaning mechanism. Gradually incinerate the bones.'

'Now you're getting it.'

'How are you planning to investigate that angle, sir? Lossuary isn't the only mortuary we use. And after all their help at Krankie, are we going to haul old Pete Gibson in to accuse him of being a mass murderer?'

'Actually, Alec, I'm already working on all of that.'

'How, sir?'

Wiley puffed out his chest. 'I've had Lossuary on my list since I started this case but wasn't sure how I'd get to investigate them without showing my hand. So, it was a bit of quick thinking on my part when we brought McArdle in on the *Toothfairy* case. When he mentioned his new battlefield dig site, I realised there would be a high probability it would uncover human remains. You following me so far?'

'Yes.'

'And that's why, when *Mysterious Scotland's* call came in, I'd already decided we would help them. In response to McArdle's anticipated request, I'd already selected Lossuary as the logistical base to manage the bones. All that was left to do was to put a person inside Lossuary to do … a little digging around.'

'You have someone on the inside?'

'Yes.'

'Who, sir?'

'Beth.'

'Beth is an undercover police officer?'

'No, Alec. She's a civilian contractor. And for the record, she doesn't know she's helping us.'

'Forgive me, sir, but I'm surprised you'd rely on Beth. The two of you are barely civil to each other.'

Wiley pulled a smug smile. 'She pushes her luck. The fact she doesn't know she's doing me a favour makes her tolerable. Do you think I'd let her speak to me like that if she wasn't useful?'

Lillico wasn't sure what to say, so he said nothing.

'I've instructed her to take DNA samples from throughout the Lossuary bone store. And those are being cross-referenced against the *Toothfairy* results.'

Lillico recoiled. 'Why would she be willing to do that?'

'I've sold it to her as a routine audit.' He pulled an ugly smile. 'She's got virtually free rein of the place this week. Though I've asked her to be discreet about it.'

Lillico could see so many procedural issues with this cross-contamination of cases, he didn't know where to start. And if Chief Super Macfarlane found out, it would be the end for Wiley. So, he had to work to force a measure of calm into his voice. 'Sir. If Lossuary are processing *Toothfairy* vics, then they've been doing it for a long time. I doubt they'll be careless if they have a police pathologist camped in their kitchen. Civilian or not.'

Wiley's shoulders dipped up and down. 'The *Toothfairy* has been active for decades. Maybe they've got sloppy?'

Lillico reacted sharply. 'Sir, that's evidence gathered without a warrant. It would never be admissible.'

For a second, Wiley looked chastened. 'If she finds anything useful, we'll find a reason for a warrant, then sweep in and legitimize it. So far, unfortunately, there isn't a single DNA match between the Cairngorm teeth and any of the bones from my off-the-books audit in Falkirk.'

Lillico relaxed a little. He was sorry to hear Beth's report. There was a dreadful logic to Wiley's hypothesis. The Falkirk location, sitting right at the centre of Scotland's transport network, was a place where no one blinked twice at the sight of a dead body. And maybe the rationale was still sound. If it wasn't Lossuary, then it could be a similar lab. He cleared his throat. 'I still wish we'd discussed this, sir. I would have strongly objected.'

Wiley sniffed. 'Because you stick too close to the rules, Alec. Meanwhile, back in the real world, I have a case to solve.'

Lillico opened his mouth to object, but Wiley spoke over him.

'Let's consider relocating the *Jacobite Alien* to another lab. We'll pretend it's just been discovered and then I'll instruct Beth to run the same covert DNA sweep she did at Falkirk. Or maybe I won't', said Wiley with a sneer. 'For the sake of your conscience, Lillico, I'm giving you grounds for plausible deniability.'

'Honestly, sir. Just because I can feign ignorance of this doesn't set my mind at ease.'

Wiley shrugged - as if he cared. 'And that's another reason we're not going public with all McArdle's chatter about aliens. I might need to haul the *Jacobite's* big ugly carcase around a few other suspect labs until we get a lucky break.'

'For the record, sir. Unscrupulous and illegal.'

'Ah, get over yourself, Lillico. It hurts no one and it might just well give closure to a lot of grieving families. And now it's my turn to be honest. I'm bothered that you would put your own squeaky-clean reputation above the grief of dozens of families …' He stopped to glower at Lillico. 'Actually? I'm bloody disappointed in you, son.'

Lillico stared at Wiley but said nothing. His boss had plunged to new depths. It looked like Chief Superintendent Macfarlane was right about Wiley after all.

'Go do some work, Alec. Shuffle numbers around in spreadsheets, or whatever the hell it is you do. This grownup needs to get some work done.'

Lillico stormed out of Wiley's office and immediately picked up his phone to call Macfarlane. But he knew he wasn't in the right frame of mind to make the call, so he forced himself to work on another task for a few minutes before circling back to consider the issue again. There was a level at which he could agree with his boss, but the flagrant disregard for evidence rules risked the success of the whole case. Using Wiley's methods, they might find the killer, only to watch a decent lawyer cut the evidence to ribbons and allow the guilty to walk free. Quite simply, there had to be a better way.

His mobile buzzed in his hand, and he looked down to see an incoming call from Beth. He accepted the connection and spoke. 'I was about to give you a call. DCI Wiley just filled me in on your freelance work.'

The delay in Beth's response was barely a breath. 'Oh, has he now?'

'And it appears Lossuary is in the clear. Wiley is getting ready to move the *Jacobite Alien* to another site.'

'Ah! There might be a problem with that.'

'What?' said Lillico, wary about being sucked into Wiley's deceptions.

Beth cleared her throat. 'I'm phoning to report a theft.'

Chapter 31

They arrived at Lossuary within the hour. Fifteen minutes later, Wiley was striding around the stainless-steel units, pausing only to toe-kick one door that was lying ajar. Glaring at Beth, he said. 'Let me check if I have this straight. The *Jacobite Alien's* bones. Every photo and every piece of analysis you've done on him is gone?'

She nodded. 'I've no idea how that happened.'

'CCTV?' Wiley barked at Lillico.

'Working on it, sir. It's motion-activated and I'm running through the last twenty-four hours at high speed. Based on the first pass, no one comes or goes.'

'And the photos taken by the McArdle's team. They're all gone too?'

Beth rolled her eyes. 'You made him surrender them all to me! His crew was left without records.'

Wiley leaned in close to Beth, so Lillico could barely hear. 'You're meant to be the eyes and ears of Police Scotland, inside Lossuary. How do you explain this?'

Beth's face flushed with embarrassment. 'I'll need to sweep my PC for viruses.'

'There must be some evidence somewhere?'

Beth shook her head.

'What about the Lossuary crew?'

Lillico stepped forward. 'Uniform are gathering them up. Pete's in the canteen and the others are on their way.'

Wiley nodded, then removed Lillico beyond Beth's hearing. 'What do you make of this?'

Lillico drew his hands up to the waistband of his trousers. 'On one hand, sir, it's a massive distraction. The *Jacobite Alien* is an archaeological discovery and is unlikely to have any connection to the *Toothfairy* case.'

'Agreed. Anything else?'

'Just that, if someone realised you were using the *Jacobite Alien* to do clandestine sweeps of pathology labs, then they might have removed it to frustrate your plans.'

'I am wondering that myself. But why steal it from here? As far as I'm concerned, Lossuary were already in the clear.'

Lillico released a pent-up breath. 'I really don't know, sir.'

'What about Beth? Was I wrong to trust her?' whispered Wiley.

'It's possible she's deflecting you from Lossuary by fabricating the DNA samples. Might be worth getting those double-checked.'

'Beth took the samples. I had the tests done elsewhere. But you're making a fair point. If Lossuary was processing *Toothfairy* victims, Beth could be protecting it.'

'Or, she might be protecting another lab by keeping us tied up here.'

'Maybe', said Wiley. 'But what would be her motivation? By preventing us from scrutinising these labs she'd essentially be protecting the *Toothfairy*.'

Lillico shrugged. 'You've already demonstrated she's amendable to a little extra cash. But the thing is, sir. She told me about the *Jacobite* theft two seconds after I told her we might be moving the bones. For your logic to work, she'd needed to have anticipated our next move, and I don't think that's plausible.'

Wiley stole a glance back at Beth, who was yawning and checking her watch. 'Fine. Let's keep an eye on her,'

'Do you want to interview her under caution?'

'No, because then she'll stop collaborating with us. Let's try and find the bones. I want to have the option of placing Beth in other labs. That way, I can keep tabs on her. If she's working against us, she'll slip up eventually.'

'And she might be entirely innocent', added Lillico. Of assisting the *Toothfairy*. And in the theft of the *Jacobite Alien*.'

'Which means it was someone else in this godforsaken shed', growled Wiley. 'Let's put the lot of them under caution and take them to the nearest station. We'll talk to Pete first.'

In the bowels of Falkirk station, Pete sat in the custody suite with his hands clasped and his usual merry expression dimmed only so far as his face rested in a state of happy bafflement. Wiley and Lillico watched him on camera for a few minutes before commencing the interview.

'He must have been onto Beth', said Wiley. 'Maybe he noticed her taking DNA samples from around the bone store?'

Lillico wiped the side of his face with his left hand. 'Sir, let's not divulge you had a civilian breaking evidence rules. And remember it was you betraying his professional hospitality.'

Wiley waved a hand dismissively. 'I'm going to muddy the waters a little. I'll not mention the *Toothfairy* murders but let's see if we can rattle him a bit.'

Lillico looked at Pete, who was now slumped back in his chair whistling, and using the table as a keyboard while he tapped out the notes of an unknown tune. 'Best of luck, sir.'

Wiley bustled in ahead of Lillico and stretched out a hand to Pete, giving him a vigorous handshake before taking a seat opposite him. Lillico kept his hands to himself and stuck to the rules.

'Pete', began Wiley. 'Thanks for your cooperation. You'll have heard that we've misplaced a few bits and pieces?'

'Of course. Beth came to me first. I can't tell you how upset I am that something like this should happen in our facility', said Pete, beaming.

'And you're aware it looks like theft? The bones are gone, and all our data related to the *Jacobite Alien* has been erased.'

'You're certain it wasn't incinerated?'

'How do you mean?'

'We have a small crematorium. Nothing fancy. Just for disposing of industrial waste relating to our work. If someone used it to burn the alien bones, the oven should still be warm.'

Wiley glanced at Lillico who shrugged, then pulled out his phone to text Beth.

'Thanks, Pete. We're checking that. I have to say, the bones might be valuable, because of their unusual appearance. That's why we're working on the basis they were stolen.'

'I'm very, very sorry to hear that', said Pete as his smile diminished far enough to indicate he was, actually, a little bit sorry. 'And I appreciate it throws the shadow of suspicion over myself and my entire team.'

Wiley gave Pete an encouraging nod. 'Where were you last night?'

'At home with Mrs Gibson. We watched TV until almost 11 pm, then we went to bed.'

'And you didn't get up at all?'

'No.'

'Can you prove that?'

'My house has the same motion detector security kit we use at Lossuary. It's quite affordable and offers us peace of mind.'

'Fine. My DC will need to see the images from last night.'

Pete nodded to affirm his consent.

'What about Hamish and Gary. Can they access your business premises without you being present?'

'They have all the codes and keys. Both have worked for me for a long time. I'd trust them with my life.'

'Good, good', said Wiley. Casting a sideways glance at Lillico. 'Nice to work with people you can trust.' He nodded again, then asked, 'Are you a hillwalker, Pete?'

Pete slapped his hands on his legs like he'd been accused of nude jaywalking. 'What, munros and the like? Ice and midges?'

'High peaks and glens. Cairngorms for example.'

Pete laughed. 'Never. Not my scene. And really? Too old.'

'You're sure? Never climbed Macdui, by any chance?'

Pete blinked but said nothing.

'Have you ever been approached by people associated with organised crime?' asked Wiley.

Pete flinched, then shook his head.

'I mean, you handle dead bodies for a living. You have the resources to store them, and it appears, to destroy them. Maybe you have some unsavoury characters asking you to do them a favour?'

Pete shook his head again.

'Perhaps they offered you money. Maybe even threatened you?'

'Mr Wiley. I work hard for an honest living. Over the years I've had some dubious people come knocking at my door. But I don't ask to know their business and I've always declined their work. And these days, most of my contracts come from the good people of Police Scotland.' Pete stopped to deliberately shake his head. 'I suspect the people you're referring to know that. So no, I don't work for those kinds of customers.'

'And Hamish and Gary?'

'They both know I'd fire them on the spot. But ask them yourselves.'

'Did you keep any photographic record of the *Jacobite Alien*?' said Wiley, switching tack.

Pete glanced down at the table. 'Normally we'd take a digital image of every box before it goes into the bone store. But Beth said you'd given instructions to the contrary.'

'That's correct', said Wiley. 'We needed confidentiality.'

'Which I support and endorse.'

Wiley allowed his hands to fall on the table, palms up. 'How could this happen, Pete? Your business was trusted because it's normally discrete and secure. How do you explain it?'

For the first time in his experience, Lillico watched the smile vanish from Pete's face. 'Gentlemen. I can't. I don't know how this happened.'

Twenty minutes later, Wiley shuffled off for a fag break, giving Lillico the opportunity to touch base with Gill McArdle. 'Did you retain any images of the *Jacobite Alien*?' he asked as soon as Gill picked up.

Gill was silent at the other end of the phone.

'Gill. Did you, or didn't you?'

'I have three shots of the bones before they were recovered.'

'Even though Wiley asked you not to?'

'I snapped them before Wiley implemented his news embargo. Honestly, I didn't think to go back to delete them. I can do that right now if you want?'

'No. Wait.' Lillico paused. 'Gill, the *Jacobite Alien* has been stolen.'

'What?'

'From right under the noses of Beth and the Lossuary team.'

'But that's …'

Lillico spoke over him. 'And the thief managed to delete Beth's digital record. Lossuary doesn't have images, because unlike you, they stuck to the rules.'

'Alex, those bones … if there's even a chance they're some form of human hybrid, they're absolutely priceless.'

'Well, for now, they're missing.'

'And you want my images?'

'Yes.'

'Okay. Give me a second.'

Lillico waited while Gill fiddled with his phone. In the distance, he could hear an eruption of shouting. 'What's going on, Gill?'

'I dunno. Some fracas kicking off over at the cat mag. The editor is tearing a strip off the layout artist, poor kid.'

'Right. Sorry to hear that. And the photos?'

'Weird', said Gill. 'Let me try my laptop. Maybe they've backed up there.'

Lillico fought the desire to multitask while McArdle did whatever it was he was doing.

'Look, Alex. I can't explain this, but I don't have the photos either.'

'How could that be?'

'I … I've no idea', said Gill.

'What about Fiona? She's down south, right? She might have some.'

'No, I watched Fiona delete everything off her camera. She was happier without them, to be honest. And Emma didn't take any. She was the only volunteer to see the remains.'

The call went silent for several long seconds. 'Gill?' said Lillico.

'Yes.'

'Why aren't you surprised by this?'

Gill exhaled deeply into his phone. 'I suspect there'll be a rational explanation. But I dig up unicorn bones for a living, Alex. Nothing surprises me anymore.'

'I guess.'

'I take it there's no obvious smoking gun amongst the Lossuary staff?'

'None.'

Again, Gill fell silent, so Lillico pressed him. 'You got any theories how all our physical evidence and digital images across three separate devices could disappear?'

Gill sighed. 'Sorry. None. But I'll tell you this for nothing – we need those bones.'

The afternoon's interviews wore on into the early evening. Wiley and Lillico interviewed Hamish and Gary, plus three drivers who worked part-time for the company. Finally, they saw a cleaner and a bookkeeper. Lillico was cross-referencing Mhairi's list of Cairngorm casualties when he spotted something worth pursuing.

'Let's wrap the up', groaned Wiley. 'We're getting nowhere.'

'Can we have one more crack at Pete? There's something I want to press him on.'

Wiley stretched and grimaced. 'Five more minutes. That's all.'

'Do you want to know what I have?'

'Just get him in here. If I find you're laying a tasty trail of nuts, I'll play along.'

It took a few minutes to retrieve Pete from the custody suite and pull him back in for questioning.

'Last couple of details', said Wiley. 'Then we'll get you dropped home.'

Pete smiled happily and clasped his hands.

'You said you've never been a hillwalker', said Lillico. 'Did you want to reconsider your answer?'

A glimmer of surprise passed across Pete's face before he shook his head.

'I'm puzzled them.' Lillico stared at his phone screen. 'Because I have a record extracted from *The Cairngorm Society's* Annual Review, recording an accident that took place in 1991.' He slid the phone across to Pete. 'This is your parent's home address, and the deceased was your father, was he not?'

Pete steadied his glasses on his face and studied the entry. 'Yes. And yes.'

'And the entry mentions your father was walking with his son when he died.'

'That was my brother.'

'But the image is of you, beside a loch. With your father I presume?'

Pete shrugged. 'I've never seen this. Someone in the family must have supplied the photo.'

Lillico nodded. 'Quite possibly. I should add, that I'm sorry for your loss. Can I ask how your father died?'

'He developed heart problems during their descent from Ben Macdui.'

'Did he die on the hillside?'

Pete shook his head. 'We'd no mobiles back then. My brother ran for help. To the ski centre at the north end. Took him three hours at a fast jog. He raised the alarm there.'

'And how soon did help arrive with your father?'

'Another four hours.'

Wiley gave a low whistle. 'He was alone for seven hours?'

Pete shrugged. 'It was a Saturday night in early May. It took a few hours for mountain rescue to raise a crew.'

'What happened next?'

'The rescuers were airlifted to the mountain and my brother led them back to Dad. It took a while. His navigation skills weren't great. Once they found him, they applied first-aid before airlifting him to hospital. Unfortunately, he died during the flight.'

'Again, I'm sorry. Are you and your brother close?' asked Lillico.

Pete slowly shook his head.

'Why not?'

The permanent smile finally melted from Pete's face. 'When our father passed suddenly, my brother and I had a difference of opinion.'

'And that was?'

'He wanted to sell Lossuary. I wanted to keep it in the family. I had to buy him out, and he made me pay top dollar.'

'I see. Could you give us his current address?'

'I can't.'

'Why not, Pete? He's your brother.'

'Because we haven't spoken in a long time. Look, what's all this got to do with our bone theft?'

Wiley turned to stare at Lillico. They could both see that for the first time, Pete Gibson looked flustered. 'Could your brother still have keys for Lossuary?'

Pete glanced up and right. 'I can't answer that question with any certainty.'

Wiley pushed his chair back noisily. 'Thanks, Pete. We'll drop you home now. DC Lillico will give you a shout if there's anything else.'

As Pete stretched and slowly left his seat, Wiley whispered to Lillico's ear. 'Let's track down this brother.'

Chapter 32

When Gill arrived at Falkirk that evening, he found two squad cars sitting outside Lossuary. He parked up and approached one of the uniforms. 'Any chance of a word with DCI Wiley?'

'Sorry, sir. He's down at the local station.'

Gill nodded his understanding then walked a few steps away from them to phone Wiley. 'Chief Inspector. Glad I caught you. I was hoping to access Lossuary to see if I can work out what happened to the *Jacobite Alien*. Obviously, I won't get inside without your permission.'

'I'm done for the day, McArdle. I'm away home to get a bite and have a think about the case.'

'What about DC Lillico?'

'Hold on a second.' The phone call became muffled, and Gill got the impression Wiley was walking.

'Alec's here too. He says he'd be delighted to give you a hand.'

'Really? Okay, good.'

'We're local. He'll be with you in five minutes.'

Wiley rang off and Gill waited. When Lillico did show up, he didn't look at all delighted.

'Looking for anything special?' he said, blocking Gill at the front entrance to Lossuary.

'Inspiration', said Gill.

'That's hardly grounds to let you go rummaging through a crime scene.'

'Granted, but assuming Beth and the whole Lossuary crew are at least under suspicion, then I'm your best chance at finding the *Jacobite's* bones.'

'I told you; he's gone.'

'Is he gone, Constable? Or is he hiding in plain sight?'

Lillico stopped and drew his hands wearily to his hips. 'This is an active investigation. If we do go in there and you see something significant, you'll have to tell me. Okay?'

'Agreed. And you're not the only one pissed off by this. I've lost the physical evidence for the most significant story we've had drop into our laps in the last year. And unfortunately, it disappeared on your watch.'

'Leaving you with an absence of proof', murmured Lillico. 'You'll hardly let that stand in the way of a good story.'

Gill rocked back from Lillico a few inches. 'What's your point, Constable?'

'You don't think I haven't read your file? One case of fictitious evidence construction, proven by your old university and more recently, quite fantastic claims about time travel. All I'm saying is, you seem to have a flexible relationship with the truth.'

Gill refused to be baited. 'The university thing is true. I made a bad decision. I fessed up to that years ago. And as for *Mysterious Scotland*? I stand by every word I've ever printed.'

Lillico pulled the door open. 'Go do your thing, Gill. But remember, this place is full of CCTV, so someone will always be watching.'

Gill nodded and stepped across the threshold; disheartened that his one big mistake still haunted him after all these years.

'And Gill. Please can we make this quick?'

Gill walked the rooms and corridors of Lossuary as if it were a dig site. He was looking for clues; for any sense of something being out of place. Most of all, he listened to his instinct. What had happened here? Were the remains of the *Jacobite Alien* still hidden in the building? If they weren't, could he find a hint where they might have been taken? But his inner voice wasn't speaking to him. It was as if the presence of all these bones created such a pervasive sense of death that even the light felt black. There was nothing here that spoke of life. Even in the company canteen, the fridge stank of spoilt milk, and a dying pot plant scraped at the single dirty window in a last attempt to escape.

'Seen anything?' Lillico asked after half an hour.

Gill shook his head. 'I assume the computers have all been collected for analysis?'

'Yes', Lillico replied.

'And your guys will do a thorough sweep for viruses or spyware?'

'Y-u-p', said Lillico, slowly.

Gill took a deep breath and walked through to the bone store with its shelves upon shelves of human remains; neatly numbered and in their place.

'Has anyone checked these boxes for signs of the *Jacobite Alien*?'

'Why would they?'

'The digital records could have been destroyed with some kind of hack. However, the bones themselves might still be here, scattered across these boxes.'

Lillico rubbed his face and slumped against the doorpost. 'That's a valid point.'

'Shall we crack on?'

'Don't you have a family to go back to?'

Gill looked up. 'My fiancée is working overseas. She's not back for another fortnight. The magazine is my only baby, and she never sleeps.'

'Grief, Gill. This could take hours.'

Gill had forgiven Lillico for his verbal barbs and now he felt sorry for the weary-looking officer. 'Alex, just go. Let the uniforms know I'm doing a record check and they should lock up after I'm finished.'

'Not strictly procedure.'

'You and DCI Wiley came to me. You guys asked for my help. And here I am. Helping.'

'Okay then.' Lillico pushed back away from the door. 'I'll need an update from you, first thing in the morning. Okay?'

Gill flexed his fingers. 'Looking at the size of this place, I might still be here.'

Gill's plan had been to look for any of the most distinctive alien bones. The elongated humerus, tibia and femur were potential candidates. If he found the skull or the dramatically extended coccyx, then he'd really be flying. But, two hours into the project, he was flagging rather than soaring. Before now, he'd only had fleeting visits to this room and hadn't lingered long enough for the concentrated smell of death and dust to seep into his lungs. Coughing occasionally, he gradually realised the Lossuary bone store was a very different experience than chancing upon human remains in a field dig. Every box in this place carried a higher emotional price tag. The bones of a young woman dating from the 1970s – case unsolved. Those of a child found in a sunken car at the bottom of a loch in 2001 – case unsolved. Gradually, he trained himself to only glance at the box labels as he tried to deflect the fact that each one represented the end of a human life, by foul means or natural causes. Added to that was the sheer physicality of moving the boxes. Lifting them onto a trolley, and then examining their contents was wearisome. Closing the lids and replacing the crates on shelves that were often higher than his head left his arms aching. Soon, he was sweating and tired.

An hour later, another uniform came in to see him. They'd just completed a shift change and would be watching from their car. Gill nodded his understanding and carried on with his work.

By 2 am, Gill was doubting the validity of this line of enquiry. He was halfway through the boxes and had seen nothing out of the ordinary, so he decided to call a halt. He'd leave a message with the uniforms for Lillico, then go home and sleep until lunchtime.

He was heaving the final box of the night onto its shelf when he heard a sound. The same guttural, throaty, clicking voice he'd heard when he'd been working alongside Beth. Gill suddenly felt the weight of Raphael's sword, lying in its scabbard and pulled snuggly against his back. He was increasingly aware of it these days, even if few people could actually see it.

'Hello?' Gill called into the shaded room.

The clicking, hissing voice came again, originating from along one of the rows. Gill walked quietly to the end of his current row and peered down the next. And saw ... nobody. The voice again. From further on. Until three rows down. And then he saw it.

The *Jacobite Alien* stood higher than the highest shelf, growling to himself as he delved through a box of bones. At least, Gill assumed this reanimated creature was the *Alien*. He was the right shape; his tall body hunched, and his weight offset by a two-metre long tail. His bones were covered in flesh; his naked grey skin reflected some of the fluorescent light above his head. Its dark eyes flashed towards Gill before its attention diverted back to the box.

'I can't find it', the creature hissed.

Gill swallowed. 'Find what?'

It threw Gill an irritated glance then held up its left hand. 'I'm missing a damn thumb.'

Gill took an involuntary step backwards.

'Ah! There it is!' said the creature, snatching something from a box and fastening it to his hand. It stood back, flexing its fingers and admiring its work.

'Anyway, McArdle', said the creature in a more considered, rumbling voice. 'I have been waiting for you. Waiting a long, long time.'

'Who are you?' said Gill, impressed by how level his own voice sounded.

The creature gave the slightest of bows. 'My name is, Sariel.'

'What are you?'

The creature waved its newly completed claw-like hand in the air. 'I could explain but you wouldn't understand. I suppose I'm not dissimilar to your motorbike-riding friend. Though I won't lower myself to such antiquated means of transportation.'

'How are you here? I mean, we had your bones …'

'Not my bones', said Sariel, flicking his left claw at Gill. 'My offspring. I don't remember his name. He was simply the fruit of my loins. And the reason for his brief existence was to facilitate this conversation we're having now.'

'You created him, just so he could die on a battlefield?'

'He was a big lumbering oaf. Ugly too – none of his father's good looks. But terrifying. He was all the government troops could think about in the opening minutes of the battle. He died gloriously in a hail of bullets.'

'His bones are missing. Are you wearing his body?'

'That frail old thing?' Sariel flexed the fingers in his now-restored left hand. 'Well, I suppose it's a cloak of sorts. Though I've made some … improvements.'

'What are you doing here?'

'I wanted to meet you in person, Gill McArdle. I hope you feel honoured.'

'How do you know me?'

Sariel dropped the bones he'd been sorting back in their box and turned to face Gill. Stepping towards him, and seeing Gill back away, the creature sank to its haunches so that its oily black eyes were level with Gill's. 'There. That's better. We can talk man to man. And yes, I've looked forward to meeting you.'

Gill felt his Adam's apple bob in his throat. 'Why?'

'Because you have so much potential, Mr McArdle. A real fire-starter. We saw your potential future in a time long ago. And now we'd like to help you fulfil your destiny.'

Gill started to edge backwards, barely containing his urge to flee from this thing. 'My destiny?'

'Why, yes! You must realise that a man like you is fated for far greater things than this?' The creature gesticulated at the boxes of bones, wiggling his long fingers in distaste.

Gill's response erupted as a shout. 'Raphael said much the same thing. Seems like a coincidence.'

'No such thing', said Sariel, rubbing his chin. 'And what did he offer you? Riches? Power? Sex with the most beautiful girls in Scotland?'

'No. And that's not what I want.'

Sariel laughed a husky, clicking laugh, before attempting a clumsy wink. 'McArdle! Isn't that what every man wants?'

'You still haven't told me what you want', said Gill.

Sariel unfolded a long bony finger towards him. 'I want us to be partners.'

'You what?'

'Yes. Absolutely! We could join forces. There are so many things we could achieve together. You could be the public face of our new enterprise. And as a token of my appreciation, I might even give you back my offspring's bones so you can admire them in your magazine.'

Gill swallowed. 'That sounds very benevolent.'

'Ah, though, it's not without cost.'

'What a surprise.'

'We should exchange gifts.' Sariel twirled his right hand in the air as if trying to grasp a thought. 'I could, for example, give you Scotland.'

'Scotland?' said Gill.

'And as a seal on our new friendship, you could give me your sword.'

Gill flexed his shoulders, comforting himself with the weight of the scabbard. 'My service and my sword? I don't think so.'

'Or if you prefer, I'll buy them', said Sariel. 'Pay a mighty price too.'

Gill's head swam with uncertainty. Was this creature real? Or was this moment a bad dream? Was his mind really capable of dreaming up something so awful?

'I'm waiting', said Sariel in a sing-song voice. 'For your answer.'

'Look, buddy', he said. 'Step back from this a moment and see yourself. What are you? A monster? A demon? Probably only the vision of a demon. You walk in here looking like something out of the pit of hell and you expect me to stoop to one knee and swear my allegiance?'

Sariel leapt to his full height and towered over Gill, his claw-like hands poised to tear Gill's flesh from his ribs. 'Why, aren't you impressed with what you see?' he growled.

Gill staggered backwards and tried to convince himself this wasn't happening. He'd read about these creatures and their power. He also believed their influence was limited; governed in some way by laws he didn't yet understand.

'You seem to believe I don't have the power to hurt you', Sariel continued. 'I assure you, I do.'

Gill recoiled as the creature leaned close to his face; smelt its rancid breath in the air. 'Even if you do, I'm not going to work for you.'

'Maybe a little demonstration would help', said Sariel, sitting back again. 'Let's think. If you're feeling so gutsy about yourself, maybe we could talk about one of the people you love? Who do you care about? Craig usually comes to work on his motorbike. It would be unfortunate if this morning he should be involved in a fatal accident. Or Fiona. Did you know she'll be working in the shadow of an ancient bell tower today? Why, a gust of wind could just …' Sariel waved his hand in the air. 'All that rubble just needs is a little nudge. And Salina?' The creature threw its head back and laughed. 'Why right now she's more than a kilometre below water in a DSV that's fifteen years old. Oh! And that storm is now a category two hurricane. It's changed course and is heading for the Gulf of Mexico.' He stopped and laughed aloud. 'What could possibly go wrong?'

'This is between you and me, Sariel. Leave the others out of it.'

'That's better, McArdle. You see? Now we're negotiating. You know what outcome you want, and I know what I want. All that's left is to discuss is the price.'

Gill shook his head. 'You think you hold all the cards? Raphael will come to my side.'

Sariel sent his withering gaze off to the left, and then for several seconds, he looked to the right. 'Point him out to me', he whispered. 'Maybe he's in disguise.'

'You know what I mean.'

'I know you haven't seen Raphael for over a year. And what you can't realise is that Raphael is bound under oath to grant me the power to kill you.'

Gill's anxiety increased as the creature revealed how much it knew about him. 'Raphael serves the Nazarene. And He could command an army and bring it to my side.'

'Oooh! An army?' The creature slid away from him and stood at the junction between four blocks of shelving with his arms outstretched. 'Do you think I'm impressed? Why I could raise an army from these bones.'

Gill spat out an ironic laugh. 'You might be able to make bones disappear; I'm still trying to figure that bit out. But as for transforming them into an army ...'

Sariel uttered a low, rumbling growl in response. Then he lifted his arms higher and started to mumble in a language Gill didn't understand. All around him, the bones in the boxes started to rattle and move. Sariel cackled once, then mumbled louder and Gill saw that the boxes starting to ooze with pink fluid. The lid popped off one and he watched in horror as flesh appeared on one of the bones. Sariel was shouting now, his hands waving in the air. Around Gill, the shelves were collapsing under the additional weight, and he was soon ankle-deep in what looked like the ghastly remains of a mass casualty event. On the cusp of panic, Gill watched, as skin wove across the flesh; the bodies of men, women and children reforming in front of his eyes. He jumped in fright as somewhere in the back of the room, a long shelving unit collapsed, knocking over another beside it. The shelves nearest Gill started to bulge with twisted corpses, erupting from the boxes. Arms sprang out towards him, and Gill started to swerve left and right to avoid being touched by Sariel's awful incarnations.

'You see?' shrieked Sariel. 'An army!'

'A dead army', shouted Gill, over the roar of collapsing shelves.

Sariel leaned forward and gesticulated at the corpses. 'Arise!' he bellowed.

At this instruction, Gill's nightmare just got worse. All around him, the corpses struggled to escape their confinement and started to get to their feet. The ones closest to Gill staggered forward, trying to grapple with him. Gill retreated, forced back by the zombie-like figure, seeking refuge in the alcove of a locked door. He was on the cusp of outright panic until he saw into the creature's eyes. And then he realised. 'They're not alive, Sariel.'

'They are alive as they need to be!'

The staggering body of the nearest corpse had reached Gill, its fingers about to grasp Gill's face.

'That's not life! That's a fraud!', Gill shouted, squeezing further backwards until he finally took refuge in a corner of the room. Feeling the weight of his sword over his left shoulder, his anger burned against Sariel for his menaces and this counterfeit life. Bellowing at Sariel, he drew his blade and struck the approaching corpse with a violent blow, causing it to collapse. Another one closed in from Gill's right and he lunged his blade, drawing it upward and witnessing the creature erupt again into a cloud of flying bones. Two more shuffled towards him, crowding the space to swing his weapon, so he grabbed his sword tip and thrust the edge of his blade across the chests of his attackers. As their bodies fell away, Gill found the sword was guiding his arm; expertly directing his strokes as he stepped forward, gaining ground from his assailants. With space opening up all around him he struck and slashed until his face and clothes were smothered in powdered bone. He faced down this phoney army until he faced Sariel, alone. The creature formed an expression, halfway between a grimace and a smile, manifesting his own double-ended spear, poised in a defensive posture.

'You see, McArdle', Sariel hissed. 'An army!'

Gill held Sariel's dark gaze for the briefest moment, and then roaring in defiance, he charged at the creature, lunging with his sword until …

Gill's roar echoed around the empty room.

And suddenly the reanimated corpses were gone.

There was no sign of Sariel.

Gill stood, holding a defensive posture. Until he heard footsteps.

'Are you alright, pal?' One of the uniforms was staring at him. 'I heard shouting.'

Gill wiped his face with his arm and looked about him. Everything in the room appeared in order. Neatly labelled boxes on robust and ordered shelves. He sheathed his sword and looked for any physical evidence of what he'd just endured. 'I … I must have fallen asleep. I was having a nightmare.'

'My wife gets those. Too much red wine at bedtime if you ask me.' The officer glanced around the room. 'Mind you, in twenty years as an officer, I've never been near a place as creepy as this.'

Gill slumped against one of the shelves while he caught his breath. 'On that, we're agreed. What time is it?'

'Just gone 2.30 am.'

'Thanks.'

'Listen. I think it would be best for everybody if you went home, pal. Come back to this in the morning with a fresh head.'

Gill swallowed and glanced around. 'Aye. You're right. I'll grab a few bits and leave you to lock up.'

Embarrassed and more than a little shaken, Gill packed up his stuff. His hands were trembling. The result of physical exertion, combined with the horror of the experience. With one last look behind him, he turned out the lights in the ossuary and walked towards his car. Behind him, the officer he'd spoken to glanced cautiously in Gill's direction while chatting quietly with a colleague, no doubt updating him on Gill's little performance. He sighed. Accumulating the badges of academic eccentricity had always been a risk in his line of work. If he hadn't already lost all his pride, he would have considered changing his name and moving somewhere far away. He pictured how he must have appeared to the arriving officer. Having a "wee turn", in front of a copper was just another passing humiliation.

He dumped his stuff in the back seat of his car and moved around the front. He was about to get in when he noticed a note under the wiper blade. He took it out, noting the Lossuary headed paper, and read. Instantly, his heart sank.

'Sorry our chat was interrupted. So much more to talk about. Meant what I said about Craig, Fiona and Salina. You have six hours, six minutes and six seconds to meet me at the top of Ben Macdui. Or if you prefer, you have eternity to live with the consequences. Speak to no one!'

Instinctively, Gill glanced at his watch to lock in the time. Had he been less traumatised, he'd have smirked at Sariel's thinly veiled reference. But in the face of the continuing threat, it was all he could do to grip the open door of his car to stop himself from doubling over. In his heart of hearts, he knew straight away he shouldn't cave to Sariel's instruction. *The Book* made strong promises about this kind of thing, and given more time, he might have figured this out. But Sariel had put Gill's dearest friends in the firing line and that was a price he wasn't willing to pay while there was something he could physically do about it. In his exhaustion, a gust of wind caught the note and carried it away. Arriving at a dreadful decision, he didn't have time to go hunting for it. Instead, he slammed the door and quickly drove away.

Chapter 33

Lillico pulled up in front of Lossuary around 9 am and pretended to himself he felt refreshed. He'd been unsettled when he arrived home the night before. As an antidote he'd slipped into a streaming series he was now regretting as it had been the early hours when he'd finally fallen asleep.

'What time did he leave?' Lillico asked the officer on duty after discovering that Gill had gone without leaving a message.

'He was away by 3 am. He looked knackered. I found him napping when I did my first circuit.'

'Really?'

'Oh, aye. Caught him in the middle of a nightmare. Lots of shouting. It's what made me come and check on him.'

Lillico nodded, remembering what it felt like to wander around Lossuary in the middle of the night.

'Thanks. Maybe he's having a lie-in. I'll give him 'til midday then give him a call. Any incidents overnight?'

'Quiet as the grave, sir.'

At exactly the same moment as Lillico was starting his day in Falkirk, Gill was leaning into the last few hundred metres of his ascent of Ben Macdui. The A9 had been mercifully quiet through the middle of the night. He'd driven hard. The only time he'd taken his eyes off the road was as he reached Krankie, slowing through the speed restrictions and glancing at the dig site, now smothered in artificial light and earth-moving equipment. The contractors had moved in and were starting to rebuild the embankment. Passing the site, he accelerated again, ignoring the speed cameras and pressing on to arrive at the Aviemore ski centre car park in under two hours. He didn't have much equipment in his car. Walking boots, his second-best rain jacket, a water bottle and two cereal bars. He'd thrown what he had into a rucksack and hit the hill as fast as he dared. Skirting the peak of Cairngorm Mountain, he'd struck across the plateau on the fastest possible route to his destination. Approaching the top, he reached the spot where Craig had been struck by the projectile thrown from above. There was no sign of their attacker from that day, but Gill suspected the culprit would be waiting for him on the rounded peak.

Gill hit the peak of Macdui with eight minutes and fifty-nine seconds to spare. He slumped into a shelter, barely more than a horseshoe of stones, and tried to get his breath back. He hadn't been there for more than a few moments when he sensed a dark presence behind him.

'My friends', said Gill, not looking up. 'Are they okay?'

'So far', hissed Sariel.

'What happens now?'

'We sit awhile. Take in the view.'

Gill said nothing, and in his shaken state, he decided it was better than anything else Sariel might have in mind.

Lillico dialled Gill's number for the third time. On this occasion, when it rang off, he didn't leave a message. It was almost 3 pm and Gill owed him a report on his nocturnal investigations. Needing to track him down some other way, he phoned the office. To his unexpected pleasure, Cassy, the girl with the dirty red mittens, picked up the phone.

'Not seen or heard from him', she said.

'Is that out of character?'

'Not particularly. He can disappear for days on end if he gets his claws into something. He gets this wild look in his eyes and shoots off to hunt down some mystery or other.'

'And was he looking like that last time you saw him?'

'No. He was pretty pissed off about the *Jacobite Alien's* bones going missing. It was gonna be a big story.'

'He didn't turn up for our appointment this morning. Is that the kind of thing he'd forget if he was on a trail?'

'Unlikely. He doesn't normally go off-grid without giving me a heads-up. Do you think we should be concerned for him?'

'I've no special reason for thinking that. But let's agree to keep in touch. First person to see or hear from him contacts the other.'

'Agreed.'

Lillico hung up and went hunting for the officer he'd met first thing that morning. Finding he'd gone off duty, he resorted to the motion-activated CCTV operated by Lossuary and chose the camera covering the bone store. And straight away, there was Gill, the camera firing every few seconds as

Gill reached for a box or lifted a bone to examine it. Lillico accelerated the footage, watching Gill working down row after row of plastic containers. Even at ten times normal speed Lillico soon got bored. Box down, rummage, rummage, then box back up again. Rinse and repeat. Box down, rummage, box back up.

It was all very dull, until the moment when Gill spun away from his workstation and stared at something out of the camera's line of sight. Slowing down the video playback, Lillico saw Gill talking to someone. But without any audio, Lillico couldn't figure out what he was saying. In the poor light and difficult camera angle he doubted a professional lip reader could do much better. Eventually, Gill started to back away from whoever he was speaking to until he was squeezed into a corner. The man's body language was strange, as if the room was full of water and this was the last place Gill could gulp some air. Gill yelled something and then reached behind his shoulder before doing a really strange thing. Clasping his hands together, he began to swing his arms right and left, lunging occasionally and starting to advance back towards the centre of the room. Moments later, the uniformed officer appeared, and Gill reached back over his left shoulder before talking to the new arrival. The officer's body language appeared wary, and Gill's face looked strained.

Lillico called over to a uniformed officer to join him. Then he ran through the video sequence again.

'What do you think is going on here?' asked Lillico.

The officer scratched his head. 'Looks like a fight, except there's nobody else there.'

'What do you think Gill has in his hands?'

The officer peered closely at the screen. 'I don't see anything.'

Lillico stepped forward through a few frames. 'Here. The light catches something in his hands. A weapon I think.'

'Sorry. I'm not seeing it.'

Lillico froze one frame and stroked the screen. 'Right here.'

The officer stopped and put on his hat. 'Your eyesight must be better than mine, Detective.'

Lillico let him get back to his duties. Who was Gill talking to, he wondered? Finding a nervous tremor coming into his body, Lillico took a time stamp from the original camera position and switched to a second one covering the opposite end of the bone store. Slowing the film to a quarter of natural speed, he checked every frame and found ... nothing.

Stepping forward to the minutes when the officer had accompanied Gill out to his car, Lillico switched to the CCTV of the car park. The light was poor here, but he could discern the two men raise hands to each other in farewell, before Gill, stepped around to the driver's side. Then he stopped and reached for a note left on his windscreen. Lillico watched Gill freeze, and when the note flew off in the wind, Gill didn't search for it, instead, he drove off at speed. Certain now that something was wrong, Lillico dashed out to the carpark. It took him twenty minutes to find the note skewered on some shrubbery. It was rain-dampened and smelt of faeces. Donning gloves from his pockets, he smoothed out the note on the bonnet of a squad car. He read the words and wondered what they meant. The only insight he could deduce with any certainty was that Gill had gone to Macdui.

Lillico was worried now. For Gill's physical welfare; for his mental state. And something else. Something about Gill's expression as he swung wildly about the ossuary. The man seemed to perceive he was fighting for his life. Lillico needed to decide if he should follow Gill, and if he did, should he tell his boss and take a backup person? Or should he go alone, making this a solo mission? So many decisions to make and with so little time. He was fretting over this when a text arrived from an unknown number.

'Kelpies. 6 pm', was all it said.

The exact location seemed vague but at least the time was precise. The brushed steel horsehead figures were only a short distance from Lossuary, so when Lillico parked up six minutes later, he still had a short time before the meeting. If that's what this was. A rendezvous with a person or persons unknown would normally require planning and backup, and yet, here he was, doing what Alexander Lillico normally thought impossible; stretching the rules. But he couldn't help feeling this meeting was important. He'd just completed a circuit of the first horsehead when he noticed two figures positioned near the second. One was crouching and staring at the ground – a woman with strange headgear that masked her face. She was in smart business clothes and not someone familiar to him. The second was the tall, muscular figure of an olive-skinned man. Wearing biker leathers, he stood with his arms folded and a concentrated expression on his face. The man was the first to see Lillico and raised his right arm in greeting, his leather jacket parting in the middle to reveal the intricate leather belt. Oh … and the guy still had a sword behind his shoulders. In the circumstances, that didn't seem weird at all.

'The forest below Gill McArdle's dig site', said Lillico, addressing the standing figure. 'We've met before.'

The man nodded curtly. 'And now, without distractions, we find ourselves in the moment I anticipated.'

'Moment for what?' Lillico retorted, determined he wasn't going to be distracted from Gill's peril for too long.

Biker-guy didn't respond. Instead, he looked down at the crouched woman and offered his hand.

Like a petulant child, the woman looked away, then huffed and let the man's powerful arm pull her to her feet.

'This is Adina', said Biker-guy. 'She will explain.'

Lillico turned his gaze to the woman. Her head covering looked like a closely tailored glass helmet, with a V-shape cut for eye slits. She removed it now and tucked it under her right arm.

'McArdle is in trouble', she said at last.

Lillico already knew that, though he wasn't about to tip his hand. 'How do you know?'

'Have you met a lady called Rosemary Solomon?'

Lillico shook his head.

'She's a friend of McArdle's. Lately, of me too. And she's a person with ... remarkable insights.'

When she didn't elaborate, Lillico shrugged. 'Which means what, exactly?'

Adina looked again at Biker-guy and gave him another irritable sigh. 'Raphael, we're wasting time here. As much as I'd love to sit and have a long chat with your policeman friend, it's all going to be meaningless unless he understands the context.'

Raphael smiled. 'Ask him then.'

'Ask him what?'

'Ask him if he understands what's happening here.'

Adina gritted her teeth and appeared ready to walk away. Instead, she threw Lillico an embarrassed frown. 'What would you say …', she began, 'If I told you Rosemary Solomon hears messages from God?'

Lillico smiled back at her, grasping the root of her discomfort. Then he looked down at his toes. 'Yeah, I believe in that.'

Adina's eyebrows shot up. 'You do?'

'Had my struggles with it over the years', said Lillico. 'But on balance …'

'Solomon thinks a demonic force is trying to kill McArdle', Adina said in a hurry. 'But she doesn't know where and she doesn't know when. But she thinks it's soon. Gill isn't answering his phone and now I'm worried.'

Lillico closed his eyes and rocked back on his heels. Adina immediately misinterpreted his gesture.

'There you go', she said to Raphael. 'I told you he wouldn't believe me.'

Lillico shook his head. 'Actually, I've physical evidence that what you've said is very real.' He reached into his pocket and pulled out the note from Gill's windscreen, now tucked safely in a clear plastic evidence bag. 'Take a look at this.'

Adina read the note and nodded nervously. 'Raph. Solomon is right. Somebody needs to rescue McArdle.'

Raphael pushed up off the statue and into a standing position. 'I agree.'

'McArdle and I aren't easy company', said Adina. 'I think I should stay out of this.'

'He needs you', said Raphael, pointing at the helmet. 'And without McArdle, the armour will never be complete.'

'Go rescue him then!'

Raphael smiled. 'That, my friend, is a task for you.'

'What?' she said, thrusting the note against his chest.

'In this situation, my jurisdiction is limited. But Mr Lillico will assist you. Or Charlie. If you can find him.'

Adina jerked her free hand and shook it at Lillico. 'Aw, c'mon, Raph. This guy isn't one of us!'

Raphael had already started to walk away. 'Are you sure about that?'

'What? Give me a hand here, Raph.'

Leaving Adina to froth in her own frustrations, Lillico trotted after Raphael's long strides. Across the man's broad shoulders hung a phrase in Latin, wrapped around the image of a roaring lion's head. Reading the words, "Rex Gladio", Lillico was certain he'd seen that image sometime in his past.

'Hang on a second', said Lillico, matching Raphael's pace. 'Haven't we met before?'

'In the woods. Remember?'

'Before that. I saw you a long time ago.'

Raphael stopped abruptly. 'You did.'

'When?'

Raphael looked away and nodded soberly. 'You were just a child. You needed encouragement.'

As Lillico glanced up at the man, he was caught in the flare of a memory he tried to keep buried. The crush of that moment in his past hit him like a punch in the chest and he had to stop and lean against the statue for support.

'Your father asked you to lie for him', said Raphael.

Lillico nodded as the consequences of that moment came surging back. Confronted by a situation no child should ever have to face, he'd found himself as the sole witness to an … indiscretion. In the blaze of emotion that followed, his mother had implored him to tell the truth. And he had. And the impact on his family had been devastating. And afterwards, when the yelling started and the police were called, he'd been removed to a neighbour's house, where a large, kind man had sat with him until the fire consuming his family burnt itself out. Amidst the emotional wreckage of everything his family had striven to build, he had clung to the stranger's precious words. 'You did well, Alex. This was never your fault.'

'You gave me something', said Lillico. 'That day my family imploded.'

'Yes, I did', Raphael replied. 'Now, go and gather Adina. You both have a task to complete.'

'To rescue Gill McArdle?'

'Yes. But more than that.'

'If I'm risking my life out there, and Adina is risking hers, I'd like to know what's at stake?'

'Do you ever play chess, Alex?'

Lillico nodded, and for the first time, he saw uncertainty flit across Raphael's face. 'Pieces are in play', Raphael continued. 'Attack and defence. Suffice to say, if Gill survives this conflict, we gain a strategic opportunity.'

'Which is?'

Raphael sighed. 'I never thought this day would come. That Scotland might approach such a perilous crossroads.'

Lillico felt his heartbeat tick up. 'Tell me.'

Lifting his gaze to the far horizon, Raphael closed his eyes for a moment. 'To gain permission to take Gill's life, our enemy made a risky wager. If he survives today, then Gill wins authority to declare *The Torn Isle*.'

Lillico dropped his hands to his sides. 'And what is that exactly?'

'A dark day', said Raphael, lifting his hand to Lillico's shoulder in farewell. 'A last resort. And a refuge to prevent an even greater calamity. And honestly, my friend. If you love this land, pray it never happens.'

Chapter 34

The sweat on his back long ago turned into a layer of damp clothes and now Gill was cold. In fact, he'd gone past cold and was experiencing disorientation, which was probably a symptom of exposure. His body seemed incapable of generating more adrenalin and he found he was transitioning from fear to despondency. He felt beaten. Trapped. And just a little frustrated he didn't know enough about *The Book* to decode this situation. What little food he'd brought was finished, and his water was running low. Adding to his discomfort, the light was fading and soon he'd be sitting in the dark with only a demon for company. And still, Sariel sat, occasionally picking at his fingernails while he stared down from the mountain peak.

'Was that you?' said Gill. 'Wandering around in the woods at Krankie?'

Sariel didn't turn. Instead, he twisted his left hand around on his abnormally flexible wrist. 'Just a little drama to get you in the mood.'

'And the bones? Was that all theatre too?'

Sariel expelled an exasperated sigh. 'They got *your* attention.'

'And the apparition we know as the *Old Grey Man*. Was that you?'

'Reconnaissance.' Sariel sniggered. 'Though I did have some fun.'

'You've been making appearances on this mountain for a hundred years, for what? Just so you could set this trap?'

'Questions, questions, questions!' spat Sariel. 'Do be quiet unless you have something meaningful to say.'

'I want to know my friends are safe', Gill shouted.

Sariel responded with a dismissive wave and said nothing.

'Kill me if you have to, but Salina and the others; they've no part in this.'

Again, the demon ignored him.

Though it made his heart race again, making small talk with a demon wasn't making Gill any warmer. Sariel seemed to hold all the cards and by trapping Gill in a long moment of passivity, there seemed little an ordinary human could do in the face of this demonic torpor. Eventually, feeling bitterly cold, he was forced to get up and start walking around the outside of the shelter, spinning his arms and making little jumps to work some heat back into his limbs.

'Don't go wandering off', muttered Sariel.

'Why am I here?' Gill complained. 'You gave me six hours to get here, and I've been sitting freezing on my backside longer than that already.'

Sariel shrugged. 'I want to get back to our negotiation.'

'I wasn't negotiating.'

'You're here, aren't you? You've recognised my power and have already begun the process of bargaining for your friends' lives. You clearly have some sense for the harm I could do them. And to you too, if I choose. So, if you believe all that, why don't you believe I could also smother you with riches?' Sariel beckoned. 'Come over here for a second.'

Rather than argue, Gill allowed his next circuit of the mountain to bring him closer to the demon.

'Look at this view', said Sariel, pointing at the layers of mist and dusk rendering the Cairngorm landscape into layers of greens, browns and faraway grey. 'I mean, the view is better from *Buachaille Etive Mòr*, but you can still see most of Scotland from here.'

'I guess.'

'How would you like to be King of Scotland?' said Sariel suddenly.

Gill thought for a moment. 'Last time I looked, we're part of a larger democracy.'

'Democracy?' muttered Sariel. 'Is that what you're calling it?'

Gill just grunted.

'Think about it. KING OF SCOTLAND', he bellowed with a flourish. 'Or, President-for-Life, if you're fussy about semantics.'

Gill coughed weakly. 'Sounds like a poisoned chalice.'

Sariel smiled an ugly smile. 'I'm being serious. It could happen you know. I could make it happen. Let's think.' He made a show of stroking the point of his chin. 'Let's hypothesise that a rotten government in London tips Scotland over the edge into being an independent republic. You've got to admit, that's realistic for a start. Then after independence, Scotland's economy crumbles because no one has the wit to comprehend what kind of financial winter the move to independence might create. Then the nationalist coalition fractures into its constituent tribes, each one wanting to pursue different agendas. At the same time, new research shows that the old family line from the time of James IV leads today to the door of popular journalist, Gillan McArdle. Rising to the call of a loving public, McArdle reluctantly accepts the ceremonial post of Scottish President and sets about unifying the nation. But the economic conditions continue to darken, and the people scream for salvation. And who is the only man coming up with solutions? A man working in tandem with an angelic being, such as myself?' Sariel jabbed Gill with his elbow. 'And then, as the tide begins to turn, the people want to reward their saviour. Whatever title they give him, you know it would be a job for life.'

'You make it sound so plausible.'

Sariel's smile was like a cat pawing its prey. 'You know it makes sense. And really? You already know you're the man for the job.'

'And the cost of all this power?' asked Gill.

'I'll need you to meet my boss. He'll be your sponsor after all. Acknowledge him as your ultimate lord and master, then with that little ceremony over and done, you can get back to the day-to-day business of being king.'

'Do you want me to say "No" right now or would you like to go through a little song and dance where I pretend to think about it?'

'You're the one freezing to death on a mountainside.'

'Then, No. These days I'm with The Nazarene.'

'Really? Poor choice.'

'It's my choice to make.'

'Oh, well. I'll ask again in the morning. If you're still alive.'

As darkness fell, the wind picked up and a dense cloud of powdered icy snow engulfed the mountain. Gill stopped his pacing as the snow came in; cold to the bone and faint for lack of calories. He realised Sariel's urgency in getting him here was about leaving him unprepared. Physically, emotionally, spiritually, unprepared. To make matters worse, no one knew where he was. He was marooned with a dark and deadly force that might extinguish his life without another word passing between them. He glanced at his phone. There was no signal. And oh, what he would have done for a five-minute call with Salina. Or Cassy, or Fiona. At that moment, Gill realised he'd never felt so alone in all his life.

Finding a spot in the stone shelter giving the most protection from the wind, Gill hunkered down and did his best to concentrate his body heat. As the night wore on, he rocked in and out of consciousness and gradually realised that if sleep took him deeply, he might never wake up. He screamed silently, pushing himself to be awake enough to seek out that small, calming voice, that intermittently was his guide.

And with the first wisps of dawn, to his great relief, the voice did come, soothing Gill and reminding him of passages he'd read in *The Book*. Tending to his concerns. Reminding him how much he was loved. Then, as he began to feel brighter, it led him through the contractual terms underlying this unholy encounter. Ultimately, the voice showed Gill he'd been deeply misled. Flooded with relief, he started to laugh.

His laugh deteriorated into a coughing fit, and he felt Sariel rapping a bony foot against his shin.

'I'm worried about you', he said. 'You're delirious.'

Gill freed one eye from the layers of his hood to stare up at the demon. 'Really? I find your compassion hard to believe.'

'Yes, really. I'm looking at you and I see so much wasted potential.'

'You sound like my father did, ten years ago.'

'There you go! A wiser man than me. Well, a man, at least.' The demon tapped his shoulder. 'Do you miss him, Gill? Do you miss your daddy?' he mocked.

'Keep him out of this.'

'Don't be shy. I can help with grief. Help you take revenge. Strike back at the people who sat back and let your father die.'

'He was an old man. It was his time.'

'Was it? Are you pretending the medics couldn't have done more?'

'They looked after him to the end.'

'Hastened the end more like. All those drugs!'

'The drugs eased his pain.'

'And your prayers ...' Sariel picked at something under one long, black fingernail. 'Didn't do any good. Nobody listening, *Sword-Bearer*? Nobody at home?'

'Go away, Sariel. I mean, properly go away. From here, from me. Forever.'

'Look, if you won't part with your sword, at least use it to save yourself.' Sariel pointed at the boulders forming Gill's inadequate shelter. 'I know it's written in *The Book* that if you were to strike these stones with the sword, you could transform them into anything you want. Food! Yes. You could turn them into a haggis supper, and a hot drink. I'm sure you have some clever words to conjure up a lovely, warm sleeping bag.'

Gill sighed. 'Is that what the sword is to you, Sariel? A magic tool that exists to serve me?'

'You were the one who compared your relationship to the Creator with a conjuring trick. That day when you sat by the river and talked magic with your friends.'

'My words were inadequate', coughed Gill. 'The Creator's gifts are real, but I won't pretend he's a vending machine.'

'A sword? Or is it a light-sabre? Or a wizard's wand. At the end of the day, really, what is that thing you're carrying unless it's a utensil to serve your needs?'

'A sword', said Gill, his teeth chattering with a sudden infection of even deeper chill. 'And I'm told it will be my honour to carry it into battle.'

Sariel made a show of looking around. 'Don't see any battle. Is there a battle? Maybe they're fighting really, really quietly?'

'Yes', said Gill weakly. 'Maybe we are.'

'Well', sniffed Sariel. 'That's religion for you. Always looking to fight with somebody.'

'Maybe in the old days', shivered Gill. 'And on behalf of all the people who suffered at the hands of misguided religion, I'm sorry about that. But this sword is raised in defence.' He coughed. 'But you'll have noticed that already.'

Sariel huffed and returned to his perch, facing the east now, apparently waiting for the first rays of sunlight.

They drove in silence until they entered the roadworks at Krankie. Slowing to the speed limit as he passed a convoy of queuing lorries, illuminated by flashing yellow lights, Lillico felt Adina bristle beside him.

'Can't you hurry up?' she snapped.

'Just passing the dig site', said Lillico, for conversation rather than any need to impart information.

Adina said nothing.

'Has Gill told you what they found in there?' asked Lillico.

Adina sat staring out into the dark, her elbow against the window, the back of her left hand pressed against her mouth. 'Nope', she mumbled.

'A strange skeleton.' Lillico suddenly remembered himself. 'Sorry, I'm not allowed to talk about the details.'

'So don't.'

'Gill thinks it might make a good story for his magazine', said Lillico, unable to bear the silence in the car any longer. 'The bones look extraordinary.'

'Super. He could bag them up and send them to me. I could stick them in my museum or something.'

Lillico felt stung on Gill's behalf. 'You don't seem to think too much of Mr McArdle.'

She sighed and wearily rubbed her face. 'I should have shot him when I had the chance.'

'Beg your pardon?'

'Nothing', spat Adina. 'I was joking, okay?'

Lillico's evidence-gathering brain wanted to press her. But her participation in this mission was already tenuous, so he let it pass. Instead, he asked another obvious question. 'Why are you so angry about doing this?'

'Isn't it obvious?' she snorted. 'I should be in Edinburgh, checking on my kids and curling up beside my husband, instead of … instead of whatever this is', she said, thrusting her hands at the road as if this gesture would neatly convey the source of her anger.

'Sorry. I'm still not sure why you're driving through the night into a potentially dangerous situation for a man you don't even like?'

'Because, when I think it through, it's the only logical thing to do', she spat. 'I don't HAVE to like it.'

'Okay but help me understand. What's your problem with Gill?'

'I DON'T have a problem', said Adina with emphasis. 'It's just … he and I did some business together. It was a tough negotiation, and at that stage, I didn't think I'd ever have to see him again.'

'What changed?' asked Lillico, sensing he was pushing his luck.

'This', barked Adina, vigorously tapping her head so her helmet flickered in and out of visibility.

'Okay', said Lillico, trying to grasp the source of Adina's discomfort.

'On the most gruelling day of my life', Adina sniffed. 'A man I hoped I'd never see again introduced me to a unique group of people. And while they're companions of sorts, they're just as perplexed by their experiences as I am.'

'Does Gill have something like your helmet? I saw him brandish a weapon on some security footage.'

'He has a sword', said Adina flatly.

'Ah. That explains what I saw on the CCTV', said Lillico.

'There's a group of us. We all carry pieces of metaphysical armour. And we'll be nothing if we don't have the sword. That's why we have to rescue Gill.'

'Aside from him being a nice guy and all?'

Adina twisted around to face him. 'You don't seem in the slightest way freaked by this.'

'By what?'

'My helmet. Gill's sword.'

Lillico licked his lips. 'I've seen something like them before.'

As the roadworks fell behind them, Lillico illuminated his blue lights and accelerated.

She turned to face the road again, then a few seconds later, swung back towards him. 'Does Gill know about you?'

'Know what?'

'Oh, come on, Detective. At least show me the courtesy of a little candour.'

Lillico thought. 'I don't think so. We were on the cusp of a conversation one day. If he'd asked me about faith, I think I would have told him where I stood.'

'But instead, you what? Bottled it and talked about sport instead?'

'No. It just wasn't the moment.'

'Men', she breathed, studiously peering off into the dark.

'What about you, Adina? Do your friends and family know you're with the Nazarene? And that you have a sparkly magic helmet to prove it?'

Adina didn't move or speak.

'There you go then', said Lillico. 'And I don't judge because you probably haven't had the right moment to tell them.'

'Gill told me why he believes', said Adina after a time. 'What he experienced on Orkney. I don't think it came easily to him.'

'I didn't know him before all this', said Lillico. 'I mean, I was aware of his face. And I suspected he a had a story, but I wasn't sure.'

Adina was silent for a full minute, then heaved out a juddering sigh. 'Aren't you curious about my story?'

Lillico glanced across. 'About your helmet?'

'Yes, but before that. What I believe and why.'

Lillico winced and hoped she didn't see. 'We can chat about our life histories if you want. I warn you though, mine's not pretty.'

'Is it ever?' Adina shot back.

'I guess. Though you'd think it should be.'

'You'd think', Adina observed. She turned to look at him. 'Do you want to start?'

When Lillico didn't respond she flicked her right hand at the air in front of her. 'Okay, it's girls first then.'

Starting in faltering steps, Adina proceeded to tell her story; her pace and volume building throughout the account. And Lillico found he didn't need to speak again until they reached Aviemore ski centre. One hour later, as he pulled his car to a standstill, he found he had tears streaming down his face.

They parked beside Gill's vehicle and waited for a snow shower to pass. Lillico discovered the late October night was inhospitably cold as got out of his car and stood in the icy carpark. He looked at Adina as she stood shivering in an oversized borrowed jacket. With her warm brown eyes and curls of hair drifting out from the edge of her hood, he suddenly had the urge to embrace her. To show some human compassion for all she'd endured. But studying her face now, he could see a different Adina from the one he'd met at the Kelpies a few hours before. Her misgivings were behind her and now she was a warrior, limbering up before a battle.

'Ben Macdui', said Adina. 'How long will it take us?'

'Are you fit?'

'As you now know, I'm ex-special forces. Means I'm probably fitter than you.'

'Four hours, if we walk hard and take turns carrying the rucksack.'

'I'll carry it first. You're gonna be talking.'

'Why would I be talking?'

'Because I've already bared by soul', said Adina, shouldering the pack and starting to walk. 'Now I want to know who the hell you are, Alexander Lillico.'

'Okay then', said Lillico. 'All being well, we should be on the mountaintop shortly after dawn.'

Chapter 35

When Gill's brain stumbled back into focus, he found he was still in a sitting position. He could just about feel his backside, but his arms and legs were numb and though he struggled, he could barely move them. The last thirty-six hours – had any of it been real? Scenes from the battle in the bone store and the demon on the mountainside flitted through his brain like a half-remembered horror movie. He tried to open his eyes but found them sticky and blurred. By shaking his arms, he eventually coaxed some life into his left hand, drawing it back and forward across his face until finally, he could see. Getting his bearings, he found they'd moved a short distance from the mountaintop. Suddenly shocked and fearful, Gill found he now sat on a high cliff. Far below him, the tips of conifers swayed in the wind. Further afield, he could see the peaks of the Cairngorm range. Even in his hollowed-out state, Gill thought it looked so beautiful.

'One last chance to change your mind', said Sariel, moving closer to stand behind him.

Gill glanced up at the creature and found the dead, grey skin was now covered by a luxurious black cloak, covered with symbols he didn't understand. Reluctant to admit it, Gill saw that Sariel looked quite regal in his robe and sash. But that didn't change what he was. Gill tried to speak but ended up just shaking his head.

'Pity', said Sariel. 'This privilege will simply be passed to another man.'

'P... P...', Gill spluttered.

'What's that, McArdle? Last minute change of heart?'

'P... Piss off, Sariel.'

The demon stood. 'I realised you'd be stubborn. Of course, you and I had to go through this little dance as the privilege was yours for the taking. But don't think for a second I haven't already offered this prize to someone else. He accepted without a murmur. And as a consequence of his wise choice, he's already emerging as a man with authority.'

Gill coughed. 'You haven't hurt my friends because you can't. You lied to me, Sariel. And I was a fool to come up here. Hurt me, if you must, because hurting my friends isn't in your power.'

'I think I'm done here. Time to die, human.'

Gill swayed a little and took a deep breath. He was trying to focus his mind on Salina; for her face to be the last waking thought his mind would have. But his brain was swimming and her face kept slipping in and out of focus.

'Tell you what, I'll offer you one last choice', said the demon, standing behind him. 'Personally, I'd like to rip you to shreds. But you've shown a lot of courage so I'm offering you the opportunity to take your own life.' He leaned out over the cliff. 'It's about two hundred metres. Bound to be a clean death. All you have to do is step out. Gravity will do the rest.'

Sariel sat down again beside Gill and started to hum an old guitar riff.

Gill smiled as his head flopped uncomfortably to one side. Led Zeppelin, *Stairway to Heaven*. There was a certain irony.

A few minutes later, Sariel tried again. 'If you do fall, you never know your luck. Perhaps your little pocket angel, Raphael, will sweep in and rescue you. Carry you off to a nice highland hotel where he'll serve a full Scottish breakfast. What do you say? Shall we give that a try?'

'He rescues me when trouble finds me', Gill rasped. 'Not when it is self-inflicted.'

'You should try', hissed Sariel in Gill's ear. 'Sssso much better than the alternative I've got planned.'

Gill wanted to laugh, but it just came out in a series of short coughs. 'You know the biggest joke in this?'

Sariel's face pulled into exaggerated bewilderment. 'Do tell.'

'This whole charade? You offered me the same deal your side offered The Nazarene', Gill gasped. 'I'm truly flattered.'

Swearing, Sariel clambered to his feet, extending the claws on his long bony fingers and screeching with rage.

'Man, that thing is disgusting', said a woman's voice behind them.

Gill crawled away from the cliff edge, just in time to see Sariel plant his feet to confront Lillico and Adina.

Lillico dug into a zipper pocket and pulled out a sealed plastic bag containing a sheet of paper. 'Got your note', he said, waving the bag in the air.

Adina covered her mouth and coughed. 'But, ugh! What did that thing roll in? As my kids would say, it's properly minging.'

'Oh! My note on Gill's windscreen!' said Sariel, dropping into a mock crouch. 'Somehow, I've overlooked this crucial piece of evidence and now the plucky police sergeant has used the clue to track me to my lair!'

Lillico looked from Sariel, to Adina, and back again. 'Yeah. Kinda like that.'

Sariel stood upright again and dropped the back of his hands onto his narrow hips. 'Really, why Raphael sees any value in you people? You're all so stupid.'

'He did find you', rasped Gill. 'And actually, he's a constable, not a sergeant.'

Sariel huffed a little laugh. 'He found me because I intended him to find me.' He waved his right hand in a circle. 'Look on this as me hitting a *three-for-the-price-of-one* deal. I get to dispose of all of you in a single mission. And as for the question of his rank? That proves Sergeant Lillico is a liar.'

'Strictly speaking, I'm a Detective Constable for another two days.'

'Why all the secrecy then?' said Sariel, stepping towards Lillico, wiggling his fingers. 'Are you undercover? Will you be telling tales?'

'None of that is your business.'

Sariel laughed. 'You people! Let me explain to your friends. You're gathering intelligence about DCI Wiley. If that's the right word to use.'

Sheepishly, Lillico shrugged.

'Oh, you really are so very wedded to the truth, Lillico. Now that McArdle knows about your little deception, he'll probably put it in his newspaper.' Sariel turned to glare at Gill. 'Or he would have, had he lived.'

'Enough!' shouted Adina. 'Before we have to listen to any more of your bullshit, I've a few points of order.'

'Points of what?' bellowed Sariel, his flying spittle reaching almost as far as Adina's chest.

'I have a source', said Adina. 'And he says you're out of contract.'

'I'm not sure you're playing by the rules, Ms Mofaz. This source?' muttered Sariel. 'Big Turkish-looking guy?'

'Actually, Sariel', wheezed Gill. 'She's right. You should listen to her.'

'Under the terms negotiated by you in the highest court in heaven', Adina continued, 'you had three attempts to end Gill's earthly life, or forfeit your collateral.'

'And I'll have each one yet', yelled Sariel.

'Well, this is what I'm saying', said Adina, holding her ground. 'You tried at Airth church on the fifth of March. Then two weeks ago, you tried here, right on this mountain. Finally, in Falkirk, in the early hours of yesterday morning, you attacked him and lost. Face it, Sariel. Those were your three chances. And now, the deposit your side put on the table belongs to Gill.'

'Deposit?' said Gill.

Sariel ignored him. Instead, he stood up and laughed. 'You dare to stand here and claim that territory, while I, a prince among demons, stand ready to rip your flimsy bodies, limb from limb?'

'Ah', said Adina. 'That's the other thing. You're not actually here. Well, not physically anyway, so the whole limb from limb thing is gonna be a stretch.'

Sariel visibly slumped a little. 'And why would you believe a thing like that?'

Adina tapped her head. 'I know stuff. I've read *The Book*. I've considered the implications and know what's real and what isn't. Your three chances are up and consequently, your physical power to hurt my associate is finished.'

Sariel spun around and did an angry little dance, looking at himself from every possible angle. 'Why? I'm an illusion, even to myself!'

'Look. I'll show you', said Adina, picking up a stone and tossing it at Sariel's chest.

The demon watched the stone pass through his body and disappear over the edge of the cliff. In response, he gripped his fists in anger and roared at the sky.

'Listen', said Adina calmly. 'You can run this scary monster lark all you want, but I'd like to look at the evidence. And I think if you could have killed us, you would have done it by now.'

Sariel cocked his head to one side. 'Really? Or am I simply treasuring that moment so I can enjoy every last agonising breath?'

'Yeah, yeah, yeah', said Adina, turning to Gill. 'Having used your three shots, I think you're using the last tool in your box and trying to scare Gill to death. Or at least, leave him so bound up in his fears for his friends he feels he can't act against you.'

Sariel's laugh had real mirth now and Gill started to wonder if Adina had pushed her confident play a little too far. Sariel suddenly pointed at Gill and at some level, Gill realised the creature could read his mind.

'You see, even the *Sword-Bearer* doesn't believe you.'

'He doesn't need to. It's me you have to answer to.'

'Under whose authority?'

Adina tapped her head and the translucent crystal helmet materialised around her skull. 'Raphael offered me a gift. Or to be exact, he allowed me to experience a gift I was given a long time ago. You see, Sariel, I know what I believe.' She stepped towards him. 'The Nazarene, Aura, Creator – I don't suspect they exist. *I know*. I won't speculate about their powers and purpose. *I know*. And as for your boss and all his lies? Trust me. I've been there. *I know*.'

Sariel guffawed. 'You know. You know. You know. Know what, in the face of all I'm about to do to you?'

Adina folded her arms. 'Lillico, would you do the honours?'

Lillico nodded, then slowly unzipped his jacket, spreading the folds aside to reveal a thick translucent belt, carved with intricate letters depicting the many names of the Creator. 'Under the authority granted in me', Lillico began. 'In respect to Gill McArdle, I charge you with malicious conduct beyond your negotiated terms. And furthermore, that you have lied from the moment you began your attack. You are hereby remanded in custody to await sentencing.' For the first time in Gill's experience, a broad smile crept onto Lillico's face. 'You're to be detained in the prison, known in *The Book* as, The Lake.'

'Maybe you didn't hear me, human. I asked, under whose authority?'

Lillico stepped towards the creature and pointed once at the sky. 'HIS.'

Sariel roared in rage and leapt at Lillico, his claws outstretched. But the blow never struck home as Sariel's form started to melt into smoke. Peering at his body in horror, Sariel watched as his feet, then his legs, and then his body, spun into a miniature black tornado. Then, with a last shriek, the smoke plummeted down into the earth.

And for several long seconds, the three didn't move.

Adina was the first to speak. Sucking in a deep breath of fresh air she said, 'That's better.'

Gill sat watching Lillico for a long moment, observing how the young officer's shoulders gradually became less square, until finally, he crumpled into a sitting position on a clump of heather beside him.

'You have the belt', Gill observed.

Lillico regarded Gill for a long second, then nodded.

'Who gave it to you?'

'Lillico has had what you might call a special relationship with truth since he was six years old', said Adina, stepping over to join them.

'I've felt the weight of the belt many times. Today, for the first time, Adina helped me see that truth has power.'

'You got this from Raphael?'

'My first encounter was years ago', said Lillico.

Gill rubbed exhaustion from his eyes. 'I almost died. How was Sariel able to push me as far as he did?'

Adina's shoulders dropped into a shallow shrug. 'Quiet simply, he lied. Lied and lied.'

'But the bones? The photos?'

'Does your phone still have any power?' asked Lillico.

Gill struggled to get his cold, stiff hand inside his jacket pocket. Eventually, Lillico reached across to help him. 'My battery has two per cent.'

'Look at your photos. Scroll to the day you uncovered the *Jacobite Alien*.'

Clumsily, Gill did so, and couldn't restrain a tiny gasp when he saw the photos of the malformed body lying in its grave. 'They're back!'

'They're not back', said Adina. 'They never disappeared in the first place.'

'What?'

'Sariel seeded doubt. Probably managed to distract you. After that, he was able to convince you they were no longer there. It was all lies.'

'And the bones we recovered to Lossuary?'

'I'd guess they're wherever you left them, in a carefully labelled box in Falkirk.'

'You're saying Sariel pulled a mind trick on what, a dozen people?'

Adina started to set up a camping stove. 'His team invented deception, Gill. And they've had millennia to hone it down to a fine art.'

Lillico also stood and wrapped his coat around Gill. 'He had three attempts to kill you.'

'And when he failed', said Adina. 'No doubt he tried to trick you into harming yourself.'

Gill nodded, embarrassed by how close he'd come to taking the bait.

'You're fortunate you had it so easy', said Adina.

'Easy?' spluttered Gill.

She shrugged. 'He attacked you head-on. Guns blazing. I think you'll find in future, our enemy will be a lot more subtle.' She dropped her hands on her hips and pitched towards him. 'Lure you into bad decisions by flattery. Tempt you to do a little good by cutting some moral corners. Anyway, that's my experience.'

'Oh, good grief', said Gill, dropping his face into his hands.

'Yay!' exclaimed Adina, flamboyantly splaying out her arms. 'The famous Gill McArdle gets to make a declaration over some island. What could possibly go wrong?'

'I'm not following', said Gill, looking up.

'Something Raphael told us', said Lillico. 'I'll tell you what little we know once we start walking.'

'Let's just get you some warm food, Gill', said Adina. 'How are you doing?'

'I feel like I've had the crap beaten out of me, then been held hostage for a fortnight in an industrial freezer.'

Lillico glanced from Adina to Gill. 'Once you've eaten, can you get off the mountain under your own steam, or shall I call for help?'

'I take it Raphael isn't coming?' Gill knew his face was pleading.

Lillico shook his head. 'Just us.'

Gill blew into his cold hands. 'I'll be fine.'

'You sure?'

'Feed me, then steer me home, Constable.'

'Actually, Gill. On that one insignificant detail, Sariel was right. In two days, I will be a Sergeant.'

Gill waved a hand to swat this information away. 'Okay. Nice to meet you, Detective Sergeant Alexander Lillico. You can talk me through that while we walk.'

'I will, once you've explained the significance of this crystal armour we're all carrying.'

Gill elevated his shoulders and felt the weight of the blade in its scabbard. 'I'll do my best. But Solomon is the one you really need to talk to.'

'Adina mentioned her', said Lillico.

'And if you thought Sariel was scary …', said Adina with the flash of a smile.

Chapter 36

'You look like crap', said Wiley without looking up. 'Where the hell were you yesterday?'

Lillico glanced at the clock. It was almost 8 am, and for once, Wiley was early at his desk. They'd taken seven hours to get Gill safely off the mountain, then another three to get the battered journalist back home to Dundee and poured into bed. Then Adina had stepped onto an Edinburgh-bound train, and Lillico had gone home to review his emails and make a few calls. By early evening he'd been ready for a shower and a night of much-needed sleep.

'Pursuing a possible lead on the missing *Jacobite* bones', was all he said.

'You didn't think to call?'

'Sorry, sir. I got distracted tracking down Pete Gibson's brother.'

Wiley brightened. 'Anything tasty?'

Lillico shook his head. 'Records show he moved to Glasgow after he sold his share in Lossuary. And that he died of lung cancer five years ago.'

'Brilliant', Wiley drawled. 'There goes another lead. And did you have any joy on the missing bones?'

'None', said Lillico. 'I left Gill working at Lossuary and he found a clue they might have been taken off-site. We spent most of yesterday on that, though it turned out to be a dead end.'

'So, you've no idea where they are?'

'My best guess, sir, is they're probably still at Lossuary. I'd wager some mix-up between the boxes. When you think about it, it is an awfully big warehouse.'

'What about the photos? And Beth's data?'

'Still looking into that.'

'Misplacing the bones is probably McArdle's fault. Where is he by the way?'

Lillico paused, wondering how truthfully, he could describe what happened to Gill without explaining Sariel's apparition. In the end, he opted for brevity. 'Gill spent Tuesday night on Macdui.'

'In this weather?'

Lillico's shoulders dipped up and down. 'What can I say? He's dogged when he's on the trail of something.'

'Right. That's another bollocking I need to give him.'

'To be fair, sir, he realises in retrospect it wasn't a good move. He was rescued off the hill by other walkers and was suffering exhaustion and the early stages of hypothermia.'

'Who were these other walkers? Not *Toothfairy* suspects by any chance?'

'Definitely not, sir', said Lillico with a straight face. 'Just a couple of good Samaritans who happened to be in the area.'

Wiley looked up and for a second, Lillico thought he saw genuine concern. 'How is he now?'

'No lasting damage. Just needs a day or two to rest up.'

'Glad to hear that', said Wiley, turning back to his screen. 'Where would Scotland be without her favourite slice of fruitcake?'

'Yes, sir.'

'While you were out doing whatever it was you were doing, I've been busy processing another batch of DNA hits.'

'More direct connections to the *Toothfairy*?'

'Yes. The profiling work you did against the Missing Persons register produced the goods. We've identified another five victims. I took the liberty of adding them to your dataset.'

Lillico moved around to look over Wiley's shoulder. His boss had indeed updated the embedded Excel tables running the charts. 'We're identifying a lot more than we expected, which is unusual. See anything new?'

Wiley shook his head. 'Lots more randomness. The only commonality is that some of them have had brushes with the law. Strengthens my conviction these people were assassinated.'

'Could the *Toothfairy* be a vigilante?'

'They were convicted of white-collar crimes, mostly. They weren't rapists or child molesters.'

Lillico nodded. The identification of fourteen victims should have yielded a breakthrough, and yet, there was no obvious pattern leading them to the killer. 'There must be clusters, sir. I still see merit in giving the vics names to McArdle's team', he said. 'They have an analyst on their team who seems to be able to see through walls.'

Wiley sighed. 'We need a breakthrough, Alec. Otherwise, my ass is on the line. So, against my better judgement, I'm going to say, yes. But they have to treat the information with the utmost confidence.'

Lillico nodded and got up to leave. But then the belt he wore, representing truth and honesty materialised heavily on his hips. It was hidden beneath his jacket, and he realised it conferred certain responsibilities. Closing the office door, he turned around and sat down again. 'Thank you, sir. Can I just repeat, I'm not comfortable with "Alec". It's Alex, or Alexander, or just Lillico.'

Wiley looked up and quizzically cocked his head to one side as if composing a suitably insulting rebuff, so while he still had a chance, Lillico continued. 'And if you're worried about your job, sir. Then there's something else you really need to know about me.'

'You've spoken to Gill?' said Lillico a little later as he slid his files onto the conference room table at the *Mys.Scot* offices. With him were Mhairi, the team's excellent researcher, and Cassy, the striking girl with the red mittens.

Cassy nodded. 'Briefly this morning. He sounded dreadful. Everyone here is quite upset about what happened. I mean, it's Gill. He makes a habit out of almost dying. But still, another hour out there and that might have been the end of him.'

'Is his fiancée aware?'

'Yes. She's cutting her trip short due to bad weather. She should be home late on Sunday.'

'Cool. I think he'll be particularly pleased to see her back safely.'

Cassy tapped her fingers with a biro. 'Gill was very cagey about what happened to him on Macdui. But he says you were there?'

'I was.'

'So, what was he doing?'

Lillico sat looking at them and wasn't sure what to say. 'It's Gill's story to tell.'

Mhairi leaned into Cassy. 'I don't think the gentlemen have had time to get their stories straight.'

Lillico shrugged. 'I'm not going to lie to you about it, but I'm not ready to divulge the truth either.'

Cassy tapped the table in front of her. 'This is important, Detective. We're glad Gill is safe, but the cat mag is running a book on what happened to him, so it's absolutely critical we get the inside track.'

Lillico shook his head. 'You're not going to get it from me.'

'This is the way I see it', said Cassy, spreading her hands out in front of her. 'An alien spaceship comes down to recover the bones of a long-dead colleague, recently recovered from a Scottish battlefield. In the course of their mission, they abduct Gill McArdle, who will of course have no memory of his experiences, before dumping his half-dead body on the mountain.'

Tell you what', whispered Mhairi. 'That's gonna make a cracking front cover.'

'To business, then. The sweepstake. Shall we say £10 each?'

Mhairi nodded.

'Lillico. Do you want a piece of this action?'

Lillico shook his head. 'I respect that these intra-office rivalries are your highest priority just now, but when you do get a moment, I'm still trying to catch a serial killer. If I'm remembering correctly, Gill did say you guys would help. But, you know, take your time.'

'You're right', Mhairi whispered theatrically into Cassy's ear. 'He is a bit straight.'

Cassy nodded and looked away. 'Cute though. When he's angry.'

'I am in the room, and I can hear you', said Lillico wearily. 'If you were two blokes talking about a woman this way ...'

'Relax, Alex', said Cassy pushing back from the table and standing up. 'We're just messing with you.'

Lillico thrust an open palm across the table. 'I've spent days convincing my boss to let me share this data with you. I've been dazzling him with your potential insights. Please, please, don't let me down now.'

'Mhairi's your girl for that, said Cassy. 'I'm gonna swing by the cat mag a couple of times looking really, really smug.' And after hitting Lillico with a professional smile, she got up and left.

Mhairi paused until the conference door closed behind Cassy. 'Sorry about that. She's a bit uppy and downy these past few weeks. Not sure what's going on.' She slapped the table hard enough to make Lillico jump. 'Right, Constable. Show me what you've got.'

Lillico opened his folder. 'I have a list of fourteen names associated with the *Toothfairy* case.'

'Associated?'

'Associated by way of their DNA. They're deceased, obviously. That's all I can say at the moment. We have dates of birth, addresses and occupations for most of them. Some have criminal records. Nothing too drastic. I'm trying to see a pattern, but I can't.'

'And you think I can add value, how?'

'The research you did on deaths and disappearances on Cairngorm; you built up quite a list?'

'We did. So, you're asking me to try and find relationships between the people on my list and the people on your list?'

'Yes. Discreetly. My boss agrees that if we find anything, you guys get first rights on the story. But only once we've charged any potential suspect.'

'Brill. Explain your data. Then I'll get right on it and see what I can do.'

Struggling to concentrate, Mhairi dropped her elbows on her desk and rubbed her temples. Cassy had a way of moving around the office when she was stressed. Darting around in short little bursts - from colleague to printer - from printer to phone - from phone to colleague, Mhairi could see Cassy was as jittery as she'd ever known her. The looming close on issue 29, plus Gill's continued absence were probably the cause of her angst.

Blocking out Cassy's harassed behaviour, it was mid-afternoon when Mhairi finally had a breakthrough with Lillico's data. Her discovery might have little consequence, but she decided she should share it with him right away. She'd have liked to walk Cassy through her logic first, but it was clear her friend and colleague didn't have the headspace, so Mhairi decided to talk to Lillico alone. She had just dropped him a text requesting a call when Cassy appeared at her elbow.

'I'm going out for half an hour', said Cassy.

'If you're going for a coffee, I'll join you. I just need to make a call first.'

Cassy shook her head. 'I'm off to Gill's flat to take him his post and a bunch of grapes. I know we've a few days to close issue 29, but unless Gill makes some decisions, we'll be in a pickle next week.'

'He said he'll be in tomorrow', Mhairi recalled.

'And what if he decides to stay off until Monday?' groaned Cassy, swinging her hands around the *Mys.Scot* pen. 'I just need to get in his face. Give him a bunch of yes/no questions, then I can be back in here before home-time and throw some order on this chaos.'

'Okay.' Mhairi paused. 'Don't be too hard on him.'

'I won't', said Cassy raising her hand in farewell. 'But I am going to extract some decisions from him even if I have to shine a bright light in his face.'

Mhairi laughed in response, just as her laptop started buzzing. Lillico was requesting a video call.

'Hang on', she said, reacting to his face. 'I'm going to have to find somewhere private.' She picked up her computer and scanned the office. The *Game and Gun* team were using the conference room, but Tony Farquharson's office was empty, so she used her backside to bump the door open and went inside.

'You got something for me?' said Lillico, as Mhairi laid her laptop down on a flat surface.

'Hmm, most of it still looks random to me but I do have one cluster emerging.'

'Anything you see could be helpful.'

'It was the McBlain surname that caught my eye. It's quite rare and I remember seeing the same name in some of our other research.'

'And the point?'

'Back in the '70s, after an accident involving school children, there was a decision to remove all the emergency shelters on the Cairngorm plateau.'

'Yeah, I remember seeing that in your notes.'

'Well, a gentleman called Angus McBlain chaired the committee approving the demolition. I looked him up and it turns out he died back in 2002. But there's a Colin McBlain on your *Toothfairy* list. And I've confirmed Colin was the son of old Angus.'

Lillico whistled under his breath. 'I don't know how you hold all this information in your head.'

'I don't. I use software. Anyway, that name stuck out. And that made me wonder if there could be other connections. So, I built a family tree of everyone on that committee and guess what I found?'

'Please, Mhairi …'

'The names of four other sons and daughters of that committee are on the list you gave me.'

Lillico was silent for a moment. 'Really?'

'Yes', Mhairi protested.

'Mhairi, that could be significant. However, these names only represent a third of our victims.'

'Agreed. But it's the only cluster I'm seeing in your data.'

Lillico's gaze left Mhairi's face and drifted into the long distance. 'Got any theories?'

Mhairi threw him an apologetic smile. 'I'm wondering if someone could be punishing the bothy committee?'

'Okay, but why? Surely if the killer had a coherent motive based on the bothies, why take it out on their children rather than strike the original group?'

'Like I said, I see a cluster in the data. I can't explain it.'

'Can you help me take this to the next level?'

'Sure.' She glanced at her watch. 'But it will have to be tomorrow. My band has a practise session this evening.'

'No problem', breathed Lillico, pausing as he assembled his next question. 'I've read about the bothy demolition. It was controversial at the time. I need to know if any individuals, families, or groups, suffered harm as a result of that decision.'

'Okay. Can you help me narrow the search parameters?'

'Yes. They would have had a child around the time the shelters were removed.'

Mhairi looked up from her notes. 'Sorry, how will that help you?'

There was another pause. Lillico was obviously weighing how much he could tell her. 'If some of the *Toothfairy* deaths are indeed revenge attacks for the bothy demolition, then why did they only begin thirty years ago? Why not from the late '70s onwards? I'm reasoning they didn't start taking revenge until they were old enough, and so if we follow that logic, they must have been a child when something occurred to trigger this retaliation.'

'I'll get back into the Cairngorm archive. They'll list any accidents or callouts linked to the bothies. I should be able to get enough info there to work out if they have descendants. Anything else?'

'Yes. If you've time, check the families of any bothy committee members who aren't on my list. If they're still alive and haven't been targeted yet, I feel a duty to warn them.'

Chapter 37

Two hours later, the phone in the Dundee office rang far longer than normal. Finally, it was answered.

'*Mysterious Scotland*. Craig speaking. How can I help?'

'You on the phones now?' asked Gill.

'Mhairi is on the line to someone in *The Cairngorm Society*, and Cassy is still on walkabout.'

'What? She's not in the office?'

'She was going to visit you, then after that I assumed she was on some secret mission for our illustrious editor. Speaking of whom, how are you?'

'On the mend. Had a chilly couple of days on Macdui.'

'The haunted mountain! Did you see our rock-throwing friend?'

'Actually, I did. Though he wasn't throwing stuff at me which helped.'

'Are you being serious? Have you had a face-to-face with Scotland's yeti?'

'Aye. I asked for a full interview but he declined.'

'Gill?'

Gill paused. He was being sucked into a conversation that neither he nor Craig were ready for. With a twinge of guilt, he chose to deflect rather than risk Craig's incredulity. 'Long story. One for just you and me on a pub night.'

'Okay', said Craig, sounding a little deflated. 'I'll hold you to that. You say you're looking for Cassy?'

'Aye.'

'Haven't seen her since lunchtime.'

'That was hours ago', said Gill. 'She only stayed ten minutes and said she'd a tonne of work to do.'

'Looking at her desk, boss. She's not been back in. Let me check with Larry.'

Gill waited while a muffled exchange took place.

'Apparently, she did call in. She's planning to meet someone promising her a lead on our missing *Jacobite Alien*.'

'Sorry', said Gill, stopping to cough. 'I haven't had a chance to tell you. We believe the alien bones are still at Lossuary.'

'Really?'

'Yeah, sorry. Mislabelled box or something.'

'Okay. Well, I guess Cassy will show up shortly, frustrated and spitting tacks about wasted time.'

'Yeah. When you see her, can you ask her to give me a call?'

'Sure. Anything I can help with?'

'It's a personal thing. Thinking about it, just leave it. I'll catch up with her in the office tomorrow.'

'No problem. Hey, Gill. You know how we used to produce a magazine from time to time?'

Gill let a few seconds pass before answering. 'Yes.'

'Might want to get our heads together. I mean I know most of issue 29 is finished, but if you want to run with any of the Krankie stuff, we need to move on it ASAP.'

'Yeah. I'll see you tomorrow. I won't be fit for much, but at least I can type. Promise you'll have my full attention until we get issue 29 in the bag.'

Arriving at 8 am on Friday morning, Gill received a muted standing ovation from anyone already at their desks. The team on the cat mag were less than enthusiastic. Misled by a rumour, the editorial staff had entered the sweepstake with various predictions explaining how Gill had met his demise.

'It was just a little frostbite, guys', said Gill, quoting his favourite movie.

They all studiously avoided his gaze, apart from the layout artist, who stared in alarm at a space just over Gill's left shoulder.

Gathering Mhairi, Craig and Larry, they made some hasty decisions about the upcoming issue. Unfortunately, nothing he'd agreed with Cassy the day before had reached the team. No one had seen or heard from her for almost twenty hours and Gill was getting worried. Sitting at his laptop in the office, he scanned through social media to see if any of her accounts had any fresh activity. He was so focused on his task, he almost leapt with shock when something cold and damp brushed against the exposed skin around his ankles.

'What the …' he gasped, shifting his legs to one side to see what was molesting him. He looked down to see a small white West Highland Terrier looking up at him. Meeting his gaze, the creature panted and gave its tiny tail a tentative wag.

'Excuse me', he said, addressing the office space around him. 'Whose is this?'

Mhairi looked up from her work and then down at the small dog. 'Sorry, he's with me.'

Gill cleared his throat. 'Did I miss the memo? Is this *bring a pet to work day*?'

'He's Cassy's', said Mhairi, turning back to her screen. 'I kinda got landed with him when Cassy didn't come back yesterday. I think he's a bit stressed so I thought it would be better to have him in the office.'

'Aye', said Gill. 'But aren't there rules about this kinda thing?'

'Dinnae tell the cat mag', Larry whispered from his desk. 'They're banned frae bringin' pets.'

Craig nodded. 'Ever since that spat between the Siamese and the Shorthaired Tabby. Man, it was rank for a fortnight.'

Mhairi sighed and walked over to gather the little white dog into her arms. 'You wouldn't do that, would you, Mince?'

'Mince?' spat Larry. 'Wha kind name's that frae a dug?'

'Cassy's idea', sniffed Mhairi. 'As in, he's as thick as …'

Craig laughed. 'That's actually quite cute. What do you think, boss?'

Gill was still trying to rub dog snot from one ankle onto the trouser leg of another. 'I'm still in shock Cassy has a dog. I thought her only hobby was swimming.'

'She can do both you know', said Mhairi rubbing the dog's ears to his obvious delight.

'It's just I didn't know that about her.'

Mhairi smiled darkly. 'Lots of things you don't know about our Cassy.'

'Yeah', muttered Gill, burdened by his worry for Cassy and the unfinished magazine they were trying to close. 'Like where the hell is she?'

Everyone shook their heads.

'Okay, let's give it to lunchtime today, then if no one's heard from her, I'm gonna call Lillico.'

'Might be better if we phoned DCI Wiley', said Craig.

Gill pulled a face. 'If I need to get something done, Lillico's my new best friend in Police Scotland.'

He turned back to his laptop to deflect further conversation and checked his task list. 'Mhairi, the DNA analysis we got from Beth.'

'Sorry, from the *Jacobite Alien*?'

'Yes. Any luck identifying it?'

'I got one hit straight away, but it didn't make sense so I'm still looking.'

'I'm still curious. What did you find.'

'Honestly, Gill. It's just garbage.'

'Let me be the judge.'

Mhairi reached down and rubbed Mince's ears. 'According to my preliminary analysis, one of our *Jacobite's* ancestors was an *Arabian Horned Viper*.'

Gill laughed before he could stop. 'A snake?'

'Told you it was useless. Biologically impossible.'

Gill leaned back, stared at the ceiling and thought. Then without meaning to, he shuddered.

'Yeah', said Mhairi. 'You can see why I didn't come running to you with that little morsel.'

He shook his head. 'In a strange way, it reinforces our speculation about Nephilim.'

'The old Biblical tale about demons having sex with people?'

'Yes. When the devil manipulates Eve in the Garden of Eden, he's characterized as a snake.'

Mhairi stared down at Cassy's dog. 'If Cass was here, she'd remind you that's a baseless myth.'

'Aye. Baseless myth', Gill repeated, getting painfully to his feet and walking towards the coffee machine. He was beginning to wonder if there was any such thing.

A short while later, Mhairi glanced at the office clock and sighed. It was almost 9 am and she knew she couldn't wait too much longer before she had to make a decision. *Calum's Road* were due to play a ceilidh that evening in one of the biggest bars in Arbroath. Okay, it wasn't exactly a big gig, but the band didn't help its reputation by dropping a date at short notice. Her anger at Cassy being a no-show at yesterday evening's practise session had mellowed into concern. It just wasn't in her character to forget, or simply decide she couldn't be bothered. So, with nothing else to do, Mhairi had gone to Cassy's flat in the hope that her friend would show up. After twenty minutes of hanging around in the stairwell, a neighbour recognised Mhairi and used the spare key to let her into Cassy's flat. She'd stayed until midnight, then with no news from Cassy, she'd gathered *Mince* and gone home. Never mind waiting until lunchtime to alert Lillico – Mhairi planned to mention Cassy's absence during their scheduled 9.15 meeting.

Since talking to Lillico yesterday afternoon, she solved one part of his problem. Amongst the annual toll on the mountains, only one family stuck out. A family of four where the only survivor had been a young girl. On the basis that this child may have nursed a grudge against the people who ordered the demolition of the shelters, Lillico had asked her to track down the names of the bothy committee. Having done that, she checked the registered lists of births and deaths, discovering that tragedy had visited all of these families, apart from one. The only committee member not to lose a family member in the years following the incident was a young man called Peter Tullen. He'd been active with Cairngorm Mountain rescue through the 1970s until resigning to take a job at an oil and gas major in London.

Tullen. That name was too familiar to ignore. Mhairi stopped and thought. 'Please God, no', she breathed.

With a growing sense of dread, she turned to *Calum's Road* web page. Each of the band members had dedicated their demo album to the person who'd most influenced their music careers. Cassy had planned to make her dedication to her school music teacher, but at the last minute had changed it to her dad. There! She could see it in black and white. Peter Tullen was Cassy's father.

Mhairi was on the phone when Gill got back from the coffee machine and was just about to place a drink on her desk and return to his seat when Mhairi waved frantically at him to wait. She punched a button to place her phone on speaker and leaned over the mic.

'Alex, I've got Gill here. Two seconds please until I fill him in.'

'What's happening?' said Gill.

'Cassy. She's in trouble.'

'You bet she's in trouble. When she comes wandering in to collect her pooch ...'

'The *Toothfairy*', said Lillico's voice from the speaker, brushing Gill aside. 'She's taken Cassy.'

Gill laid his coffee to one side and hunched over the phone; the strain in his limbs chased away by the rising emergency. 'She? What? How do you know that?'

'Look, I'm on my way to you and I'll be there shortly. Mhairi has discovered a cluster in the *Toothfairy* killings. Go ahead, Mhairi.'

Gill looked at Mhairi.

'You asked me to look into the Cairngorm's bigger tragedies. One of the worst was back in November '74, when two families were climbing Macdui in fair weather', said Mhairi.

'On the descent, the party got hit by a blizzard. Conditions were so dangerous, they decided to find emergency cover at a high-altitude bothy known as the Curran Shelter. When they couldn't find it, the Burnside family had two sons in their early teens and decided to get off the mountain to head for the Corrour bothy.'

Gill nodded. 'I know it.'

'The other family, the Peytons, had a teenager plus a nine-year-old girl in their group. Fearing she was already succumbing to hypothermia, they split from the other family and kept looking for the Curran Shelter.'

'Hang on. November '74?' said Gill. 'That shelter had been demolished by then.'

Lillico butted in. 'The procurator fiscal reported that the family were using an out-of-date map. The bodies of the parents were found protecting their daughter. That poor kid was the only survivor.'

Mhairi pulled up a file. 'Five *Toothfairy* victims identified from the DNA in their teeth were offspring of people serving on the committee that recommended the demolition of the Cairngorm shelters. On the basis of that, I did a search on the rest, and I found that every committee member has lost a person in their family, apart from one.' Mhairi stopped to swallow. 'Cassy's dad was on that committee.'

'And you're connecting that to her disappearance?'

'Yes. Cassy has a sister, but I spoke to her this morning - she's safe on Raasay. And Cassy has been missing for twenty-four hours.'

Gill's mind reeled as he considered the implications of this.

'Thing is', said Lillico. 'I believe the Peyton's surviving daughter has to be linked to the *Toothfairy*.'

'So, we need to find her. Immediately! What's her name?'

Mhairi turned to look at him. 'We know who she is, Gill. Because she's listed in the Cairngorm records. I'm sorry. I should have recognised her name when the DNA results were emailed across from Lossuary.'

'Mhairi, you've already done amazing work. Just tell me.'

'It's Beth.'

Half an hour later, Lillico threw his unmarked squad car onto the pavement outside the *Mys.Scot* offices, the blue lights, still flashing. Gill and Mhairi joined him outside before he had time to enter the building.

'Beth seems to have baited Cassy with information on the missing bones', said Lillico. 'Any idea where they might have gone?'

Gill still looked physically frail. 'Alex, I'll do everything I can to help, but isn't this a police matter?'

'As much as I'd like to hang around Bathgate until 10 am watching Wiley scratching his arse, we need to be quick on this', said Lillico.' We three are the only ones with any insight on this case. I think we've the strongest chance of sorting this together.'

'Besides', said Mhairi. 'Cassy is a friend.'

'Okay', said Gill, running his fingers through his hair. 'You said Cassy's family was the last one to be attacked. Is there any significance to that?'

'Not as far as I can see', said Mhairi. 'Her dad was on the bothy committee but was a relatively junior member.'

'He used to be mountain rescue, right? I've heard Cassy bragging about his superhero credentials.'

'He was, but if the records are right, he'd already moved south by the time of Beth's tragedy. So he wasn't involved in recovering Beth or the bodies of her family. The fact that the family was in London for a spell may have made him harder to track down.'

'You said it happened in November. What date?'

'The first.'

Lillico leaned in. 'You realise that's today?'

'Meaning, it's a significant day', said Gill. 'Retribution on the last family associated with the committee on the fiftieth anniversary of the disaster. What will she do?'

'She'd go somewhere significant', said Mhairi. 'But where?'

'The site of the shelter?' Lillico suggested. 'Where her parents died.'

Gill shook his head. 'She's done that already, by laying the teeth of her victims. You say there was a fourth family member?'

'There was a brother', said Mhairi. 'Records show his body was discovered just short of the Corrour bothy. The fiscal decided the family had realised they weren't going to find the shelter and sent the son to call for help.'

'That's a tragedy', said Gill.

'And the location will be significant to Beth', Lillico added.

'Agreed', said Gill. 'If there's any logic to her actions, that's where she'll be.'

Lillico dropped his hands on his hips and slowly shook his head. 'Long way to drag a hostage. And that's assuming Cassy was able and willing to walk.'

Mhairi jerked a hand in his direction. 'She must have been tricked into it.'

'Yeah, possibly.'

Lillico ran a wary eye over Gill. 'You realise this takes us back to Ben Macdui?'

Gill nodded. 'Mhairi needs to stay here. She's the one who understands the data.'

'Agreed', said Lillico.

Gill pulled his waistcoat tight around his body to fend off the chill. 'Macdui is hours away. We need to get to Cassy as fast as we can.'

Lillico was already punching a number on his phone. 'Jump in. I'll sort us out a ride.'

Chapter 38

Oscar woke with a hard white light illuminating the bothy's tiny windows. Snow had fallen since their arrival and the wind had pushed dusty flakes against the glass all night. Since it stopped an hour ago, a thin winter sunlight had broken through, amplified by the early-season snow on the mountains all around the bothy. The floor was hard and cold, and the four-season sleeping bag barely felt up to the job.

A glance at the time confirmed it was past 8 am. Meanwhile, the Tullen girl was still sleeping. They'd arrived just before nightfall, bedding down in the frozen room. Later, they'd been disturbed when a party of walkers had arrived in the small hours. At first, Oscar had worried the new arrivals would complicate today's plans, but they'd left again a few hours before sunrise; under pressure to complete the Lairig Ghru circuit before they ran out of daylight for a second night. The disturbance added to the bitter cold that had kept them awake for a couple of hours.

After another short doze, Oscar glanced again at the time. The appointment wasn't far away. Meanwhile, it was hard to know how long it would take the Tullen girl to realise she was in danger. Until then, they'd continue to play their little game.

'Morning, Cassy', said Oscar as a solitary roommate started to stir.

'Morning', Cassy shivered. 'Oh man, it's absolutely Baltic in here.'

'Did you notice our visitors?'

Cassy spun her head around from the comfort of her sleeping bag. 'Are they gone already?'

'Couple of hours ago.'

'They were noisy buggers.'

'Aye. And then they only stayed about four hours. Maybe they worried last night's snow would slow them down.'

'Should we be worried?' asked Cassy.

'I don't think so. The men I mentioned are coming to us, so we don't need to walk any deeper into the hills. They should be here quite soon. They'll tell us what they know and then we can head back to Braemar.'

Cassy shivered. 'Still don't understand why we couldn't have met up in a Starbucks.'

'Well, it's like what we were saying yesterday, and you'll know this from working on an investigative magazine. Sometimes you have to push the extra mile to get the story.'

'And why you? I mean, you're not a Detective. Couldn't you just have kicked this over to Lillico or Wiley?'

'Our visitors are personal contacts of mine. They'd not talk to a cop. That's why I called you.'

'Gill might have been the better choice. He'd love the cloak and dagger around this little encounter.'

'It had to be you, Cassy. I so enjoyed working with you on the Krankie dig. And you appreciate the importance of the bones. I wanted to have another woman by my side, so you see, you're the only person I could call.'

'But why the secrecy? I'd feel better about this if I could at least talk it over with the guys in the office.'

'Because I promised my contacts I'd respect their confidentiality. And I always keep my promises.'

Cassy rubbed her hands together. 'I hope it's worth it. I'm not sure I'll ever be warm again.'

'I'll find my stove and make us coffee', said Oscar, struggling out of the sleeping bag and pulling on an extra layer. 'To pass the time, why don't you tell me something about yourself?'

Cassy huffed. 'You heard what little there is to tell, yesterday on the walk here. Too much work. Not enough life. And when I look in the mirror, I don't see much balance.'

Oscar nodded and put a match to the Trangia stove. 'You have a sadness about you. I mean you're a bright bubbly person on the surface, but I can tell you're someone who carries great pain.'

Cassy stopped leaning on her elbow and lay back down again. 'That's all a bit deep for first thing in the morning. I don't normally bear my soul to a new friend until at least my second caffeine hit.'

'I don't mean to pry. Just making conversation.'

'What about you? You married?'

Oscar's headshake was just a tremor. 'Never. You?'

'Nope.'

'Kids?'

Cassy left a long pause. 'One. Years ago.'

'Ah. Sorry. Emotional minefield. I should shut up.'

'It's alright. I don't talk about him enough.'

'Did you lose him?'

'In a way. His father stole him from me. I haven't seen him since he was three years old.'

'That's dreadful, Cassy.' Oscar left a polite pause. 'What age would he be now?'

Cassy rolled over and didn't respond. For a minute she busied herself extracting her cold limbs from her bag and quickly pulling on some clothes. 'These guys we're meeting, how do you know them?'

'In a professional capacity. I've worked with them for years now. And their fathers before them. It's a long-established family business.'

'And you're certain they know what happened to the bones of the *Jacobite Alien*?'

'Oh, absolutely.'

'Okay', said Cassy, walking to the window and rubbing condensation off a small pane of glass. 'Coffee first, then I'm going outside to run around in the snow.'

Oscar watched the Tullen girl wading through the foot-deep snow, hurling dusty handfuls in the air and making ineffectual snowballs because the grains of ice were too cold to stick together.

After a while, Oscar called out. 'You never asked me.'

The girl stopped running and stood panting as her breath crystalized in the air. 'Asked you what?'

'Apart from checking my marital status, you didn't invite me to tell you something about myself. Don't you think that's rude?'

Cassy shrugged. 'Sorry. I was barely awake. I didn't realise you wanted a deep and meaningful.'

'Well, are you?'

'Am I what?'

'Going to ask?'

The Tullen girl folded her arms across her chest. 'Fine. Why don't you tell me something about yourself?'

Oscar nodded thoughtfully. 'Today's a big anniversary for me.'

'Oh, yeah?'

'Fifty years ago today, my family died.'

Her mouth dropped open. 'That's awful. I'm so sorry.'

Oscar shrugged. 'All three of them. On the same day.'

'Gosh. I can see now why you wanted to talk about it.' Cassy paused. 'How did they die, if you don't mind me asking?'

Oscar pointed at nearby Ben Macdui, its peak shrouded in a passing snow shower. 'My parents died up there. They died trying to save me.'

'My gosh. You must only have been a kid.'

'I was nine. Would you like another coffee?'

'Looks like we need to wait some so, yeah, please.' Cassy stopped messing around and came to stand by Oscar. 'What was your family doing out here?'

'My folks were keen walkers, always had been. We were following one of the recognised trails when the weather turned bad.' Satisfied the Trangia stove was now warming nicely, filling the cold air with billows of steam, Oscar carried on. 'There was another family walking that day, but they abandoned us when I got too cold to walk. My dad was a reliable navigator and knew these hills better than any of us. He decided we should hole up in one of the storm shelters, so he gathered me in his arms, and we walked and walked.'

'What happened?' Cassy asked.

Oscar glanced back at her. 'We never found the shelter. My parents did what any loving father and mother would do; they formed a shield around me with their bodies.'

'Oh, that's awful.'

For a brief second, there was warmth in remembering. 'You won't know this, but my dad used to call me, Oscar.'

'Okay.'

'It was his pet name for me.'

'It's cool. Why did your dad call you that?'

Oscar shrugged. 'I loved acting ever since I was tiny. In fact, I still help an amateur dramatics society in Stirling. When I was a kid, my dad told me that someday I'd star in a big film and win an Oscar, and over the years the nickname stuck.'

'It's obviously important to you. Does anybody nowadays still call you that?'

'A few. I still use it as a pen name when I'm acting, or if I'm blogging, or as a codename when I'm doing a little work on the side. You know. Off-the-book stuff.'

'I get it', said Cassy. 'A little anonymity. And a nice way to remember your father.'

Oscar sighed. 'The nicest thing would be to live in a family again. Doesn't look like that's gonna happen.'

The Tullen girl had stopped having fun and stood rubbing her hands together in her blood-red mittens. 'What happened to your brother?'

'He went for help. To be precise, he headed for this bothy', Oscar said, pointing at the stone hut. 'But by then, they'd left it too late. His body was found … around about where you're standing.'

Something dark crossed the Tullen girl's face as if she'd started to realise her presence here wasn't an accident. And perhaps the circumstances weren't benign. 'And is that why we're here? Because of this anniversary?' she asked.

'It is.'

Her face rucked into a frown. 'Meaning, it's nothing to do with recovering the bones of the *Jacobite Alien*?'

Feeling a little shame for the deception, Oscar turned away. 'Those bones won't be seen again.'

'How can you be certain?'

'Because they remind me of something very dark. So, I decided to burn them. I used the Lossuary incinerator and left it to cool before I reported the theft.'

The Tullen girl threw out her hands. 'For goodness sake, why?'

'That doesn't concern you.'

The Tullen girl now looked deeply unsettled. She thrust out her face and chest and shouted, 'Why am I here then? What the hell does any of this have to do with me?'

Oscar didn't feel like explaining. This wasn't about Cassy Tullen. It concerned the promise a nine-year-old child made on a mountain, cocooned amongst the frozen bodies of her family. None of the other kills had known why they were singled out. That they were substitutes for their parent's debt.

'All you need to know, Cassy, is that I established a covenant the day my family died. I promised each of them that I would find out who was responsible, and I'd make them pay.'

'Responsible?' spat the Tullen girl. 'Your father took his young family to the top of Britain's second-highest mountain in November. That's culpability right there!'

Oscar's eyes flicked in the direction of two walkers, making their way into the southern mouth of the Lairig Ghru, and just about to pass the footbridge leading to the bothy. The Tullen girl noticed too and immediately started to back away. Suddenly alert to the danger she was in, she reached up with both arms and turned to yell at the distant walkers. The walkers stopped, and hearing cries for help, they picked up the pace as they crossed the footbridge. As the Tullen girl started to run towards them, Oscar followed, confidently striding through the snow.

'That woman is threatening me', said Cassy, breathlessly as she reached the two men. Both were in their early forties with thick beards, one red, one black, and both flecked with ice.

Oscar stopped and faced the three figures as they in turn stopped and faced her. Finally, the thrill of the chase brought a trickle of excitement. But … only if the next few seconds played out according to the plan. Oscar took a deep breath.

'Mick? Monty? Nice to finally meet you guys face to face.'

'Wasn't in the plan', growled the black-bearded one in a Glasgow drawl. 'This business has had a rule for thirty years. We never lay eyes on each other.'

'Sorry', said Oscar, pointing at Cassy. 'But this girl is a live one, no pun intended. She rather got away from me.'

It took a few more seconds for the Tullen girl to realise she'd been duped and belatedly she tried to dash away. But the dark-bearded guy was ready for her and a swift kick to one of the girl's ankles sent her sprawling in the snow.

'Grab her, Micky', he said.

Mick leaned down to grasp the girl's arms behind her back, while Monty, walked up to Oscar and leaned deep into her personal space. 'We said, no faces. Not now. Not ever.'

'It was an accident', said Oscar, throwing up her hands in mock despair. 'Look, just do what you came here to do, then you can be on your way.'

'And after?'

Oscar shrugged. 'I'll do what I came to do. And then … we'll carry on as normal.' Swallowing nervously, Oscar hoped Monty didn't see. Perhaps the man realised that Oscar seeing his face had been no accident. By finally setting eyes of the Drumchapel crew, this was in effect, a signature on her own death warrant. But there was still the hope they'd follow through on their deal first.

Monty continued to stare. In the face of a kinder man, his dark eyes would have been appealing. In Monty's face, they presented the gaze of a calculating predator.

'Okay', he said at last. 'Then afterwards, we merry three need to have a wee talk.'

He took a step back from Oscar and drew a hunting knife from a sheath strapped somewhere about his abdomen. 'As you claim to be so squeamish, you might want to look away.'

Oscar nodded. 'Yeah, gimme a second. I don't mind after, but this part of the job leaves me cold.'

Turning around, Oscar started to walk back to the bothy. The Tullen girl meanwhile had recovered her senses sufficiently to register what was about to happen to her. With her face still half buried in the snow, she started to kick and squeal. Oscar started to walk faster. As a pathologist, the dead were never a problem. But for personal reasons; for reasons pertinent to this mountain, this same professional couldn't bear to be around when someone passed from life to death. It took two minutes to get back to the bothy door where one last glance back at Mick and Monty, confirmed they both now crouched over the Tullen girl, waiting for Oscar to finally step out of sight. Sighing, Oscar stepped inside the bothy. It was obvious that once they were done with the Tullen girl, Oscar would be next. Tipping the rucksack upside down, Oscar unwrapped the Glock 19 from its hiding place. It wouldn't be enough to keep the Drumchapel crew at bay forever, but if it was as convincing here as it was on stage of the Stirling Art Centre, then it might buy her a day or two. Time enough to deal with the Tullen girl. Time enough to fulfil this covenant.

Chapter 39

Lillico came off the phone to the Police Scotland control centre, fretting about how the next hour would play out. There was only one helicopter available in the Central Belt at short notice. A weather-beaten AW159 Wildcat – an old gunship recently retired from the British Army. It had been rebadged and refitted, and was due to be transferred to HM Coastguard. Arriving at Dundee airport, it touched down long enough to collect Gill, Lillico and his two-man armed response team.

'Detective. Explain why we've a civilian on board?' demanded the senior firearms officer.

'Essential intelligence' replied Lillico, ignoring the man's tone. 'If the hostage isn't where we think she is, then Mr McArdle will be helping me figure out what we do next.' He nodded at Gill as if to reiterate this and saw again how exhausted Gill appeared. If things turned nasty at the bothy, he hoped Gill would have the resources to deal with it.

'Okay, but we still can't deploy. I'm waiting for authorisation.'

Lillico held up his phone. 'Just came in.'

The officer glanced at his own phone and then looked at his colleague. 'Okay then. Use of force is authorised.' He glanced again at Gill, as if willing Lillico to change his mind.

'Can someone confirm exactly where we're going', said the pilot over the intercom.

'Corrour bothy at the south end of the Lairig Ghru', said Lillico. 'Immediate threat to life.'

'Beth will hear us a mile away', said Gill to no one in particular.

'If you want me to mask our approach', said the pilot, 'I can help with that.'

'Anything you can do', said Lillico, slamming the door closed. 'Let's go.'

Gill had never been in a helicopter before. He watched as the ground receded, then the aircraft pitched forward, and with a burst of acceleration it roared out over the River Tay and headed for the sea.

'Our flight plan takes us up the east coast, then inland north and west from Stonehaven', said the pilot over the intercom. 'We'll hug the mountains and enter the Lairig Ghru from the north end. I estimate we will be arriving at the target area in 25 minutes. When we arrive, we will threat-assess before touching down. Is that understood?'

'You suggested you can bolster our element of surprise?' quizzed Lillico.

There was a muffled conversation as the pilots conferred on tactics. Moments later, the senior pilot came back on. 'Leave that one to us.'

'If you people need to talk, you can switch to a private channel', said the co-pilot.

Gill nodded at Lillico, who met his gaze and nodded back. They had no idea what was waiting for them. Or whether it was already too late. On both of his last two visits to Macdui, Gill had faced supernatural opposition. When he'd surveyed the old gunship as it touched down, he'd noticed it had been stripped of its external weaponry. He wasn't sure it would have done them any good, but he rather wished it was all still in place.

Lost in his own thoughts Gill watched the Angus coastline rush below as the helicopter climbed to five hundred metres. Soon they were over rural Aberdeenshire and Gill felt his heart beating hard in his chest as he saw the Cairngorm mountains loom up rapidly on the port side. The helicopter climbed again, speeding over a forest fringe towards the Aviemore Ski Centre. Banking right as it followed the foot of the mountains it soon took a sharp left turn as it passed over the Chalamain Gap at low altitude. Now, lying before them, almost straight, and thirty kilometres long, the Lairig Ghru, filled their forward view.

'Two minutes', said the pilot.

Gill's stomach leapt somewhere inside him as the nose of the craft tilted lower, and the engine pitch increased. He'd walked this, the longest, deepest glen in Scotland, with Craig a few weeks before, and it had taken them all afternoon. Today, the same landscape flashed by him in seconds. The high valley walls seemed to devour them as the pilot eased his altitude down to one hundred metres until Gill felt they were scraping the valley floor. He stared into the gap between the pilots and out at the terrain. He knew this was a wide U-shaped valley and remarkably straight. But the craft was so low, the canyon walls screamed past the side windows. To anyone on the ground below, the noise must be deafening. And their sound wave would reach the bothy only a few moments ahead of them. What would they do then? Touch down, or engage Cassy's captor from the air? At this point, it was a cloud of unknowns.

Lillico caught Gill's attention again and tapped his mic, but Gill just shook his head.

'Safeties off', said the senior firearms officer, rather matter-of-factly. And all around them, the valley walls roared past them in a blur.

'Fifteen seconds' said the pilot. 'Stand by for air-brake manoeuvre.'

'Used to fly these things in the army', said the co-pilot to no one in particular. 'This feels like the good old days.'

And suddenly, the bothy was in sight, crouched at the foot of a mountain called 'Devil's Point.' Beyond it, the Lairig Ghru emptied into a wider open valley bathed with inviting sunlight.

The engine pitch roared again, then eased as the pilot air-braked over the bothy and spun the craft clockwise so those on board could survey the scene. To Gill's horror, he could see the prone body of one person, while a second and third faced off against each other, oblivious to the arriving craft.

Two minutes earlier, winded and dazed after falling hard, Cassy was only catching snatches of conversation between her abductor and the new arrivals. Her ankles burned where she'd been kicked, and her head was spinning. Partly because of her fall, and in part because one of the brutes had his knee pressed below her shoulder blades. He clasped her hands together and forced them into the small of her back. She tried wriggling a few times, but nothing budged in his vice grip. Forcing herself, unnaturally, to relax, she focused on her breathing, using all her energy to suck in air. Another snatch of conversation passed which she didn't quite hear. And then bizarrely, a couple of minutes of inexplicable silence when nobody spoke. The pressure on her back eased a fraction and she was able to breathe more deeply.

'What do you want to do?' said the man leaning on her.

'It's simple', the other guy replied in a low voice. 'Oscar's seen us now, so we need to get rid of her.'

'Shite, man. She's the best cleaner we've ever had. How do we do business without her?'

'We agreed the rules. We start bending them now, that's the beginning of the end, my friend.' He sniffed. 'There'll be other cleaners.'

'Maybe. But not like Oscar.'

But Monty sounded impatient. 'Are we still discussing this? Oscar is one of the few people who could rip the lid off our business. No way I'm risking that. Okay, Micky?'

Mick coughed in the cold air and spat. 'Okay then. But don't moan to me when the day comes and we've a freezer full of product and no one to shift it.'

Monty just grunted. 'I'll sort Oscar. You fix that one.'

Cassy heard the crunch of snow as Monty moved off in the direction of the bothy. Then after a few steps, he paused. 'You hear that?'

'Hear what?' said Mick.

Moments later there was a roar overhead as if a Typhoon jet had thundered down the glen, twenty metres above the ground. Mick swore as they were hit by a blast of cold air, and for a fraction of a second, he lifted his knee from between Cassy's shoulder blades. She knew immediately it would be her only chance.

Chapter 40

The roar and air-rush of the aircraft almost took Mick off his feet. As his grip slackened, Cassy spun from her front onto her back, forcing her captor onto his knees. For a moment, he straddled her, and their eyes met in a moment of terrible intimacy. If Mick was caught out by this, Cassy was not. Death had come for her, but she wasn't going without a fight. As Mick found his balance again, Cassy's right knee came up with such force into the man's groin that he pitched over her shoulder and fell on top of her, face-first into the snow. In as long as it took Mick to gasp in agony, she'd pushed him away and was already on her feet.

Above them, the copter spun in a circle and roared back towards them, descending as if it was about to land. But Cassy ignored it. If there was help on board, it was coming too late to save her from Monty.

Monty spun around, his blade already in his hand. He glowered at Mick who was bellowing in the snow. Then glanced at the copter slowly coming down to land. And finally, he looked at her.

Cassy stood and faced Monty. She shuffled a little on her feet to check her stance, then forced her arms and shoulders to relax. Monty didn't have time to hunt her, and she didn't have the strength to run. If he still meant her harm, Monty would charge at her. She'd lost her mittens during the fight, so she flexed her fingers, trying to force some feeling into her frozen hands. And then she waited.

Monty's charge closed the gap between them in three terrifying seconds.

Dropping her left shoulder as she flung her right foot backwards in an arc, with her left arm rising in front of her as a counterbalance, she leaned back just far enough to avoid the thrust of Monty's blade. A fraction of a second later, as the man's right arm passed in front of her, Cassy's body movement still spinning to follow the arc of her right foot, synced with her attacker. Harnessing his momentum and gripping his extended arm just at the moment she planted her right foot, forcing Monty to trip over her. The result wasn't tidy, but it met the needs of the moment as Monty crashed onto his side, eyes wide in alarm.

Switching both hands to grip the wrist on his extended arm, Cassy stood over him, the blade in his hand pressed flat against her abdomen. The fall had winded him. But she knew if she didn't press her advantage, he'd be on his feet again in a flash. So, she pulled his arm straight and twisted it with all her might.

The blade sprung free as Monty screamed in pain.

As the copter touched down, it tossed snow in the air for a full thirty seconds. When the pilot finally gave the all-clear, the armed officers exited by separate doors and ran in a crouching posture with weapons raised towards the figures on the ground. Gill made to follow them, but Lillico grabbed his shoulder. Tearing free of him, Gill spilt out into the snow and followed the guns. The air was still full of ice blown up by the copter and from a distance of fifty metres, he could only see one person standing.

'Hands!' yelled the lead officer. 'Hands where we can see them.'

Ahead of them, a diminutive female figure in a coat that was probably one size too big for her, raised her hands in the air.

'Cassy', shouted Gill, as he ran ahead of the armed response. He sprinted the last few metres and threw his arms around her. The officers meanwhile fanned out left and right to cover the two prone figures.

'Are you hurt?'

'I … no, I don't think so.'

Gill could feel her shaking in his arms. Even as he gripped her, the shaking got worse.

'I … I don't feel very well', she said, slithering away from him a few steps, falling into an untidy crouch, coughing and retching.

One of the pilots had emerged from the copter with a revolver at the ready.

'Blankets', shouted Gill, and the man nodded and turned. A minute later, he was draping a fleece over her shoulders and a crash blanket over the top of that.

'What happened?' he asked.

'They tried to kill me', Cassy mumbled, after a pause. 'Thought I'd be scared. Then I remembered … You can't hurt someone who already feels dead.'

'Cassy?' said Gill, moving to embrace her.

But she held up her hands and pushed away from him. He watched her stagger to a nearby rock, where she sat down, and sat with her arms wrapped around her face for the next fifteen minutes.

Looking red-eyed and drained, Gill finally coaxed Cassy into the relative shelter of the bothy and pressed a mug of coffee into her hands. Lillico and the firearms officer were in conference with one of the pilots. Beth sat sullenly in a corner, her hands bound behind her back. The Glock had been secured and the junior officer held it in an evidence bag.

'You're lucky we didn't shoot you', said the firearms office. 'Waving a fake gun around like that.'

'I wish you had', said Beth.

Setting eyes on Beth, Cassy started to lurch towards her, her left fist slowly drawing back.

'Wait', said Gill, realising what was about to happen. 'We have her now.'

'And someday, the Tullens will pay', said Beth weakly.

'Yeah?' spat Cassy. 'Bring it on, bitch.'

'Whoa', said Lillico gently, before inserting himself in Cassy and Beth's line of sight. 'Let me get a few details from you, then the Wildcat crew are going to get you and Gill off this mountain. Cassy? Can you do that for me?'

Cassy lifted her gaze from his chest to his face and unclenched her teeth. 'Yeah.'

'The two guys outside', said Lillico looking at Cassy. 'They tried to hurt you?'

'Yes.'

'Kill you?'

'That was their plan.'

'So what did you do?'

Cassy's eyes flitted to the ceiling and a flicker of a smile crossed her face. 'Trained in taekwondo at High School. Nothing very clever – I was trying to impress a boy. Which was pointless really because I … I … I …' Cassy stumbled as her reminisces ran out of road.

'You took them both down?' pressed Lillico. 'With martial arts you learned as a schoolgirl?'

'When I do anything', Cassy hissed, pausing to wipe her nose, 'I aim to be the best. Got a problem with that?'

Lillico lifted his hands. 'I believe you. Just tell me a little of what happened?'

Cassy nodded, her eyes fixed on Lillico as a frown spread across her face. 'The second guy, the one with the knife. I dislocated his arm. Or broke it. I don't really give a damn. And the first one? Yeah, I think his baby-making days are behind him.'

'They're both in a bad way', said the firearms officer. 'Their injuries aren't life-threatening, but they're both in extreme pain.'

'No rush then', said Cassy gripping her coffee.

'Gill', said Lillico. 'You said you've seen those men before?'

Gill nodded. 'They tried to kill me six months ago when I was working on the Isle of May.'

'Okay', said Lillico. 'I'll read them their rights, then I'll place them in custody. We can sort all this out in Bathgate once we're all warm and dry.'

From outside the bothy, came the sound of a slower, heavier craft.

'Too many of us for our little ship', said the pilot. 'We've called in one of the heavy lifts.'

Gill steered Cassy towards the door before turning to Lillico. 'Coming?'

'I need to wait here for the Crime Scene folks', he answered.

'Okay', said Gill. 'Cass. Let's go.'

'Wait, Cassy', said Lillico, suddenly.

'What?' snapped Cassy.

Lillico had started to bite his lower lip, his eyes flicking around the other faces in the room. He shook some tension out of his body and took a breath. 'You did great today.'

Cassy's pause was painful for everyone in the room. 'Thanks, Alex. And really? Part of me wishes they'd won.'

Chapter 41

George Wiley sat scowling at a mug of tea while Lillico shuffled papers in front of him, referring back and forth between sheets of numbers and his laptop. He'd decided the conference room in Bathgate nick was bigger and better equipped than his last posting, but didn't like it because the view was "crap".

'Any time you're ready, *Sergeant*', Wiley said with emphasis. No doubt he resented being back in the nick on a Saturday.

'Got somewhere to be, sir?'

'Yeah, Lillico. On Saturday mornings, I normally coach the Corstorphine girls, under-fives polo team. Just bloody get on with it.'

Lillico's eyes glanced up from his computer to Wiley then back again. 'Sorry, sir. Got quite complicated in the end.'

'We only have four more hours to charge her, or our apprentice dentist is gonna walk.'

Lillico didn't look up, smiling instead as he finished his prep. 'Don't worry, sir. It won't come to that.'

'Well, you see, Alec …'

'Alex. Sir.'

'Alex. Sure. You see, I'm a little concerned your wee stunt in the mountains was an attempt to bag the limelight.'

'Not my style, sir.'

'Going solo like that …'

'There was an immediate threat to life. After our last case review, I realised you'd cracked it, sir. There always was a link between some of the victims. But not them all. That's what threw us. You correctly deduced there were two motives at play.'

Wiley blinked a few times. 'Aye, well … I could feel we were getting close. The randomness of the killings did appear to be the work of contract killers. But the teeth? They convinced me there was a motive beyond money.'

'Exactly, and of course, once Mhairi cracked the logic behind the victims selected by Beth, or Oscar, as she's known to the Drumchapel crew, the path led to the door of her final intended victim.'

'And we're sure Beth was paying for these hits by acting as a "cleaner" for the Drumchapel gang?'

'That's the way it's looking. We've traced Beth's digital footprint and there is no sign of any financial incentive.'

'And how many victims in the end?'

'Six descendants of the original Cairngorm Committee that demolished the shelters, but hard to say about the rest. The teeth give us at least nineteen more, but we may never know.'

Wiley nodded and stared down at the table. 'Bloody hell.'

'This is a huge case, sir', Lillico whispered. 'You're going to get masses of press attention.'

Wiley nodded quickly and self-consciously reached up to straighten his tie. 'The question we need to answer before we charge her is, how was she disposing of the bodies?'

'That's what I've been working on. But I've got most of it now.'

'Please, tell me. Before I get old and grey.'

'Beth worked as a contractor. She spent most of her working week with Police Scotland and its predecessor forces. But she also did evening and weekend work at two universities attached to teaching hospitals.'

'And?'

'Teaching hospitals use human cadavers to train new doctors. Once in the system, the bodies are opened up, operated on, and eventually, most are dissected.'

'That's disgusting.'

'Only way to do it, sir. And wholly necessary for educating our next generation of doctors. And it gave Beth an opportunity. You see, when someone who has donated their body to science dies, the respective university has to act quickly to repurpose the corpse into something ready for the students to work on.'

'I'm sure there's a queue all the way to the bakers to do a job like that.'

'Exactly. These anatomists have to be highly trained, empathetic to relatives of the deceased and yet have the emotional detachment to treat the expired human body as a training tool.'

'You're saying that Beth drip-fed her victims into anatomy laboratories?'

'That's what I've found, yes.'

'But you can't just turn up in a van and unload a body in the middle of the night? Someone would notice.'

'Indeed. There are consent forms to be signed and checked. And when the donor dies, there are procedures. Phone numbers to be called. Technicians on duty in the event of a call out.'

'And you know how she got past that lot?'

'I do. It's simply that she had time on her side. We can talk to her in a minute about why she did the things she did, but what's clear is, she'd been preparing this for a very long time.'

'How long?'

'She started forging consent forms as far back as the early 90's. Gradually she built up a portfolio of fake donors with a spread of profiles. People of different ages and genders. When she got a body, she'd match it to one of her dummy profiles and set the wheels in motion.'

'But all those other checks?'

'She obviously made sure the bodies only became available on nights when she was on duty. I suspect when we dig around some more, we'll find she had access to a cold store of some kind. Or maybe her Glasgow "suppliers" handled that aspect. Once she had a body and a date for processing, she would make an emotional call to a university on a burner phone. This alerted the anatomy department about the death of a "donor", and of course, only on the nights when Beth was on duty to go pick up the body. After that, it was just a question of whether the resulting cadavers were kept in one piece, or if their profile wasn't ideal, meaning they had to be …'

'Broken up for parts', finished Wiley.

'Either way', said Lillico, 'She had to prevent accidental identification. Fingerprints, tattoos and of course …'

'Teeth', whispered Wiley.

Lillico nodded.

'But why keep the teeth? Why risk attracting attention? It's what did for her in the end.'

'An offering to her family's memory? Paying the mountain? Guilt – a plea to be caught?' Lillico speculated. 'We can ask, but I doubt we'll ever get an answer.'

Wiley blew out his cheeks, letting the scale of Beth's deception wash over him. Then he leaned over and rapped the nearest stack of papers with his knuckles. 'And you're sure you can prove this?'

Lillico nodded. 'It will take a forensic analyst months to unravel it all. Perhaps longer if we have to sample all the body parts stored in local universities. But I've got enough data points to persuade a judge what her game was.'

Wiley slowly shook his head. 'This is bloody good work, Alex.'

'Thank you, sir.'

'I just hope she doesn't try to mitigate her crimes by pleading insanity.'

'Given the high degree of planning over many years, I doubt that plea would stick, sir.'

Wiley surprised him by reaching across the table and offering Lillico his hand. 'When we're on our own, you can drop the formality. Just call me, George.'

'Thank you ... George.'

Wiley pulled back and stood up. 'Shall we go catch a killer, Alex?'

Lillico smiled and gathered up his papers. He was just following his boss towards the door when Wiley stopped abruptly. 'And while we're having this cosy little chat, can I just add one tiny thing?'

'Sure, George. Go for it.'

Wiley snarled over his shoulder. 'Don't you ever spend six F-ing grand of my budget on a helicopter ride, ever again. Not without asking me first.'

'You realise we could do a Zoom call, or meet in an office like normal people', muttered Gill as George Wiley strolled up, hands in pockets and twenty minutes late for their Sunday afternoon appointment. The bright November sunshine, which had briefly washed over Edinburgh's Princes Street Gardens like a cleansing balm was surrendering to a cloud of approaching rain. The pleasant weather didn't compensate for the fact that he'd sacrificed a big chunk of his afternoon to be here in person.

'You know me', said Wiley, pulling on a fag. 'Always a sucker for fresh air.'

'No Lillico today?'

'Nah, in the light of his hard work, I gave him a couple of days off.'

'I wasn't sure about him at first', said Gill. 'But now I've worked with Alex, I can see he's a handy guy to have around.'

Wiley drew on his cigarette while he thought about this. 'Aye, it's looking like it.'

'So, Detective Chief Inspector. As much as I enjoy our little get-togethers, I assume this isn't a social call?'

Wiley nodded. 'I wanted to let you know that Mick and Monty Galloway have been formally charged with six counts of murder as part of the *Toothfairy* case.'

'Only six?'

'Those are the ones I can prove without any doubt. We might charge them with more at a later stage.'

'Right.'

'And they'll also be tried for the attempted murder of Cassy Tullen, in November of this year and Gillan McArdle, on the May Isle in March.'

'Glad to hear that', said Gill, giving a satisfied nod. 'What about Mick's daughter, Lillian?'

'Although she part of the group that attacked you on the May Isle, I don't have enough to give her anything more than a slap on the wrist. We're gonna have to leave her in play.'

Gill gritted his teeth for a moment, then resolved to look on the bright side. 'Maybe after this, she'll choose a different path.'

'Maybe she will', said Wiley, stopping to clear his throat. 'Suffice to say, I wanted to thank you for your assistance. DS Lillico says your team provided valuable skills.'

'Thank you. I'll pass that on to Mhairi. She did a great job.'

'That means all reporting restrictions are lifted. You're welcome to write about the *Toothfairy* case in any way you see fit.'

Gill nodded. He hadn't expected that. And while he couldn't offer Tony Farquharson the bones of a human/alien hybrid, he could now present the inside story on the biggest news item in Scotland. It would mean a dash to the finish on issue 29 if they were to add new material, but at least he had the best team in the business. For now.

'Though, it might be prudent to run any articles you write past Lillico', Wiley continued. 'If there are sensitivities or anything that might prejudice our trial, he'll be the man to spot it.'

'I can live with that', said Gill. 'And trust me. I don't want to publish anything that might allow those butchers to get off.'

'We're agreed then, which brings me to the next thing.'

'What thing?'

'Our new case.'

'Hang on a second. What happened to your pitch about me doing you a one-time favour?'

Wiley smirked and tossed away his cigarette. 'Look at it this way. As the head of *Special Investigations*, I'm gonna get a lot of weird shit across my desk. You'll benefit by association.'

'George. One of my best and dearest people was almost killed on this job. Why, under heaven, would I ever want to work with you again?'

'Because', said Wiley, 'I've got a cracker for you.'

'I can't imagine any circumstances under which I'd take another case from you people.'

Wiley brushed his knuckles against Gill's elbow. 'Walk with me a minute. If you're not intrigued, you can slink away.'

Gill peered into Wiley's eyes, almost buried in the fleshy layers of the man's face. It wasn't a pleasant experience, but he did see sincerity. Better still, he felt a tug somewhere in his subconscious. That vague, in-between place where his faith and his instinct reached beyond the veil.

'Okay, George. You've got twenty minutes before I get on a tram to meet my fiancée off her flight. Tell me what you've got.'

Six hours after Wiley met Gill in Edinburgh, Chief Superintendent Macfarlane lingered in the car park at Ratho Bridge. He resented being called out on a Sunday and Lillico being fifteen minutes late wasn't helping his mood.

'About bloody time', he huffed to himself, as Lillico's unmarked squad car drew up and parked facing him.

The earlier showers that had rumbled off and on all afternoon had now consolidated into a proper thundery downpour, so Macfarlane flashed his lights to alert Lillico he should come over.

Nothing happened for a few seconds until Lillico's lights flashed back at him.

'Stupid bugger', he spat, flicking his lights long and hard enough for this junior officer to have no doubt about his intentions.

Again, a short delay and then Lillico's lights flashed back at him. And still, he didn't come.

Macfarlane swore, and drawing his collar around his neck, stepped out of his car and splashed through puddles to reach Lillico's passenger door. He stepped in and angrily slammed it shut.

'What the hell …', he began, stopping when the driver turned around to face him.

'Chief Super!', said Wiley, sounding like he was feigning surprise. 'Sorry, but DC Lillico … my apologies, … DS Lillico was unavoidably detained. When he said he was meeting a contact, I thought he meant a snotty little grass from Sighthill.' He smiled an ugly smile. 'But I should have known when I saw your motor.'

Macfarlane made ready to leave again. 'This is a personal matter between me and your DS.'

'But while you're here, sir', said Wiley. I wanted to thank you for setting me up with *Special Investigations*. I think you'll agree, it's a fair match to my unique skills.'

'Yes. I mean … you did a fine job closing the *Toothfairy* case. That one could have run and run.'

'Been chained to my computer all day', Wiley continued. 'Answering messages of congratulations.' He swung his hands in a dramatic flourish. 'Yeah, I really seem to have found my niche with this one.'

This time Macfarlane did get as far as opening the door, rain immediately finding its way through the crack and onto his face. 'Well done, DCI Wiley. Carry on.'

'Was there something you wanted to talk to Lillico about?' Wiley bobbed his shoulders. 'Any little message you wanted me to pass on?'

Macfarlane thought desperately. 'I wanted to thank him for giving evidence in DI Mackinnon's trial. We got the right result and I know it wasn't easy for him.' He stepped out of the car and then as an afterthought added. 'He's a brave man your DS. Maybe a little too brave, do you think?'

'And wedded to the truth, sir', said Wiley. 'Either it will be the end of him …'

'And wouldn't that be unfortunate', said Macfarlane.

'And of course, if the job doesn't kill him …' Wiley continued. 'We'll probably end up working for him.'

Macfarlane winced, then slammed the door. He'd be damned if the day ever came when he'd report to Alexander Lillico. Not after this little stunt.

Chapter 42

The team endured a hard start to the week making changes to the magazine without Cassy's guiding hand. After a couple of days in London, Tony Farquharson returned to the office on Wednesday morning and immediately caught Gill's eye. Four days had passed since the Lairig Ghru clash and Gill was busy. Reluctant to be dragged away from his desk, he lingered in Tony's doorway and declined the offer of a seat.

'How's Cassy?' Tony asked, unpacking his briefcase.

'Recovering', said Gill. 'She called this morning and said she'd be in this afternoon.'

'Ask her to come and see me. I'd like to offer her any support I can.'

Gill nodded and made to move away. But Tony wasn't finished.

'I'm seeing frenetic activity in the *Mys.Scot* pen. Care to give me an update?'

'We're rejigging issue 29 to pull in material on the Krankie dig.'

'Is this your *better-than-a-waterhorse* archaeological find? The one you still haven't told me about?'

Gill considered his response for a second. 'No. That turned out to be a dead end.'

'What's causing all the excitement?'

'We have a big crime story. Mhairi's desk research was the breakthrough that caught the *Toothfairy*, and now we have permission to publish some details.'

Tony immediately brightened. 'That's awesome, Gill. But hang on. Is Cassy okay with this?'

'She won't be mentioned by name.'

'Still, we should run this by legal.'

'Already done', said Gill. 'Check your emails; it's all there.'

'Thanks.' Tony paused. 'I'm sensing a little irritation, Gill. Are we having a falling out?'

'No, Tony. I'm just a little disappointed.'

Tony folded his arms. 'What's the problem?'

'Your golfing buddy. The one who fast-tracked us onto the Krankie dig. You must have realised I'd be curious?'

'Ah', said Tony.

'And while Roddy Canmore is no longer part of the Scottish Government, a dozen keystrokes in Google reveals that he now sits on Transport Scotland's Highway Committee.'

'It was just a lead for a story, Gill. He's been trying to kiss and make-up ever since that bust-up around his father.'

'But after the things he said about us? How can you possibly trust him?'

'Yes, he's a bully. But you let him get to you. And at the end of the day, you run a magazine, but I have to run a business. That means shaking hands with people I don't always like.'

'Could we agree, for the future, we're not going to take any more jobs from him?'

'It was just a dig, Gill. In the end, everyone came home safely.'

'Just a dig, Tony. Where we worked side by side with a serial killer for three weeks. Three weeks when Cassy was vulnerable.'

'That was a coincidence, Gill.'

'No such thing.'

'Well, I don't see how Canmore could have known. It wasn't as if he was in league with Beth Peyton.'

'It makes me wonder where Roddy gets his information. And who he's taking orders from.'

'What are you suggesting?'

Gill shrugged. 'Just speculating.' He tapped the door frame with his knuckles. 'Can I get back to work, boss? Lots to do.'

Tony flicked his chin. 'One last thing. About the dig.'

'Yes?'

'There was a rumour going around. You know what this place is like.' Tony paused to form his words. 'There was a suggestion ... somebody seemed to think you'd found bones ... indeed, the full skeleton ... of an alien.'

Gill couldn't suppress a wide smile. When Tony said out it loud like that, the very idea of the *Jacobite Alien* sounded so ridiculous.

'No. Don't worry about it', Tony continued after seeing Gill's face. 'Just someone having a laugh.'

Gill nodded and excused himself.

Back in the meagre privacy of his own workspace, Gill scanned around to make sure he wasn't being observed. Shielding his phone close to his body, he called up the remaining images of the *Jacobite Alien* and pondered what to do.

After her arrest, Lillico confirmed that Beth had used the Lossuary incinerator to burn the bones of the *Jacobite Alien*. And before she committed herself to the Lairig Ghru, Beth had deleted all her files on the subject, expunging everything on the official record. Now, it was as if the *Jacobite Alien* had never existed. What had motivated her to do that was unclear, though Gill could imagine a malign influence manipulating her to cover its tracks. Or was it simply that Sariel had haunted her in the same way he had tried to control Gill? That somehow, by burning the bones she was declaring her desire to be rid of him? Either way, Beth's decision had left Gill with only three crude photos, grabbed in haste on his own phone on the day the bones were discovered. And would they be enough to convince a sceptical world that he'd had in his possession the bones of a Nephilim? Him – Gill McArdle, with his unreliable methods? And even if he could persuade some part of his audience, what good would it do other than sell a bunch of magazines? Considering his decision carefully, he paused and practised Solomon's advice. Listen to the voice! So, he cleared his mind and asked the voice to speak.

After a few seconds he'd heard nothing, so he asked again.

And a third time.

This time, as he felt fingers drawing across his upper back, peace wrapping around his shoulders, like a soft towel laid upon a child emerging from the sea. Embracing him. Drying him. Telling him he's loved. And then, a woman's gentle voice behind his ear…

'Let Sariel's mongrel child rest in peace.'

The voice faded and with it, the embrace gently withdrew. And Gill was alone again.

Taking a deep breath, he deleted the photos, cleared his memory backup and purged the last physical record of the *Jacobite Alien* from history.

Then he sat for a moment, contemplating the consequences of his decision, and realised that ultimately, some stories were too dark to be told.

His debt of friendship towards Arnold Broadbent was another burden on his conscience. Typing him an email, Gill explained that the big story he'd been working on hadn't played out as he'd hoped. But he did have the results of a four-hundred-year-old field trial, experimenting with gunpowder as a preservative of organic materials. Results were in and there were thousands of photos to choose from. He pressed 'send' and fully expected Arnold to bite.

With that all done he contemplated what he should do next and was filled with a sad foreboding that life around *Mys.Scot* was going to get a lot harder. And it wasn't long before his friend and office manager asked for a private chat.

A few minutes later, and with a heavy heart, Gill followed Cassy into the conference room and gently closed the door.

Composing himself opposite her, he took a deep breath. 'What's up, Cass?'

'Sorry. I've not been myself these past few weeks.'

'Are you kidding? After everything you've been through …'

'No, Gill. Since before then. I've been out of sorts for a while.'

'You've been doing a great job. We're the best team in the business because you're in it.'

'Thing is, Gill. I've been thinking about Tony's offer and have decided I need to take some time out.'

'After what happened last week, you should take as long as you need.'

'No. More than that.'

Gill shifted his gaze from the table to her face. 'Is this you resigning?' he said, gently.

'No! Well, yes. Oh, I don't know. I just need to go and sort out my head.'

'Can I help?'

'Thank you. But I don't wanna talk about it.'

'I understand. When do you need to go?' He shrugged. 'For how long?'

Cassy looked away and for the first time in their three years together, Gill saw despair in her face.

'Answer to the first question is, immediately. The second answer is, I dunno.' Her eyes flicked up to his face. 'Sorry to leave you in the lurch. You've still got Mhairi.'

'We'll cope. I don't think she relishes doing your job but she's certainly competent.'

'I'll come back if I can. I promise.'

Gill's head had sunk, involuntarily onto the tabletop. Doing this job without Cassy was going to be a struggle. Pushing this unhappy thought to one side, he knew in his heart of hearts that his first duty was to his friend. Sitting up, he reached across and grasped her hands. 'Some things are bigger than work, Cass. Go and do what you need to do.'

'Thank you. Gimme a couple of months. I'll be in touch.'

Gill cleared his throat. 'Will you be suspending *Calum's Road*?'

'I need to chat to the girls, but yes, we're closed to new bookings.' She grimaced. 'Unless of course, they chuck me out of the band.'

'I gather you *are* the band', he said with emphasis. 'And without wanting to pressure you; you're *Mys.Scot* too.'

'I'm here 'til the close of issue 29. And I'll definitely be leading the gig on Saturday night.'

'You sure about that? I don't want to pressure you.'

'Definitely. My issues are slow burn rather than an instant disaster.'

'What are you going to do?'

Cassy looked down sadly at her hands. 'I need to go back to the last place where I was standing on solid ground. I'm going home to Raasey.'

Gill got slowly to his feet. 'Okay then. Let me give you a hug that leaves you in no doubt you're my friend. My life is better because you're in it. Quite simply, you're the best, Cass.'

Chapter 43

'Do we do it now?' said the little girl, looking up at Gill. She was beautiful, in the cream satin dress, adorned with a purple sash. Her twin sister's ribbon was red.

'Just a few more minutes, Esther', whispered Gill.

'Where did you find them?' asked Salina. 'They're gorgeous.'

'Alice Trevelyan's kids', said Gill. 'I'll introduce you later.'

He stared at Salina, spellbound by the life in her flashing eyes. On a work day, she was a woman whose lovely figure and natural poise meant she looked great in scruffy jeans and a hoody. Today she looked glorious in the cream silk wedding dress her mother and sisters had made for her.

Standing at the threshold of a barn door somewhere in rural Fife, Gill and Salina peered over the girls' heads into the light-filled room. Behind them, hay bales and the remains of an ancient tractor hinted that on most days of the week, this was still a working farm. On this Saturday evening, however, the old stone building had been transformed into something entirely different.

Salina grasped the back of his black tartan waistcoat and gave it a tug. 'Are you nervous?'

'Terrified', said Gill. 'Never been much of a dancer. Almost as bad as diving Loch Ness.'

'Not about that', she said. 'About life together?'

'What's to worry about?'

'I fly DSVs to huge depths for a living, and you make archaeology look like an extreme sport.'

He half turned to face her. 'You're saying, you don't see us growing old together? That's dark.'

'I'm not saying that. Just, with what I do, with what you do, and we look at the forces arrayed against us …'

'You're forgetting our secret weapon.'

'I'm not. Just saying, no one lives forever.'

He leaned across and kissed her. 'Day at a time, Sal. Let's enjoy every minute.'

'Do we do it now?' asked the girl with a red sash.

Gill crouched to talk to the twins. 'Any second now, Grace. Just hold on.' They were interrupted as the Ceilidh band struck up, demolishing the conversations around the room and signalling the evening was moving into a different phase. Gill had heard *Calum's Road* were good. He hadn't realised they were this good. As if sensing his surprise, Cassy looked across at him and winked. He stood up and smiled back at her, glad that for tonight, she could see past her troubles. But he couldn't help asking himself, if she'd been invited as a guest, rather than booked as a musician, would she have come? Either way, he was delighted she was here and looking amazing. For once, her trademark baggy shirt had been substituted with a stunning black dress.

Salina gave him a bruising nudge. 'A week ago, I was diving the Mississippi Delta. Suddenly I come home, and I'm married! Is this what's life going to be like with you?'

Gill stared at her with what he hoped were loving and serious eyes. 'Call me, "Mr Spontaneous" from now on.'

She laughed. 'With this level of catering? Not in your skillset, my love.'

'Your mum helped me plan it all. Bringing the wedding forward was something I discussed with your dad.'

She threw her hands out in protest. 'I was ambushed! Literally frog-marched down the aisle!'

'You were not! You smiled the whole darn way.'

For a second, Salina disappeared into herself, and Gill remembered the sacrifices Salina's parents had to make to pursue their own true love.

'Thanks for doing the whole traditional thing', she said, looking at her feet.

'I wouldn't call this traditional', said Gill, glancing around the makeshift dance hall. 'Although your dad and I briefly discussed doing it on a trawler.'

'A nautical theme! What happened to that lovely idea?'

'Your mum', said Gill, curtly.

Salina laughed. 'There's a woman you don't cross in a hurry.'

The band came to the end of their intro sequence and the alcohol-fuelled audience clapped enthusiastically.

Gill leaned over to whisper. 'Okay, girls. Go for it.'

Esther and Grace ran ahead of them, flinging flower petals in the air to create a cascade of reds, pinks and purples. With their baskets empty, they dashed to take up their positions at the edge of the improvised dance floor.

Cassy took the mic and yelled loud enough to wake the dead. 'Ladies and gentlemen, WE ARE, *Calum's Road*. AND this is our first dance. Please welcome … the bride and groom.'

Chapter 44

<u>Editor's comment – Mysterious Scotland, issue 29</u>

For this issue, Mys.Scot was invited to excavate part of the old battlefield site at Killiecrankie. During an exceptionally wet dig, we found the debris of war alongside the remains of the fallen. Evidence of man killing man. Brutal and ugly. And unfortunately, it was ever thus. Scotland's beautiful landscape has suffered battles ever since our ancestors evolved the dexterity to throw a spear.

During our survey, we stumbled across evidence of a serial killer in a case the newspapers are calling the Toothfairy. A terrible business that brought about the deaths of at least two dozen people. Some of those deaths were motivated by vengeance. Others no doubt by greed, cravings or misfortune. The case is complicated by the involvement of several parties and our coverage of these crimes will be limited so we don't prejudice this continuing investigation. Ultimately, we will leave the final judgment to a jury of our peers. But I'm left wondering what is happening to this country? When you try to picture a Scotsman, what do you see? A romanticized image of a strong man in a kilt? His eyes glistening with determination to do right by his family, clan and country? How then did the old virtues that underpinned our society erode so thoroughly? Did the kirk preach too long? Probably. Were our leaders and ministers found to be as frail and craven as the rest of us? Undoubtedly. Or is it simply that we're losing the ability to show a little care for our neighbours? I don't have all the answers and I suspect I never will.

In the search for some light relief, while working in Killiecrankie, I took the opportunity to do a little hill walking. Climbing Britain's second-highest peak, I found myself on Ben Macdui with another member of the Mys.Scot team. We tramped through mist to emerge at the top in brilliant sunlight – a rare treat! And the excitement didn't end there because, during our descent, we encountered a rare phenomenon known as the "Old Grey Man". According to folklore, this wraith accompanies struggling climbers during the moments when their lives hang in the balance, and its appearance has been recorded in the logs of many respected mountain men. Sometimes this apparition encourages the climbers, but more often than not, seeks to terrify them off the mountain. Of course, in our own enlightened times, we know these spectres can't be real. Their physical appearance is simply a trick of the light, where the walker's own shadow is projected onto a fog bank during a weather event called temperature inversion. And as for the psychological effects? Of course, these can be explained away by the stressful conditions; the isolation experienced on the mountain during a moment when one's life is at risk. And so, in experiencing the Old Grey Man, I found myself asking other questions. When I'm under pressure, do I lean towards rationalism or folklore? Do I look for explanations in science or the supernatural? Or in reality, to answer life's toughest questions, should I look to both?

During this busy month, all these issues have left me pondering. Man against man. Dogma over tolerance. Angels fighting demons, in our schools, workplaces and government. And however, you see this world, and whether you believe in the supernatural or not, it isn't hard to perceive Scotland as a battlefield between good and evil. Please hear me on this. I'm not standing in judgement on our nation, its leaders or its people. The words on this page are simply my grief. Why are we not a kinder, more tolerant, and ultimately, more prosperous community? Why do we tolerate any shadow cast over this beautiful land? Stand with me on any mountain top, or at the head of any glen, and you'll know. This Mysterious Scotland looks so much better, bathed in light.

The End

If you have enjoyed 'The Ice Covenant', I would be so grateful if you could leave a review on the site where you bought the book. And please stay in touch. There is so much still to come.

Tormod Cockburn

The next adventure is ...

This Emerald Veil

Cassy Tullen has gone home to Raasay to lick her wounds. But before long her indomitable spirit is rising again to challenge the dark forces in her life, and take back what is rightfully hers. She's all alone, with the odds stacked against her. That's until the day she meets a fierce, freckle-faced girl on the bus from Harris. If these two powerful women can comprehend each other, Cassy might just have evened the odds.

Gill McArdle, meanwhile, is on the island of Iona, searching for the burial places of the kings. What began as an orderly archaeological dig risks disintegrating into a treasure hunt, and Gill suspects sabotage from new enemies as well as old. As the pressure mounts on him, Gill still values decency. But he's done running. This time, he's coming out fighting.

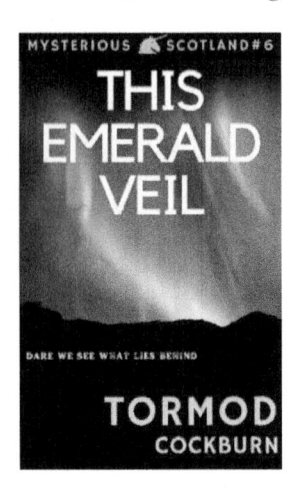

Join the Reader's Syndicate at TormodCockburn.com

Or click on the thumbnail

Mysterious Scotland Reader's Syndicate

Join our Readers Syndicate at TormodCockburn.com for new publication alerts and for free material. We'll be adding more free material, exclusively available to members of the Syndicate.

Mys.Scot

Acknowledgements

Firstly, an apology to everyone who correctly identifies the cover photo as *Buachaille Etive Mòr* rather than *Ben Macdui*. Macdui's a beast, but the Herdsman just takes a better photo. And it is mentioned in the book…

As ever, I'm very, very grateful to my beta readers, especially Julia for her forensic analysis of the plot. You guys make a better book.

A shout out to the archaeologist who once walked me to the door of a bone store like the one portrayed in 'Lossuary.' And for the words he uttered that became the inspiration for this story – 'Wouldn't this be a perfect place to hide a body!'

Talking of bodies … my thanks to Garry Thompson for his insights into pathology labs. Any errors applying this information are all my own.

My thanks to The Cairngorm Club, for their meticulous record keeping, going back to 1893. Also, to all the good citizens who continue to maintain the Corrour Bothy, and other places like it, as a safe haven for any weary walker needing to get out of the weather. Also, to the writers, Nan Shepherd, John Geiger and Patrick Baker, for their inspirational words. And especially to the bard himself for Lady Macbeth – an enduring case study into the destructive power of revenge.

And finally, to all those friends I've shared Scotland's mountains with over the years; Angus, James, Kirstie, Rick, Kevin & Phil. Celebrating every beautiful viewpoint, and every safe return.

Printed in Great Britain
by Amazon